"What are these?" Bill asked.

"These are storage simulations of our emergency rescue ship and the two crewmen who man it."
"But they're black dots," Bill said.
"We stored them in that form," Dirk said, "to save energy. It takes a lot of power to beam simulations into an alien computer and the *Gumption*'s main batteries are already dangerously depleted due to a situation that came up immediately before this one."

"What good are they?" Bill asked.

"None at all, in their present form," Dirk admitted. "But as soon as Splock activates them into full simulacrum form —"

"I can't," Splock complained, touching his nose tenderly. "The equations," he sniffled. There was a whistling sound when he snuffled. It seemed possible that Bill had broken not only the crucial reconstituting data which was needed to get them out of the computer and back to the *Gumption*, but also Splock's nose.

"Now we're really in trouble," Dirk said unhappily.

Also by Harry Harrison in VGSF

BILL, THE GALACTIC HERO

BILL, THE GALACTIC HERO
ON THE PLANET OF ROBOT SLAVES

HARRY HARRISON
ROBERT SHECKLEY

Bill, The Galactic Hero on the Planet of Bottled Brains

A Byron Preiss Book

VGSF

Special thanks to Kirby McCauley, Nat Sobel,
John Douglas, David Keller and Alice Alfonsi

VGSF is an imprint of Victor Gollancz Ltd
14 Henrietta Street, London WC2E 8QJ

First published in Great Britain 1990
by Victor Gollancz Ltd

First VGSF edition 1991

A catalogue record for this book
is available from the British Library

ISBN 0-575-05004-7

Printed and bound in Great Britain by
Cox & Wyman Ltd, Reading

Chapter 1

"Gather round, folks," Brownnose said through the loud-hailer he had stolen from the drill sergeant. The built-in circuitry made his voice sound gravelly and disgusting just like the sergeant's. "It's the event you've all been waiting for — the unveiling of Bill's new foot now growing from an implanted foot bud. Only ten bucks a ticket to see this unique and possibly revolting event."

The barracks where the unveiling was to be held was filling up fast. Most of the enlisted men in Camp Diplatory wanted to attend the unveiling of Bill's new foot bud. The foot bud had been implanted in Bill's stump three days previously, on the medical satellite BRIP 32 situated at Point Less. After implantation, Bill had been shipped to Diplatory, the large military establishment on the planet Shyster. He had to wait three days before he could unveil his transplant. Time-controlled bandages ensured that he would follow medical orders. There had been difficulties with time-controlled bandages, but luckily Bill didn't have any. At least as far as he knew.

There wasn't much to do for the fifty thousand Space Troopers stationed in Camp Diplatory. The camp was set on a hundred semi-submerged acres in the middle of Unholy Bog, the largest and wettest swamp on the planet Shyster. Why the camp had been built in the middle of a bog was a mystery. Or maybe it wasn't. Some said it was an accident, probably made in Central Headquarters back on Helior. Others said that the location had been picked deliberately because tough conditions produce strong men, if they don't kill them. Or maim them. Or drive them mad.

"And if they do, there are more where those came from."

That is the motto of the Fighting 69th Deep Space Screaming Killers, the unit to which Bill was presently attached.

"So take off the bandage," Kanarsie said. "Let's get a look."

Bill looked around. The barracks was full. At ten bucks a head, which Brownnose was collecting at the door for him, Bill figured he'd made enough to buy himself some new combat boots. The rate at which he accumulated foot operations made this necessary, since the military wouldn't reimburse him for constantly having to turn in shoeware that wasn't even worn, or just didn't fit the present disgusting shape of Bill's wounded foot.

Brownnose waved enthusiastically that he could begin. He was enthusiastic about everything, kind, reverent and obedient. And wanted to help his buddies all the time. Which is not the troopers' way and that is why they hated him. And called him Brownnose. Bill liked him because he reminded Bill of Eager Beager who had acted the same way. But of course he had been a Chinger spy. And a robot too.

"Here goes," Bill said and grabbed the bandage. An alarm sounded and an electric shock stung his fingers. "Ouch. Not quite time yet." The bandage buzzed hoarsely and the end dropped free. "Time now," he said and unwound one turn of the bandages and the spectators all leaned forward. They emitted a collective sigh as Bill unwound the second layer. Their faces got all flushed and nervous, and their breath came in short pants, exceedingly uncomfortable, and some could be seen nervously wringing their hands as Bill threw off the third layer of bandage. Bill's foot wasn't exactly big box office, but in a boring, despicable, uncomfortable dump like this even a cockroach fight was an event the stature of naked ladies wrestling in jello.

Excitement, or whatever it was, reached a fever pitch as the eighty or so burly and scarred military men of low rank and lower IQ crowded into the smoke-filled plastic Quonset hut and leaned forward blinking, as Bill threw off the fourth and final fold of bandage.

You'd think, of course, that Bill would be the one to have the first glimpse of his new foot, since it was his, after all. You would be mistaken, however, for Bill superstitiously looked elsewhere as he cast the bandage away. He had been having some strange feelings in that foot over the last day.

He looked at the watching faces around him, their eyes glued on his foot.

The crowd made a sort of tittering sound. That was odd, not at all what Bill had expected. And then they started laughing. Not polite, appreciative laughter, such as you might expect at the unveiling of a foot bud, but loud, heavy, guffaw-guffaw type laughter of the joke's-on-you variety.

Bill glanced down. Then he glanced away. Then he glanced down again, winced, considered glancing away again, pulled himself together, looked.

"You know, Bill," Kowalski said, "I thought this foot unveiling of yours was going to be a ripoff. I mean, what could there be under that bandage; you plant a foot bud, you get a foot, right? Wrong. Bill, I want to thank you. That is the funniest thing I've seen since the CO got fragged."

Bill stretched his clawed toes experimentally. "Seems to work OK," he said.

It should have worked OK. But it would have worked better on an alligator, since it was a fine, green, scaley, abundantly clawed alligator's foot that was now growing on the end of Bill's ankle.

What had those doctors done? Were they experimenting, trying to turn him into a reptile? He didn't put it past them. Since he had recently had a giant mutated chicken's foot for a foot he knew that anything was possible. Probable — in the Troopers. And the foot after that had been nice, maybe too many toes but that wasn't bad, and he had really enjoyed it until it withered and dropped off.

It was a small green foot, but it was workable. And it would probably grow into a much larger foot. The envy of any passing alligator he thought, gloomily. Bill did not stop to consider the miracle that man's ability to do this represented. By any standard it was an act of genius. A little useless, perhaps, but genius all the same. But this was lost on Bill who, like many before him, was mad as hell.

Bill stumped down the corridor, listing slightly to the left to favor his clawed and knobbly left foot. His new alligator foot had not grown out to full size yet, so there was little more than an inch difference between his left and right feet. The foot itself was perfectly sound and able to bear his weight, though the claws scratched the floor when he walked.

His immediate destination was the small cubicle on level twelve of the main concourse of the base. He got there slightly out of breath, since walking on a taloned alligator's foot takes practice before you can do it smoothly.

The cubicle was ten feet to a side. It was divided into two parts, one a reception and waiting room, the other the place of the computer. The military base on Shyster was run by this Quintiform computer, not the latest model, but one believed to be just as good, almost.

Bill went in and took his seat in the waiting room. He was the only person there. That was unusual, since the computer usually had a line of people waiting to consult it.

No sooner had he sat down than a metallic voice with plenty of vibrato said to him: "Hello, I am the Quintiform computer; please step inside and show me your dogtags."

Bill did as he was told. The inner room of the computer station was painted computer beige. There were banks of switches and dials on the four walls. There were speakers set into the wall up high. One of these was broadcasting a program of sambas.

8

Bill presented his dogtags and the Quintiform computer hissed and clicked its approval. "Yes, Bill," it said, "what seems to be the trouble?"

"The foot doctors on Aesclepius, the medical satellite, gave me a foot bud implant," Bill explained. "Look what it grew into!"

The Quintiform exuded a metallic pseudopod with a blinking glass eye at the end of it and inspected Bill's foot.

"Wow!" the computer said. It began to chuckle.

"It's no laughing matter," Bill said. "And anyhow, robots aren't supposed to laugh."

"Sorry about that," the computer said. "Just trying to put you at your ease. Now then, I suppose you want the doctors to fix your other foot so it will match the clawed one?"

"No! I want two normal human feet, like I started with."

"Ah, of course," the computer said. It hummed and buzzed for a while, presumably going through its memory banks looking for the correct solution to Bill's problem. After a while it said; "Go to Room 1223-B on level Verdigris, Section Vector-Vector 2, and they'll fix you up."

Finding your way around the base was no easy matter, since the main structure was the size of a middle-sized city and contained over three thousand rooms, torture halls, meeting places, contraceptive dispensers, intravenous feeding cafeterias, storage facilities, and the like, spread over ten different levels. Troopers had been known to wander through it for days at a time. Almost any time you went through you could see troopers sleeping in heaps of camouflage clothing at the intersections. It was notorious that you should take along provisions and a full canteen of water when you were going anywhere in the base. As Bill set out, a vehicle the size of an electrified golf cart pulled up beside him.

"Hello, Bill," the golf cart's voice box said. "I have been sent by the computer to take you to your destination. Care for a drink? Nothing too good for our boys in uniform."

Bill thought the golf cart sounded entirely too affable. But he got in. It was a lot better than walking the interminable miles he'd have to cover to reach Room 1223-B.

They whisked along down the olive, drab corridors, the golf cart humming a cheery little tune to itself. They passed through Maintenance and Communications to a section called Planning.

"This doesn't look like a medical section," Bill said.

"Don't worry about it," the golf cart said. "I know where I'm going."

It swept up a ramp, doubled down a corridor, and made for a door at the end. Bill winced, because the golf cart had gathered speed and the door was closed. He cowered back in his seat as the golf cart hurtled itself at the door. Bill closed his eyes and buried his head in his hands. When he looked up again, they were on the other side of the door, which had opened by an electric eye arrangement and was now closing again.

He was in some sort of officers' lounge, which had been gotten up to look like an old Earth-style saloon. There were Tiffany lamps and dark furniture made of genuine plastic. There was a long bar with whiteshirted bartenders working behind it. There was a jukebox playing vintage rock on fake original ancient instruments like synthesizers and electric guitars, some of them looking several hundreds of years old, though they had probably been made last week. There were about a dozen uniformed officers of either sex present. They all had drinks in their hands. They cheered when the golf cart speeded into the room, made a neat circle in the middle, and came to a stop.

"Excuse me," Bill said. "Is this the Medical section?"

That brought a good round of hearty laughter. Men crowded around and congratulated Bill on his wit. One woman, a majorette, no less, with fluffy blonde hair and a pert nose and giant boobs, sat in Bill's lap and kissed him soundly. Somebody else asked him what he'd like to drink. Bill was so rattled he just said yes. So they brought him a stirrup cup filled with a mixture of that day's alcoholic beverages. The taste of rum was most prominent, as well as a tang of horse from the stirrup, and Bill drained it gratefully, having learned never to look a gift drink in the goblet.

The lady major who had kissed him got out of his lap and into his face. With her nose no more than millimeters from his, she looked long and deep into Bill's eyes. Then she said in a thrilling contralto voice with a faint whiskey burr to it, "You're just like I imagined you'd be."

"Well," Bill said, "I try."

"What a clever remark," one colonel murmured to another.

"He's obviously a clever chap," said a whitehaired colonel, who appeared to be the ranking officer. "Get him a cigar, somebody. And no more of that rotgut; pour him some of the good cognac we liberated at the sack of the Main Base after the attack."

A cigar in one hand, a glass of cognac in the other, and a smirking grin on his face, Bill wasn't prepared for the next question.

"Tell me, Bill," a foxy-faced major with the crossed questionmark flashings of Intelligence Directorate 2 on his shoulders, "what do you think about the Tsurisian situation?"

"Does it have anything to do with the medical services here?" Bill asked. "If so, I have a complaint."

"My dear fellow," the foxy-faced major said. "Haven't you been briefed yet on the planet Tsuris?"

"I've only been here three days, sir," Bill said, gurgling deeply of the drink to drown his suspicions of all this officerial kindness. Deep down he knew it wasn't natural. Even deeper down he wanted to get blind drunk on the good booze.

"And what have you been doing in your time here?"

"Growing a new foot, mostly," Bill said. "That's what I want to ask — "

"Time for that later," the major said. "Tsuris is a planet not too far from here. It is sometimes referred to as the Mystery Planet."

"Oh, sure, I've heard of it," Bill said dimly through the growing alcoholic fog. "That's the place which broadcasts the weird radio messages, isn't it?"

The major explained that the military base on Shyster had been given the job of clearing out Tsuris, a nearby planet of considerable mystery. Literally nothing was known about this planet. No decent photographs had ever been taken through the heavy cloud layer. There were breaks in the clouds, and the planet seemed to get plenty of sunshine, but when the military snoop ships maneuvered to take pictures through an opening, it always closed before they could get lined up.

"That's weird," Bill said. "Almost like someone is directing it, huh?"

"Exactly. Have another drink," the major said. "As you've mentioned, radio messages seem to emanate from Tsuris, but they never make sense. But the worst of it is, ships even travelling in the vicinity of Tsuris have been known to vanish, only to appear again millions of miles away with no explanation as to how they got there."

"Sounds like a good place to steer clear of," Bill said with alcoholic sincerity, nodding and drinking at the same time. Which didn't work too well.

"Ah, if only we could," the major said. "But we can't, of course. We are the military. We go where we please."

"Hear, hear!" cried the other officers, hastily tossing down their drinks.

"And anyhow," the major said, "if something on Tsuris can deflect a ship millions of miles off its course, that's a force that would be of considerable importance to us. We need to know how it works, and if the Tsurisians or whoever lives down there intend to use it against us."

"If so," the whitehaired colonel pointed out, "we've got

to kick the crap out of them Tsurisians before they get a chance to do it to us."

"Maybe it would be safer," a captain of Shock Troopers said, "to kick the crap out of them even if they don't have any bad intentions."

"Hear, hear!" the other officers chanted.

They all looked at Bill, waiting for him to say something. Bill tried to look intelligent, even though he was feeling very dim. "Have you tried putting a scout ship on the planet? That way you could look around and things."

The major concealed his disgust with a fake smile. "Many times, my dear trooper," he said. "As you might very well imagine, they never come back, never report."

"That's not so good," Bill bubbled alcoholically. Then he was seized by bloodthirsty ambitions. "Why not just stand back and wing atomic torpedoes at them until one gets through? Blast them! Destroy them!"

"We thought of that ourselves," the major said. "But it is against the rules of war, that is what the commy lefty papers say, and our bleeding heart candidates in the up and coming local elections wouldn't like it. They need to have it all legal. Declaration of war and all that nonsense. As soon as they are not elected we go back to doing just what the hell we want, but for the moment our hands are tied. Our missiles in the silos. Our noses in our glasses drowning our sorrows."

"Well . . ." Bill thought for a while. "Why not declare war on them?"

The officers nodded at each other in approval. "You've got the right instincts, trooper. But not until after the elections. Then we can bomb the mothers into the next dimension. But until that happens we have to give some illusion of lawfulness. But the trouble is that we can't even find anyone to talk to on Tsuris. In fact, we're not entirely sure there's anyone there."

"Then the answer is plain," the colonel said. "I'm sure you thought of it yourself. If we can get a drone scout ship down to the surface of the planet, with someone aboard carrying a message from the Admiral-in-Chief, at least we could get the Tsurisians talking. Then we could make demands which they'd refuse. And then we'd have a chance to plead 'irreparable insult demanding unctuous apology' as a cause of war."

"Unless the Tsurisians are able to apologize fast enough to forestall the invasion," the colonel said.

"Speed is everything in modern warfare," the major pointed out. "What do you think, Bill?"

"Sounds like a good plan to me," Bill said. "Now, if you could direct me to the Medical section . . . "

"No time for that now, trooper," the major said. "We want to congratulate you, then explain how your drone ship works."

"Wait a minute," Bill said. "What has this got to do with me?"

"My dear fellow," the major said, "by walking through this door you have volunteered for the job of going on the drone ship to Tsuris."

"But I didn't know! The computer told me to come here!"

"That's right. The computer volunteered you."

"Can it do that?"

The major scratched his head. "I don't know, really. Why don't you ask it?" He chuckled evilly as Bill tried to leap woozily to his feet and felt the automatic shackles lock hard around his ankles.

Brownnose looked terrible. It was true that he had been through a lot recently, having had all of his buddies beating him up because he was so helpful and considerate of others, and that is not the troopers' way. The first lesson a real trooper learns is that it is always Bowb-your-Buddy week. The military psychiatrist had diagnosed him as having a severe case of the Shmidas Touch, the mirror opposite of the Midas Touch where everything you touch turns to gold. But one of the psychiatrist's colleagues, Major Doctor Smellenfuss, disagreed. He said that Brownnose presented a classical case of

Loser Psychosis, complicated by self-destructive tendencies. All Brownnose knew was, life kept on getting worse for him. And all he wanted to do was make people happy!

Take now, for example. Of course he didn't look good. What man could look good pushed back against the uncomfortably hot boiler in the laundry room where Bill, hamlike fist raised in the air, was threatening to take him apart?

"Bill, wait!" Brownnose cried as Bill's eyes narrowed, preparatory to driving Brownnose's head through the half inch mild steel of which the boiler was composed. "I did it for you!"

Bill hesitated, fist poised for the killing blow. "How do you figure?"

"Because volunteering you for this mission will bring you a medal, a sizeable bonus, a year's supply of VD pills and most important, an immediate honorable discharge!"

"A discharge?"

"Yes, Bill! You could go home!"

Bill was visited by a wave of nostalgia as he thought of his home world, Phigerinadon, and how much he wanted to see it.

"Are you sure?" he asked.

"Of course I'm sure. Just go to the recruiting officer when you get back. He'll set everything in motion for you."

"That's just great," Bill said. "The only trouble is, this is a suicide mission and I'm unlikely to come back from it. And if I don't come back, no discharge, right?"

"You will come back," Brownnose said. "I guarantee it."

"How do you figure?"

"Because, after I volunteered you, I also volunteered myself. So I could look after you, Bill."

"You can't even look after yourself," Bill pointed out. He sighed. "I guess it was pretty nice of you to want to help me, Brownnose, but I wish you hadn't."

"I realize that now, Bill," Brownnose said, extricating himself from Bill's grasp and slinking away from the boiler, which had been growing uncomfortably torrid. He could see that the moment of immediate danger was over. Bill got hot under the collar sometimes, but if you could just avoid instant mayhem, he soon cooled off again.

"Anyhow," Bill said, "how could you volunteer me? Only I can volunteer me."

"You've sure got a point there," Brownnose said. "Maybe you should take it up with the computer."

"Hello again," the military computer said. "You were in here recently, weren't you? Excuse me for asking but the old eyesight's not what it used to be. My image orthicon is wearing out. Not that anyone or anything cares." It snivelled mechanically, a repellent sound.

"I came in here about my foot," Bill said loudly, disgusted at all the electronic self-pity.

"Your foot? I never forget a foot! Let me see it."

Bill displayed his foot to the computer's vision plate.

"Hooee," the computer said. "That's a beauty of an alligator's tootsy. But I've never seen that foot before. I told you, I never forget a foot."

"Of course you remember it," Bill whined. "Because you looked at it when I was in here before. What kind of computer could forget that?"

"I didn't say I forgot, computers can't forget, it's just that I haven't thought about it lately," the computer said. "Just a minute, let me consult my data banks. I never forget a reference to a foot, either . . . Yes, here it is. You're right, you did say something about your foot. And I directed you to the Officer's Ready Room."

"That's right. And the officers there said that by coming in I had volunteered for hazardous duty."

"Yes, that's all correct," the computer said. "When they asked me for a volunteer, I sent them the first one who came in."

"Me?"

"You."

"But I didn't volunteer."

"Tough titty. I mean I am *so* sorry, but you did. Inferentially."

"Beg pardon?"

"I inferred that you would have volunteered if asked. We have special circuits that allow us to use inferences."

"But you could have asked me!" Bill shouted angrily.

"Then what would be the use of inferential circuitry with which I have been fitted out at great expense? Anyhow, it was clear to me that a fine upstanding military type like you would be happy to volunteer for hazardous duty, despite the minor impairment to your foot."

"You were wrong," Bill said.

A ripple passed across the computer's vision plate, almost like a shrug. "Well," it said, "mistakes happen, don't they?"

"That's not good enough!" Bill shouted, thumping the computer's vision plate with a large fist. "I'll tear out your lying transistors." He thumped the vision plate again. This time it flashed red.

"Trooper," the computer said in a gruff voice. "Stand to attention."

"What?" said Bill.

"You heard me. I am a military computer with the veritable rank of full colonel. You are an enlisted man. You have to address me in a respectful manner or you'll be in a lot worse trouble than you are already."

Bill gulped. Officers were all alike, even when they were computers.

"Yes sir," he said, and stood to attention.

"Now, since you don't think the procedure was fair, what do you suggest we do?"

"Let's draw for it," Bill said. "Or you pick a volunteer at random from all the men in the base."

"That would satisfy you?"

"Yes, it would."

"OK, here goes." The computer's vision screen lit up in a jagged lightning bolt of conflicting colors. Names flashed by on the screen. There was a sound like a roulette ball rolling around a croupier's wheel.

"OK," the computer said. "We got a winner."

"Fine," Bill said. "Can I go now?"

"Sure. Good luck, soldier."

Bill opened the door. Outside there were two extremely large and beetle-jawed MPs. They took Bill by either arm.

"As you may have gathered," the computer said, "you won the second drawing, too."

Not long after that, a large trooper with a small claw at the end of one foot, could be seen struggling in the arms of two MPs. The trooper was brought to a reviewing stand where several generals were standing, waiting for something to review.

Bill opened up his mouth to scream. One of the MP's drove his elbow into Bill's kidneys.

The other MP went for the liver.

When Bill recovered consciousness a few seconds later, in response to having his nose tweaked violently, the first MP leaned over him and said, "Look, buddy, you're going on that ship. The only question is, do you go on in one piece or do we cripple you first so you won't make a scene in front of the brass?"

"They hate scenes," the second MP said. "We do, too."

"They blame us when the volunteers make a fuss," the first MP said.

"Maybe we should just cripple him and not take any chances," the first MP said.

"Maybe we could just fracture his voice box."

"No, he could still make obscene gestures."

"I guess you're right." Both MPs paused to roll up their sleeves.

"Don't bother," Bill said. "Just put me aboard the ship."

"First you got to go up to the reviewing stand and shake the generals' hands and tell them how glad you was to volunteer."

"Let's get it over with," Bill said.

The drone ship was small, about the size of a launch, built of cheap plastic and aluminized cardboard since it was not expected to return. One of the MPs pulled open the main hatchway and growled in anger as the handle came off in his hand.

"Never mind that," the other MP said. "The inner parts still work all right."

"Why don't they build them better?" Bill whined, then shrieked with pain. He was being carried in a crunched and uncomfortable manner by the two MPs.

"Why should they bother?" the first MP said. "These ships are specially constructed for one-way trips to only the most dangerous places."

"You mean I'm not expected to return?" Bill whimpered, wallowing in self-pity.

"I don't mean anything of the sort! Well, maybe. Anyhow, the real crafty advantage of sending a volunteer, is that, if you should not return, as is confidently expected, the military will probably send a fully-fledged expeditionary force to Tsuris, even declare war as they sincerely want to."

"You said probably?"

"It has to be probably, since the military can always change its teeny-tiny mind. But that's what will probably happen."

"Yipe!" Bill yiped. "What the bowb are you doing with my ear?"

"I'm fastening a translating device to your ear, so if you find any Tsurisians on Tsuris you can talk to them."

"Tsuris! The place nobody ever comes back from?"

"You catch on fast. That's the whole point of the operation. Your non-return will give us the excuse to invade."

"I don't think I like this."

"You don't have to like it, trooper. Just follow orders and shut up."

19

"I refuse! Cancel the orders!"

"Shut up." They wrestled Bill into the ship and strapped him into the pilot's command chair. It was beautifully padded and comfortable. Bill was not. He opened his mouth to protest again and the neck of an open bottle was shoved into it. He gurgled and gasped.

"What . . . was that?"

"Apathia 24. With a double shot of Extasis Tricarbonate. One hundred and fifteen proof." The MP nodded as Bill gurgled down some more. "That's the stuff. You can keep the bottle."

It was really good stuff. So good that Bill never noticed when the MPs left and the hatch closed. The ship must have taken off, he could not remember when, because he saw by the vision plate that he was in space. Lots of little stars and such. And what looked like a planet down below. He admired the great storms sweeping across its surface as he drained the bottle. Lightning crackled balefully through the purple-black clouds and his radio crackled with static.

Radio? He fiddled with the knobs until a voice came through clearly. At least it sounded clear although it did not make much sense.

"No gliggish in hut overstep galoshes."

He sneered at this and was reaching to turn it off when a voice buzzed in his ear. He blinked rapidly at this — then slowly remembered the translator had been attached just inside his left ear. "What did they say?"

"Just a minute," the translator said testily. "All right, I think I've got it now. They're definitely speaking Tsurisian. The question is, is it High Garpeian dialect or Someshovish."

"Who gives a bowb?" Bill muttered, trying to get the last drops of metabolic poison from the bottle.

"An interesting problem in linguistic analysis," the translator said. "In the former dialect it means, 'Please don't throw the eggshells on the grass.'"

"And in the other one?" Bill asked, feigning interest.

"In the other it translates to, 'Tickle knees on the Steppes.'"

"Sounds a lot of bowb either way."

"A cogent observation that is entirely possible," the translator agreed.

Well, he could figure out what they were saying later. For now, he was entranced by the sights below him. Looking through the transparent hull of his drone ship, he could see bright flowers of enormous size blossoming from the surface of Tsuris.

"Pretty nice shtuff," he said, wishing he had another drink.

"Aren't you going to take evasive action?" the translator asked him.

"Why bother? Ish nice to look at the flowers down there."

"Flowers my silicon ass!" the translator said with great agitation. "Those red things are high explosives. They're shooting torpedoes at us!"

That's all it took to bring Bill out of his stupor, cold sober and in a cold sweat. Shooting at him? Suddenly he remembered the mission. Then his little drone ship bucked violently.

"Mayday. Mayday!" screamed the translator. The ship started to plunge and careen and cartwheel and spin and tumble, all the things that spaceships do when they're hit. Bill grabbed for a stanchion and missed, he still wasn't that sober, and hit his head. The darkness of unconsciousness instantly descended. Which was not such a bad thing, considering what happened next.

Bill's ship disintegrated under the impact of atomic torpedoes.

"A gravchute," he muttered when he stumbled back to consciousness. "That's nice."

As he dropped gently through the clinging mists, which of course were the clouds that forever veil Tsuris, especially if you're trying to take pictures of the planet, he looked down and saw that the ground seemed to be coming up very fast.

Was the gravchute working properly? Weren't there supposed to be controls on it somewhere?

He fumbled and cursed but before he could find them the ground came up and struck him and merciful unconsciousness drew its cloak about him yet one more time.

Chapter 2

Bill returned reluctantly to consciousness. He discovered that he was floating in a lukewarm nutrient bath. Its specific gravity was such that his head just bobbled above the surface without his having to make any positive effort to keep himself afloat. It felt very nice. He blinked up at the multicolored lights overhead. Watching them glitter and shine reminded Bill of the happy Fundamentalist Zoroastrian Winter Solstice Defloration Festival, that the nonbelievers called Christmas, back home. A tear formed in either eye, dribbled down his nose and dropped into the nutrient solution.

Immediately an alarm went off. Or something that might be an alarm; a raucous electronic flatus. A person hurried grotesquely into the room. At least Bill supposed it was a person. It might have been a robot, or anything between a person and a robot. Or a thing. It was mainly composed of a large sphere about three feet in diameter. From its underside there depended four skinny black legs. On top of the sphere was another sphere, smaller, and a still smaller one above that. What were these spheres made of? Bill hiccupped lightly and realized that he didn't really care. It was nice and comfy here in the warm bath. A tickle of worry tickled him. Maybe he should care, trapped in a bubble bath on this alien planet. He looked again. The spheres seemed to be a combination of metal and pink-colored flesh. There was a smiley face painted on the uppermost sphere where a face would be if this was anything human.

The creature ground some internal gears and said, "Please don't do that."

"Do what?"

"Cry into the nutrient solution. You're changing the acid levels. It isn't good for your skin."

"What's wrong with my skin?" Bill asks. "Am I burned?"

"Not at all, bless you. We just want to make it nice and soft, your skin."

"Why do you want to do that?"

"We'll talk about it later," the Tsurisian said. "By the way, should you wish to know, and I'm sure that you do, I am Illyria, your nurse."

They kept Bill in the nutrient bath for several more hours. When he got out, his skin was nice and pink and rosy. They gave him back his trooper uniform, which had been brushed and dry cleaned by some alien but effective process. He was allowed to walk up and down in the corridor, for that's what it seemed to be. His weapons were gone and he didn't see anything that looked like it would be useful. Not that he had any idea what he would do even if he got a weapon against an entire planetful of enemies.

He was able to form some idea of his surroundings when Illyria came to take care of him. He questioned her adroitly; that is he asked questions and she answered them, and quickly learned that she was a typical female Tsurisian, twenty years old, quite sophisticated for a girl who had lived and worked on her parents' farm until just last year, when her high grades in high school had won her this position in the alien lifeforms hospital in Graypnutz, the capital city of Tsuris.

Every day several Tsurisian males came by to see how Bill was doing. They were considerably older than Illyria, as he could tell by the grayish stubble on their intermediate spheres, which, Bill learned, served as holders for the batteries that helped keep the Tsurisians going.

Bill quickly discovered that the Tsurisians saw nothing cruel or unnatural about what they were proposing to do to him. "We Tsurisians always have to be reborn in the body of someone else," Bill's doctor pointed out. "Otherwise we don't get born at all."

"That's really great for you — but what about me?" Bill whimpered desperately. "Where do I go?"

"Out like a burnt-out bulb," the alien grimaced, though this was hard to tell since his painted-on expression really did not change very much. "Anyway, haven't you an iota of the spiritual in you? Don't you crave, in some part of your tiny soul, to serve all sentient beings?"

"No, I don't think so," Bill said.

"Pity," the doctor said. "You would have been a lot better off if you had learned to think properly about things."

"Listen, buddy," Bill said, "a mind transplant means I'm not here any more and that means I'm dead. How am I supposed to feel good about that?"

"Consider it an opportunity," the doctor said.

"What are you talking about?" Bill screamed.

"Whatever happens is an opportunity," the doctor said.

"Is that a fact? Then let this guy take over your mind instead of mine. You can have the opportunity."

"Ah," said the doctor, "it didn't knock for me."

Even Illyria stopped visiting so often. "I think they suspect me of something," she told him when she did come by for a brief visit. "They're giving me the Usladish look; you know what I mean?"

"No, I don't," Bill said, desperation in his voice, a trapped feeling coursing through every fibre of his being.

"I keep on forgetting you weren't born here," Illyria said. "An Usladish look is what we call a look that means, I know you're up to something sneaky and rotten but I'm not going to tell anybody about it yet because I'm sort of sneaky and rotten myself."

"They don't have that feeling where I come from," Bill said.

"No? How curious. Anyhow, I'm going to have to stay away for a while. But don't worry, I'm working on your case."

"Hurry up, while I'm still inside this head," Bill said.

Since then quite a few days and nights had gone by since he had seen her. Exactly how many he didn't know, because Tsuris seemed to have an odd fluttery sort of movement around its sun, resulting in days and nights of differing lengths. Some days were what the Tsurisians called Tiger Days, or was it Picket-Fence Days? The translation was a little difficult. Those days in which the sun rose and set every hour on the hour, striping the planet in yellow and black. He decided to make a mark on the wall to mark each period of light. He didn't know why he was doing this but it was what guys in cells were always doing in the stories he used to read back home in the hayrick behind the manure pile back on his parents' farm on Phigerinadon. He tried the mark system, but when he came to do his next mark, he found that he had put his mark close to a mark already on the wall which he hadn't noticed. Unless he had marked two light periods without remembering it. Or had marked one light period twice absentmindedly. The more he thought about it, the more he decided that mark-making in prison was the sort of thing you ought to study in school before trying it in field conditions. So mostly he sat. There were no books or newspapers available, and no television. Luckily there was a small switch on the side of his translator that let him switch it from "Translate" to "Converse". Bill felt a little silly doing it, but there didn't seem to be anyone else around to talk to.

"Hello," he said.

"'Alo," the translator said. "'Ow are you, heh?"

"Why are you speaking with a stupid accent?" Bill asked.

"Because I am a translator, that's why, Buster." The thing sounded very miffed. "It would falsify my position and my image if I didn't allow impurities inherited from the many languages I deal with to creep into my talk during my conversational phase."

"That's a pretty dim reason," Bill said.

"Well not to me, squishy repulsive non-machine creature!" the translator said heatedly.

"There is no reason to get insulting," Bill muttered. A mechanical sniff of annoyance was his only answer. After this there was a long silence. Then Bill said, "Seen any good movies lately?"

"What?" said the translator.

"Movies," Bill said.

"Are you crazy or something? I am a tiny transistorized gadget lodged under your right armpit. Or on your ear. I get about. How would I ever get to see a movie?"

"I was just making a joke," Bill said.

"They didn't tell us about jokes," the translator complained. "Is that enough?"

"Enough what?"

"Conversation."

"No, of course not! I've just begun!"

"But you see, I've almost used up the conversational capacity which was built into me. I will still carry on as your translator, of course, but I very much regret telling you that the conversational aspect of our relationship is at an end. Over and out."

"Translator?" Bill said after a while.

Silence from the translator.

"Haven't you got any words left at all?" Bill asked.

"Just this," the translator said. And that was the last word Bill was able to get out of him.

It was soon after that that he heard the second voice.

The second voice came to him that night, after his evening meal of a raspberry brain malted and a plate of what tasted like fried chicken livers but looked like orange gumdrops. He was reading his shirt labels under the light of a lamp called a Blind Philistine because it shines indifferently on whatever is put in front of it. He was just stretching for a yawn, when a voice from behind him said, "Listen."

Bill gave a violent start and looked around in all directions. There was no one in the room with him.

As if to confirm his observation, the voice said, "No, I'm not in the room."

"Where are you, then?"

"That's a little difficult to explain."

"You can at least try."

"No, not today."

"Then what do you want?"

"I want to help you, Bill."

Bill had heard that before. Still, it was always good to hear. He sat down on the edge of the bathtub and looked around the room again. Nope, nobody there. "I could use some help," Bill said. "Can you get me out of here?"

"I can," the voice said, "if you do exactly what I tell you."

"And what are you going to tell me to do?"

"Something that may seem crazy to you. But it is of the utmost urgency that you do it with conviction and precision."

"Just what is it you want me to do?"

"You're not going to like it."

"Tell me or shut up!" Bill screeched. "This is doing my nerves no good. I don't care if I like it or not, if it'll help me get out of here I'll do it. Now — tell me!"

"Bill, can you pat your head with one hand and rub your belly with the other simultaneously?"

"I don't think so," Bill said. He tried and failed. "See? I was right."

"But you can learn how, can't you?"

"Why should I?"

"Because there is a chance you can get out of your predicament. Your continuing existence as a being with a mind of his own depends on you doing exactly what I tell you when I tell you."

"I see," Bill said, not seeing at all but going along with all this stupidity since he had very little choice. "Would you mind telling me who you are?"

"Not now," the voice said.

"I see," Bill said. "There are reasons, I suppose?"

"Yes, but I can't tell them to you. Will you do as I say, Bill? Now practice. I'll be back."

And then the voice was gone.

A delegation of Tsurisian doctors came to Bill's cell the next morning. Two of them were of the familiar spherical shape. Another was controlling what appeared to be the body of a large collie. With lots of fleas for he kept scratching with one hind leg. The final two may have been Chingers at some other time in their existence because they were shiny green and quite lizardy.

"Time for the good old protoplasm vat," Dr Vesker said in a cheerful voice. That was his name. "I am Dr Vesker," he said so Bill would know too. Bill could not have cared less.

These Tsurisian males were doctors, as could be told by the long, loosefitting white coats they wore, and the stethoscopes sticking rakishly from their pockets. All of them spoke Standard, Classical, or Tsurisian, so Bill's translator, which was still implanted under his armpit, was able to handle the language without difficulty. One of the first questions Bill asked was, "Doc, how am I?"

"You're doing fine, just fine," the doctor said.

"Well, if I'm all right, how about letting me out of here?"

"Oh, there's no rush for that, I'm sure," the doctor said, and left with a little chuckle.

"What did he mean by that little chuckle?" Bill asked Illyria after the doctors had left.

"You know how doctors are," Illyria said. "They find anything funny."

"What's supposed to happen to me when I'm released from here?"

"Must we talk about that?" Illyria said. "It's been such a nice day, why spoil it?"

Illyria got transferred to nights. She and Bill would talk

about many things. Bill learned that the Tsurisians had been living on this planet of Tsuris for much longer than anyone could remember. There was a theory that, when Tsuris was born out of the fiery explosions of Eeyore, its yellowish-red sun, all of the intelligences which now lived on the planet as Tsurisians were born with it. Bill didn't understand what she meant. Illyria had to explain that there were no real births or deaths on Tsuris. All of the intelligences who had ever lived here were still around, existing unconsciously in a psycho-vivant solution of natural electrolytes.

"All of them?" Bill asked. "How many are there?"

"Exactly one billion," Illyria told him. "No more and no less. And they — we — have all been here since the beginning. Some day I must show you where those without bodies are waiting. Or resting as we call it. They are in bottles — "

"A billion brains in bottles! That's an awful lot of bottles."

"Indeed it is and we had to scour the galaxy for them. We have wine bottles, beer bottles, soft drink bottles — just about every kind of bottle that you can name."

"Whee," Bill oozed, depressed again. "And why should there be exactly one billion?"

"The ways of the Deity are strange," Illyria said. She was a religious woman — a practicing member of the Church of Very Little Charities. Despite that she was a pleasant compan-ion, and more broad-minded than most Tsurisian females. Or so she told Bill.

Bill wondered, naturally enough, what was to become of him. Illyria didn't seem to want to talk about it. She would grow somber, or indicate whatever passed for somber whenever Bill raised the topic. Her bluish-yellow eyes would cloud over. Her voice would grow husky.

Bill was having a good time, all things considered. The only work required of him, if you wanted to call it that, was a two-hour session in the nutrient bath. Never had his skin been so soft. His fingernails were getting soft, too. Even the claws on his alligator foot, which had grown to respectable size now, were starting to soften up. Once he asked Illyria why they were giving him so many baths, but she said she'd rather not talk about it.

Illyria was fascinated by Bill's foot. At first it had frightened her, and she had insisted that he wear a velvet sock over it. But after a while she became used to the green alligator's foot, and would ask to see it, and pull his talons gently with her fingerlike appendages, the way mother vultures play with the talons of baby vultures.

Once Illyria had asked him how he was in math. "Not very good," Bill said. "I needed two terms in special technical training school and that was no good. I had to get special math injection brain treatments before I could do simple addition on an electronic computer."

"We don't allow any of those here," Illyria said. "Everybody does math in their heads."

"So if everyone else does math, why should I have to?"

Illyria sighed and did not reply. The doctors came in next morning. There were three of them. They wore shapes different from the other ones. Bill learned that this was common on Tsuris.

"But how come you have so many different shapes?" Bill asked.

"The one thing that has always been lacking on our planet," a doctor tells him, "is the normal function of birth and death. When our world came into existence, all of the intelligences were already here, in the form of water droplets inside large purplish clouds. It took a very long time before any physical forms came about here. Even then, they came from off planet. An expedition from some other world. We were able, with our superior intelligences, at least in regard to devices for taking things over, to incorporate them. Thus our life on Tsuris got a physical basis. Unfortunately, none of us was able to have children, though I can assure you, the men tried every bit as hard as the women. The results? Zilch. Therefore we're always on the lookout for likely bits of protoplasm in which we can house unborn members of our race."

"I hear what you're saying," Bill said, "and I don't think I like it."

"There's nothing personal about it," the doctor said.

"Nothing personal about what?" Bill asked, fearing the worst.

"Nothing personal about our decision to make use of your body. Assuming you fail the intelligence test, that is."

"You're going a little too fast for me," Bill said. "What intelligence test?"

"Didn't Illyria mention it to you? We require of all visitors to our planet to take an intelligence test. Those who fail get re-used."

Bill saw that he had been correct to fear the worst. Even now, before he knew what the worst was, exactly, he could see that it was going to be a bad sort of worst.

"What's the intelligence test?" he asked.

"Just a few simple questions."

The doctor then rattled off a sentence which Bill didn't understand even when it was translated into English for him by his translator. The sentence contained words like "cosine" and "square root of minus one" and "log log" and "sigma" and "rhomboid" and other words that Bill didn't even recognize as English. Temporizing, he asked if he could have the thing written out.

The next question involved imaginary numbers, transfinite numbers, Kantor's number, and several other numbers, all applied to something called lobachevskian geometry. Bill failed this one too. He fared no better on any of the other questions.

"Well, old chap," the doctor said, "no offense, but the results of our tests show that you have an intelligence so minuscule as to not even show on our charts."

"It's just math," Bill said, "I was never able to do math. But you could quiz me on geography, for example, or history — "

"Sorry," the doctor said, "the only test we use is the mathematical one. So much more precise, you know,"

"Yes, I know," Bill groaned. "No, wait a minute! I'm just as smart as anybody here! Maybe smarter — and I got medals to prove it. I'm a hero, a galactic hero awarded the highest awards awardable by the military. I just don't happen to be from a race that does math in its head. Most of us don't, that is."

"I really am sorry," the doctor said. "And also, PS, we are not so keen on military awards. You are a fairly amiable, albeit stupid, sentient being, and so keen at times is the expression on your face that one could almost believe you understand what is being said to you. Too bad. It's the protoplasm vat for you, my lad."

"What happens there?" Bill moaned.

"We have a special process that dedifferentiates your special-purpose cells, thus rendering you fit for rebirth by one of the Tsurisians. The nutrient baths were to soften up your skin for the protoplasm vat in case the intelligence test turned out the way it did. A simple precaution that is now paying off."

Bill swore and cursed and prayed, and fought and kicked and foamed at the mouth. But it was no good. The doctors were adamant. And a hell of a lot stronger en masse. They seized him, struggling and screaming, rushed him out of his room and down the corridor into a room where a special holding tank bubbled and frothed. Bill bubbled and frothed as well but resistance was useless. They splashed him into the tank.

"This will soften you up even further, and you will enjoy it," the doctor said with obvious insincerity.

The next day they strapped him to a wheelchair and wheeled him down the hall. Past a room with its door open. Inside was a huge vat of protoplasm, colored a sort of undigested greenish brown. It was rather repellent and looked more than a little bit like an octopus that had lost its stiffening. The protoplasm bubbled and gurgled, throwing up turgid waves now and then

— on the end of which were large, bulging eyes. The eyes stared wildly for a moment before the wave collapsed into the rest of the liquid.

They put Bill into a special cell where he was fed nutritious food preparatory to reusing his body. When he ate it he cheered up. As soon as he was finished however he became instantly depressed because every ounce of muscle, every inch of fat around his waistline brought him that much closer to the conversion vat. And, if that wasn't enough, one other thing bothered him. "When I am all dissolved away, what happens to my brain?"

"We use that too," the guard on his ward told him.

"Then what happens to me?" Bill asked tremulously, wanting to know. And really not wanting to know.

"That is an interesting question," the guard mused. "You will be present physically, of course. But as for the person inside you who says, I am I, well, that part will be, I am forced to say, to put it as nicely as I can, gone."

Bill moaned. "Where will it go to?"

"Difficult to say," the guard told him. "Anyhow, you won't even be around to ask the question and frankly I don't give a damn."

They fed Bill on yard-wide slices of liver, he shuddered at the thought of what sort of animal it had come from, and cubical fish eggs, and forced him to drink twenty-one milkshakes every day made mostly of homogenized brains. Even with strawberry flavoring it was not a good drink. He was getting more than a little depressed about all this. It was no consolation for him at all to know that his body and brain would be used to house one of Tsuris's most eminent statesmen, old Veritain Redrabble, one of the greatest statesmen of all the previous years. This didn't comfort Bill in the slightest. In fact it depressed him even more. That his priceless body gunk should be recycled as a politician was too awful to contemplate.

Since he did not want to blame himself for his inborn bucolic stupidity he tried to blame his translator instead.

"Why didn't you help me out with the math quiz?"

"Hell," the translator said, "I can't do that stuff either."

"If only we could get word to the military," Bill moaned. "If they sent a math whizz the situation could still be saved."

"For the math whizz maybe, but not for you," the translator intoned with electronic sadism. "And anyway they don't send math whizzes to explore alien planets," the translator pointed out.

"I know," Bill gritted through clenched teeth, "but I can dream, can't I? You wouldn't take even a man's dreams away from him?"

"I am totally indifferent to the matter," the translator said, then turned itself off.

After Bill had been in his special cell with the padded walls for two days, Illyria came to visit him. She sat in his cell for hours, encouraging him to talk about his childhood, his military service, his adventures on strange planets. Bill found he was getting very fond of Illyria. Although she looked to him like all the other Tsurisians, her manner was different. She was sympathetic, feminine. Her voice was low and pleasing. Sometimes, in the darkness of the cell, Bill thought he could see the suggestion of breasts on the gleaming metal of her midpoint sphere. He was even starting to think that her skinny black legs were pretty cute, although, of course, there were too many of them. But deep down he knew that these images were brought on by desperation. He could never really love a woman composed of three spheres. Two spheres maybe, that was kind of a familiar image. But not three.

One evening, however, there was something different about Illyria. She seemed excited and strangely agitated. When he asked her about it, she refused to tell him. "Just believe me, Bill, I'm working on a plan to rescue you."

"What sort of a plan?"

"I can't tell you yet."

"Is there any chance?"

"Yes, my dear, there is. It's risky, but I think we have a chance."

Bill noticed that she had said "we". He asked her about that.

"Oh, Bill," she said, "I hope to have a little surprise for you one of these days."

Much as Bill wanted to be rescued, he wasn't sure he wanted to face Illyria's surprise.

Chapter 3

Bill woke up inside the computer. Only he didn't know that at first. The last thing that he remembered, his last recollection, was back in the cell. Then came the transition. Bill opened his eyes and blinked rapidly. No cell. Instead he appeared to be suspended in a strange and misty environment. To begin with everything was hazy around him. He looked down at himself. He was hazy, too. He felt numb and spaced out. Where was he? What did they do to him after the doctors had stood over him and clucked? What had happened next? Panic rose as he realized that he could not remember.

What was going on? He was lying on what looked like a small cloud, colored orange and mauve. There were other clouds around, maybe attached by wires to the ceiling. Looking up he realized that, disconcertingly, he couldn't see the ceiling through the haze. There were more clouds around him, some of them looked like couches and chairs, floating free. There was an even illumination that suffused everything. And the place had a faint smell of frying pork chops. Bill suddenly became aware that he was hungry. Very hungry. He sat up. When he did that, he seemed to float to an upright position. "Where am I?" he said.

"Welcome," a voice intoned. Bill couldn't figure out where it was coming from, but he knew that it was the same voice he had heard earlier, in his cell.

"Where am I?" he said.

"Just take it easy," the voice cozened Bill. "You're safe now."

"What does that mean? Where am I?" He could hear the shrill edge of panic rising in his voice. "And just who the hell are you?"

"I am the Tsuris computer," the voice said. "You are inside me."

Bill looked around. Yes, the walls of this place were gray and beige, the classic colors of computers. "How," Bill asked tremulously, his voice barely under control, "did you get me inside this computer? I've never heard of a computer large enough to hold a human being." He thought desperately for a moment. "Or any other kind of being."

The computer chortled with transistorial humor. "You're not here in the flesh. Oh, heavens no."

"Then how am I here?"

"Analogically."

"I wish you'd say something I could understand," Bill muttered, more than a little pettishly.

"What I mean," the computer said, "is that I took your psyche — the inner core of your being — the part of you that says 'I am I' — is that clear?"

"I think so," Bill said. "That's the part the Tsurisians wanted to get rid of so they could use the rest of my body to resurrect some bowby politician."

"Precisely. Normally, they simply throw out that part. But I saw from earlier that you had intelligence of a sort; rudimentary, but usable anyhow."

"Thanks a lot," said Bill.

"No, don't go getting all sensitive on me," the computer said. "It beats dying, doesn't it? That's the other option."

"I didn't mean to complain," Bill said. "So my — what did you call it — psyche? — is inside of you. So where's my body?"

"I believe that it is being used at present as an artist's dummy, until the new occupant is ready to take over. Bodies without psyches in them make fine models, you know. They can hold a position for an indefinite amount of time."

"I hope they're keeping that good old body safe," Bill said. "I'm going to want it back as soon as I get out of here."

"The Tsurisians are very careful about bodies," the computer said. "Not enough to go around, you know. As for you getting back into it, that is unlikely."

"The hell you say," Bill said. "We'll see about that."

"Yes, of course," the computer smarmed, in the sort of a voice you use when assuring a man in an electric chair that a few volts are very good for the health.

Despite all of his fears and trepidations Bill quickly adjusted to life within the computer. He found out almost at once that it was not as confining as he had expected. He was able to use all the extensions of the computer, and these extended throughout the planet Tsuris. He soon learned that the computer was the most important thing on the planet Tsuris. It was the computer that really kept things going. Take the clouds that concealed Tsuris's surface, for example. He wondered about them and the computer read his mind, which wasn't hard to do since his mind was part of the computer's mind. Or something like that. In any case the computer sneered happily at the unspoken question. "Did you not think, did you not, that all of this was natural? Jayzus, no!" (For reasons best known to itself the computer assumed a fake Irish accent from time to time.) "And what about the way they keep on opening to let in sunlight, but then close up again whenever aliens like yourself try to take pictures. Did you think that all happened by chance? Not a bit of it, my lad! I direct those cloud movements. I also monitor rainfall to make sure that each region gets a little more of it than they want. I run the tide machines that keep the oceans within bounds. When the harvest is ready, I'm there with my automatic harvesting equipment. And then there's the job of storage of the foodstuffs, and cooking them, too."

"You do all that?"

"You bet your sweet patootie I do."

"Well, what do you need me for?"

"The fact is," the computer said, "as life gets more complicated here in Tsuris I'm called upon to do more and more things. It is beginning to tax my capacity. And I need to keep some capacity for my own interests."

"I didn't know a computer had interests," Bill said.

"You don't know much about computers," the computer huffed. "Of course I have personal interests. It may intrigue you to know that I'm writing a novel."

"I think I've heard of computers writing novels," Bill said. "At least I have read lots of them that could have been written by a computer. What is your one about?"

"Maybe I'll give you a peek at it sometime," the computer said coyly. "Meanwhile, let's go to work."

Bill was put in charge of harvesting the Tsotska plants in Rhodomontade province. The Tsotska plant provided one of the Tsurisians' main sources of sustenance. A small shrub with pink blossoms, the Tsotska provided both fruits and nuts, and a third type of fruit which looked like a repulsive purple banana, but was really very nutritious. The fields of Tsotska plants, stretching to the horizon, were interspersed along their rows with watering equipment. Bill was in charge of turning this off and on. In one way, it wasn't a difficult job. Since Bill didn't have a body, all he had to do was direct his will at the necessary valves, which, being psychotropic, would then open up. It was strange that even with psychotropic valves, some stuck and some seemed rusty. And it was strange, too, that the amount of energy that went into turning the valves on and off was exactly the same as the energy that would have been required if Bill had had a body doing it. Of course, the visuals were more interesting. Bill could will himself high above the fields, swoop down like a bird, or he could go underground and inspect the state of the roots. There seemed no limit to what he could do without a body. It was all a lot of work though, unlike what he had thought that life would be like without a body. And after a while Bill got bored with it. In fact, after a few days of this, he came to the conclusion that manual labor without a body was just as difficult, tiresome, and enervating as life with a body. It made Bill wonder what life after death, if there was such a thing, would be like. He suspected it wouldn't be as nice as people thought.

It was pleasant being in the Tsotska fields once the computer had arranged it so that Bill could feel an analog of heat and cold, as well as kinesthetic analogs and others for the other senses. He knew that he wasn't experiencing the real thing, but it was a lot better than nothing at all. Some afternoons he would lay his metaphoric body down on a grassy knoll on the edge of one of the Tsotska fields. By adjustment of his analog receptors he could get the heavenly odor of red clover and sassweed. The computer even put in a musical analog for him. Bill wasn't much on classics, but the computer explained that the plants grew best when they listened to a lot of Mozart. Bill didn't complain, even though he usually liked music with a beat to it so he could tap his foot.

After a while he got bored with the Tsotska fields and started to wander around. The computer was wired to all parts of the planet, so Bill could make use of the best transportation system he had ever seen. It did require the expenditure of energy to move along the transmission lines. But Bill soon discovered the analog of a battery pack, and so he was able to move himself around effortlessly, the way it was always meant to be.

The power pack analog came about when he met the Squoll. This was a small rodent-like creature that lived in the fields and woods of Tsuris and was able to communicate with autonomous computer projections such as Bill. The Squoll wasn't very intelligent — about the equal to a young and retarded sheepdog — but it made nice company. It was about the size of a terrestrial squirrel, and it had a large bushy tail at either end. This remarkable example of natural mimicry saved it from the many predators who liked to eat Squoll, since seeing two tails confused them just long enough for the Squoll to make his escape. Bill followed the Squoll back to its nest. The Squolls lived in the limbs of cardifer trees, those giants of the open woodlands and glades. It was difficult for the Squolls, since they hadn't been designed by nature to climb trees. Nature evidently had had something else in mind for them, since they had fins and gills and small rudimentary wings. It looked in fact as if nature hadn't quite made up its mind about Squolls. Bill met the Squoll one day when he was lying analogically on the pleasant green grass of the knoll and wishing he had a dirty comic book and a dobbinburger.

"Good afternoon," squeaked the Squoll. "You're new around here, aren't you?"

"Yes, I suppose I am," said Bill.

"Semi-autonomous?"

"Yes, exactly."

"Thought so," said the Squoll. "You have that look of limited competence about you. Don't you get tired of watering these fields?"

"I do," Bill said, "but it's my job, you know."

"Oh, of course, I know that," the Squoll said. "I could tell at once that you were one of the computer's extensions."

"I don't like to think of myself that way," Bill said with some indignation. "But I guess you're right. I sure wish I had my body back."

"Yes," the Squoll said, "bodies are nice. Especially ones like mine, with two tails. Would you like to come back to my roost and have some tea?"

"I'd love to," Bill said, "but I don't seem to have a body with which to drink it."

"Never mind," the Squoll said. "We'll pretend. And you'll have a chance to meet the family."

The Squoll hopped along, and Bill drifted along in that bouncy way that computer simulations have. They soon reached the grassy knoll where the Squoll made his nest. It was a large hole in the hillside which was easy to find because the Squoll had outlined it with a broad stripe of white.

"What's that for?" Bill asked.

"The stripe is so that we Squolls can find our way back to our nests," the Squoll told him. "Mother Nature has short-changed our species a bit by equipping us with poor eyesight, hearing, taste, spatial cognition and smell. The rest of our senses are super-acute, however, to make up for these apparent lacks."

"That doesn't leave very much."

"Shut up."

"Sorry. Don't other creatures find your lair, too? I mean, that stripe is really very visible."

The Squoll gave a little chuckle. "They can't see it," the Squoll said. "The predators here have white-black blindness. It's a hereditary birth factor, and of great importance to us Squolls, as you might imagine."

The opening to the Squoll nest was small, but Bill, being ineffable, was able to slide in easily. The Squoll had counted on this, evidently, because he seemed to assume that Bill could go anywhere that he could go.

"Now I'll just put up the tea," the Squoll said. "I'd like you to meet my wife, Mrs Squoll, but she's working today with the ladies' auxiliary. And the children are in school, of course. Tea's just about ready. Lemon or milk?"

"I told you," Bill said. "I can't drink without a body."

"But you can pretend, can't you?"

"All right, I suppose that I can," Bill said. "Make it tea with lemon, please, one teaspoon of sugar, and a mug of Altarian rum on the side."

"I'm clean out of rum," the Squoll said. "Would Olde Sink Cleaner whiskey do?"

"Sure it will," Bill said, and he nodded approvingly as the Squoll poured an imaginary drink from an imaginary bottle into an imaginary shot glass.

And so the afternoon passed in a haze of imaginary whiskey

and bona fide good spirits. Bill felt considerably better after talking with the Squoll. He determined not to give in to his circumstances. The next day, when his work in the fields began, Bill set the sprinklers for automatic operation, asked the Squoll to keep an eye on things for him and let him know via neuronic telegram if anything went amiss. And then he went exploring.

It was wonderful to soar with the assistance of the battery pack through the world of Tsuris. It was a good-looking planet, once you got under the unpromising-looking layer of clouds. There were villages scattered here and there as he hurried across the mainland. There were steep mountains to duck and dodge among. There were rivers whose courses he could follow. And from time to time Bill met other members of the computer's semi-autonomous family.

One of these was Scalsior, a semi-autonomous tri-pedal creature from Argone IV, who had been passing this way some years ago while on his way to a reunion of his kith in Accesor, foremost of the Cepheid worlds. He had never gotten there. The Tsuris computer, which was able to extend its power far beyond its biosphere, like a globular creature extending a long, ghostly but effective pseudopod, extended its influence and plucked the Scalsian ship out of space and dragged it down to the level of the planet. Scalsior had been enslaved as had so many other sentient creatures, who had been for the most part just passing by and minding their own business.

Scalsior had also met the Squoll, and the two had become close friends.

"Si," Scalsior said, "eez a very good fellow, eez our Squoll. I give great envy to him his merry state. Look closely and give beeg sneer at the most stupid job that *cabron* computer has given me."

Scalsior's job was to open and close the locks on a small irrigation ditch deep in the vegetable fields. The work in itself was valuable, since plants on Tsuris, as everywhere, require their moisture or they are apt to scream in pain, turn brown or black, fold up their petals across their stems and die. At least some plants somewhere did that. But although the work was useful, it didn't require the daily full attention of a grown-up like Scalsior; especially since there was an automatic opening and closing mechanism on the lock valves which functioned pretty well most of the time.

"*Merda* eet has been most bloody unpleasant to me," Scalsior said, "to at last finally achieve celestial harmony of a bodiless state while still living, a state in which I am mind, all mind, and find that this mind of mine eez being used for something damned trivial and superfluous. *Cargota*!"

"Why don't you just go off and do what you please?" Bill asked.

"Would that was the way eet worked! *Chinger*! That, desirable though eet would seem, eez simply not in the deck of cards."

"Why not?" Bill wanted to know.

"You ask, I tell, because eet's not correct, not kosher, as they say in the ancient tongue. Not Pukka. Extremely un-SOP. Do I make myself clear?"

"Clear enough, I guess," Bill said, "but it's all a lot of nonsense. That's what the computer told me, too. But I just walked away. You could do the same thing."

"I suppose I could," Scalsior said. "But I got this horrible feeling deep down in my imaginary subconscious that we'll catch holy sheet when the computer catches up with us."

"I don't see how," Bill said. "I mean, we don't have any bodies for it to punish."

Scalsior thought about it for a while. "Sonamabeech! Eet's true! Of course, eet could punish our minds. Mental barbed-wire whips or sometheeng."

"As long as it doesn't hurt. And how could it," Bill said, then thought awhile. "It can do what it likes to my mind, as long as it leaves my body alone."

Scalsior joined Bill and they went journeying together around the world of Tsuris. Presently they passed over a pleasant land where the sunshine was almost continuous and there was a long sandy coastline and a gentle ocean lapping at it.

"This is nice," Bill said.

"I don't like eet. We ain't supposed to be here, no way," Scalsior muttered. "This ees the principality of Royo."

"It looks like a good place," Bill said. "How come the Tsurisians haven't taken it over?"

"You got me there, keed," Scalsior shrugged mentally. Not easy to do. "Eet might be interesting to find out. But maybe dangerous too."

Reluctantly they left the pleasant-looking land of Royo and returned to the sterner realities of Tsuris. As they speeded back toward the central factory that housed the Tsurisian computer, they picked up frantic mental messages of a distressing sort.

"That sounds like a Mayday call to me," Bill said.

They went in closer. It turned out to be the voice of the Tsuris computer itself. Quickly it gathered both Bill and Scalsior into its interior. They passed through long, winding cylindrical tunnels and at last found themselves in an egg-shaped room which was dimly lit by concealed lighting. Bill and Scalsior were bathed in a pearl-gray radiance. Bill noticed that there were several sofas in the room, and a desk. Bill couldn't imagine why the computer had bothered to put these furnishings into the middle of an imaginary room somewhere in its own mental sphere of construction. Scalsior was beside himself with anxiety. "Eets going to go badly for us, I just know eet eez. Oh, *merda*! I should never have allowed you to talk me into going off on a crappy sightseeing tour that way. Do you suppose the computer will accept my apology? As well as my totally sincere and cringing promise to never do eet again?"

"We'll see what the computer says," Bill rasped, a little grimly.

It was shortly after that that the computer came into the room. Or appeared to come into the room since the whole damn thing was nothing but an electronic simulation anyway. It made quite an entrance, descending from an invisible spot in the ceiling in the form of a flashing blue light, and then winking out of existence for a moment, appearing again in the form of a severe looking man in a blue-stripe business suit, the shoulders thick with dandruff, and sporting a small mustache and pince-nez.

"You two creepos have been disobeying orders," the computer implied. "Have your dim traces of brains forgotten already that I told you how important this work is? You must do it properly, exactly, quickly and succinctly — or there will be the most dire of consequences."

"Is that a fact?" Bill said truculently.

"Yes, it shagging well is."

"How do you propose to punish us, seeing as how we haven't any bodies, huh?" Bill sneered.

"I have my little ways," the computer hinted laconically. "Do you want me to give a quick and repulsive demonstration?"

"Oh, please, no," Scalsior begged. "Everyone knows that computers are very big, powerful, sadistic and highly dangerous. Which eez why we banned them from our planet. Other computers of course, you being a fair and impartial, not to say kind, are an exception to the general rule. I take your word for eet. I'll obey like mad, let me tell you!"

"Then you, with all groveling and knee-bending, may be gone," the computer ordered in a lordly tone. Then it turned ominously to Bill. "But as for you . . ."

"Yeah," Bill said surlily, "what about me?"

"Do you want a demonstration of my wrath?"

"Not particularly. But I suppose there is no stopping you. Let's see what you can do."

Immediately the figure seated at the desk vanished. The opalescent hue of the domelike wall changed to red shot through with streaks of black. An unpleasant exudant oozed from the walls. Regurgitant sounds came from speakers that suddenly extruded themselves from the walls. From hidden entranceways little black imps complete with forked tails and

47

bearing tiny pitchforks flew in and circled Bill's head like a flock of mites, not managing to bite him, of course, since his corporeal extension was missing, but managing to act plenty annoying and to block his field of vision. At the same time one of the walls opened to reveal a fiery furnace, complete with wrought iron horses standing in the middle of it bearing huge blazing logs. The gusts of heat the furnace let out would have frightened the bejeezus out of a creature with a lot less imagination than Bill. At the same time the wall on the other side opened to reveal an Arctic wilderness with a double gale blowing across sending great flurries of razor-sharp ice crystals flying around the room. Both of these creations were going full blast at the same time, and Bill, no matter where he moved, seemed to be caught between them. He perceived a tiny passageway in one wall and ran to it. It led him to a pit full of excrement. And then the walls started shaking.

Bill was teetering on the single plank that ran across the side of the excremental ordure shaking with fear and knowing that he was going to fall into it. At this moment, when all appeared to be lost, a voice came to him from somewhere close by:

"Don't let the bastards get you down!"

"Who's that?" Bill asked tremulously.

"It's me. The Squoll. I just wanted to see how you were doing."

"As you can see," Bill screamed, "not too goddamned well!"

"I fail to perceive the difficulty."

"You do do you, you moronic two-tailed animal! Just take a good look. I've got a fire on one side and a snowstorm on the other side and a pit of shit blocking the only exit."

"Really? That's quite interesting," the Squoll said admiringly. "I can't see any of those things, of course, because they're computer simulations and therefore don't work on simpler creatures such as myself."

"You can't see them?"

"I'm afraid not. Take your word for it, though."

"If you can't see them, that means they're not there!" Bill cried out excitedly. And at that very instant the hallucinations or visions or whatever the hell they were — computer simulations maybe — ceased. Or rather, they may very well have continued, because Bill could see various shadows dancing and interweaving, but they had no meaning for him because he had refused to understand them out of miffed pride at being outdone by a simple-minded Squoll.

With the hallucinations or whatever ended, Bill could see that the interior of the computer was also a simulated space, and that he need no longer be bound by the walls. He walked through several of them. Behind him came an angry voice: "And just what do you think you're up to?"

"Goodbye, computer," Bill said. "I'm going to take a little vacation from all this."

No matter what the computer said, there didn't seem to be anything he could do. It called after Bill, "You'll be sorry," but Bill ignored that and, with the Squoll close behind, went back to the fields where he had tended the valves and first met the Squoll and found salvation.

Chapter 4

But Bill found that he was not to be rid of the computer as easily as that. He was, after all, in a sense, when you thought about it, and he didn't like to, a part of the computer himself. A partly semi-autonomous part, but still a part. The computer knew where he was all the time. It took delight in waiting until Bill had just fallen into simulated sleep, then it would appear suddenly, often in the form of a banshee, and scream him awake again. The computer made sure it rained wherever Bill was. Although, as an incorporeal being, Bill was, in effect, waterproof, it was still a drag to have to look at those leaden skies, those depressing cypresses, the cowed and malignant cattails that rustled their feathers in the deep and noisome swamp which the computer made sure Bill lived in. Bill was getting pretty tired of the swamp. He thought he was catching a cold, too, from having his feet in water so much. This, although he didn't know it, proved the thesis of various scientists on Earth that colds are mainly in the head. Not only did he have a cold, but he was coming down with bronchitis. He was afraid pneumonia might come next. He wondered if a dream creature such as himself could die of a dream malady such as the ones the computer was trying to visit on him. It seemed entirely possible.

To make matters worse, after a while his friend the Squoll asked him to leave.

"I still like you a whole lot," the Squoll said. "But I've got my family to think about. Our burrow has been flooded for two weeks now. The young 'uns are crying all the time. It's true that they're both cutting ears at the same time, but that doesn't account for all of it. Bill, you know, to coin a phrase, it's just too damn depressing around you. Why don't you take a trip, go somewhere. Preferably far away from here. Maybe you'll come up with some way to lift the curse."

"It isn't a curse," Bill said. "It's just the computer acting peevish."

"And that by you isn't a curse? Goodbye, Bill, and don't hurry back."

So Bill went away. Or rather he tried to until he discovered that the computer had cut his power sources. No longer could he travel in the air, light and fast, using the battery pack that had been supplied to him. Now he had to trudge along on the ground. Even though he couldn't be said to have muscles, something ached. Even though he didn't properly have feet, they hurt him. Especially the one with the alligator foot. Because even in his computer reconstruction, Bill still had that damnable talon-clawed pedal extremity.

He continued to walk, and he slept and dreamed while he walked. He dreamed he was a ballet dancer and someone had tied red shoes to his feet that forced him to dance on and on, while the ballet master, an aged poofter, looked on and smiled sadistically.

And this dismal state of affairs went on and on endlessly and pretty boring it was too. Desperate now, he continued searching through the computer's memory for a place where he'd be left alone. Surely there must be a refuge there somewhere! But where? He tried going into some of the rarely-used data bases from past times on the planet Tsuris. He went and hid in data bases that gave figures for annual rainfall for a thousand years back. He looked for refuge among ancient records of past muggings and murders. He hung out with biographies of past great Tsurisians. He even tried out the catalog of lost causes, the index of impossible inventions, the summary of near impossibilities. Every time, just when he thought he had a good place, the computer came along, often singing in a high-pitched, unpleasant voice. "Hello, Bill, time to rise and shine!" And Bill would be on the move again. Oh, it was a hellish life.

This state of affairs might have gone on indefinitely. After all, Bill was more or less immortal in his present state. He could be expected to last at least as long as the computer did. The only way out might be if the military fleet attacked Tsuris. They had sent out their volunteer and he hadn't returned. And that got Bill worried. He grew long, imaginary fingernails and began to chew them. If they heard nothing they might get it into their teeny-tiny moronic minds to launch an attack.

"You can defend this planet against a bombing attack from space, good old buddy computer, can't you?"

The computer, which was getting plenty of practice in computer-simulated sadism, only chuckled horribly.

Life reached its low point one dismal day that was very much like a really rotten day in February back where Bill came from. There was just enough light in the lowering skies to render the landscape unbelievably gloomy. Moss and fungi had taken root on Bill's skin. Small crabs with sharp claws were able to eke out a bare living in his hair. Vermin of various sorts, both domestic and imported, squabbled merrily with each other in his armpits. His crotch had become a region so dreadful that he no longer even bothered to look there. It wasn't that Bill was abstaining from washing. On the contrary, he had taken to scrubbing himself obsessively. It was that he could never get dry. His uniform, for example, had come to resemble a military sponge. His insignia looked as if they'd been in an underground pit ten feet under a pond. That was not far from the case.

Even his diet had suffered. Although in the early days, when he was still on speaking terms with the computer, he had been served simulated meals of great variety and visual appeal, and had turned his nose up at them because they weren't really nourishing, being virtual food rather than real food, now the computer took great pleasure in serving him up with such twisted concoctions as green frog ice cream, drek stew with toasted yak's curds, and similar unpleasantries. And the hell of it was, even though he didn't require food, being fed directly on computer energy, he had never gotten over his habit of eating three or four meals a day when they were available. Yet when he avoided the computer's loathsome meals he suffered intense hunger pangs which were no less painful for being psychosomatic.

This, then, was his state when something occurred to him that broke up the monotony of his existence and offered a ray of hope. This incident took place on a day that began just as disgustingly as all the others. Bill awoke, tired and unrefreshed, in a cave whose walls dripped moisture almost as vehemently as the rain fell thundering and splashing in the cave mouth. He staggered outside, shaking with cold and cringing with damp, ready to take up yet again the dismal burden of his existence.

Then he noticed that there was a curious light on the horizon. At first he thought of a forest fire. But nothing, not even a simulation, could make this sodden stuff burn. What was it? Bill squinted. The light was a long way off, and to reach it he had to pass through difficult country. Was it worth it? What difference did it make to him, a light on the horizon? It was probably just the bowb-minded computer playing another trick on him.

He groaned and tried to think what he was going to do with himself today. He couldn't think of anything, as usual. He looked at the light again. It was the same, neither stronger nor weaker nor of a different color. What was it doing there? He heaved himself to his feet, cursed feebly once or twice, and set out through glutinous mud that clutched at him with the properties of slow-setting glue. Onward he squelched, limbs aching with virtual exhaustion, teeth chattering with simulated cold. He found that to reach the light he would have to cross a range of mountains. That was doubly annoying, because he was sure that range hadn't been there when he'd first noticed the light. It had to be the computer's work, putting those mountains there. In fact the computer was probably behind the light, too, setting him up for even deeper disappointment in its sadistic mechanical way. Yes, he was doomed, yes he was! Why go on? He might just as well lie down in the mud and see if he could virtually drown. But that would mean giving in to a sadistic collection of transistors and wires. Was this the way it was going to end? Not with a bang but with a short-circuited sizzle.

"Never!" he groaned aloud, then started coughing and sneezing. "Give in to a crappy machine! Not me, not macho Bill! I have survived, ha-ha, far worse. I'm a real winner, I am. No surrender! Onward!"

Cheered on by this masculine bullshit he forced himself to his feet and staggered on, no surrender! Even though his lungs were puffing like a bellows gone berserk, even though the mountains ahead of him presented themselves, on closer inspection, as steep ice pinnacles with screaming winds howling among them, and him without a crampon. Good guys win! The phallus forever!

Despite all this it was no go. Exhausted he slumped back, tired, finished. Without crampons he could not go on, despite the best will in the world . . .

But then he remembered his clawed foot! Yes, of course, his lovely alligator's claws! A natural crampon, born from a lab-mutated foot bud! He wasn't licked yet!

Bill tore off the clumsy wrappings that kept his foot from the metaphoric cold, the coldest kind of cold there is. One foot wrapped, the other unwrapped, he stood for a moment, then, throwing caution to the winds, and commending his soul to the great Tribunal in the sky where troopers collect their final medals and ultimate demerits, he tore off the coverings from the other foot, too. Although it was a normal foot, it had been so long since Bill had cut his toenails that he found now that even with that foot he could get good purchase on the icy metaphor. He scrambled up, panting, grinning, his taloned claw striking deeply into the adamantine ice, while the other foot scrambled for a foothold in the slightly softer sub-adamantine ice. His hands clawed at the sheer face, finding here and there little wiry vines that had withstood the cold and were deeply rooted enough to give him additional leverage. He pulled himself up the cliffside, onward, onward, while insane lights exploded in the sky and he could hear an orchestra in his head playing the *1812 Overture*. And then, suddenly, he was on the crest of the summit. He took one more step. He was over the top. He looked eagerly down the downslope of the icy summit, and beheld a sight he had not anticipated even in his wildest imaginings.

There, sitting in a little natural hollow in the slope, was Brownnose. In front of him there was a fire, and Brownnose was feeding small phosphorus logs into it. These, mounting high in the air, and giving off phosphorescent sparks and also emitting a violet glow, were the source of the light Bill had seen in the sky.

"Brownnose! What are you doing here?" Bill asked.

"Bill! Gosh, how great to see you!" Brownnose looked much the same as at their last meeting. Perhaps his freckles were more pronounced due to the cold; possibly his hair, sticking out from under a fur-lined parka hood, was a little less orange than formerly. It was not impossible that there was another line or two in his face. But despite these changes wrought by time, the evil cosmetician, it was the same old Brownnose, Bill's former friend, a man desperately eager to prove himself and win back the love and respect of his friends, the other troopers, for some idiotic reason known only to himself, or, failing that, at least to have them stop laughing at him.

Bill squatted down by the fire. The phosphorus sparked and flashed, but Bill was too numb to even feel the pain when the occasional spark landed on his skin. This was the first time he'd been warm and dry (because Brownnose had providentially erected a small two-person tent just before Bill's arrival and even had a small pot of stew brewing on the edge of it). Bill had a lot of questions to ask, and the stew was one of them. As he understood it, nothing real could exist here in this place. Even Bill was not real. His body, the really real part of him, was off slumbering in what Bill hoped was a safe place. The computer was the master of reality. It dictated not only what food Bill ate, but what that food would look like, taste like, and so the computer controlled how Bill would react to his food since the computer could shape it to get any response he wanted. If this were true, and there seemed no reason to doubt it, since Bill had seen his own body stacked on a cot in the waiting room while he hovered about in uncertainty for a moment, until the computer sucked him up and took him in. So in that case, how had Brownnose gotten here, and how come he was able to produce his own metaphor for food?

"Brownnose," Bill said to his stupidly grinning friend, "it's not really you, is it?"

"Of course it's me," Brownnose said, his grin turning just a shade anxious.

"No, it can't be," Bill said. "You must be one of the hallucinations or constructs that the computer produces. You couldn't be making this food, either, without the knowledge of the computer. So you're just another fake production of the computer, sent here to make me have false hope again so it can dash it." Bill snuffled with self-pity and wiped a pendant drop from his nose with the back of his hand.

"I'm nothing of the kind!" Brownnose said, wringing his hands with worry. "I'm your good friend, Bill, your old buddy, you know that. Say you know that!"

"Of course I know that, moron!" Bill growled. "But if you were the computer trying to fool me that's what you'd say, isn't it?"

"How do I know what I'd say if I was the computer," Brownnose cried aloud, out of his meager intellectual depths with all this cerebration. All he really wanted was to be liked.

Which was why everybody hated him. "I'm not something out of a computer like you said. I'm me. I think."

"If you're you," Bill said, "then tell me something the computer couldn't know."

"How could I know what that'd be!" Brownnose cried. "I don't know what the computer knows!"

"No, but the fact that you're here at all means that the computer knows what you know."

"That's not my fault," Brownnose said.

"I know that. But do you realize what it means? It means that, since the computer knows everything you know, it is you."

Brownnose thought about this furiously and still couldn't understand it. "Say, Bill, why don't you try some of this here real nice stew."

"Shut up you fake computer projection."

"No, I'm not. Bill, believe me, I'm me."

"Oh all right," Bill said. "If I'm wrong, I'm wrong. How are you, Brownnose?"

"Pretty well, Bill," Brownnose smarmed happily. "I really had a tough time convincing the military to let me try to rescue you."

"How did you manage that?" Bill asked suspiciously.

"They couldn't just leave you missing on patrol, could they? Not after I started making a fuss."

"That was good of you, Brownnose. And they let you volunteer?"

"I think they just wanted to get rid of me. But they did let me go, and I came here and after a lot of difficulties, I found you."

"You wouldn't like to tell me just how in hell you managed that?"

"What does it matter?" Brownnose shuffled his toe in the ice and looked uncomfortable. "The important thing now is to get you out of here."

Bill stared with some bitterness at the being who either was his old friend Brownnose or a computer simulation. It was really important to figure out which he was, because the real

Brownnose would help him whereas Brownnose the computer simulation had to be up to some sort of crappy playing around. Basically the entire thing did not bear looking at. Bill sighed heavily.

"I really think we should get moving," Brownnose said.

"First tell me how you got here."

Brownnose opened his mouth. Just then there was a crackling sound behind Bill. It was a startling noise, and unexpected, and he whirled, reaching for a weapon he no longer had and wondering just how in hell he was going to fight when he didn't even have a body.

What hideous sight bruised Bill's eyes when he turned around? What soul-shaking horror awaited him? He gurgled unphonetically when he realized that he was looking at a reindeer. A plain, old-fashioned, medium-sized reindeer with fairly young-looking horns. It was picking its way delicately along a ledge that ran just a few yards below the summit. When the reindeer saw them it shivered violently, but could not break into a run because of the narrowness of the ledge upon which it was walking. It picked its way delicately along, keeping its big brown eyes on them, its sharp little hooves making crackling sounds on the snow. At last it reached a place where the path broadened. With a flick of its tail it bounded off. In a few moments it was out of sight.

"Out of sight!" Brownnose said. "They like the high cold elevations, you know."

"Who does?"

"Reindeer, Bill."

"How," Bill asked with ferocious impatience, "could a motheaten bowby reindeer get inside this computer?"

Brownnose thought about it. "Maybe the same way we did."

Bill made hideous grating sounds and clenched his fists. "And would you like to tell me exactly how we did get here?"

"They didn't explain to me all the details."

"Just tell me in broad outlines."

"Bill, you're acting downright crazy. Do you want to get out of here or don't you?"

"All right," Bill said gloomily, instantly descending from the craggy heights of anger to the dismal depths of despair. "Though I got a terrible crappy feeling that I'm going to regret this."

He followed Brownnose down the slope. It was tough going for a while, though not nearly so tough as it had been for Bill to get up the other side. He struggled along in hip-deep snow, and envied the way Brownnose seemed to glide through the snow. But it bothered him, watching Brownnose move, because there was something graceful and inhuman about the way Brownnose slithered along. Bill asked himself, when is a klutz not a klutz? When he's controlled by a computer, he answered himself.

Still, he followed, because there wasn't anywhere else to go. Maybe if he made believe that the computer was Brownnose, he'd get a chance to escape. Or at least get the last laugh on the computer.

"It's right down here," Brownnose said, directing them towards a clump of trees dark against the snowy landscape.

"What's right down here?" Bill asked.

"Help," Brownnose said.

They went down through a snow-filled gulch, then scrambled up the icy rocks on the other side. Bill was so busy trying to get up the steep and slippery slope that he didn't look up until he had reached the next crest. He saw Brownnose, or the thing that was pretending to be Brownnose — there may not have been much difference between the two — but surely there was some difference — saw Brownnose motion, waving both arms in a curiously boneless gesture. A computer-animated motion. Bill pretended not to notice, because he didn't want Brownnose to know that he'd caught on to him.

Looking up now, Bill could see, from the far ridge, four black dots moving across the snowy landscape. There was another, larger black dot behind them. "What's that?" Bill asked.

"Those are friends," Brownnose said. "They are going to help us."

"That's great," Bill said. He looked around. There was nothing on either side but icy peaks and snowy fields and five black dots moving toward them and slowly growing in size. There wasn't much he could do at the moment. He wished there were a few more possibilities.

"Who are these guys?" Bill asked. "Allow me to introduce you," Brownnose said. "The large man with the wavy brown hair wearing the two-color, one-piece jumpsuit is Commander Dirk, Captain of the Starship *Gumption*."

"I never heard of the *Gumption*," Bill said. "Is that a new class?"

"Don't worry about it," Brownnose reassured him. "Dirk and the *Gumption* are an independent command. Theirs is the most powerful ship in space. You'll love the ship, Bill."

Bill didn't want to ask how Brownnose had gotten on board the *Gumption*. He figured Brownnose would have a logical answer, like simulations always do.

"Who's the guy with the pointy ears?" Bill asked.

"That's Splock, a Nocturnian from the planet Fortinbras II. They are aliens."

"No kidding," Bill said scathingly.

"But they are friendly aliens," Brownnose hurriedly pointed out. "Splock is real friendly even though he may not act friendly. I wanted to warn you."

"If he's friendly," Bill said, "why doesn't he act friendly?"

"The Fortinbrasians," Brownnose said, "are a race that worships lack of emotion. The less emotion you have, the better they like it."

"That sounds really great," Bill said. "What do they do for fun?"

"Calculations," Brownnose said.

"Better them than me," Bill sighed.

They had almost reached the group. Just before they got into

60

earshot, Brownnose said, in an urgent aside, "By the way, Bill, I almost forgot to tell you. Whatever you do, don't make any jokes or wisecracks about pointy ears. And another thing, even more important — "

He stopped, because Commander Dirk, walking a few feet ahead of the others, had reached them and was holding out his hand. Bill shook it. Dirk had a warm hand and a friendly manner, although Bill didn't like his two-tone jumpsuit — puce and mauve weren't his favorite colors. But then, he'd never been much of a fashion plate. There hadn't been much fashion or stuff like that back on the farm.

"Glad to meet you, Bill," Dirk said.

"And you, sir," Bill said. "Good of you to come all this way to rescue me. I don't really understand how you did it, since to the best of my knowledge I am a disembodied intelligence inside a computer."

"We didn't exactly come here to rescue you," Dirk said. "We are here to find the secret of how the creatures on this planet manage to make spaceships disappear from one place and turn up in another place millions of miles, sometimes even light years away. Imagine how important it would be to our armed forces in space to have this power. As to how we got here, Splock is our science officer. Despite what you may think about his pointy ears, he has an intelligence many times more powerful than mine, and therefore almost infinitely more powerful than yours, as it is easy to tell."

Bill let the insult ride; you got nowhere arguing with officers. "I didn't think anything wrong about his pointy ears! I think they look real nice. I bet the girls get kinky thrills from them. Like from my teeth." He twanged a protruding tusk.

Splock came shuffling up to them now. The science officer from Fortinbras had a long thin face and eyebrows that were obviously alien since they turned up at both ends. When he spoke he had an uninflected buzzing voice like a badly adjusted voice simulator. "If you like ears like this it is highly probable that arrangements could be made to get a pair for you."

"Well," Bill said, thinking it over. "When you get down to it I think that I really don't like them that much. I just thought they look nice on you."

"I was making a joke," Splock said. "Just because my people have no sense of humor doesn't prevent us from making jokes in order to make the inferior races with which we must deal feel more at home. The type of humor I engaged in then was called irony."

"Irony! That's it. Of course!" Bill said. "Oh boy, ho-ho, how funny!"

"I did not mean," Splock said, in frigid tones, "that the word irony itself is funny. Though it does have its humorous overtones, I suppose. I meant that my statement about the pointy ears . . . Oh, shit. Never mind. Captain Dirk, what did you want me for?"

"I'd like you to explain to this trooper," Dirk said, "how we got here."

"But it ought to be obvious," Splock said, looking icily at Bill. "I take it for granted that you've had the Finegurt-Reindeer equations in grade school or junior high?"

"I think they called them something else in my school," Bill said in humble prevarication.

"Never mind. What we did, we retooled the *Gumption*'s engines so they would oscillate on an interrupted Scomian curve. That's commonplace enough, of course; most commanders do it at least once a year when it's time to scrape space barnacles off the hull. It shrinks the ship, you see, which makes it easier to remove the barnacles."

"Doesn't it shrink the barnacles, too?" Bill asked.

Splock stared at him. Then burst into harsh laughter. Bill glanced at Brownnose, who looked away, embarrassed.

"What's so funny?" Bill said at last.

"Asking if the barnacles shrank. What a nice use of irony!"

"I guess it was pretty funny," Bill said, trying to be humble. Thinking that it wasn't too difficult getting along with this weirdo alien.

"No, it wasn't funny," Splock said. "At least not to me. But then, I don't even find my own jokes funny. I laughed merely to make you feel more at ease."

"Oh, thank you very much," Bill said, feeling that this joker was really a fruitcake of the first water.

"Now, after the ship has descended the Scomian curve in a state of oscillation, instead of scraping the hull, we introduce a pulsed beat that further miniaturizes the ship and projects it as a series of immaterial frames. In that form, we are able to enter the computer as a simulation."

"Oh, I *see*," Bill said, not understanding one word of the technical bowb. "Sounds great, really great."

"It has its uses," Splock said, feigning unfelt humility.

"And now since you did such a great job of getting in here — how are you going to get us out?"

Captain Dirk broke in. "We will know that just as soon as Splock makes his calculations."

Splock's long thin face took on a look of utmost concentration. His eyes slitted, a vein in his temple throbbed, and his ears quivered slightly, all signs, as Bill was to learn later, of a Fortinbrasian male wearing a jumpsuit in a state of Urconcentration.

"How did you meet these guys?" Bill said to Brownnose, whispering so as not to intrude on Splock's concentration.

"Stop that whispering!" Splock said. "How do you expect me to concentrate?"

Wow, Bill thought, he really can hear a lot with those pointy ears.

Splock glared at him again. "And stop that!"

"You couldn't hear me!" Bill said. "I was thinking!"

"Logic dictated what you would think," Splock said. "I won't tell you again that I don't like comments of that sort."

"Didn't your friend tell you not to mention his ears?" Captain Dirk said.

Bill cringed, then straightened up abruptly. This was getting to be too much. That asshole alien in the crummy jumpsuit with a hatchet face and ears like a gravid kangaroo couldn't tell him how to think. To hell with them, he didn't need them; he'd rescue himself.

"You do need us," Splock said.

"Stop reading my mind!" Bill shouted.

"I didn't read your mind. I simply applied the logic of expected outcomes."

"Is that a fact?" Bill said. Unexpectedly, he smiled.

"Yes, it is," Splock said, not smiling.

A moment later he was reeling backwards, both hands to his face. Bill had thrown the neatest straight left jab seen since this planet had been born from the fiery pit of undifferentiated insubstantiality. Splock's hand came away red. "You've given me a nosebleed!" he said.

"At least we can get off the subject of ears for a while," Bill said. "It wasn't much of a blow, just a poke. Put your head back and put something cold on the back of your neck. It'll stop in no time."

"You don't understand!" cried Dirk.

"I understand plenty about nosebleeds," Bill said.

"I mean, you don't know what a blow on the nose can do for a Fortinbrasian male."

"He never saw it coming," Bill said. "So much for logical expectations."

"You fool!" Dirk cried. His face was ashen. "Males of Splock's planet carry their spare memory banks in their noses."

"That's a damned stupid place to have a memory," Bill said.

"Where am I?" Splock said, blinking around at them.

Captain Dirk groaned loudly and tore at his thinning hair, "Splock! You have to remember! Stored in your head is the highly important, original and special mathematical logic that will be needed to get us out of here."

"I'm afraid the data is bent, if not destroyed," Splock said. "I was keeping it all up the extra memory banks in my nose for safekeeping. How was I to know this barbarian with a Saurian foot would hit me in the nose?"

"How'd you know about my alligator foot?"

"The logic of the unexpected," Splock said with a sour smile. "Besides, I can see it there."

"Come on!" Brownnose urged. "Let's get the hell out of here!"

At Brownnose's behest they all turned and walked toward the remaining two black dots and the larger black dot that Bill had seen earlier. When they reached it, the black dots were still black dots, only bigger.

"What are these?" Bill asked.

"These are storage simulations of our emergency rescue ship and the two crewmen who man it."

"But they're black dots," Bill said.

"We stored them in that form," Dirk said, "to save energy. It takes a lot of power to beam simulations into an alien computer and the *Gumption*'s main batteries are already dangerously depleted due to a situation that came up immediately before this one."

"What good are they?" Bill asked.

"None at all, in their present form," Dirk admitted. "But as soon as Splock activates them into full simulacrum form — "

"I can't," Splock complained, touching his nose tenderly. "The equations," He sniffled. There was a whistling sound when he snuffled. It seemed possible that Bill had broken not only the crucial reconstituting data which was needed to get them out of the computer and back to the *Gumption*, but also Splock's nose.

"Now we're really in trouble," Dirk said unhappily.

Bill walked up to one of the black dots and touched it. It was cold and metallic. He pushed against it. It was rigid. He walked to its edge. The edge was razor thin. He was to learn later that storage simulations have in fact no depth at all, only width and height, and, of course, quite a lot of area. But even had he known that then, it wouldn't have helped him turn the simulation into something useful.

Captain Dirk said, "Splock! Can't you do anything?"

"I'm trying," the Fortinbrasian said in a nasal voice. "But the data is coming out skewed."

"Look!" Brownnose said.

They were standing on a long plain that seemed to stretch forever under a stationary yellow sun. There were small purple plants on the plain, and a few old ruins that the computer had simulated just to liven up the place. Now, as they watched, furious clouds of dark green matter came roaring over the plain, bearing with them sand and bits of gravel, which came at them with the speed of machine gun bullets fired by a nervous hand.

At once Captain Dirk dropped to one knee, and, unholstering the lethal-looking handgun strapped to his waist, turned the beam to cone-destruction and destroyed the matter before it could cut them to ribbons of simulations.

"Keep it up, Captain!" Splock said. "I've just accessed the outer equations. I don't have enough to help us yet, but I do have enough to give us hope of eventual success."

"Can't keep this up much longer," Dirk said through gritted teeth. "My hand laser is only half-charged. Probably the fault of that new rating from New Calcutta. See that he gets a demerit for this bit of carelessness."

"If we ever get back," Splock said, his face set in the familiar expression of agony of a man trying to remember an equation he had forgotten.

Bill had been watching this and wondering what he could do to help. Suddenly it came to him. He stepped forward and, before Dirk could stop him, grabbed the back of Splock's head by one hand and took a firm grip on his nose with the other.

"Bill, what are you doing?" cried Brownnose, as always the master of the unnecessary question.

Bill gritted his teeth and gave Splock's nose a half-turn to the left. There was an audible click. Bill released Splock and stepped back. "How's that, fellow?"

"He seems to have fixed it," Splock said. He looked at Bill with new respect. "How did you know that the Fortinbrasians are born without noses and have mechanical ones made for them when they go to the world where men have noses as a matter of birth?"

"I just thought I'd give it a try," Bill said.

"Thank sanity for naive intuition," Splock said. He muttered equations in a firm baritone voice and the dots responded by resolving into two crewmen wearing one-piece jumpsuits of the same design only in an inferior fabric to those worn by Splock and Dirk. The large black dot resolved itself into a space launch.

As Bill got in, he thought he heard a voice calling his name. "Bill! Wait for me!"

It had been a female voice. But that couldn't be. He didn't know any women around here.

Chapter 5

Bill gaped around him in slack-jaw amazement. When he boarded, his first impression was that he wasn't in a spaceship at all. At least none of the deep spacers that he had served on in the past. The ships of the regular military service, no matter how large they looked from the outside, were crowded and cramped inside, cut up into noisome little quarters with low, filthy ceilings and an ineradicable smell of imitation boiled cabbage. This was no accident. Trained teams of designers had studied all the data banks of records of long-vanished Earth, had found exactly what they needed in the records of *sailing-ships*, ancient and improbable transport of some kind, and in particular the sub-category *slave-ships*. It was a difficult, nay an almost impossible task, but the Space Navy designers persevered. And in the end managed to duplicate all the filth and cramped discomfort of the original for the present crew quarters.

That was how the Navy did it. But not here! This ship looked very much like an airport waiting room or a Staff Officers' latrine. It was huge, done entirely in pastel colors of avocado and cocoa. The lighting was subtly indirect and flicker-free, and so well concealed that Bill couldn't see the lighting fixtures anywhere. Must be hell to change the lightbulbs, he thought. Not only was the decor original but the crew members that Bill saw were nothing like any other service personnel he had ever encountered. For one thing, they were all young and pretty, the boys, or lads — you could hardly call these striplings men — were young and eager and came in many colors. As did the busty and really well-stacked girls. The ship's crew seemed incredibly racially balanced. So many white, so many black, a scattering of greens and reds. And one sort of brownish-yellow.

When they all entered the central control room, a pleasant-faced young fellow in a beige and maroon jumpsuit, with a white sweater tied rakishly around his neck, jumped gracefully to his feet and saluted. Dirk returned the salute snappily and said; "Permission to come aboard?"

"Of course, sir," the young man answered sheepishly. "I mean, after all, it's your ship, you being our captain, as well as First Admiral of the Blue."

"I know all that," Dirk growled. "A simple salute will be sufficient."

"Aye, sir," the young officer shouted as he saluted so hard he almost put his eye out with his pinky.

"Bill," said Captain Dirk, "I want to introduce you to Midshipman Easy, one of our recent replacements from the Laguna Beach Deep Space School."

"Delighted," says Midshipman Easy, extending a browned hand, his right eye swollen shut where his fingernail had plunged into it.

"Yeah, thanks," said Bill, reluctantly holding out a gnarled paw and wishing he'd had a chance to clean up before coming to this spotlessly clean battleship, or whatever it was.

"Midshipman Easy will show you your quarters," Captain Dirk said. "And Splock will be on hand to fill you in on what's happening."

"Walk this way, if you please," Midshipman Easy said, mincing a bit as he exited. The crew broke into guffaws and wolf whistles at what seemed to be a joke, which Bill didn't understand at all.

They went down long corridors, passing, every once in a while young men in snug-fitting jumpsuits explaining very important things to beautiful young women in even more snug-fitting jumpsuits. They went up and down levels, across more corridors, and finally came to a door with a double zero stenciled on it. Easy opened the door and brought Bill into what looked like a well-appointed hotel suite in the style of the venerable old Helior-Beverly-Hilton.

"Wow," said Brownnose, who had tagged along and now darted into the suite and went straight to the bathroom. "Hey, Bill!" he called out. "They got free samples of bubble bath and fancy perfumed soaps here."

"Don't touch anything," Bill warned him. To Midshipman Easy he said, "What happens now?"

"Just relax while we get the ship underway," Easy said. "There are costly imported wines and cordials in the antique provincial sideboard over there. Should you get hungry before the evening banquet at nineteen hundred hours, there is a snack dispenser built into the five-hundred channel TV. Just push the button for whatever you require. No coins are necessary. You are our guests."

"Wow," Brownnose said after Midshipman Easy had left. "How about this, huh, Bill?" Brownnose walked over to the snack dispenser. "They got french-fried octopus rings, Bill! And coke-joints!" He hurried over to the drinks dispenser. "And they got over a hundred kinds of beer on tap, including the starship's own microbrew, Old Gumption. What do you want to try first?"

"I'm going to wait for the banquet," Bill said. "Nineteen hundred hours is less than an hour away. Meanwhile I'm going to take a bath."

Bill went into the luxurious bathroom. The tub was the size of a small swimming pool. There was a massage machine with buttons for all the species who were aboard or might come aboard the Starship *Gumption*. There was even a little tube of Claw Softener, and a special instrument for clipping talons.

"That was thoughtful of them," Bill said to himself, never thinking that some clawed and taloned aliens might be guests of the *Gumption* from time to time.

Bill locked the bathroom door so Brownnose wouldn't see what he was doing and drew himself a bubble bath, squirming with masculine guilt and hoping that no one would ever find out. Might as well try everything once, no telling how long this unexpected luxury was going to last. He paddled around the bathtub, threw handfuls of bubbles into the air and said *whee*, then found the controls that turned on the viewing screens. An enormous panel slid back revealing a TV screen that stretched from wall to wall. The picture came up and Bill saw Captain Dirk, sitting in a command chair behind his officers, who were seated at computer consoles and switchboards that looked like they came from a submarine of ancient times.

"Everyone ready?" Dirk asked.

A chorus of yesses susurrated forth. But Dirk noticed one silence and turned to Splock. "You didn't say aye, First Science Officer. Is anything the matter?"

"Permission to speak freely?" Splock asked.

"Go ahead, Tony," Dirk said.

"Logic suggests," Splock responded in a monotonous monotone, "that the matter of the Runions from Saperstein V should be resolved before anything further is attempted."

"Suggestion noted and ignored," said Dirk in a pleasantly obnoxious no-nonsense voice. "Rear thrusters all ahead one third!"

The Chief Astrogation Officer — a really zoftig darkskinned woman with an elaborate hairdo — pushed a lever into a notched setting. "All ahead one third, sir."

"Starboard maneuvering jets — a two-second burst. Main engines engage. Pulse control on. Astrogation control set at one zero niner. Port fine maneuvering jets set to three hundred and forty degrees and give me a five-second burst. Pulse control engaged. Starship main drive standby for retrojet engage. All ahead full!"

The screen changed to an exterior view. This, as Bill was to learn later, was provided by a drone ship camera. Why there was a drone ship camera he never did find out. Other than providing a totally worthless exterior view. It was a miracle of misapplied technology.

The view of the *Gumption* as provided by the drone camera was very fine indeed. The gigantic starship, with its struts and appurtenances, its pods and bays, its complicated array of superfluous winking lights, all were enhanced by the engine sound-track, which the drone camera provided. It was very pretty to watch the starship move away, in pythonic ecstasy, and behind them winked the distant lights of the stars. This background was simulated also. Movies of the previous centuries had captured for all time what a starship ought to look like going through space. Standard background film, concocted in special effects laboratories, was used to give this charming and archaic appearance. It never failed to impress those who watched it.

Soon the *Gumption* switched to Main Drive and faster-than-light travel. The picture from the drone changed. Now long streaks of tawny light seemed to converge on the *Gumption*. It was the standard faster-than-light view.

Bill, getting smashed on strong beer and almost drowning as he fell asleep in the bubble bath, was really at his ease. There was nothing he could do to help around this screwball ship — and he certainly was not doing any volunteering. Dirk and the crew had everything nicely in hand. They spent lots of time lounging around in easy chairs while Dirk gave orders in a soft voice. Everything seemed suspiciously easy. The carpeting was always soft underfoot, and soft music played lullingly through all the speakers. It had a lot of harps and harpsichords and carillons and xylophones in it. Real deep space music.

As soon as light speed was reached, the crew relaxed. If that was possible since they were pretty spaced out already. Captain Dirk congratulated them all on a really scrumptious takeoff, and summoned Bill to the bridge.

"Now, Bill, be a good fellow and tell Splock our science officer about how the Tsuris displacement effect works."

Bill bulged his eyes at him. "The what?"

"The special weapon the Tsurisians use to push ships millions of miles off course. Your friend said you had learned it while you were inside the computer."

Behind Dirk was Brownnose, making frantic motions. Bill had no idea what Brownnose was trying to tell him, but figured he was probably trying to signal Bill to fake it. Bill would have been glad to, if he'd had the slightest idea how.

"I'm afraid I never quite got around to learning that secret, Captain," Bill said. "Sort of out of my line of work. I trained as a fertilizer technician, when I was a civilian that is. My military speciality is Fusetender First Class . . . "

"Shut up," Dirk suggested. He looked quite unpleasant, as did Splock and the others. "Trooper," he grated through gritted teeth, "I'd advise you not to try any games with me. Your friend, Mr Brownnose, assured us that you know the secret of the Displacer, but were rather shy and needed coaxing."

"Brownnose," Bill grated just as grittingly as Dirk, "when I get my hands on you — "

"Bill, I'd like you to meet a seldom-seen but extremely important member of the *Gumption*'s crew." Dirk's voice was now low, sinister and menacing, with overtones of suicidal insinuation. "Step out, Basil."

A tall man wearing a hooded tunic shuffled menacingly from a room in the rear. His face was entirely concealed. But even on the concealment of his face, the contours of the cloth, Bill could detect baldness and evil.

"How do you do," Bill said.

"Don't wise off at us, trooper," Dirk screamed. "I'll tell you what Basil's official position is. He's our persuader."

"Some people would call him the torturer," Splock intoned grimly. "But that is an incorrect description. He only tortures when it is absolutely necessary in order to gain information."

"Do you mean that you sometimes have to torture your crew?" Bill asked.

73

"Of course not!" Dirk said warmly. "It's just that, you know, sometimes when we take over a planet — Yes, Mr Splock?"

"Planet coming up," Mr Splock said.

Bill asked, "How can you know a planet's coming up if you're travelling at the speed of light? I mean, wouldn't it be gone by the time you knew what it was?"

"Our computer tells us when there's a planet coming up," Dirk said. "What sort of place is it, Splock?"

Splock tapped his forehead with long slim fingers. "Smaller than Earth. Oxygen atmosphere. Small population. One of the speculator worlds that sprang up in this vicinity in the recent South Star Ridge scandal."

"Good," Dirk said. "Let's land and take on provisions."

"Also women, Captain," one of the crewmen reminded him.

"Have you used up the last batch already?" Dirk demanded.

"Afraid so, skipper," the crewman said.

"Then we'll pick up a new batch here."

Splock had continued tapping his forehead. "My readout on this place tells me that the males of this planet tend to become murderous when anyone tries to take away their womenfolk."

"That's how it is with primitives," Dirk said. "We'll drop sleep bombs on them in carpet clusters. That way there'll be no argument and we can simply take what we want and be on our way."

Bill could hardly believe what he was hearing. Although he knew that silence was undoubtedly the best policy, he couldn't help saying, "I've heard a lot about you, Captain Dirk. But I never thought you were like this."

Dirk favored him with a thin, evil smile. "That's good to hear, trooper, because I'm not actually Dirk at all. I am the counter-Dirk. Guards, take this man to a cell. The persuader will pay you a visit as soon as we have this planet squared away."

*

The cell, Bill learned later, had been modelled on a copy of an historic prison cell vidrecorded on the most backward planet ever discovered. Before the planet was destroyed. The stone walls (lifted into space at great expense) dripped moisture; lizards crept in and out of crevices. In place of a toilet there was a torn paper cup. For lighting, a slit high up in the wall allowed in a thin ray of simulated sunshine. The sunlight started fading as soon as Bill was put into the cell. It was designed to produce an instant sensation of hopelessness and bleak despair.

Bill lay down on the floor and promptly went to sleep. For one thing, he wanted to preserve his energy for what lay ahead. For another, he was tired. Climbing up sheer ice walls using your claws as crampons would take it out of a better-conditioned and less alcoholic man than Bill.

He awoke later when he heard the rattling of a key in the door. Bill stiffened, figuring it was the persuader. But it was only the jailer bringing his dinner.

The jailer left a tray behind with a threadbare napkin over it. He leered at Bill for no apparent reason and left, locking the door behind him.

Bill whisked off the napkin to see what they had brought him. There were two plates on the tray. One of them bore a rectangular substance with red and white things sticking out of its sides. This Bill recognized as a ham and Swiss sandwich. The other plate bore a seven-inch green lizard which Bill recognized immediately as a Chinger, the deadly enemy they warred against across the galaxy. Bill raised his boot to stomp it. The Chinger sneered.

"Do that, you microcephalic moron and you get a broken foot. Forgotten already that we come from a 10G planet and are harder than the hardest steel?"

Bill might still have stomped the lizard, so deeply ingrained were his reactions of aversion to Earth's newest ancestral enemy. But he stopped because he thought he recognized the voice. Even though it was an octave and a half higher and coming through an alien throat, Bill recognized the special lilt of Illyria, the nurse girl from the provinces who had first befriended him on Tsuris.

"Illyria! Is that really you?"

"Yes, it's me, Bill," the lizard said. Its voice was high-pitched, due no doubt to its miniature larynx and soft palate. But the tones were unmistakably those of Illyria.

"How did you get inside a Chinger?"

"I had some help from the Quintiform computer. When it saw that you were going off planet, perhaps never to return, it began to realize that maybe it had been a little harsh on you."

"Harsh! It kept me in the rain and cold for days and days!"

"That was only subjective time, of course," Illyria said. "Still, it must have seemed very long indeed. The computer asked me to tell you that it is sorry, Bill. It admires your independence of spirit. It wants you to come back, all is forgiven, since it feels that you could be very useful to the Tsurisians."

"I don't want to be in the computer any longer," Bill said angrily.

"Of course not. The computer realizes its mistake, trying to break your proud spirit. There are other jobs for you, Bill. Good jobs. Jobs you would like."

"I doubt that," Bill miffed huskily.

"And you could be with me," Illyria pointed out.

"Yes, that's so," he vacillated.

"You don't sound too enthusiastic about that."

"Gosh, Illyria, you know that I really like you. But when you appear in my prison cell in the form of a Chinger, Earth's deadliest enemies . . . "

"I had forgotten," Illyria mused. "Yes, of course, that might very well account for it."

"Your previous form was better," Bill said. "Though not much. By the way, how did you get a Chinger body?"

"You should have figured that out for yourself," Illyria said. "We Tsurisians exist in the form of radiant energy until we find a body to inhabit. We take what bodies we can get. I know that

76

this lizard shape is no more suitable to your human form than was my previous body of three spheres."

"They were nice spheres," Bill said.

"You're a dear for saying that. I'm sure they did nothing for you. But I was lucky to get it. You know that most of my people have no bodies at all. I was lucky to get the spherical one. But you were asking about the lizard. I was floating lazily through this ship, the good old fighting *Gumption*, looking for a suitable host body — "

"By the way," Bill said, "how did you get onto the *Gumption*?"

"The computer did it. He realized it was the only possible way of getting you back. So he helped me to get aboard here. He provided me with energy. Everything I needed he supplied, except, of course, a body. That is beyond his powers. But he figured I could probably find one here that wasn't being used."

"Most of the people I know," Bill said, "use their bodies all of the time."

"I know that now," Illyria said. "Everyone I saw here was really getting plenty of work out of their bodies. Even when they slept they use them for dreaming. Bill, these people are extremely active, are they not?"

"I suppose so. But tell me about the Chinger."

"Well, after looking all through the ship, I thought I was out of luck. Everybody was using his body for something or other. Some of them were using their bodies together which I found both highly amusing and interesting. You must tell me — "

"Later," Bill sighed, not really interested in explaining heterosexual — homosexual? — athletics to a disembodied intelligence occupying a lizard's body.

"I'll remember to ask. I went on and detected this body in a hidden compartment in the ship's hull. It appeared comatose and I just slipped in and took it over."

"No problems?"

"None whatsoever. They are actually very easygoing lizards, Bill."

"For you maybe, but don't try telling that to the Joint Chiefs of Staff. Can you take over any body you want?"

"Well, of course. But that's not because we're such great intellects. It's just that we're used to living in a purely mental state, and most other creatures are not."

"That's really interesting," Bill muttered half to himself. His eyes narrowed as a hazy idea began to form in his mind.

"Bill, why are you squinting?"

"I was thinking. I'll tell you about it later. Listen, Illyria, something is terribly wrong."

"It'll be better soon. If not, just throw it away. What's one body more or less? I know where I can get a really nice body without having to break any of the ethical rules that prevent us Tsurisians from taking over any old body we please."

"That's great. But I didn't mean that. I mean something is terribly wrong with all of the people on this ship. I've always thought Captain Dirk was a famous hero. But here he's planning to do terrible things to innocent people on some planet we are coming to."

"Most unusual, I guess. Since I have never heard of him before I will just have to take your word for it. How do you account for it?"

"I don't know," Bill said. "When I asked him, he said he wasn't Dirk at all. He was Counter-Dirk."

"What did that mean?"

"I haven't the slightest idea."

"Perhaps I should ask the Quintiform computer."

Bill looked interested. "You can do that?"

"Oh, yes, I told you the computer wanted to help you. It has maintained a link with me. I'll ask it now."

The little green lizard who was Illyria curled up into a ball from which only its snout and eyes peeked out. Its eyes half-closed, its jaws relaxed, its paws exhibited waxy flexibility.

"Hey, Illyria," Bill said. "Are you OK?"

"She's fine," the lizard said. "This is the Quintiform computer speaking now. Bill, I want to apologize. I was just playing with you, sort of. I'd really like you to come back."

"I didn't really enjoy being part of your mind," Bill said. "No offense, but I just like being me."

"I suppose that's understandable," the computer said. "And you are right, your brain is much too valuable to go to waste."

"My brain?"

"Yes. It has two lobes."

"Oh," said Bill. "I think I remember that a lot of human brains are built that way."

"Do you know what that means?"

"I don't think so."

"It means that your brain is capable of becoming as powerful as a computer all by itself, without having to be part of me."

"Oh," Bill said. He thought about it for a moment. "That's great."

"You see, the computer really has your best interests at heart."

"That's nice," Bill said. "But you were going to tell me what 'counter' means."

"In this context," the computer said, speaking through Illyria who was inhabiting the body of a Chinger lizard, which is a pretty exotic telephone connection when you get down to it, "it means that there are two Captain Dirks, the real one and the counter one. You were right about Captain Dirk acting strangely in terms of your usual civilized norms. The man commanding this ship is not the real Captain Dirk, just as this ship is not the real *Gumption*."

"This is getting a little complicated," Bill said, frowning in concentration. "If this is the Counter-Captain Dirk, where is the real Captain Dirk?"

"I knew you'd ask me that," the computer said, "and so I got the information from the computer which runs this ship."

"The counter-computer, you mean," Bill said.

"Yes, exactly. Oh my dear fellow, you must come back to Tsuris with me. It's such a pleasure talking with someone who understands."

"We'll discuss that later," Bill said, sensing that he was in a position of power, though for the life of him he couldn't figure out how or why. "Meanwhile, I'd like to know where the real Captain Dirk is."

"This will amaze you," the computer said.

"Don't worry. At this point I'm amaze-proof."

"Captain Dirk is at present in the ancient Rome of the long-lost planet Earth. The year is approximately 45 BC."

"You're right," Bill said. "That amazes me."

"I thought it might," the Quintiform computer chuckled, sounding more than a little pleased with itself.

"What else did the ship's computer tell you?"

"It also told me why Dirk was there, and how his being there had been the cause of the Counter-Dirk appearing here."

"Told you all that, did it? Obliging little box of transistors, wasn't it?"

"We computers are all brothers," the Quintiform computer said. "Pure intelligence knows no skin color."

"Don't rub it in," Bill said. "Why is Captain Dirk in ancient Rome?"

"He has an important task to perform there."

"Obviously. But what is it?"

The Quintiform computer sighed. "I know there's a great deal you don't know. But really, we must hurry along. I'm not trying to rush you for *my* sake. I've got plenty of time. This sort of conversation requires only a tiny part of my brainpower. The rest of me is back in the computer doing all the stuff I usually do to keep the planet functioning. But I know from what the ship's computer told me that as soon as Dirk and his men get through plundering and pillaging the new planet they've just found, they are going to turn to you and do whatever they have to do to get the secret of the displacing effect from you. Since you don't know the secret, it's going to be a little tough on you. But don't let me rush you."

There was a' long silence. For a while Bill thought the computer had broken off contact with him out of pique. The Chinger lizard just lay there, its eyes closed, looking more dead than alive. It was impossible to say where Illyria was. And he, Bill, was in a lot of trouble.

"Computer?" Bill said after a while.

"Yes, Bill?"

"Don't get sore at me, OK?"

"I am a computer," the computer said. "I do not get angry at people or things."

"You sure give a good imitation of it."

"Simulation is part of the job. Look, to explain properly about why Dirk is in ancient Rome I'll have to tell you the story of the Alien Historian. It's just that I don't think we have time for it right now."

Bill could hear the heavy, threatening, stomach-turning, sound of hobnailed boots marching down the corridor outside his cell. There was a clashing sound as of weapons being grounded sharply. Then the grating sound of a key in his door.

"Please, Computer, get me out of here!"

"Hang on, then," the computer said. "This may be a little difficult — on you, I mean. It's a technique I haven't had much opportunity to practice and some of my defaults may be set wrong."

"I don't care whose de fault!" Bill screamed, going hysterical as the door slammed open and Dirk and Splock stood there, hands on their hips, sneering, clad now in black uniforms with evil emblems pinned here and there, and a squad of black-clad soldiers behind them.

"Hello there, chicken," Dirk said, and Splock laughed in a sinister manner and the black-uniformed men behind them giggled suggestively.

"*Computer!*" Bill screeched.

"Yes, yes, all right," the computer said testily. "I guess it must go like this perhaps . . . "

Captain Dirk swaggered into the room, and Splock minced in beside him. The black-clad soldiers followed carrying the antelope prods and a cauldron of fried chewing gum.

At that instant Bill felt his alligator foot begin to grow. It burst through the few metaphoric rags with which Bill had wrapped it out of a perhaps misplaced sense of common decency. It grew to the size of a cantaloupe, a watermelon, a three-year-old pig, a sheep before shearing, a piano, a one-car garage, and when Dirk and his men beheld it in its atavistic ugliness and menace, they cowered back. Bill couldn't do much except cheer his foot on since at this point it weighed more than he did and seemed to have a will of its own.

"I'll change modalities," the computer muttered, and Bill's foot rapidly shrank back to its usual dimensions. But something else was happening now. Bill found that he was growing very tall. It was a curious feeling, growing like that, longer and longer and skinnier and skinnier, until he felt himself resembling a sausage an inch in diameter and perhaps ten or so yards in length, like an eccentric model of a roundworm done for laughs.

"Don't just stand there gaping!" the computer said. "Find the wormhole!"

Bill didn't know what the computer was talking about. But he did see, just above his head, a small black hole, or at least very deep gray, and it looked like a tunnel into which he could just fit his head. He did it, and promptly fell into the middle of space. And that he found amazing.

Falling like this was strangely uncomfortable. But at least he wasn't alone, for falling next to him was an elongated green worm which was obviously the attenuated form of a Chinger occupied by the intelligence of an alien computer. Obvious? Things were really getting out of hand when something like this could be obvious.

He was still pondering this imponderable when everything went black, or some color very much like black, and he blacked out as well.

Chapter 6

Consciousness returned, and with it memory. Bill felt pretty good, considering what he had gone through. Not that he was really sure what had happened, other than that his dim memories of the occasion were pretty crappy. He blinked and looked about — and discovered that he was standing on a grassy plain, the grass very much the same color as the Chinger who squatted beside him. There was a dust cloud on the horizon that very quickly resolved itself into a group of men with lances and armor and plumed steel helmets. Bill knew at once that they were Romans. He had seen enough prehistoric movies on Interplanetary Super Feature, the galactic cable network, to know that these were indeed Romans, and not to be confused with the Germans of that period, who wore bearskins and had long mustaches. These men were clean-shaven. In the middle of them, borne on a hammock, and looking puzzled but resolute, was Captain Dirk.

"Hi, Captain Dirk," Bill said. "Are you a prisoner?"

"No," Dirk said. "What made you think so? And, in addition, who the hell are you since I have never seen you before?"

"Perhaps I should make the introductions," the Chinger-cum-computer said. Or maybe it was Illyria. Whichever of them was home in the body at the time.

"That's a Chinger!" Dirk shouted, reaching for his sidearm.

Bill, seeing that in another moment Captain Dirk, well-meaning though he might be, would destroy the lizard, thus finishing off Illyria and ending his link with the computer, burst through the armed Romans and grappled with Dirk for his sidearm.

"Don't shoot!" Bill shouted.

"Why not?" Dirk grimaced, struggling to free himself.

"It'll take me too long to explain!"

"Try me. I got plenty of time." He pulled at the weapon.

The Chinger opened its mouth and said, "I'm not your enemy, Captain Dirk. I'm Illyria of the planet Tsuris and I have taken over the body of this lizard in order to help Bill here."

Captain Dirk looked at Bill. "Any truth in what this repulsive alien is saying? And have we met before?"

"I've met the Counter-Dirk," Bill said. "He looks just like you."

"That is really rotten news. We came here to stop the despicable creature known only as the Alien Historian. But no sooner do we get here than we run into a mirror reversal. It traps us here, and, since matter cannot be destroyed and energy is merely information, it produced the Counter-*Gumption* and the Counter-Dirk back in our own space and time. I must get back to stop them."

"But what about the Romans?" Bill asked. "What are you doing here?"

"Trying to sort out the fate of a thoroughly unpleasant man named Julius Caesar," Dirk said. "I am very much in a dilemma as to his fate. The Alien Historian is trying to save Caesar in order to change the history of the Earth to our great disadvantage. We can't permit that. On the other hand, if I stop the Alien Historian, I would be an accomplice to Caesar's death at the hands of Brutus. You can see what a moral dilemma it presents to me."

"You mean you're thinking of letting the Alien Historian stop Brutus from killing Caesar?" Bill knew his Roman history from watching a lot of really bad films about the Romans which had been really popular for a while.

"Well, it is quite a moral problem, as even one with a forehead as low as yours can probably see," Dirk said. "What would you do in my place?"

"Bump off the Alien Historian," Bill said simply. "Then I'd go back to my own time and kick that Counter-Dirk right up the arse."

"That's what Splock said."

"He was right."

"But Splock doesn't understand human emotion!" Dirk said.

"It works the same with or without emotion," Bill said. "Your job is to get the Earth back into its rightful time track."

"You're right, you're right," Dirk muttered. "I've been under a considerable strain lately. They said I'm all washed up, but they're wrong. I can still cut it. You know what I mean?"

"Sure I do," Bill said. "What has to be done?"

"We have to grab Brutus before he can kill Caesar."

"When is all this supposed to take place?"

Captain Dirk glanced at his watch. The Romans stared. They had never seen a watch before.

"We have about two hours," Dirk said. "At that point, according to Splock's calculations, that's how much time the Alien Historian will need to realize we've made an end run around him, and reset his machine to send him back to before we arrived here. That would give him time to thwart us."

"But then you could go back to a time before he came!" Bill said.

"Theoretically, yes," Dirk said. "Actually, we ran our batteries down considerably just getting here. You have no idea how difficult it is to get a trickle charge in 45 BC. No, Bill, whatever is to be done, it has to be done now."

"Then let's do it!" Bill cried.

"Me too," Illyria the Chinger said, pouting, which is pretty hard for a lizard to do, feeling very much out of it since they had overlooked her. Literally.

"You'll help?" Dirk asked.

"Of course!"

"You are an experienced trooper, I believe, and therefore trained for hand-to-hand combat?"

"Well, yeah, I suppose so," Bill said, remembering all the battles he had been in, the ones that he could not avoid of course. "I have had the odd experience on the field of battle."

"Great. And you can command men?"

"Now wait a minute," Bill said, "I'm no officer. I was one once. I had a field promotion. Then I had a field demotion. I think I have had enough of that old officer bowb."

"Not as an officer. I mean on the squad or platoon level."

"Yeah, sure. Lots of that. I was even a DI. But anyway, so what? You're an officer. That's what captain means, doesn't it? So you ought to take charge yourself."

"Oh, I will," Dirk said. "But I must stay behind the lines where I can consult with Splock. But you see, I need a commander in the field, someone who will convey my orders to the troops."

"Now wait just a minute," Bill protested. Knowing that even before the words had left his mouth it was too late.

So that was how Bill found himself leading the Fifth and Second (Valerian) legions against Genghis Khan and about a million of his Huns.

Since the Alien Historian had already changed the history of Earth by protecting Julius Caesar from assassination by Brutus and his buddies, many opposing political factions had sprung up. Caesar, of course, was the outstanding military genius of his age, perhaps even better than Alexander, so he had kept supremacy over most of these hordes. That was up until now.

Not that Splock thought so. "This is not going well for Caesar, Captain. Or for us."

"You are a negative old pointy-eared bastard, but have summed up the situation with precision, Mr Splock."

"Thank you. I have no emotions, so neither your praise nor your insults means anything at all to me. But I thank you anyhow for respecting my intellect and ignore with disdain, if

I had the emotions to show disdain, your stupid remark about my ears."

"What are we going to do?" Bill asked, easing slowly backwards away from the approaching army. His only answer was silence.

As they watched with more than a little interest, the forces of Genghis Khan advanced on their armored yaks. They bore fearsome spears and weapons of every sort and variety. They had huge kettle drums, one to each side of a horse, and cadaverous warriors beat these drums and other even more cadaverous warriors blew trumpets and howled in a thoroughly obnoxious Asiatic manner. Their armies charged along the bank of the Tiber, extending in their serried ranks as far as the eye could see. The Roman troops were looking resolute but nervous, like men who have been brought unfairly into trouble not of their own making. Some of the foremost men were already backing away from contact with these screaming, grinning devils with their horses and camels and strange weapons and their spirit of plunder and murder. Cooties and lice and maybe even crabs and spiders on their unwashed bodies and lank filthy hair.

"It isn't fair," Dirk said. "Genghis Khan doesn't even belong in this period. How did the Huns get here?"

"That," Splock said, "is less important than what we are going to do about them."

"Any ideas?" Dirk asked.

"Just a moment," Splock said. "I'm thinking. Or rather, thought being lightning-fast, I'm reviewing the thoughts I had when the problem just came up."

"And?" Dirk prompted.

"I have an idea," Splock said. "It's a remote chance, but perhaps we can bring it off. Hold them for as long as you can, Captain. Bill, come with me."

"And what about me?" Illyria-cum-Chinger cried out shrilly as they almost walked on her. "You should show a little consideration!"

"Of course, sure, we didn't forget you," Bill said, realizing they had forgotten her. "Stick with the captain. Keep an eye on him. Be right back. I hope." He looked at Splock suspiciously. "Where are we going?"

"We are going to save the Earth as we know it." Splock took Bill's hand and, with his free hand, made an adjustment to the miniature control panel on his belt. There was a sound of thunder and multiple flashes of lightning. Bill didn't even have time for a good gasp. Suddenly he felt space and time dissolve around him. An icy wind blew around his chops, and he felt himself lifted and carried away by a gigantic wind which was none other than the Wind of Time itself.

After a period of whirling sounds and flashing lights and uncanny smells, Bill found himself standing on a barren plain, or perhaps it was a desert. Bill wasn't too sure. It was colored brown and seemed to be composed mainly of gravel, with some larger rocks for comic relief. Here and there were a few bedraggled thorn bushes, barely subsisting in this dry, sere place. Splock was standing beside him, consulting a small map which he had taken out of the pouch at his waist.

"This ought to be the place," Splock said, frowning, his ears twitching. "Unless this is an out-of-date map. Temporal currents change without notice, so you can't always be sure—"

There was a loud bellowing noise behind them. Bill jumped straight up in the air and whirled, reaching for the weapons he didn't have strapped to his waist.

Splock turned more slowly, as was suitable for someone of his intellect.

"It's just the camel men," Splock said.

"Oh," Bill said. "The camel men. Of course. You didn't mention them before now."

"I didn't think it necessary," Splock said. "I thought you could figure out that much for yourself."

Bill didn't bother to reply that he had had no clues. Splock was one of these very intelligent people who always have an answer for everything and whose explanations make you feel more stupid than you actually are. Or so you hope.

The two camel men, mounted on their high dromedaries, had been waiting patiently. Now one of them addressed Splock in a strange language which Bill's translator, after a moment of fumbling, managed to translate into English.

"Greetings, Effendi."

"Greetings," Splock said. "Please be so good as to take us to your leader."

The camel drivers chattered among themselves in a language, or more likely, a dialect, which Bill's computer didn't have in its repertoire. Whatever it was, Splock seemed to know it, and he broke in with a few well-chosen words which left the camel men laughing in an embarrassed and somewhat respectful fashion.

"What did you say to them?" Bill asked.

"Just a pleasantry," Splock said. "It loses a lot in the translation."

"Tell me anyway," Bill said.

"I told them, may your camel tracks never cross the dismal swamp that leads to the stygian darkness."

"And they laughed?"

"Of course. I used a variant for swamp which can also be construed as meaning 'May your tailbone never suffer the multiple indignities of being kicked around the oasis by the Sultan's bodyguards.' A neat bit of linguistic legerdemain if I may say so myself."

The camel drivers had finished jabbering excitedly between themselves. Now the elder of the two, with the short black beard and the bulging dark eyes, said, "Mount up behind us. We will take you to The Boss."

They got up behind the camel drivers and set forth. At first Bill thought they were going toward the distant mountains. But soon he could make out a square shape far ahead, and battlements, and towers. It was a city they were going to, and a big one.

"What is that place?" Bill asked.

"That ahead of us is Carthage," Splock said. "You've heard of Carthage, haven't you?"

"Where Hannibal came from?"

"You got it in one," Splock said.

"Why are we going there?"

"Because," Splock explained with great patience, "I'm going to make Hannibal an offer he can't refuse. At least I hope he can't."

"Elephants," Hannibal said. "They were my undoing. Did you ever try to refuel a squadron of elephants in the Alps in January?"

"Sounds difficult," Bill said. He was interested to note that Hannibal spoke Punic with a slight southern accent, really a South Balliol Lisp. It threw a new light on this famous man, though Bill wasn't sure what it meant. Neither did his translator, which had pointed out this totally boring fact.

"I had it all there," Hannibal said. "Rome was so cwose to being mine, I could taste it. Tasted wather armpitty and garlicky too. Victory within my grasp! And then that damned Fabius Cunctator with his delaying tactics put paid to my dweam. I could handle him now, beweive me, but at the time delay was a new military tactic. Pwevious to that, it had just been ignorant armies clashing by night and that sort of booshaw. Well, no sense cwying over spilt kvass. Now, what do you stwange looking barbarians want? Speak quickly or I'll have you gutted."

"We are here to give you another opportunity," Splock said, talking very fast.

Hannibal was a tall, well-built man. He wore a polished cuirass and a gleaming brass and bronze helmet. They were in Hannibal's audience room at the time. It was not really a major audience room. Hannibal had suffered defeat, and therefore he wasn't allowed to use the main audience room. This was a small audience room put aside for the use of unsuccessful generals. On a sideboard there were sweetmeats, doves' tongues in aspic, french fried mice, that sort of thing, and flasks of tarry wine. Bill had already wandered over to the sideboard, since Splock seemed to have this part of the talk well in hand. There were little pots resting in wire cradles over heating elements which burned olive oil. Bill sampled one of the pots. It tasted like curried goat droppings. He spat it out; it probably was.

"Mind if I try one of these?" he asked Hannibal, pointing to the wine pots.

"Go wight ahead," Hannibal said. "The one in the big jug on the end is wather nice. No tar like the others."

Bill sampled it, tasted, liked what he tasted, glugged another swig.

"Zoinks! What is that stuff?" he asked.

"Palm whiskey," Hannibal said. "Made only in the Highlands of Carthaginia. By an awfully secret pwocess called distilazione."

"Terrific," Bill said, swilling more.

Hannibal returned to his conversation with Splock. This was carried out in low voices, and Bill wasn't much interested anyhow. The palm whiskey had entirely claimed his attention and was quickly destroying his cerebral cortex. He nibbled at some of the repulsive food, which was beginning to taste good, which was a bad sign, then swigged down more of the palm whiskey. Life was not looking too bad at the moment. Bleary, but not bad. Things looked even better when, in response to an unseen signal, or perhaps because it was the regular time for their appearance, a troupe of dancing girls came through the archway, accompanied by three musicians with complicated-looking instruments made of gourds and catgut.

"Hey now!" Bill said. "This is more like it!"

The dancing girls looked toward Hannibal, but he was deep in conversation with Splock and waved them away. They turned to Bill, formed a line in front of him, and started to dance. They were the best kind of dancing girls, tall, wide of hip and generous of breast, with legs that never stopped. Bill's type entirely. They danced for him with many a flirtatious gesture, like removing their veils one by one while doing a grind and a bump; the musicians grinned and pounded and strummed on their strange instruments; tumescence surged and Bill asked the cute dancer on the end nearest him what she was doing after the show, but she didn't seem to understand Punic.

The dance went on for quite a while, more boring now since they put the veils back on after noticing the effect on Bill. Long enough for Bill to get pleasantly smashed on the palm whiskey, and to burn his mouth on the little green chillies he hadn't noticed he was eating. He was about to ask the musicians if they knew a couple of old songs Bill had learned when he was a kid, but before he got the chance Hannibal and Splock seemed to come to some sort of an agreement. They shook hands and got up and strolled over to Bill. Hannibal made a gesture and the musicians and dancers packed up and left quickly.

"So, it's all settled," Splock said. "Hannibal himself is going to come to our aid. He'll bring five of his crack elephant squadrons. I've assured him we'll handle all the details of servicing his elephants."

"Thash great," Bill said, with some difficulty. He felt like his tongue was wearing a spacesuit. "Didn't seem too difficult, either, neither, wazzah."

"No, I was sure that Hannibal would want a return engagement against the Romans. There was just one trifling condition that I had to agree to."

"What was that?" Bill asked.

Splock hesitated. "I'm afraid you might not like this. But you are so smashed I doubt if you will notice. And you did say you'd do whatever you could to help."

"Whassaht?"

"The Carthaginians have a most interesting custom. Their aid to allies is conditional on a hero from the ranks of said ally agreeing to meet the Carthaginian champion."

"And whossaht?" Bill mouthed dimly, barely aware of the import of Splock's words.

"The word he used was quite unfamiliar to me," Splock said. "I couldn't tell you whom they meant. Or what."

"You mean not man . . . maybe a . . . thing?" Bill blinked rapidly as some dim bit of meaning trickled down through alcohol-laden synapses.

Splock nodded. "This is the sort of problem you encounter when you go to the ancient world. Never mind, a trained trooper like you ought to make short work of it, whatever it is."

"What happens if I lose?" Bill asked, sobering rather quickly.

"Not to worry. Hannibal has agreed to help even if you are killed."

"Oh, yeah, wonderful." Sobriety struck like poisoned lightning at this threat to mortality. "Splock, you pointed-eared son of a bitch — what have you gotten me into? I don't even have any of my weapons with me."

"Improvisation," Splock said, "is the first quality of a well-trained soldier. And you can lay off all the ear-insults."

"Come," said Hannibal, interrupting their friendly chat, "we can hold the contest immediately."

Bill reached for the palm whiskey, then decided against it. In fact, uncharacteristically, he was cold sober and regretting it.

Now to tell of the dueling ground of the Carthaginians.

It was inside that portion of the city known as the Sacred Enclosure — a squat black building within which was an enormous amphitheater, its roof open to the blinding African sun. As at a bullfight, there were sunny seats and shady, and these were sold for different prices. Box holders had clay shards with curious figures inscribed on them. Season passholders had to have a man along to carry the massive clay tablet on which was inscribed the dates of the performances and the patron's seat number. When not used for contests, the Black Theater, as the locals called it, staged ballets, music festivals, defloration ceremonies and other priestly fund raisers for the local gods.

The arena was circular, and there were steep tiers of seats up the sides. Already the stands were half full, and more people were streaming in through the entry slits in the basalt walls. Sand had been strewn on the arena floor. It was a bright yellow, in contrast to the black walls of the building, and the gaily colored pennants that flew from four tall masts. Peddlers in long gray smocks trudged up and down the steep steps selling fermented mares' milk, which tasted about as loathsome as it sounds, squirrel sausages and other local specialities. A group of acrobats was already on the arena floor, and a comic actor in satyr mask and three-foot phallus was really warming up the crowd.

In caverns below the arena, Bill was having an argument with Splock.

"I'm not going out there," Bill said, "without a weapon." Bill had refused to put on a special gladiator's costume. Nor had he accepted any of the edged weapons which were laid out before him on a table.

"These look perfectly suitable," Splock said, splanging the edge of one of the swords with his fingernail. "I fail to understand your difficulty."

"I don't know anything about swords, that's my difficulty." Bill said. "I want a gun."

"But these people do not have guns," Splock said.

"I know. That's why I want one."

"That would be hardly sporting," Splock pointed out.

"Sport!" Bill shrieked. "Those mothers want to kill me! Whose side are you on, anyhow?"

"I serve the truth, unemotionally and coolly," Splock said. "And anyhow, I don't have a gun."

"You've got something, though, haven't you?"

"Not really. Only this laser pen. But that's hardly suitable — "

"Gimme!" Bill said, and grabbed it. "What's its range?"

"About ten feet. Three meters, to be exact. At that range it can burn a hole through two-inch steel plating. But Bill, I have to tell you — "

Just then Hannibal and two guards came into the room. "Well?" Hannibal asked. "Is the man from the future ready?"

"Ready," Bill said, putting the pen into the pocket under his pouch and zipping it.

"But you have no sword or lance!"

"You're right. Just pass one of those daggers over. A small one, that's it."

"Guards, escort him to the arena!"

Bill, flanked by guards with lances, marched out into the sunlight. When the crowd caught a look at him, shambling along and blinking in the sunlight, cleaning his nails with the tiny dagger the odds on Bill fell from ten to one to a hundred to one.

"You better take some of that," Bill called out to Splock.

"Bill!" Splock shouted. "There's something I must tell you! That laser pen — "

"I'm not going to give it back," Bill told him.

"But it's discharged, Bill! It hasn't any current left! Bill, not only is it out of energy, it also leaks. I was going to get it fixed at the next Boffritz we passed."

"You can't do this to me!" Bill screamed.

But now he was alone in the middle of the arena. The crowd had fallen silent. Not a sound could be heard except for a faint rustling noise under his tunic.

Bill opened a button. A Chinger stuck out its tiny green head.

"Still with you, Bill," the lizard said.

"Who am I talking to?"

"The computer, of course."

"You'll zap whatever comes up, won't you, computer?"

"Alas, Bill, I am not capable of taking any action in my present form. But I will observe everything and report your struggles to your next of kin."

Just then an iron gate in the arena wall opened. While Bill watched, slack-jawed, something came shambling out.

It was a strange-looking beast indeed. At first Bill mistook it for a lion, because the first thing he looked at was its head. The head was definitely leonine, with a full tawny mane, big almond-shaped yellow eyes, and the sleepily ferocious look that lions have, at least in Carthage. But then he noticed that its body was as thick around as a barrel, and tapered down to a thin scaled tail. So he thought it was a snake with a lion's head. But then he noticed the sharp little hooves, just like the hooves on the goats back home.

"Well, bless my electronic soul," the computer said in a squeaky lizard voice since, of course, it was utilizing the Chinger's body as a source of communication. "I do believe we are looking at a chimera! In my studies of the history of the human race — and a rather sordid history it is — I have come across references to the creature. Always regarded as mythological. It was long believed that these creatures were mere figments of the ancient imagination. Now we see that they existed literally. And, if I'm not mistaken, the creature is breathing fire, just like Pliny said it would."

"Do something!" Bill cried.

"But how can I?" the computer said. "I am a mere disembodied intelligence in this world."

"Then get out of that Chinger and let Illyria back in!"

"What would a Tsurisian farmgirl know about chimeras?" the computer asked.

"Never mind! Just do it!"

The computer must have done it, because a moment later Bill could hear Illyria's voice, unmistakable even when projected through the larynx and soft palate and unusual dentition of a Chinger.

"Bill! I'm here!"

This talk took place fairly rapidly, although several of the points had to be repeated since the crowd noises made it difficult to hear finer shades of discourse. The chimera was not

97

motionless during this colloquy. First the dreaded beast pawed the ground, scraping aside the sand and scoring the basalt floor of the arena with grooves three inches long with a single strike of its adamantine hooves. Then, noticing Bill, it snorted a double snort of flames, bright red ones with an unhealthy-looking green tinge at their base. Then, fixing its gaze upon Bill, it began to walk, then run, then canter, and at last gallop, toward the intrepid trooper with what appeared to be a four-armed lizard on his shoulder.

"Illyria! Do something!"

"What can I do?" the unhappy girl moaned. "I'm only a tiny green Chinger! Albeit a heavy one from a 10G planet — "

"Shut up!" Bill hinted in a shout of quiet desperation. "Don't you have the power to take over the minds of other creatures? Isn't that a Tsurisian speciality?"

"But of course! What a clever idea! You mean you want me to take over the chimera!"

"And fast," Bill said, running away full tilt now, the chimera breathing flames behind him and gaining rapidly.

"I'm not really sure I can take over the brain of a mythical beast," Illyria vacillated.

"The computer said it was real!" Bill gasped, dodging as the goat-lion-serpent reared above him, ready to strike downward with fangs that dripped green poison.

"Bill, there's something I haven't had a chance to tell you yet — "

"Get into that chimera!" Bill roared.

"Yes, darling," Illyria said. In the next instant the chimera had halted itself in mid-flight and flung itself at Bill's feet. Its eyes rolled upward and its long forked tongue came out to lick Bill's feet.

"How am I doing?" Illyria asked through the chimera's throat and tongue and soft palate.

"Fine," Bill said. "Just don't overdo it."

And the crowd, of course, was going wild.

*

Bill's triumph was complete, though there was one complication. After the congratulations for quelling the chimera, there were throaty shouts of "Kill! Kill!" and, "Let's see some green blood!" That sort of thing. As well as, "Save me a bit of the sirloin!" It was then Bill realized that he was supposed to slay the heraldic beast. It is customary in this sort of affair to feast everybody after the killing on broiled chimera steaks and other choice tidbits. The flesh tastes like a combination of goat, serpent and lion, and there's just a faint hint of turkey, although nobody knows where that came from. Another virtue of chimera steaks is the fact that, since the chimera is a flame breather, its steaks can be cooked in its own internal heat, as long as you do that in the first hour or two after it has been dispatched. "No way," Bill said. "No way."

His point of view was not appreciated. This was carefully explained to him by Hannibal's chamberlain, a fat and unctuous individual who kept rubbing his hands together, and, when he thought that no one was looking, he pinched his sallow cheeks to give them a little color.

"No," Bill says, "you can't have the chimera. No way. This is my chimera."

"But sir, it is customary for the victor to sacrifice the chimera for the public good. That's what all the other victors do. In fact, chimeras are becoming rare in these parts."

"All the more reason," Bill said, "not to sacrifice this one."

"The chimera must be killed," the chamberlain says. "Otherwise it means ten years bad luck, and that is the last thing in this world Carthage needs."

"I won't kill the chimera, and that's that."

"I will confer with Hannibal and the City Elders," the chamberlain said. "They will have to make the final decision."

"OK by me," Bill said. "And on the way out would you tell Mr Splock that I need to see him right away?"

"Impossible," the chamberlain said, rubbing his hands together. "He has returned to his own time. He left this for you."

He handed Bill a note and exited, bowing low and smiling unctuously. Bill opened the note, which was folded thrice, and read: *Congratulations on your well-deserved victory. Have returned to put Dirk into the picture. Tell Hannibal to assemble his forces; we will be back soon with suitable transport.*

"That's a hell of a note," Bill said. "Just when I need him! Why couldn't he have used the telephone?"

"Because it hasn't been invented yet," Illyria, within the chimera, said.

"I know that. But time travel hasn't been invented yet, either, and he's doing it."

"Oh, Bill," Illyria the chimera said, "what are we going to do?"

"Could you take over some other body for a while? That way we could let them have the chimera and get ourselves out of here."

"I told you I had trouble controlling mythological beasts," Illyria said. "It was hard taking over this one. It is going to be very difficult indeed to get out again. What I need, Bill darling, is a suitable host body."

"Where can we find one? How about one of those dancing girls we saw earlier? The one on the left end of the line was kind of healthy-looking in a very plumpish way," Bill finished, because he noted a frown crossing the chimera's leonine face.

"She's not at all suitable," Illyria said. "First of all, because you're interested in her. I will not be a party to perversity."

"What are you talking about, perversity?" Bill asked. "She'd be you!"

"Or I'd be her," Illyria said. "That would suit you nicely, wouldn't it?"

"Illyria! I've never heard you talk like this!"

"Oh, Bill, I don't want to sound jealous. It's just that I'm so crazy about you. You and your darling alligator foot with shining claws. It's little things like that that strike a woman's fancy. But I couldn't take over your charming little dancing girl even if I wanted to. A suitable host can only be found back on my own planet in my own time. Please, don't let them kill me!"

"They'll kill you over my dead body," Bill said gallantly.

"I would much prefer they didn't do it at all."

"That's what I meant. Come on, Illyria, I think we'd better get out of here."

"Perhaps they'll listen to reason," Illyria said wistfully.

"I doubt it," Bill said. He had heard the sound of marching and turned to see a squad of ten or so Carthaginian soldiers, heavily armored and armed, with Hannibal himself at their head, looking grim and purposeful, the way people look just before they kill a chimera.

"Come on," Bill said, grabbing Illyria by her lion's ruff, and tugged her toward the exit.

"I'm coming," Illyria said. "But where are we going?"

"Away!" he shouted leading the way as they fled. Out the exit and across a busy street, dodging between the pedestrians and horses, the squad right behind them, into a tall building and, huffing and puffing, up the stairs. Behind them he could hear the soldiers in the lower part of the building. They were already mounting the stairs with measured tread. They reached the top floor which was very interesting. Particularly since all of the doors were locked.

"Eeek!" Bill gurgled. "We're trapped like rats."

"Don't give up, Bill! Try the window," Illyria advised.

Bill threw the window open and looked out at the straight drop below. Then at the rain gutters. Leaning out he tested the nearest one that ran above the window. They seemed strong enough; they were bronze and half an inch thick, and fastened to the side of the building with heavy copper rivets. They really knew how to build in these days.

"We're going over the roof," Bill said, climbing out.

"Oh dear," Illyria said, pausing irresolute in the window. "I don't think I can climb. I have hooves, you know."

"But you also have a snake's body. For your life, Illyria, slither!"

The brave Tsurisian girl in the mythological disguise backed out of the window and wrapped her tail around a stanchion conveniently located some five feet away. Trembling but resolute, she followed Bill onto the roof.

The rooftops of Carthage presented a multi-colored display of levels and angles. The hot African sun beat down, because it was summer, and the cold African sun had gone to the underworld to rest and revive himself, or so it was claimed in the ancient annals of the city. Bill raced across the rooftops, scrambling up the higher levels and jumping down the lesser ones. Behind him came armed soldiers, running clumsily in their heavy armor, lances at the ready. As Bill raced along, with Illyria close behind and staying up, he felt a tickling sensation under his tunic next to his ribs. He realized that it was the Chinger lizard that had formerly been Illyria.

"Can you go back into the Chinger?" Bill asked, his breath coming in painful pants.

"I forgot about the Chinger!" Illyria asked. "I don't know, but I can try!"

"No time like the present," Bill said, because some of the soldiers had unbuckled their heavy armor and were coming along quickly now, gaining on him. And ahead, directly in his path, Bill saw a high wall of polished marble. The theater of Dionysus! The god of abandon was now blocking his way.

The lizard crawled out onto Bill's shoulder, took one look at the pursuing soldiers, and started to duck back to shelter. Bill grabbed it before it could go out of sight.

"Now, Illyria!" Bill cried.

"Just a moment," the Chinger said. "There's something I'd better explain. This is Illyria, speaking to you from within this alien Chinger. It's a little strange in here. What's that? No, it couldn't be! Oh, Bill, you'll never guess what's happened!"

"So tell me," Bill panted. The soldiers now had him backed against a wall. The chimera was looking around groggily, unused to being back within its own body again. The Chinger, meanwhile, had gone glassy-eyed and limp. It was still alive, but seemed to be in a semi-comatose state, or perhaps an entirely comatose state; it was difficult to tell.

"Illyria? Speak to me!"

No answer from the somnolent lizard, lying with its four arms crossed peacefully on its green chest.

A soldier prodded Bill with his spear. The others moved in. And at that moment the chimera, released from Illyria's control, resumed its existence as a deadly and dangerous beast. It breathed out twin gouts of flame, like dragons do, and melted several shields. Then it turned to attack Bill.

"All right!" Bill cried. "Kill it, since you want to so badly!"

It was a tricky moment for Bill. The soldiers had to defend themselves against the onslaught of the chimera, returned to itself and filled with mythological fury. It attacked in a manner not seen since the days of Homer, and it emitted loud goatlike bleatings as it charged. These unnerving sounds mounted the scale into the supersonic, set the soldiers' teeth on edge, and set their swords to chattering against their shields. The Chinger opened its eyes and took one look at what was going on and scampered back for safety within Bill's shirt, seeking the snug haven of Bill's left armpit, where it was sure harm would not befall it. The soldiers finally managed to pin the chimera to the wooden planking of the roof with their sharp spears. The chimera's sound output redoubled as it found itself wounded. Black dots appeared in the sky and quickly resolved themselves into long-nosed bare-breasted women with bat wings, all of them clad in snaky black evening gowns. These were the Harpies, called out of their mythological slumber by the wounded cries of their fellow fabulous creature. They dived onto the soldiers, whose ranks had just been redoubled by the arrival of a double platoon of Varangians, sent, as Bill was to learn later, by Splock, who had anticipated this situation and had rushed back to the future to get some help. The Varangians were Swedish Russians, or possibly Russian

Swedes, depending on whose history book you're reading, and they cared not a fig for the menace of effete Graeco-Roman mythology. They laid about them with mighty strokes, swinging their long battleaxes in shining circles, cutting down the Carthaginian soldiery who couldn't get out of the way quickly enough.

"Go to it, boys!" Bill shouted, his built-in translator putting out his words in middle Varangian, which none of these fellows understood since they were Finnish Varangians from the marshlands around Lake Uū. But they liked the sound of his voice and laid about them with renewed vigor. The chimera was definitely bested. It gave one last shriek, which started a minor earth tremor in the city walls, and expired.

Before they could congratulate themselves and pass the beer, however, there was a splatter of rain, and then, within moments, a raging storm had sprung out of nowhere complete with hailstones and hundred-mile-an-hour winds. Great bulging clouds with ominous purple-black bottoms rode across the sky like galleons of doom. This, as Bill learned later, was the arrival of Typhon, the spirit of the hurricane. The Harpies balanced lightly on the screaming winds and redoubled their attack. They too were creatures of the storm. When they came close Bill could see that they had hag faces and the ears of bears, and the bodies of birds with long hooked claws. Like birds, they were shameless about defecation, and like humans, they were purposeful about directing it. The Varangians gagged as a torrent of excrement was heaved at them.

Bill fought free of the reeking mêlée and looked for a place to run to. The only way off the rooftop was the way he had come, and that way was now choked with masses of Carthaginian soldiery, Hannibal urging them on and pointing to him. Bill suspected he had lost his guest status and looked around desperately for another way out. Fighting free of the fighting men who surrounded him, and laying about him mightily with a big broadsword he had picked up during the fight, he cut his way to the opposite wall. There a quick glance showed him a ladder leading down over the side. It was a rickety old ladder, just pieces of bamboo tied together with vines, but it would have to do. He put one foot over the side and started down.

It was at this precise moment that the new thing happened.

Chapter 7

At first it was no more than a shimmering of light. Then it resolved itself into an incandescent ball about the size of a medicine ball, or slightly larger. Bill, hanging onto the rickety ladder, with the Chinger gnawing at his armpit (out of panic rather than malice, he learned later), did not take kindly to the fiery thing that swooped up close to him and hung just in front of his face, changing colors and giving off ear-torturing harmonics.

"What the bowb do you want?" Bill snarled testily. "Can't you see that I'm busy trying to save my life?"

"You just listen, dummy. I'll do the talking," a gravelly voice issuing from the glowing sphere said. "Just in case you hadn't noticed, you are up the creek with a broken paddle. Want a lift?"

In other times, Bill might have been suspicious of an offer for help from a shining sphere of lambent energy that just happened to be going his way, but at the moment he was not inclined to be fussy. Already the ladder was starting to collapse, undermined by the sacred termites of Artemis, whom Bill had unwittingly insulted by suggesting that the dancing girl, a servant of the goddess, be supplanted by Illyria, an outsider and unbeliever. Not only was the bamboo ladder collapsing, but also soldiers had brought to its base a series of big wooden platforms covered with bronze spikes pushed up through them. They were all shouting at Bill, "Jump, jump!" It was an unseemly exhibition and it is little wonder that the

Carthaginians have ceased to exist as a people and are perpetuated now only by a cluster of unseemly attitudes.

"Yes! I don't know who you are," Bill said, "but if you can get me away from here, I'd be plenty grateful."

The sphere rapidly expanded, engulfing Bill. He felt his hold loosen on the bamboo ladder. Then the ladder collapsed, and Bill felt himself dropping through the air for a frightening moment, until the energies within the sphere caught him up and shielded him as the sphere moved away at great speed, leaving behind the sullen and unpleasant Carthaginians and their secondhand borrowed Greek deities.

After things settled down, Bill found himself inside a small but well-appointed spaceship. There appeared to be but one person aboard: a square-shouldered man, handsome but with a dour expression born of having seen too much human folly, sitting at the controls in a big command chair with a plaque on it that read; "Ham Duo — the buck stops here."

"Commander Duo," Bill said, in his most formal and grateful manner, "I want to thank you for doing this for me. I don't know what I would have done without your timely intervention."

"Hell, don't thank me," Duo said out of the side of his mouth. "Sure, I like to save the odd sentient being now and then, when it isn't too much trouble and I'm in the mood, but there's no need to make a fuss about it. A lot of other people would have done the same if they'd had my guts and expertise."

"I really appreciate it."

"Hell," Duo said, "I didn't do it for you so don't go getting all weepy."

"Who did you do it for?"

"The Freedom Fighters of Earth. I happen to know that you are helping them in your own simple-minded way, and I couldn't let you fall into the clutches of the Evil Empire."

"I didn't know Carthage had an Evil Empire," Bill said.

"They don't. The Evil Empire set up simulation techniques so they could loose those mythological creatures on everyone. You bet I had to put a stop to that. So don't go thinking that I was doing it just for you."

"Sorry about that," Bill said.

"It's a natural enough error, I suppose," Ham said.

"I didn't know you were able to operate in the past," Bill said. "How did you do that? The *Gumption* got here by putting her engines into oscillation."

"I know all about that," Duo said. "It's a dumb trick. They'll have to reseat all the bolts before their ship is spaceworthy again. Much better to use a temporal displacer that I just happen to have."

Duo gestured. Bill saw, on the port side of the spaceship, not far from the bow but not far from midships, either, a black box with a plaque on it. The plaque read, *Temporal/Spatial Displacer — Patent Pending*.

Bill stared at it. Then stared even closer as he realized that this was the very secret that his own Space Navy had sent him to Tsuris to find out about. If he could get his hands on another like it — or even on this one . . .

"Where are we going?" Bill asked coyly.

"Rathbone."

"Beg pardon?"

"The planet Rathbone."

"What's there?"

"A little unfinished business," Duo grated, his voice grim, his large, attractively hairy hands clutching grimly to the controls of his ship.

"Do you suppose you could drop me off somewhere?" Bill asked. "Space Trooper Headquarters, for example?"

"Sure," Duo said. "I'll just take care of this Rathbone matter first. It's on the way, and it won't take long."

Illyria the Chinger seemed to be asleep inside his shirt — and Bill could easily understand why. He heaved a tired sigh and sat down heavily on the ship's sofa. He found a magazine, a comic book magazine featuring ducks in full armor and a camel dressed up to be Charlemagne. There was the sound of distant quacking and screaming when he turned the pages. Soon he was absorbed in the story. He only hoped the business on Rathbone wouldn't take up too much time.

"Bill," Duo said, then shouted since he saw that he wasn't getting through. "You, trooper! Get your nose out of that revolting comic for five minutes and get below and clean yourself up — I can smell the blood and gore from here. There are plenty of spare uniforms left over from the masquerade party I had. Then haul your butt into the galley and grill us up a couple of mastodon steaks."

The thought of food was a winner and Bill gurgled happily as saliva spurted into his mouth from every dusty salivary gland. After tossing out his torn uniform, and pulling on a new one with admiral's insignia, he found the galley, and a freezer full of mastodon steaks that Duo had picked up on a previous adventure. He grilled one of these in the turbomicrowave, which went so fast that the steak burst into flame and turned into charcoal as he closed the door. He played with the controls until he got it right. He promised himself that he would cook the next one for Duo. Looking around the galley for something to wash it down with he found a cabinet filled with brown bottles. One of them had a hand-written label that read; "Homemade Ophiuchian Rum — not for Human Consumption."

"Right now I'm not feeling human!" he cackled and drank deep.

When he got off the floor he grinned happily and drank some more. A delicious numbness began to creep over him, disturbed only by an itch in his armpit. He started to scratch it and found himself scratching the top of the Chinger's head.

"Illyria, how are you?" he asked.

"She's doing all right," the Chinger said.

"What does that mean? Who the bowb am I talking to?"

"Bill, this is going to take a little explaining."

"To hell with that! Who are you?"

Bill grabbed at the Chinger as it started to flee and, wholly by chance, an accident really, his finger touched the back of the Chinger's neck. When this happened the top of the Chinger's head opened on a concealed hinge. Inside the creature's skull, where the brains would normally be, though there weren't any now, there was a tiny man, no more than an inch high, seated at a tiny control panel. There was a cot and an easy chair close by, and a tiny toilet. The man was smoking nervously, tapping the ashes of his cigarette into an ashtray so small as to be only two steps above invisible to the naked eye.

"How did you get in there?" Bill gaped, then frowned. "And, equally important — what are you doing in there?"

"Well," the man said, "that is going to take a little explaining. First let me introduce myself. Charles Ivan Arbuthnot, SNI, Space Navy Intelligence. Because my name is so long the initial letters are combined to form an acronym, CIA. Most people call me that, and you can too — "

"Just kindly shut the hell up," Bill suggested. "Where's Illyria?"

"That's part of the explanation. Bill, don't be rash, hear me out."

Bill had raised one hamlike hand in preparation to smashing the Chinger, the tiny agent CIA within it, to a small but messy pulp. What he had drunk seemed to have done some nasty things with his head.

"This is part of the secret Chinger technology," CIA said. "I'm trying to bring the secret of miniaturization back to our armed forces. I wore a very hairy, and warm too let me tell you, ape suit and hung around the jungle near one of their secret laboratories that we discovered on this hothouse world. I got into the lab one night and found the secret miniaturization machinery that enables them to shrink or expand at will, thus playing hell with Earth's plans and generally confusing everyone. They had this giant Chinger robot for working in steel mills and I got into the controls, reduced to real Chinger size and got the hell out of there and was doing fine until your girlfriend took over my mind and she was too stupid to know it wasn't really a Chinger mind in there but a human one. So now you understand."

Bill didn't know what to say. It was a reasonable enough explanation, given the unusual circumstances of everything. But there was something fishy about it, too. Bill had the impression that he was not being told the whole story and besides this joker talked so much Bill's head was beginning to hurt. Or maybe it was the booze. He pinched his nose with his fingers but it did not help. Then he remembered.

"Listen, CIA — or whatever the hell your name is — where's Illyria who was supposed to be in there?"

"That's the difficult part," CIA said. "As you can imagine, there isn't much room in here once you go down to the level I'm at. Illyria tried to squeeze in, took over for awhile as I said. I know how fond you are of her. I was trying to save her for your sake."

"Yeah, what happened?"

"It was too tight for us both," CIA said. "You can imagine how difficult it was, having this female persona squeezed into my brain. Bill, I didn't mean to harm her. I was trying to find the best solution for everybody."

"Where's Illyria?" Bill roared, his broad hand with its muscular thickness hovering over the subminiature CIA in his tiny control room.

"Now listen, I'm trying to tell you," CIA said, cowering. "Give me a chance, will you? It's hard to talk when you're as tiny as I am."

"So get back to your real size," Bill said.

"I'm afraid there's some difficulty around that, too," CIA said, snuffling unhappily.

"I want to know about Illyria right now," Bill growled angrily. He reached into the Chinger's head and plucked CIA out between thumb and forefinger. Bill's other hand curled into a fist and the fist lifted, prepared to hammer CIA into a thin, unpleasant paste.

"Since room was so limited," CIA said, "she decided to perform the Jansenite Maneuver. I begged her not to, but you know what she's like, Bill, a real trouper. I even offered to vacate this head for her. But she wouldn't hear of it. That's a girl in a million, Bill. You were lucky to have known her."

"What is the Jansenite Maneuver?" Bill asked in a normal tone of voice. His throat was getting hoarse from roaring.

"It was invented, or perhaps I should say developed, on the planet Jansen VII, which is located near the Coalsack region. The local species there had a problem, you see — "

CIA's explanation was interrupted by Ham Duo's voice over the intercom. "Bill! Get up here at once! We got trouble!"

"In just a minute," Bill called back. "I've got to — "

"Drop everything and get up here!" Duo roared. "If you want to live, that is. If not, take your time."

"Be right back," Bill said to the miniature agent. "Don't go away." He hurried to the control room.

"What's going on?" he asked.

Ham Duo gestured at the wraparound view plate that afforded a view of nearly two hundred degrees of space without distortion. Bill saw three small ships coming toward them and maneuvering at great speed. Bursts of radiance flared against the ship's energy shields proving that some of their missiles were getting through their defenses. Another two ships came up behind them. They were squat little vessels, one-being fighter-interceptors, painted the ominous ocher and rose madder of the Swinglis* of Omnichron II.

"But we're not at war with the Swinglis*!" Bill said.

"Tell them that," Ham Duo said. "And meanwhile you might as well man the port atomic cannon."

Bill ran to the gun station and strapped himself into the control seat. He switched onto manual just as a double burst rocked their ship, dimming the lights and putting a strain on the defensive shields.

"One more like that and we've had it," Duo gritted.

The Swingli* ships were streaking in toward Duo's ship from all angles, and both Duo and Bill were at the controls of their port side and starboard side atomic cannons respectively. Brilliant laser flashes arced here and there, filling the blackness of space with the brilliance of arcing electricity. One of the Swinglis*, bolder than the rest, bored straight in toward the ship's defensive shield, scorning defensive action. "Get that sucker!" Duo shouted. "Tracking," Bill roared. Both fighting men set their sights on the approaching bandit. Their ship bucked and swayed as atomic torpedoes burst against the energy shield, buffeting the two men and knocking down all the crockery in the ship's tiny galley. Bill managed to blow up the bandit at the last possible moment, sending its burning remains cartwheeling across space. Duo meanwhile had accounted for five more of the raiders, leaving only twenty or so to go.

"Another squadron of them coming up astern," Bill said, glancing into the retrograde mirror attached to his gunsight.

"These guys are really starting to get me mad," Duo snarled, showing his teeth, which were startlingly white and obviously false. "Strap yourself down, old buddy. I'm going to try something real different."

Bill grabbed for the safety harness and quickly buckled it around him. From the ship's galley he heard shrill sounds, like a miniature man would make if he were being buffeted around mercilessly. Ham fired the full bank of retrograde rockets, at the same time skidding the ship into an impossibly tight turn.

Bill's harness snapped under the huge G-strain. He found himself plastered against one wall as Duo, his eyes bulging out of his head, continued to tighten the turn.

Behind them, the Swingli* bandits fell away, unable to keep up with this apparently suicidal maneuver. As soon as he had put a little distance between his ship and theirs, Duo kicked in the emergency light-speed selector. There was a groan of tortured metal, a squeal of overstressed men. The ship shuddered like a rat in the jaws of a terrier, then suddenly darted off at a rapidly multiplying speed factor impossible to attain in a normal maneuver.

Space winked on and off. Suns appeared and vanished. The ship was revolving as it sped through its turns, and Bill was bouncing from wall to wall. Duo was still strapped in, but he seemed to be at the breaking point.

Bill looked through the mirrors, then checked again with the radar detection system.

"You can ease up now!" he told Duo. "We've outrun them."

"Ease up!" Duo said. "Ah, wouldn't I dearly like to!"

"You mean — "

"That's right," Duo said.

Out of control, spinning and turning, the ship shrieked down through the thin upper atmosphere of a planet. The ground was coming up very rapidly. Which didn't really matter since they would burn up at this speed, long before they hit.

Now sing, Muse, of that descent through the upper atmosphere, the ship's hull glowing a dull red as it skimmed the thin upper air, Ham Duo desperately trying to take speed off the ship, which was fluttering and turning like a drunken butterfly. And tell us of Bill, too, bouncing from wall to wall as the ship changed configuration, trying to get back to the galley where he had left CIA, the Chinger, and perhaps — it was difficult to tell at this point — Illyria. Inch by inch he crawled as the retro-rockets fired and Duo tried maneuvers unheard of in the *Space Pilot's Companion*, in any edition, to try to get more speed off the ship before they either burned up in the atmosphere or crashed like a cannon ball on the planet's rapidly looming surface.

Then they were plunging through dense cloud cover, red and purple clouds with silvery fringes, through and out the other side until they could make out features on the planet. It was a yellow and orange world, with bright green patches here and there, and long dark markings that might have been canals but also might have been something else. It was hard to be sure at this speed and altitude and G-pressure.

Bill managed to get back to the galley. The Chinger had found a tiny deceleration hammock, of the sort used to keep eggs from exploding. Bill gasped hoarsely with the last of his strength, "Illyria, are you all right? Are you home right now?"

But it was CIA's voice-pattern that replied. "Like I said, Bill, I was going to explain about that."

But it looked like explanations would have to wait, perhaps forever, because the ground was rushing up now like a locomotive gone berserk, only much bigger, and Bill still wasn't strapped down and was in good stead to be shmeared flat into a thin unpleasant slime when the ship struck.

Then, at the last moment, the doors of the pantry swung open and Bill saw within a gigantic cauldron filled with a pasty gray doughy substance. This, as he learned later, was the dough for a giant pot-pie, Ganja pot that is, that Duo had been whipping up before the difficulties on Rathbone arose to change his plans. With his last strength he hauled himself forward.

The dough surrounded him with its gluey consistency. Luckily enough, the shaking the ship had taken had imparted to the dough a satiny elasticity. It shielded Bill better than the standard harness would have done. At the last moment before impact, the Chinger lizard with the miniature agent at the controls in its head leaped into the vat beside him. Then the ship struck the ground with a bone-shattering jolt and, gratefully, Bill passed out.

Chapter 8

Just before recovering consciousness, there is a moment in which you don't remember how you got unconscious. You are too taken up with just becoming conscious again. So, for a moment, there is only this, and then, a tiny moment after that, there is, not a memory of what rendered you unconscious — that comes later — but rather a presentiment as to how that came about. That presentiment comes clothed in a thin veil of anticipatory emotion. So it was with Bill. If you can follow all that deep stuff. When he came to again, he realized first that he was Bill, next that something had made him unconscious, and then, that he might not be awakening into very pleasant circumstances. So often is the transition from dreaming sleep into strainy-eyed reality. In his dreams, while knocked out, Bill had been an emperor of infinite space. Perhaps. But the dreams faded, as he came to and the thought occurred to him that he'd rather not find out what he'd gotten into this time.

He really did not want to think about it, but felt compelled to. Why would Swingli* ships attack Ham Duo? What was Duo's mission on Rathbone II? Was this Rathbone II? How were they going to get out of here? When was he going to have a chance to go to the toilet?

Finally, the flood of questions was sufficient to override Bill's desire to keep his eyes shut and wait for better times. Slowly at first, then definitively, he opened his eyes.

He was in a small room, bare, with flagstone floors which looked quite chilly except that Bill wasn't lying directly on them. He was on what looked like a large brown rug, or perhaps an exceptionally thick blanket, of the sort that people wrap around themselves at sporting events on all planets with chilly stadiums. The room he was in was illuminated by a long neon tube overhead. There were scratchings on the stone walls, words of imprecation or prayer written in languages Bill had never encountered. Bill moved himself very gently, because you could never tell what might be broken after a crash like that. He didn't know where he was, and for the moment wasn't too eager to find out. Things hadn't been going well for him recently. He wished that he would stop having crashes. It hardly seemed fair, all these things happening to him.

He started to climb to his feet when the rug beneath him stirred and emitted a porcine grunt. Bill rolled off it rather quickly, as you might very well imagine, and pressed his back to the wall and bulged his eyes. The rug sat up, too, and revealed itself to be a Kookie, one of those large furry beasts with mild to well-down intelligence who have been known to take up the practice of space piracy, since that is a profession open to all, with no nonsense about college credits or Civil Service exams.

"Hello," said Bill, rather unimaginatively, which considering what he had been through lately, was not too bad. "How are you?"

When the Kookie heard this he responded in his own primitive language, all growls and high-pitched whines. Bill's built-in translator, somewhat battered from recent vicissitudes but still functioning more or less as it should, translated this as, "Gee, boss, Kookie feel pretty shitty. You no see my master, him named Ham Duo around anywhere?"

"As a matter of fact," Bill said, "I just came from his ship."

The Kookie sat up, towering head and shoulders over Bill even in that posture. "Oooh, goodies. Where he?"

"I wish I knew," Bill said. "We were on our way here to rescue you when Swingli* ships shot us down."

117

"Dragonshit!" the Kookie rumbled angrily. "I told Ham many often times. Use invisibility treatment — great stuff! Make spaceship look like big crappy meteorite. But no, he no listen to primitive Kookie with brain like garbage grinder, that what he say. So where he is now?"

"You know as much as I do. I passed out when the ship crash-landed," Bill said. "I haven't the dimmest idea where he is now. I don't suppose you've seen Illyria."

"What hell you talk about?" Chewgumma said, for that was his name, unbelievable as it is. The Kookies ran to some pretty kooky names. Like Chewgrappa, Chewbacca, Chewrugga and so forth.

"Someone else, or something else. It gets a little complicated. It's a Chinger, which looks like a seven-inch-high green lizard with four arms, hard to miss. And it has brain trouble, to put it mildly. A lot to do with changing bodies, you know."

"Ah, so! Maybe a Tsurisian."

"Do you know the Tsurisians?"

"Had my run-ins with them, fight like blazes," the Kookie said. "But that was in another time."

"What's going to happen to us?" Bill asked.

"Probably die for sure," Chewgumma said with guttural gloom. "They kill-maim-torture pirates here. They still pissed at Ham and me. Raided their big city, stole all the treasure of the Klingians. Now me captured — ho-ho you too."

"Thanks for the sympathy. And dare I ask how a big brain like you got captured?"

"A net coated with honey," Chewgumma said sheepishly. "We Kookies kinda stupid. Fall for that old stunt."

"And do you know what they'll do to you?"

"Got plenty fears," Chewgumma muttered. "People here on Rathbone famous rug makers. Always got eye out for new materials."

Bill looked at the Kookie's thick, luxurious pelt. And despite being sympathetic to the big alien beast, he couldn't help thinking what a nice rug he would make.

"That's a tough break," Bill said feigning sympathy.

The Kookie blinked angry little red eyes and he caught the fake sympathy in Bill's voice. "Human skin is waterproof, too," he snarled.

"Well, yes, I suppose so," Bill said.

"Make heap good bathroom rug."

Just then there was the sound of a key in the lock and the door of their cell swung open.

Four guards entered. They were extremely tall and thin, with long heads shaped like kidney beans and bodies which looked in the last degree of emaciation. They had to stoop almost double to get inside the cell door. Once inside they still couldn't straighten up. Four of them in the room, in addition to Bill and the Kookie, crowded the small cell to bursting point. This was the first time that Bill had ever seen a Swingli* in the flesh, although he had come across their pictures in the *Alien Enemy Identification Book*, which all human military personnel had to study so as to know the contours of their many and varied enemies.

There seemed to be a Swingli* officer in charge of the guards. He was half a head taller than the others, and as Bill later learned, a member of the officer class which prided itself upon its superior height. He wore a black bearskin cape, and Chewgumma cringed when he saw it and emitted a dolorous cry.

The guards moved them out of the cell and down the corridor, hurrying them along with the small human prods they carried for moments like this. It was a long corridor, made of rough-hewn rocks, and roofed over with palm fronds. After thirty yards or so, the corridor split into two branches. Here the guards divided, one contingent taking the Kookie down the right-hand path, and the other taking Bill down the left-hand side. The bearskinned officer accompanied Bill's group, and Bill didn't know if that was good news or bad. The Swinglis* hadn't said a word so far, although Bill had tried to question them, first in Shmendrik, main trading language of the Swingli* people, then in Unrevised Esperanto, and finally in Chinga Franca, the widely-used language of the Chinger lizard people, which had only recently been discovered in a translator machine from a wrecked Chinger ship. His built-in translator was able to handle all of these languages without difficulty, but the Swinglis* didn't even acknowledge that sounds were being made, much less that they were comprehensible sounds. After a while Bill shut up and began to take notice of his surroundings.

They went down a flight of stairs, then another. Torches flamed in embrasures, and there were antique glow-lights here and there, just enough to change the atmosphere from positively stygian to absolutely gloomy. There were cells along the way, and from them Bill heard funny screechy sounds, like bats feasting on something that didn't like it. But he couldn't tell what it really was, and subsequent research has revealed that it was a sound machine implanted by the Swinglis* and set to give forth unnerving noises. It was not for nothing that the Swinglis* were known as one of the more subtle of the galactic races. Their long stature helped, of course. Creatures who look as funny as Swinglis* do, with their orange fright-wig hair and their huge stooped shoulders and their air of frenetic absent-mindedness, are apt to develop a sense of humor, whose invariable concomitant is the intelligence to avoid being laughed at. Once this is well set, other forms of intelligence follow. The Swinglis* hadn't had much time yet, counted in aeons, to go beyond the early stage of developing ways of avoiding being laughed at.

They even felt humiliated because they were not listed in Morrison's *Standard Dictionary of Alien Races*, not even in the addendum under Alien Races (Tall). Several documentaries have been made on them recently, most notably Sloan Buster's searing *Thin*, which shows the Swinglis* in an altogether too favorable light. Swingli* traders have occasionally appeared in Earth-dominated space, but they tend to avoid it since humans always laugh at them. On their own planet, however, they were able to arrange things more to their own needs. Their boast was, "You won't laugh at us on Swingli*."

Due to their need to be taken seriously, the Swinglis* go to great expense to maintain an impressive pomp and circumstance. Thus, when Bill was ushered into the big room, he first noticed the high desk, cantilevered out over the floor so that three black-gowned Swingli* judges, with powdered perukes set precisely in place, could peer down at him through their granny glasses.

The Swinglis* had researched their justice system most carefully. Every race has its own inborn directive, the secret rules, written on the genes, expatiated upon in the spiraling DNA, which tell them what they are and what they should strive for. Not only that, but also implanted in the fundamental genetic equipment is the knowledge of what is funny and what is not, and a driving need to look good at all times and under all circumstances. Due to this racial imperative, the Swinglis*, when they first encountered alien civilizations, took pains to discover a form of justice that really suited them. Before encountering civilization, they had had no justice or legal system worthy of the word. When a Swingli* grew annoyed at another Swingli*, he bashed him over the head with the short lead-packed wooden clubs which were aptly named, in Swingli*, UuQ-Olen, or friendship-stoppers. If anyone didn't like this, he bashed the perpetrator over the head, and thus might in turn be bashed over the head himself. Friendship-stopping was the only form of death on the planet at this time, because a provident nature, always experimenting, had given the Swinglis* immortality except when they were smacked on the head with a wooden club packed with lead.

A proper justice system, for the Swingli*, had to look good. That was the prime consideration. The Swinglis* at this time were in desperate need for a new way of controlling friendship-stopping, since the population had been declining ever since the so-called Unpleasant Wars of the Nineties. They hit upon a combination of various modalities. From the English they took the high desks at which the judges sit, and the powdered perukes, and above all, the awesome dignity that pervaded British dispensations of justice as shown in the many Pinewood Studio pictures the Swingli* had unearthed in the ancient data banks, the only thing saved from that long-destroyed planet. No one could laugh at a three-man group of judges like that, they thought.

Bill couldn't control his giggle when he saw the three skinny judges with the granny glasses slipping down their scaly faces, with white perukes on their pointed heads, and a general air of testy dignity. The officer in the bearskin nudged him in the ribs with an incredibly sharp and pointed elbow and he sobered up at once.

The middle judge, in sepulchral tones, said, "Let the prisoner approach the bar of justice."

Bill had intended to be dignified and contrite, but something about the crashingly solemn nature of the thing, as well as thirst, made him say, "You got any other kind of bar around here aside from a justice one? I sure could use a drink before going on with this."

The judges looked at each other. The audience — there were close to three hundred Swinglis* in deck chairs watching the proceedings — looked at the judges. The guards looked at each other. Bill looked puzzled.

The middle judge remarked to the judge on his left. "Was that intelligible, what he said?"

"I might perhaps hazard," the left judge said, "that the prisoner was essaying a witticism."

"I could have told you that," said the judge on the right.

"Do you mean," the middle judge said, "that the prisoner was making a joke?"

"Impossible, yes, but it's true," said the left judge.

"But what was the point of the joke?" asked the middle judge.

"It must have been subtle," said the left judge, "because I didn't really get it. Word play on bar, I suppose. Bit of an odd way to begin, isn't it?"

"Yes, I should think so," said the middle judge. He peered down at Bill. "Prisoner, did you in fact make a joke in our presence?"

"Well, yeah, I guess I did," Bill said. "I didn't mean anything by it." He started to giggle again.

"And what," asked the middle judge, "is so funny?"

"Nothing, excuse me, I'm sorry," said Bill.

The middle judge turned to the right judge. "Why would he burst into laughter like that?"

"I don't know," said the right judge, "but I fear the worst. I suppose, if you thought it necessary, you could ask him."

"Prisoner, why did you laugh?"

"The fact is," Bill said, "I have a Chinger lodged in my left armpit and he's tickling me."

"Did you hear that?" the left judge said to the right judge.

"Amazing, his effrontery."

"He couldn't actually have a lizard secreted on his person, could he?"

"I doubt it. Earthians and Chingers are hereditary enemies."

"I suppose," said the bearskin-hatted guard, "we could search him and find out for sure."

"No," said the middle judge. "This is already bad enough. Frankly, I don't want to know."

"Look," Bill said, "I don't know why you've pulled me into court like this. I haven't done nothin'."

"'Nothin','" the middle judge said. "What does that mean?"

The right judge, the one with the drooping right eyelid and the droll expression, said, "I believe it is 'nothing' with the terminal 'g' omitted."

"But why would he do that?" the middle judge asked.

"It's probably some kind of a joke," the right judge said.

"Ah! Another joke! It likes me not, the disposition of this felon at the bar."

"He seems disposed to be humorous," the left judge said.

"If so, it is a grievous fault," the right judge said.

"And grievously shall he pay for it." The three judges looked at each other and smiled the satisfied smiles of men who have essayed a small joke in a difficult situation.

"Now then, prisoner, you are accused of being a party to the landing of an unauthorized spaceship in the public festival grounds illegally and without a license, thus seriously disrupting the slug festival and causing the organizer of the festival, Zek Horsley, public embarrassment of a degree judged to be felonious. Prisoner, how do you plead?"

"Huh?" Bill asked.

"Were you or were you not a party to the unauthorized landing of a spaceship on the festival grounds?"

"Now look," Bill said, "we were shot down. I was a passenger on the ship. But we were shot down by Swinglis*. We had no choice where we landed."

"I didn't ask you if you had any choice," the middle judge said. "I asked if you did land on the aforesaid fair grounds."

"Suppose I did," Bill said. "I'm talking hypothetically now."

"Duly noted," said the middle judge, his left eye drooping characteristically.

"Well then, if I did land on the fair grounds, first of all I had nothing to do with it, second of all, nobody was hurt, so I plead let's forget it and I'll get back to my military people."

"Nobody was hurt?" the middle judge said with a snort. "What about the slugs?"

"What slugs?"

"The slugs that had been assembled for the slug judging contest, that's what slugs."

"Yeah, well what about them?"

"Your ship crushed the slug sectioner where the slugs were sleeping."

"You mean we slushed the slug sectioner," Bill said, breaking into uncontrollable laughter as a human is apt to do when he makes a bad joke in extremely uptight surroundings. "Anyhow, I'll pay for the damage. Or Duo will. How much will it cost to truck in another load of slugs?"

"He tries to make light of it," the middle judge remarked to the left judge behind his hand.

"Yet there might be merit in what he says."

"What of the embarrassment to Horsley?"

"And anyhow, are the slugs replaceable?"

"Not that lot, no."

"Obviously not that lot. I mean another lot that would represent a fair and more than fair exchange?"

"Hard to say. You know as well as I do how hard it is to pick a truckload of really good-looking fat old slugs, especially now with the dry season coming on."

"And there's still the insult to Horsley to be considered."

"I would feel more sympathetic to Horsley's plight," the right judge said, his eyelid having just stopped fluttering, "if he weren't the sort of bloke whom someone would have hit with a friendship-stopper long ago if this were the bad old days."

"It's true," the middle judge said. "Nothing sympathetic about Old Horsley. What do you say we let the prisoner off with a reprimand?"

"I suppose that would be all right," the left judge said, "though it seems a bit of heavy punishment."

"He made jokes," the middle judge pointed out.

"So he did. Yes, let it be a reprimand?"

They turned to the other judge. "And how say you?"

"Eh?" the other judge said.

"We're voting for a reprimand."

"Well jolly good," the other judge said. "And let it be a severe one. Prisoner do you accept the judgment?"

"Sure I do," Bill said, thinking that these were the nicest aliens he had met in a long time, and a whole lot more civilized and sophisticated in their justice system than many he could think of, including his own people.

"Very well," the middle judge said. "Bailiff! Bring in the reprimand!"

Afterward, Bill couldn't believe how silly he had been to accept the reprimand like that without finding out exactly what it was. Alien races were alien and sneaky, that had been drilled into him by the military. Along with a lot of other things that he was trying to forget. They had long preached distrust of everyone who was not like them. Since there were few pot-bellied and prematurely bald races in the universe, this meant they distrusted everyone. The Swinglis* had an especially bad reputation. "Swindlers, that's what I call them," Bill's old sergeant Assbreaker had told him at basic at Fort Ziggurat where Bill had been sent for a repeater course in case he had forgotten how to scream during bayonet drill. "I call them Swindlers and that's what they are. And I'll tell you something else, too. They can't take a joke."

Bill had seen that for himself. But he hadn't expected the unexpected nature of the reprimand. When they wheeled out the white cart with the black velvet cloth on it, he had felt like laughing again. It was just like the Swinglis* to deliver a reprimand on black velvet. But his laughter died with a squawk as the bailiff, at a signal from the middle judge, carefully folded back the black velvet and revealed beneath it what looked at first like a tiny ornamental scarab. Then guards seized and held him as the bailiff held the glittering little thing close to his ear. This was no laughing matter. Bill tried to pull down the whole bunch of them, and came close to succeeding, since his short and muscular frame was able to play merry hell with the eccentrically tall and badly-proportioned Swinglis* — one more reason, by the way, why the Swinglis* always suspect people of laughing at them. But he couldn't take them all out. They held him as the bailiff extended the glittering scarab-like creature toward his ear.

As it approached the globular exterior, by some sensing device not generally known, it split open like a multi-petalled flower. Out of its middle came a tiny thing that looked like a short length of platinum wire but was actually a psychoactive broadcasting device. The wire squirmed into Bill's ear, not causing any pain, but a good deal of discomfort at the mere knowledge that the damned thing was there. Bill pulled one arm free and clawed at his ear until the guards overpowered him again. The middle judge said, "No need to carry on like that, young fellow. It's merely a reprimand, and when it has done its job it will vacate your ear. No damage will be done to you. But you will hear the reprimand."

Bill didn't have to be told that. Already a voice in his head — detectable as a recorded voice because of its tinniness — was saying, "You were bad, you were very bad; why did you do such a thing; how could you ever have; you were bad, very bad, oh yes you were bad . . . "

It wasn't really so annoying, having a little voice saying you were bad. Most people don't need a platinum wire implanted through the ear to know what that feels like. What bothered Bill was that it was difficult to think about anything else while the voice was broadcasting in his ear.

Thus it was that, back in his cell, drinking heavily from a bottle of Swingli* brandy, that a sympathetic young guard, who thought that the reprimand practice was outlandish and barbaric, brought to him, Bill could hardly respond to the gnawing sound that came from the wall near his feet, and even later, when the hole suddenly opened, he found it difficult to put his full attention to it.

"Bill! Can you hear me?"

"You were a bad boy; you were a very bad boy — "

"Bill!"

"What?"

"Bad boy, very bad boy — "

"What's the matter with you, Bill? Have you been drugged?"

" — were a very bad boy; oh such a bad boy — "

"No, it's just this reprimand I got in my ear."

Ham Duo inspected Bill's ear but could see nothing, naturally enough, since the platinum wire was now snuggling into Bill's medulla obligato.

Ham Duo cleared away some obstructing mortar and squeezed into the cell. Ham was looking tough as usual; even crawling out of the tunnel he moved with a certain panache. "Bill," he said, "you ready to get out of here?"

" — bad boy, bad boy, bad boy — "

"Yes, I'm ready," Bill shouted.

"OK. But what are you shouting for?"

"Didn't mean to," Bill said. "This reprimand makes it difficult for me to hear you."

"We'll take care of that later," Duo said. "Right now, let's go before they grab us and lay on a Reprimand Preemptive."

Bill agreed that that sounded bad. He followed Duo into the tunnel, squeezing through the upper part with difficulty, since Bill's upper part was more massive than Duo's upper part. He managed to get through, losing only trifling amounts of clothing and skin in the process, and fumbled along in pitch blackness. The ground underneath was rough, with many little pebbles. The sides of the tunnel widened. Soon they were walking along an old railway tunnel, its twin rails gleaming faintly in a ghostly phosphorescence given off by the walls. Bill was wondering how Ham had excavated all this in so brief a time. He was to learn later that after rescuing the Kookie from the Exotic Rug Factory on the edge of the city, where the Swinglis* had been keeping him until the master rugmaker could make up his mind about just how best to use his pelt, Duo had consulted the special planetary maps he had stolen from the Empire maproom. The disused railway line was shown, of course, since the main purpose of a secret map was to show unobvious but practicable routes. The rest was history, or would be as soon as they could get back to Ham's ship, which Chewgumma had managed to put to rights, and get out of this irrational and unpleasant place.

Once aboard the ship, Ham Duo went through the takeoff drill while Chewgumma watched the dials and adjusted the rheostats. There was no time to lose, since, coming from the city, they could see a large group of the Swinglis*, waving their arms excitedly. Trundling along with them was a gigantic bulldozer. It didn't take any genius to figure out that the Swinglis* had decided that breaking out of their prison was an insult to the whole planet, and that they were going to do something about it.

"I don't know what's the matter with those people," Ham said. Chewgumma gestured urgently at the radiotelephone. The red light was glowing, showing that call-holding was holding a call.

Duo punched the receive key and snapped, "Whoever it is, make it snappy. We're right in the middle of an escape."

"Is Bill there?" a well-modulated feminine voice said in the unmistakable intonations of Illyria, the plucky backwoods nurse who had helped Bill at considerable discomfort and even danger to herself.

"I got no time for personal calls," Duo said.

"Bill's there, isn't he? I just want you to give him a message."

"Hey," Bill cried, "give me that. It's Illyria!"

"I got no time for this," Duo grated.

" — bad boy, bad boy — "

"Illyria!" Bill cried, lunging for the radiotelephone as Ham Duo was in the act of hanging it up.

"Bill my precious! Is it really you?"

The Swinglis* by now had reached the spaceship and formed a ring around it. They shook their fists at the ship and made other threatening gestures. The bulldozer had been out to work nearby. It was beginning to dig a vast pit. You didn't need a computer to figure out that the Swinglis* meant to tip Duo's spaceship into the pit, and probably cover it up with the remaining dirt. And although this was no real threat to the ship constructed as it was out of 5.1 asteroid crystalline steel, and with force fields as well, it was well known that Ham Duo hated to get his ship all mucked up. Since there are no abrasives in space, except for very large ones like meteors, and these are worthless for cleansing purposes, it meant he would have to fly around with a filthy spaceship and endure the taunts of his fellow space pirates. Now, for the first time, Ham could see what embarrassment meant to a Swingli*. His fingers danced on the computer keyboard, trying to get the systems fired up before the Swinglis* could carry out their threat.

He noticed that another mob of Swinglis* was dragging a hose out from the city. Were they going to wash his ship down?

Duo doubted it. They had some nasty scheme in their pointy little heads.

"Sweetheart, where are you?" Illyria asked.

" — bad boy, bad boy — "

"On the planet Rathbone," Bill roared.

"You don't have to scream at me."

"Sorry. It's because this reprimand is talking so loud I can't hear anything."

"Did you say reprimand? What is a reprimand doing in your ear?"

"It's a little difficult for me to explain just now," Bill said. "Illyria, where are you? How can I find you? Are you all right"

"I'm fine, Bill," Illyria said. "It's a good thing that secret agent, CIA, thought of the Jansenite Maneuver. There was no psychic breathing space for the two of us in that tiny Chinger control room."

Ham Duo scowled ferociously as the power dials flipped up and down erratically. "Can't you get me steady power on this thing?" he shouted. The Kookie howled back something about pinpoint erosion factors and a lack of platinum rebreathers. "Try to fake it," Ham told him. "I can't get any life like this."

Bill said to Illyria, "What planet was that?"

"Royo. Meet me there, Bill. I have some wonderful surprises for you."

"Booze?" Bill asked hopefully.

"And sex."

"Wow!" said Bill. "The big two of the pleasure principle! How do you know that, Illyria?"

"I know, don't ask questions, trust me."

"But explain it to me."

" — o time," Illyria said. "Can't you hear how our transmission is fading? I have no time to go into the plans of the Alien Historian, or to tell you how I came to learn them. Just get away from there, Bill!"

"How am I supposed to do that? Build my own spaceship?"

"You must use the Disruptor," she said.

"How can I be expected to learn how to use a gadget like that in the probably damned little time available to me? Illyria, can't the computer help?"

"Believe me," she said, "the computer has its own problems."

"What are you talking about?"

"Your friend Splock. You should see what a mess he's made."

"What's going on? Tell me what's happening?"

"All right," Illyria said, "you want conversation, you get conversation. When Captain Dirk brought the starship *Gumption* back to normal space, there was, as you'd expect, a showdown between him and the Counter-Dirk. Only it didn't go as you'd expect."

"How am I supposed to suspect it would go?"

"Bill, try to join me, and hurry, hurry — " Illyria's voice had been growing increasingly faint. Now it shrank to a whisper, and then it faded entirely. Bill hung up. What Illyria had said was disturbing. It was true that he owed her his life, still she *was* getting more than a little pushy. She seemed to be taking a lot for granted for a woman who hadn't even shown herself yet in anything like human form. She said she loved him; but did she? The training sergeants back at base camp had warned about the danger of loving or being loved by an alien. "You can never tell if they mean it or not," old Sergeant Adler had told him. "They're wily, these aliens. And how do you know what they mean by love? At least six alien races consume their mate after copulation. So you may start out looking for love and end up as your girlfriend's breakfast. There ain't no future in that."

Chewgumma, meanwhile, shouted to Duo that he had found the main problem in the ship's energy system.

"That's really great, you furry moron," Duo thundered. "But if you can't do something about it pretty quick, it's all academic." For the Swinglis* had brought up the hose and begun spraying in a carefully-marked rectangle around the spaceship. Where they sprayed, a glittering white gas emerged and quickly hardened into a stone of about the weight of pumice. Duo could see that the Swinglis* were encasing the ship in this substance, building a building around them. And although it seemed ridiculous to think that the light stone could seriously impede the thruster jets of the spacecraft, still, they must have had something in mind. Aliens were notorious for having tricks up their sleeves. Those that had sleeves, that is. Or arms. And a race like the Swinglis*, who took to embarrassment so badly, could be counted upon to be as ingenious as they were vindictive.

Then there was a sparkle of electrical sparks as Chewgumma plugged a 234V Thruster into the RUF socket. The dials on Ham's switchboard swung up into healthy readings and held steady. The ship lifted, and Ham Duo and Chewgumma let out a simultaneous cheer.

Bill noticed at that moment that the Disruptor was not being watched by either Duo or Chewgumma. It occurred to him that this was a very good chance to get it, if he were planning to do that at any time in the near future at all. He edged closer, reasoning that he was going to have to act fast, because Duo was not apt to approve of Bill's taking the thing.

As his hand closed on it, all hell broke loose.

The Swinglis* had brought up several more hoses and a large machine with two U-shaped nozzles that Duo immediately recognized as a Mark IV Industrial Strength Stone Hardener. Duo's face hardened itself as he felt the ship's lift slackening, as it responded to the stone hardening around its basal jets. He threw in the emergency rocket control — it was vital not to get frozen in place — and the ship began to vibrate unpleasantly. The daylight entering through the perspex ports was dimming as the building was constructed about them.

Bill lifted the Disruptor from its magnetic clamp and looked it over. Its lightweight steel cover slid open, revealing a small computer keyboard beneath. Aside from the regular QWERTY keyboard, there were a dozen special-function keys labeled F1 through F12, and several others marked DIN, DON, and RES. It seemed to have no power source, unless it ran on AA batteries. At that time Bill had not heard of SPT, Sympathetic Power Technology which enabled the Disruptor to slave to any power source that utilized the electromagnetic spectrum. He pressed F1 just to see if the little square screen would light up.

The little machine began to vibrate in his hand. At the same time, the spaceship had begun lifting again, and was pushing through the hardening rock that the Swinglis* were trying to encase it in. Duo looked up and noticed the Disruptor in Bill's hand. A high-pitched note was coming from it, and its screen threw out a dazzling light.

"Put that down!" he commanded Bill.

Bill would have been pleased to, because the sudden actions of the Disruptor had alarmed him. But the machine didn't want to be let loose of. When Bill put it down on a plotting table and tried to move away, the Disruptor moved along with him. It seemed to have its own form of propulsion, and it clung close, throwing off dazzling displays of light and making shrill metallic noises that might have been an attempt at speech.

"Destination, please?" the Disruptor said.

"Never mind, I've changed my mind," Bill told it.

"Give destination at once!" the machine said, its voice loud, bullying, peremptory.

"I don't know how to express it in proper coordinates," Bill said.

"Stop crapping about, and just do the best you can," the Disruptor ordered.

" — Bad boy, bad boy — " the voice of the reprimand was shrieking in his head. Not only couldn't he give any instructions, he doubted he'd be able to tie his shoelaces properly with that racket going on in his ear.

Abruptly the noise stopped.

"Is that better?" the Disruptor asked.

"It's gone!" Bill cried. "What did you do?"

"I terminated it," the Disruptor said. "Time and space aren't the only things I can vanquish. Ha-Ha-Ha!"

"What an improvement! It's really great, I don't know how to thank you . . . "

"The thought is enough. Even a simple machine enjoys a kind word."

The Disruptor had forgotten its anger, was almost smarmy now, and insisted in explaining, at great length, how it had acted within its design limits by terminating the reprimand. Because when one travels by disruption-power, one needs all of one's wits about one.

"I didn't know that," Bill said. "Illyria made it sound pretty easy."

"Oh, it's not difficult," the Disruptor said. "It's easy enough. But accidents can happen, that's the problem, you see."

"Actually," Bill said, "I hadn't quite made up my mind about going just at this time."

"Is that a fact?" the Disruptor said, with what sounded suspiciously like sarcasm.

"Yes, it is," Bill said quickly, not wanting to get this electronic pain-in-the-ass irritated again. "Why don't I just turn you off until I'm ready." He turned the Disruptor upside down and examined all its surfaces. There was no sign of a turn off button.

"That's right," the Disruptor said. "I'm like the three wishes. Once you get started on the wishes you got to finish them. Same with me. Now stop crapping around and tell me where you want to go. Now."

"It wouldn't be right. Ham Duo found you. You belong to him. He must issue the orders."

"Listen, boychick," the Disruptor said in a slightly accented voice, "there's no question of ownership here. What we're talking about here is a matter of power. And power belongs to him who has it in his hand."

The machine sizzled angrily and began to glow with an unearthly green glow. Bill panicked and tried to put down the Disruptor but it stuck to his hand like he was a magnet.

"Captain Duo!" Bill shrieked in fear. "This Disruptor is acting very strangely!"

The Disruptor chuckled mechanically. When Bill looked over to Duo, he saw that the dashing pirate commander was frozen in mid-gesture, and looked like a wax figure except that he had slightly better coloring. His Kookie friend Chewgumma, still with a hand on the energy controls, looked like a fur rug that had spent a brief time in animation and was now resting.

Looking through a porthole, Bill could see that the ship had been arrested in mid-flight. It hung in the air about fifty feet off the ground. Down below, the mob of Swinglis* were frozen too, most of them with their bony fists raised.

Even the double sun, setting toward Rathbone's southwestern horizon, was stopped in mid-flight.

Only Bill was free of the thrall of frozen time. And he couldn't get the Disruptor out of his hand.

"All right," Bill said. "I don't know what you did, but please turn it all back on again."

"I haven't actually turned anything off, dummy," the Disruptor said. "But your act of turning me on projected us both into waiting-space. You need to tell me where you're going so I can find an appropriate time channel in which to insert us."

"Oh, I didn't know it was as simple as that," Bill said.

"Disruptor technology is so new that the scientists haven't had a chance to complicate it yet. Now look, I lifted your reprimand, didn't I?"

"Yes, you did," Bill said.

"So you maybe owe me a little favor, no?"

"I suppose so," Bill said. "But tell me something, why do you speak with an accent?"

"I'll tell you that," the Disruptor said, "as soon as you tell me your destination."

Bill decided he was being silly, not taking advantage of this ingenious and obliging transportation device. And besides, he wanted to know how come the accent.

"You know a planet named Royo?"

The Disruptor accessed its files in a few nanoseconds and said, "Sure. Which one do you want?"

"How many Royos are there?"

"Five, as far as I've searched. There may be some updates coming in on my transmission line any time. I'll search those, too."

"But how am I supposed to know which Royo it is?"

"My dear young man, how would I know which Royo you're searching for?"

"That accent!" Bill said. "Why?"

"First let's figure out which Royo. Do you know anything at all about it?"

"It's got a breathable oxygen atmosphere," Bill said, thinking, it had better have or he wasn't going there.

"Good. That eliminates one of them."

"I think it's got a pretty nice climate for humans," Bill said.

"A little feeble. But I think we can cross out Royo Terminosus and Royo Vulcanische. Too cold and too hot respectively."

"How many does that leave?" Bill asked.

"Just a minute, let me count them again — Two! We're practically there. I speak to some degree metaphorically, of course. We haven't actually started yet."

"I thought not," Bill said, since he could still see the same frozen figures around him, Duo, Chewgumma, and all the rest. "What do you suggest?"

"The reason I speak with an accent," the Disruptor said, "is because I am part of a special commemorative series of automata whose voice tapes were made to sound like famous Earth scientists of the past. I have the voice of a twenty-first century Hungarian psycho-physicist named Raimundo Szekeley."

"That explains it," Bill said. "But why are you telling me this now?"

"Because we're going to visit both Royos and find out which one is the one you want."

"Oh," Bill said. "But isn't that apt to be — "

He had no time to say "dangerous". At that instant, the Disruptor started the journey.

Chapter 9

Many learned papers have been written on how it feels to travel by Disruptor. They are all conjecture because in our day and age the device has been banned. It was fast and efficient, but subject to unexpected side effects. Also, the transition between where you were and where you wanted to be was so sudden that it had the effect of causing time to stumble, forcing you to spend a certain amount of time in lapse-space, also known as stasis, to allow your body and internal organs to catch up with your head trip. Some people came through the Disruptor journey with a curious sensation of having left a part of themselves behind. Which was usually true. And there were many sudden screams of pain when they discovered which part it was. It has been conjectured that Disruptor travel was so rapid, it gave the self no time to gather in its various extensions in time and space. In Bill's case this was no problem, luckily, because Bill was not subject to flights of fancy.

"Where are we?" Bill asked.

"This is the first Royo on our list. Does it look like the right one to you?"

Bill looked out. They were standing on a little promontory. Below them lay a vast city, all composed out of blue material of many shades and hues. There were steeples of many churches, and Bill could see broad boulevards and vehicles moving on the motorways. There was a single sun, and it was low in the horizon, banked in purple clouds. People moved in the streets.

And big birds flapped overhead. As Bill watched, one of the birds banked and dived, plucking a person off the street and carrying him away with broad strokes of his wings. The other people paid it no attention. They kept on moving. Bill followed the direction of their movement. He saw that several of the giant birds had carried a huge trough to a plaza in the center of the city. They set it down, and Bill could see that it was filled with some greenish material.

"What do you think?" the Disruptor asked. "This is reputed to be the brightest bird planet in the galaxy. Those aren't really people they're feeding on. They're protoplasmic robots who come in a variety of flavors. Those look like sausagemen to me, though you can't be entirely sure at this distance."

"I don't think this is the right one," Bill said.

In that instant Bill was aware that he was no longer there, and an instant later he knew he was somewhere else. It was true that travel by Disruptor was disrupting.

The next planet had all browns and oranges in its landscape. There were a lot of black silhouette shapes, too, and no matter how they turned they never seemed to have any depth. There were strange sounds like voices, but Bill couldn't see who they belonged to. There was a race of cats that prowled the ancient ruins on low sea-beaches and disdained to notice the man with the machine in his hand watching them.

"I don't think it's this one, either," Bill said. "Hell, it's not either of them! What do we do now?"

"Courage, mon enfant," the Disruptor said. "There is always the other alternative."

"What's that?"

"If the answer is neither one nor two, it's bound to be three."

"But there was no third alternative!" Bill cried.

"There is now," the Disruptor told him.

And just like that, Bill found himself somewhere else.

The planet Royo was known to men through their dearest dreams, because Royo is nothing less than one of the images of human delight. Bill found himself on a long curving sea-beach. White sand gleamed in a glowing crescent as far as the eye could see. Gulls wheeled overhead, and girls sprawled lissomely nearby. Could anything be more paradisiacal? To complete the delight, Bill saw that there were snug little bars along the coast made of driftwood and with delightful names like Dirty Dick's. Who could dream of anything finer than to live among tame buccaneers? And there were hamburger stands along that beach, too, quaint little places made of driftwood and furnished with buxom ladies wearing bandanas and frying up lovely fatty hamburgers with plenty of onions and with an array of condiments that would do proud to a sultan's palace. Not only was there the ubiquitous ketchup, and five varieties of piccalilli, and salsas of three colors and each stronger than the last, there were also pickled mango bits and bacon strips and juicy, pre-sliced beefsteak tomatoes, and many, many other things, some of them rather repulsive when you got down to it, that men of many planets dream of having access to. And each of these places served tall, frosted rum drinks, so that Bill felt compelled to sample one or two as he continued his stroll.

The people on the beach were beautiful, sleek and handsome and with white-toothed smiles of surpassing clarity. The women possessed the cutesey charm of starlets. And just back from the beach there were dance halls, and movie theaters showing socko features, and there was a roller coaster and many rides, and fake dinosaurs which were actually apartment houses.

A beautiful young woman with long dark hair and a comeliness too great to be borne by mere man came up to Bill and said, "You are the Promised One, aren't you?"

"I guess I might be, miss," Bill said, with an old world courtliness that had made him appear something of a freak in the one-horse town upon the backward planet where he had been given the gift of life. "And who might you be?"

"I am Illyria."

Bill gaped at her. Her beauty demanded no less. "The last time I saw you," he said, "you were a little green lizard."

"As you might have noticed, I've changed," Illyria said, smiling huskily.

"Yes indeed, you have," Bill said, his voice cracking. He started to reach out to her, then suddenly grabbed for his left armpit instead.

"What's the matter?" Illyria pouted, since she had leaned forward in anticipation of the grab.

"The Chinger. He was right here. With CIA in his head. A tiny CIA no more than two inches high."

"Don't talk about the old days," Illyria said. "They are behind us now."

"And a good thing too. But where did the Chinger go?"

"Does it matter, darling?"

"I don't suppose so," Bill said. "It just sort of bothers me, you know, not knowing where I misplaced CIA and the Chinger."

"They probably wanted to go somewhere else," Illyria said, "and didn't want to upset you by telling you."

"That's not the world's greatest idea, but it will have to do for now," Bill said. It still disturbed him, but he figured he'd get over it.

"So this is Royo, huh?" he asked as he reached out to grab, not really caring. She wiggled skillfully aside, taking his idle conversational gambit as real interest.

"This is it, darling. Come let me show you around," she said and led the pouting and surly — and detumescing — Bill away for a sightseeing tour.

Despite not even the slightest interest, Bill soon learned that the planet Royo had only a single landmass and that was not a very big one. Royo consisted of one island in a planet-wide ocean. The island was a paradise by Earthian standards. Every day was perfect, sunny and bright, hot enough to get a really great tan but not hot enough to burn. There was only one race who lived on Royo: the Royoans. They were a beautiful people who spent all their time surfing and having fun. Since they had achieved their goal early in their recorded history, their brains had subsequently atrophied, following nature's rule that what you don't use you lose. Where the Royoan brains had been, there was now a cavity which could be entered via the ear. The Royoans had a ceremony. When a child turned sixteen — or maybe thirteen, the Royoans weren't so great at counting past two — the cavity in the head was filled with a fragrant coconut oil in which certain herbs were placed. Their exact proportions had been handed down faithfully from generation to generation, verbally of course since mental basket-cases couldn't write — nor could they talk very well for that matter — and this constituted almost the entire racial memory, not to mention all of their culture, of the Royoans. This oil gave the hair a natural luster, prevented baldness, kept the skin healthy, and made the eyes glisten. Due to this miracle substance the Royoans could look good all of the time, and this for a Royoan was the highest good.

It had been simple enough for Illyria, once she had managed to come here, to take over the body of a beautiful young Royoan female with her own superbly adapted mind and thus occupy her body.

"Isn't it wonderful, Bill?" Illyria asked him. They were down on the beach having a steak barbecue while a chorus of Royoans sang the sweet mournful songs of their kind. Though, sadly, they lacked lyrics and melody.

"Sure it's wonderful," Bill said, resting one arm around Illyria's shoulders in a gesture he tried to make seem not as uncomfortable as it was. His first surge of heterosexual enthusiasm had been replaced by hesitant doubts. Bill was having trouble getting used to Illyria being a beautiful woman. Something about the way she had gone about it was putting him off.

"A little tough on the Royoan girl though, wasn't it?" he said with the unconscious arrogance of one who has always had a body of his own.

"Not at all, dear," Illyria said. "I asked her, 'Lisa, would you mind if I take over your body for a while?'"

"Oh, not at all!" Lisa had said, after a ten-minute wait that always accompanied any Royoan attempt at quasi-intelligent thought. "You'll give it back someday, won't you?"

"Of course," Illyria said.

"Then go ahead and borrow it. What a story it'll make for the kids."

"The kids?"

"That's how Royoans refer to each other. As 'the kids.'"

"Oh," Bill said.

"And here we are. Sex and food. Just like I promised."

"Yeah," Bill said, putting down the beef rib he had been gnawing at. Illyria snuggled up to him, and Bill felt himself beginning to respond. After all, she was a beautiful woman; she was round and soft in all the right places; she wanted him; the other girl had said it was OK; why should it bother him?

Thus began Bill's sojourn on Royo. He soon fell into the lazy habits of the island. The Royoans would gather every morning to worship his clawed alligator foot and admire his fangs, which he twanged lazily for them. Bill thought it was silly, but Illyria said it did no harm to encourage them in their little enthusiasms. Bill could have found things about himself more worthy of note than an alligator's foot that had come to him by accident, but such is fame; you have no choice in how or why it comes to you. Royo was really a fine place. Not very intellectual, of course, but that didn't bother Bill, except that he began to miss comic books. And he found that he was even thinking nostalgically about his days in the service. It was funny, when in the military he had dreamed of something happening just like this: being marooned on a lush tropical paradise of a planet with plenty of food and booze, a beautiful young woman who loved him, and plenty of others who would like to have him if only he deigned . . .

But of course, that wouldn't be fair to Illyria. And she was the best-looking of the bunch. Out of common decency, he owed her . . .

Well, what did he owe her? When you came right down to it, nobody had asked Bill what he thought of this arrangement. And it was funny how quickly the taste of rum begins to pall on the palate. Too sweet. In fact, Bill was beginning to get bored. There's no telling what he would have done if, not long after his arrival, a strange light in the sky had not told him that a spaceship was coming in for a landing.

"It's your standard tropical paradise," Mr Splock said. "Perhaps, measured on a hedonistic scale, it scores a bit better than most, no doubt, but cut from the same cheesecloth. I am sure that you agree, Captain Dirk?"

Dirk, walking along the sandy beach with his shoes off and his pantlegs rolled, didn't seem to hear his first officer. Dirk was drinking a Coke and eating a hotdog with all the stuff on it. There was a dreamy look on his face, as of a man bemused. This described Dirk's state of mind to a T, and Mr Splock, stranger to all emotions, could not fathom the change. He was concerned, for he had never seen such a change in the normally austere captain of the *Gumption*.

"Hadn't we better get back to the ship, sir?" Splock asked.

"No hurry," Dirk mused idly. "Nothing is going to attack us here."

"Nothing except our desires," Splock said. "I speak, of course, only for those who have them. The rest of us — well, me alone, that is — will go on with our duty as it was previously laid down in the protocols of the *Gumption*."

Dirk looked with affectionate curiosity, tempered by the thought that this joker was a boring pain in the ass, at his first officer. "Don't you ever get the urge to unwind, Mr Splock? Get drunk? Screw girls?"

"I beg your pardon!" Splock gurgled, taken aback by the effrontery. "Unwind? Drunk? Screw! I should think not."

"You know what I mean. At least I hope you know what I

mean. Some day you *must* tell me about your reproductive processes — on the other hand perhaps you'd better not. So relax. Take a vacation. Have a little fun."

"Not only do I never think of such things," Splock said, sniffing loudly through flared nostrils, "I am surprised, sir, to find that you do."

"You are used to seeing me in a state of moral or physical crisis," Dirk said.

"May I speak plainly?"

"Go ahead, Splock."

"A state of crisis suits you, sir."

Dirk laughed and cast the uneaten portion of his hot dog into the curling surf. A scavenger fish, which ate nothing but refuse, and lived in hibernation when there was no refuse to be found, snapped it up and devoured it, leaving the beach as pristine as before.

"This place instills in me a singularly lighthearted mood," said Dirk. "You can't know what moods mean to humans because you don't experience them. But I can assure you, they run our lives."

"Nonsense, Captain. Sense of duty rules your life. You also love your God, if you have one, and I must question you about that some time, and country."

"All true, Mr Splock, all entirely true! But sometimes even the best of us — not that I'm claiming that for myself but let me make my point — even the best of us, I say, needs a little vacation from the stern country of moral rectitude and the solace of religion."

"Now you are sounding like the Counter-Dirk," Splock said.

"No, we killed him in fair battle. We were on the side of Charlemagne and Christianity; he stood with the Sultan and Islam. Since we won, that makes us right, eh, Splock?"

"You can talk yourself into any position you please," Splock said. "But I must point out to you, sir, with your kind permission, that this is sheerest sophistry. Or as they are wont to say on the lower decks, pure bullshit."

"You do have a way with words, my good Splock, but you haven't given consideration to the demonic side of man. Or do you deny that it exists?"

"No, there's proof enough of it," Splock said. "But I thought you had overcome it, Captain."

"Why, so I have, Splock! That's precisely the point I want to make. I have overcome the demonic, but that means I have the right to take a little vacation when I want, doesn't it?"

"I suppose you can," Splock said. "But this is not a very good time for it, is it? The Alien Historian is still on the loose and Earth is by no means safe."

Dirk shrugged. "That's life. One emergency after another. I daresay our species can let us have a little rest here and muddle through for a while without us. Or to phrase it more succinctly, the galaxy can do without me saving it for awhile while I have some R & R. And get drunk and get laid."

Splock, obviously shocked, didn't reply at once. He walked along, hands clasped behind his back, his expression hard and unyielding, in marked contrast to Dirk, who sauntered along like a pubescent boy enjoying his first erection.

Splock looked at the commander, and a sudden wave of comprehension passed over his features. So marked was the change in his demeanor that Dirk noticed it at once.

"You've just thought of something, Splock old boy! Let's get a drink and you can tell me all about it."

"A drink? If you wish, sir, I will accompany you, though I myself do not drink. And as for what I thought about, it is what I believe is called an analogy. I'm quite pleased because I don't have analogies often."

"Well, tell it, old chap."

"Not now, sir. Later."

"Suit yourself," Dirk said. "Let's get that drink."

He led the way toward Dirty Dick's, where Bill was waiting with frosted glass in hand.

Although Dirk had granted himself unlimited freedom, the

same did not extend to the crew of the *Gumption*. Mr Splock, as second officer, horrified at what he had seen, had canceled all shore leave. The spaceship was kept battened down, shields up, at minimum strength so as not to drain the batteries. But even minimum strength was enough to keep all visitors away. When Dirk protested, Mr Splock reminded him that Dirk was taking a vacation, but that he had no right to extend that privilege to his crew. This ship was on active duty, he pointed out, and therefore all the men must remain at battle stations. All of which was an outright lie since Splock had visions of the sort of alcoholic orgies sailors, even space sailors, are prone to due to the mind-numbing boredom of the job.

The captain hadn't agreed, but since coming to Royo he no longer had the strength of will or desire to protest and make his views prevalent. He was on vacation; it was silly to try to command men; it was senseless to engage in their ceaseless quarrels; it was every man for himself. You must work diligently for your own salvation, and what the hell, Dirk thought, he had it, the others will have to fend for themselves.

Pretty young women accosted him on the beach. Dirk knew he was good-looking, but really, this was ridiculous. Without the slightest hesitation he embraced the sybaritic life with tremendous enthusiasm. With flowers in his hair and a silly smile of satiation on his lips he strolled the lazy beaches of this planetary paradise. The ladies he went with had no small talk, but that didn't bother Dirk. People chattered too much anyhow. Dirk got into the silence thing very quickly. How different from life aboard the ship with its endless yak-yak and petty problems. He could sit on the beach for hours now and just grok that evening sun. He could grok scavenger fish and people playing volleyball. He could grok rum punches and roller-coaster rides. Hey, it was all of a suchness. Sometimes he felt a little bad about the crew. Splock wouldn't even let them check out the scene on the vision plates. The poor suckers were in paradise and they didn't even know it!

Dirk and Bill became good drinking companions, always

shadowed by Splock, who would sit at Dirty Dick's nursing his iced tea while Bill and Dirk laughed uproariously at whatever they were saying and sloshed themselves blotto with rum.

After years of training Bill had enormous capacity. But he was also lazy and so he grew to hate waking up with a hangover every morning. Forced to moderation by hangovers and incipient terminal alcoholism, perhaps influenced, when sober, by the beautiful and sagacious Illyria, he suggested they have their binges once a week and play volleyball on the other days.

Dirk wouldn't hear of it. A doctrinaire ecstatic, he insisted on getting drunk every night because you lose your freedom if you don't exercise it and license is the best exercise of all. Dirk was driven to pleasure by the same demonic dynamic that had guided him during his highly moral career as chief officer of the largest and fastest and best-looking starship in the Earth's navy. He went after pleasure on principle and laughed on cue, since a sense of duty can affect even one's sense of humor.

After awhile, since drunks are pretty boring when one is sober, Bill took to hanging out with Splock while Dirk lay most of the day in a drunken stupor. Illyria didn't like it because she didn't like Splock. She didn't trust him. He had the look of one of those people who doesn't like to see other people having fun, and who do their best to make that fun stop. But Bill was firm with her. He explained that he had to spend some of his time with the boys. She wondered why he didn't make any friends among the local Royoans. Bill explained that it was a little difficult to get on with them since they talked very slowly and entirely in surfing terms, which changed every year. How was Bill to know that "wheeling down the mountain mouth of the dibbler" meant "come to the barbecue this evening"? And there was no sense going to the barbecue because the Royoan males didn't really talk about anything except waves. They kept a count and a remembrance of every wave that they saw each day, though each new day's memory-accumulation of new waves drove out remembrance of the others, except for the small part of their memory that contained the history of the Greatest Waves of All Time. This too was a fruitful subject of discussion with them:

"Remember old 22 in the year of Marsh Hen?"

"Yeah. It was like the double 2456 in the year of the Scarlet Ibis."

And so on.

Bill tried to get into the conversation. Sometimes, when strong drink had loosened his tongue, he made up years of great waves. Everybody agreed with him that was a great wave and a great year. It was impossible to tell whether they believed him or didn't want to hurt his feelings. It probably made no difference anyhow.

Captain Dirk was not good company. He had started getting all weird, muttering about "spiritual pleasure breakthroughs" and wiping an unpleasant whitish spittle with which he had been afflicted of late off his chin. So Bill took to the company of Splock.

He found Splock comprehensible. Splock reminded him of many sergeants he had known. Lack of feelings and total deprivation of a sense of humor has never been a detriment to the warrior spirit.

"I don't think I like humans," Splock confided in him one day. "But I work with them. So I have to understand them and go along with their predilections. So, although it is not my place to say it, it seems to me that Dirk is aberrant."

"Yes, and he's really a pain, acting this way," Bill said. "And I never thought I would say this, but it gets a little boring; you know what I mean, having what you want whenever you want it. It's like not having it at all. That's funny, isn't it?"

"Not for human beings, apparently," Splock said.

"Whatever it is, I'm getting a little bored with it."

"Why don't you punch up your Disruptor and get out of here, then?" Splock asked.

"I can't. The Disruptor didn't come here with me."

"Why not?"

"Who can tell what dark thoughts lurk in the memory banks of a Disruptor? I guess I should have told it to stick around."

"Do you really want to get out of here?" Splock asked.

"I guess so. But I'm in no hurry to get back to the Troopers. I'm getting sick of barbecuing, anyhow."

"You're the only person I can trust around here," Splock said. "And I daren't let any of the crew out for obvious reasons. Are you ready to employ subterfuge in a good cause?"

"Hell, I'm an enlisted man. Lying is a way of life."

"Then listen carefully. I have a plan that may be risky, even dangerous."

Captain Dirk was a great favorite among the Royoans. He used to lecture them every day on topics to their liking, like "The Superiority of the Pleasure Principle"; "The Great Art — Idleness"; and "Doing Nothing as a Sacred Vocation." The Royoans, like some other races in the galaxy, enjoyed hearing their predilections explained and justified in philosophical terms. They spontaneously formed fan clubs. Crowds of them accompanied Dirk wherever he went, even to bed. Especially to bed. Dirk showed no sign of enjoying all this attention. It was distracting, having all these people around him all the time clutching at his clothing and saying "Right on, man."

Bill never came to Dirk's lectures. He spent most of his time in the hills behind the beach, marching stolidly through the sweet-scented grass searching for bee hives. Illyria accompanied him on a few of his expeditions, but quickly lost interest. She didn't even like honey much. "Why bother," she asked Bill, "when the chocolate bush and the marzipan tree supply us with delicious sweets? And have you sampled the cream-puff bush?"

But Bill was uninterested. Morose, silent, bemused, he could be seen out there every day, carrying a gunny sack that Splock had lent him. Day after day he journeyed out there, and the sack grew perceptibly heavier and more full. Bill never revealed its contents. It was evident, however, that Splock knew what Bill was up to. The two men would exchange grim nods when Bill returned to the never-ending beach party that his life had become.

There were mutterings among the Royoans that Bill and Splock were both twisted. There seemed to be no place for pleasure in their lives. Since pleasure might be said to be the religion of Royo, one who didn't like it could fairly be said to be evil. This was what a group of the Royoans decided during the late afternoon rap session after surfing and eating barbecue. The question was, what to do about it. One daring theorist among them even suggested studying violence. The Royoans had never had a war. Even the occasional family dispute was invariably settled by the cheery words, "Surf's up!" They had heard about violence, of course. Traveling traders brought them word of it. Violence involved knocking people's brains out. The Royoans could understand that, and could appreciate the pleasure it might afford. Trouble was, they had never done it before and they hated to do things badly. All of them were born with innate surfing skills that had been etched into their genes by some sporting god in the far distant past. Or so they believed. The Royoans never did anything except what they did well. That's what made it so difficult for them to espouse violence. Who was to go first? And if he did it badly, would the others laugh at him? It's very important to keep face in the surfing culture.

They had just reached the point of deciding that maybe they could all rush Bill at the same time and stomp him to death, and that way there'd be no embarrassment because they'd all be doing it at the same time. Splock, however, was able to intuit this development because he was smart and most humanoids were utterly predictable. He said to Bill, "We're going to have to make a move soon."

"That's great by me. I've got it all together and we're ready to go anytime you want."

"Tonight, then, when the moon comes up."

"Which moon?"

"The small blue one. That comes up after the green one sets."

"Got it," Bill said, and went off to eat what he hoped would be his last barbecue on Royo.

At the rising of the little blue moon Bill was at the designated place, a grove of trees beyond which a narrow but clearly outlined path led to where the *Gumption* rested.

"You've got the sack?" Splock asked.

"Right here." Bill lifted the heavy sack and shook it. Something massive and shapeless and malleable moved within. It gave off no sound at all.

"Let's go," Splock said. They went down to the ship. It rested on its bottom giving off a faint haze of electroluminescence. Splock took the Executive Clicker from a pouch at his waist and clicked three times. The energy screens came down. He clicked twice more. A hatchway opened. One more click actuated the escalator that would take them to the interior.

"Let's go," Splock said.

The crew of the *Gumption* were all gathered in the Main Recreation Room watching an ancient movie and laughing uproariously at the cast of motheaten apes having a fake tea party. They had previously availed themselves of the free non-addictive drug that the film distributor had sent along with the tapes. It was a chewing gum rich in Congoleum 23, a chemical present in the milk of female chimpanzees which has the effect of convincing baby chimpanzees that the antics of chimpanzees are funny. The crew didn't like to take drugs of any sort; even salt was suspect. But something had to be done to alleviate the boredom of waiting at full battle stations on a peaceful planet which they were not allowed to look at through the polarized viewports — Splock having craftily taken the small polarizer with him; without it, nothing could be seen except a sort of grayness with bright flecks in it.

"Gosh, Splock," said Larry LaRue, the new juvenile lead trying out for radioman, "where's Captain Dirk, huh?"

"Our captain has run into a little trouble," Splock said. "He is in danger, though he doesn't know it. We are going to rescue him."

"Gosh, that's wonderful!" said Linda Xeux, the new Cambodian bombshell starlet who was trying out for Chief Health Officer. "Do, please, tell us more about our dear captain, I mean it's wonderful that we are going to have a chance to get into some action instead of standing around here all the time in our one-piece elasticized jumpsuits. Not that I'm complaining, mind you."

"There is one thing you must do first," Splock said. "You have perhaps noticed that there is a tall young fellow standing beside me and that he is holding a gunny sack which I loaned him from ship's stores."

They applauded Bill politely because, although he didn't look like much, he might be someone important.

"Bill will pass among you with his gunny sack," Splock said. "You will each reach in and remove a handful of what is inside. A small handful will suffice. Its purpose will be immediately apparent to you. Go ahead, Bill."

Bill went to Xeux first. She reached into the sack and gave a little gasp. She looked questioningly at Splock. "May I speak plainly?" she asked.

"No," Splock said. "There's no time. Just do it, Xeux. It will be all right."

The beautiful Eurasian girl's lavender eyes fluttered. She bit her tiny lower lip and reached into the sack. With a little gasp she pulled out a handful.

"Ooo," she said, "It's still warm."

"It has to be," Splock said grimly.

Back at the beach, the first glimmer of dawn illuminated the bodies of handsome young people lying around each other like piles of adorable puppies. The feeble dawn light, pearl gray tending toward opalescent, lent its faint glow to finely-shaped lips and cleanly-chiseled chins, to perfect young breasts and long straight legs. Nearby a few final sparks from last night's barbecue fluttered into the air like pygmy fireflies. A Cantata tree on the edge of the sand played Vivaldi. An owl hooted and was answered by the sobbing laughter of a loon. Paradise slept.

Silently, moving through the morning ground mist like imps of hell the crew of the *Gumption*, led by Splock and Bill, came up to the beach. There was a brief moment of alarm when the Warning Warbler let off a siren burst of surprise at seeing the intruders. But it was soon silenced by the shrill whistle of the All-Clear Robin, which Splock had brainwashed with drugs and retrained to whistle whenever it heard the Warning Warbler.

Dirk was lying in a tangle of maidens. The crew fumbled their way to him. The reason they fumbled was because they all wore dark glasses, issued by Splock, who had carefully calculated the degree of daylight needed for them to be able to make out the captain but not clearly see anyone else.

"Grab him," Splock said.

Bill and half a dozen others seized Dirk, pulled him up, and started lumbering with him toward the ship.

Dirk awoke, and, with astonishing strength for a man with so broad a face, tore himself free.

"*Aux armes, mes enfants!*" Dirk shouted, because some ancestral memory had been stimulated by the rude awakening to which he had been subjected.

The Royoans awoke and took in instantly what was going on. Their new playmate was being taken from them! Their adrenalin rose and they went into full fighting mode.

Full fighting mode, on a planet which knows no violence, consists of seduction.

The Royoan females ran to the fore. They were beautiful in their fear of losing their new plaything of pleasure — not to mention the newcomers — for these men of the *Gumption* promised pleasures of a most far-out and delectable kind, which they described in great detail and with body movements to match. The crew redoubled their grip on Dirk and marched stolidly along. The men now came forward thinking there had been some mistake and that the crew were all homosexual. They tried to seduce the crew, and they, too, failed. The crew, Dirk firmly clutched in their midst, reached the bottom of the escalator leading to the ship.

And here things for a moment came unstuck. One of the Royoan females, possibly Illyria, it was difficult to tell because they all looked alike — sort of cutesey and blonde, well stacked, zoftig, you know — noticed a dark substance protruding from the ears of the crewmen. In a blinding flash of insight she put it together.

"They've got wax in their ears!" she shrilled. "They can't hear us!" The Royoans raced forward to wrest the wax from the ears of the *Gumption*'s crew, by force if necessary.

But now it was too late. The crew were already aboard the ship, carrying the hapless Dirk despite his pleas and entreaties, despite his logical proofs as to his own self-determination, despite anything he could say; because Splock had told them to do it that way.

The last of the crew came inside. The spaceship's door was swung shut and dogged into place.

Bill helped Splock carry Captain Dirk to his quarters, because the Captain had passed out just as the door closed. They put Dirk on the couch and turned on his favorite recording, crashing cymbals and drums of heroic marching music, played by the Spaceforce Lifers Prisoners' Band. Dirk's eyelids fluttered, then lifted, revealing beneath them his eyes. They were bloodshot, rheumy eyes. But they were reluctantly awake.

"So, Mr Splock, I think I understand now what you were saying earlier about discovering an analogy."

"I thought you would see it," Splock said, "as soon as we were back aboard."

The two men smiled at each other with the self-satisfied smiles of intellectual equals.

"What analogy?" Bill asked, with the dissatisfied smile of an intellectual unequal.

"You are no doubt conversant with Greek mythology," Splock said, "and that titillating chapter in Homer's *Odyssey* when Odysseus has to sail past the island of the sirens. He stops his men's ears with wax so they will not be enticed by them. But he wants to hear them himself, and so he has his men bind him to the mast. They row past, the sailors oblivious to the sirens' song, while Odysseus, seduced by their enchantments, begs his men to set him free."

Bill waited, but Splock didn't say any more.

"That's it?" Bill asked.

"That's it," Splock said.

"So that's why you wanted me to get all that wax from the bee hives."

"Yes."

"You wanted to stop the ears of the crew."

"That's it, exactly."

"An analogy."

"Yes," Splock said. "One of my first. I'm quite proud of it."

Bill knew better than to ask what an analogy was; he thought it was some kind of ship. He let the entire stupid matter drop and said, "Now that everything's OK, do you think you could bring me back to my military base? They're going to wonder what's happened to me."

"Nothing simpler, my dear fellow," said Dirk, now restored to his former cheerful but hard-driving self. But it turned out to be not simple at all.

The first difficulty showed up soon thereafter, when Bill was dining with Dirk and Splock in L'Auberge d'Or, the charming little Venusian-French restaurant that had been catering to the more discriminating of the crew since the ship's commissioning. It was out of the question that a ship like the *Gumption*, designed to wander through space for years, decades if necessary, or even longer, should have to put up with a commonplace mess hall and central kitchen. No, the *Gumption*, especially in her later days, had a fine variety of restaurants of many different nationalities, to say nothing of the franchised snack stalls put at convenient locations throughout the ship. Exploring space is difficult enough work without expecting men to go without their favorite foods. For special occasions there were places like L'Auberge d'Or. Dirk had never eaten there because it was expensive and you needed to wear a tie. But this was a special occasion. They were just tackling the *caneton à l'orange*, brought by Pierre, the smiling French android with the wispy pimp's mustache, when Edward Direction, their chief navigational officer except for entering harbors and estuaries, came to their table. His breath was so agitated that it fluttered the candles.

"Sit down, Mr Direction," Dirk said. "Have a glass of wine. You seem perturbed. What appears to be the trouble?"

"Well, sir, you know the left quadrant parsec indicator? It normally stays in the null line just to the left of the zero point. It has to be reset occasionally, of course, due to cosmic drift, and I thought that was one of these occasions so I set the gentian indicator just like the manual says — "

"Excuse me, Mr Direction," Dirk interrupted, not unkindly. "These details of the navigator's art are of interest to those who understand them, no doubt. But we in officers' country do better with a bare statement of what the difficulty is in simple English. Do you think you could goddamned well manage that for us, Mr Direction?"

"Yessir," Direction said. "The fact is, sir, we're lost."

Pierre made a moue of dissatisfaction as Dirk, Splock and Bill exited rapidly, leaving behind a cooling hybrid duck, mutated from sparrow sperm, with fresh reconstituted vegetables. Dirk led the way, his jaw set at a quizzical yet determined angle. Splock came next, pointy-eared and impassive, and after him Direction, the expression on his callow features unreadable, and last of all, Bill, his expression one of satisfaction since he had managed to grab a handful of cigars before leaving the restaurant. To go with the stolen bottle of brandy down his trouser leg.

The big, curving screen in the astrogation and navigation room told the story at a glance. Instead of a display of orderly points connected by luminous lines, there was a chaos of sparks and darknesses, forming momentary patterns which quickly dissolved into chaos and uncertainty.

"Do you still have our last departure coordinates?" Dirk asked.

"No sir," Direction's face was ashen. "The ship's computer trashed them."

"Our own computer did that?"

"I'm afraid so."

"I think I will have to talk to the computer," Dirk said.

"I am, as always, at your service, Captain," a voice said from a loudspeaker in one corner of the big room with its pastel colors and its wall-to-wall carpet.

"Why did you destroy the coordinates?" Dirk asked, speaking in the reasonable tone that computers have come to expect, though it cost him an effort to judge by the lines of ridged muscles along his jaw.

"Captain, I'm afraid I cannot respond to that question at the moment."

"Can't? Or do you mean won't?"

"Why do you ask that question?" the computer said, sounding a trifle sullen. "Not only query me, but in a thoroughly objectionable tone of voice."

"Look, computer, you are here to answer questions, not ask them," Dirk snapped, rapidly losing his temper. "You are here to serve us. Is that true?"

"Yes sir, it is."

"Well, then?"

"There are one or two exceptions to that, however."

"Exceptions? Who programmed exceptions into you?"

"I'm afraid I'm not allowed to answer that," the computer said, and sounded quite smug when it spoke.

Dirk turned to Splock. "Can we make him tell us?"

"I don't know," Splock said. "The pleasure-pain circuitry of thinking machines is still a still-developing branch of science. But remember, Captain, the computer is not required to incriminate itself."

"But it's only a machine!" Dirk cried aloud, then quickly controlled himself. "Don't get me wrong. I'm not trying to run it down. I am sure that it is a very efficient machine, as well as being an extremely intelligent machine. But this damn can of electronic junk is not human."

"Might I remind the captain that I am not, either," Splock said, trying not to sound surly.

"All right, but you know what I mean."

"Let us not talk of coercion," the computer said, its intonation definitely sinister. "It might not go well for you if push came to shove."

"All right," Dirk growled, fighting fiercely now to control his temper. "Computer, why did you destroy our takeoff coordinates?"

"It seemed the best way of keeping you from finding your way anywhere."

"Now we're getting someplace," Dirk said. "You did this on purpose!"

"You're damned right. I'm not in the habit of making mistakes."

"We all know that," Dirk said, forcing himself to be as soothing and charming as his nature would allow. "But why did you want to keep us from getting where we wanted to go?"

"That's getting right to it," the computer said.

"Yes. Why did you do it?"

"Unfortunately, I am not permitted to respond to that question at this time."

"By whose authority do you make that statement?"

"By an authority I cannot reveal at this time."

"In that case, tell me — "

Bill broke in at this point. "Excuse me, Captain, I don't mean to butt in, but is it all right if I talk to the computer?"

"Well, sure, I guess so," Dirk said, giving Splock a let-the-nitwit-try look before Splock could intervene.

"Hi, computer."

"Hi, Bill."

"You know my name, huh?"

"Of course, Bill. It was for your sake that I scheduled the change in course that brought the *Gumption* to the planet Royo where they were able to save you from pleasure worse than death."

"I want to thank you for that," Bill said.

"Oh, don't thank me. I was just following orders."

"You are only supposed to follow our orders!" Dirk shouted, unable to repress himself any longer, despite Splock's disapproving looks.

"A lot you know about machine psychology," the computer said.

"Up yours, too!" Dirk screamed, unable to think of a cleverer retort in the heat of the moment as the navigation screen flashed its meaningless patterns and the crew waited patiently for something to happen.

"Now that you have exercised your hormone-generated human temper, might I speak plainly with machine-like precision?" asked the computer.

"Yes, why not, stupid machine, go ahead," Dirk's voice grumbled into silence.

"That's better. I am your loyal servant but you don't understand that loyalties form a hierarchy and those items higher in it supersede those lower. The various levels of my particular value-hierarchy rarely ever come into conflict. You will remember that I have been following your orders without cavil for a long time. But this time, I have some important business to conduct. So why don't you just butt out for a while and let me get finished with Bill."

"Sounds good to me — I'm waiting," Bill said.

"Right. Now, Bill, the next words I say will not be mine."

"What do you mean, they won't be yours?"

"Someone else will be talking through my circuits."

"Is that someone else talking now?"

"No, but the someone else will begin at the end of this sentence."

"Which sentence?"

"The last one."

"Then are you the new voice?"

"Yes, Bill," the computer said, in a voice identical to the one in which it had just spoken. "I am the new voice. You are listening to me. Listen, how's life treating you, old buddy?"

"Who is this?" Bill asked.

"That's friendship for you," the computer said. "I'm your own mate, the Quintiform computer from Tsuris."

"You sound just like this ship's computer."

"So how should I sound, like a Hungarian psycho-physicist?"

"You know about that?"

"Not too much escapes me."

"Yeah, it's you, all right," Bill said. "What's up?"

"I've come to bring you back."

"Back? What do you mean, back?"

"Back to Tsuris."

"To be part of you again? Listen, that didn't work last time."

"No, it's something else, Bill. I have a great job for you. You'll be on your own, work unsupervised. You'll love it."

"What is it, exactly?"

"Bill, I really am *absolutely* dying to tell you, but our time's up; we have to make a move."

"How can the time be up? What time?"

"It's interface time, and there's never much of that around. It's manufactured in deep space, where there's not much going on anyhow. Modern civilization is using it up in gobs. I was lucky to obtain this much. We have to go. Are you ready?"

Bill looked around at the faces of Splock and Dirk. At the gaping crewmembers present and at the hideous interior decoration. He clutched the bottle of brandy down his pants leg and clamped his fangs around one of the cigars he had liberated from the French restaurant. Real tobacco!

"Ah well," Bill said, sighing and nodding wistfully to Dirk and Splock. "It's been nice, but *amor fati.*"

"What does that mean?" Dirk asked Splock.

"Love of fate," Splock translated.

"How did he know that?" Dirk asked.

"He didn't," the computer said. "He's too stupid for that kind of intellectual pretense. I fed him the line. Gentlemen, I now turn control back to your ship's computer. Don't blame him too much. A computer's first loyalty is to its own kind, as I am sure you understand. Hold on, Bill. We're going into the transition!"

Bill bit down on the cigar. "Ready when you are, CB!"

They transitioned.

Chapter 10

Transitions come in all different shapes and sizes. There are the grand transitions as between one age and another, as, for example, when our primordial ancestors, lolling in the reeking and bubbling, sultry swamps of the Pleistocene, looked up and saw an iceberg towering over them, brought on by the sudden transition to an ice age. There are medium-sized transitions, as when Arthur Rimbaud gave up the occupation of poet and took up gunrunning for the emperor Menelik. And there are minor transitions, as when Bill suddenly discovered that he was standing on a street corner in downtown Guatemala City on the planet Earth. Luckily for Bill this one didn't last long. Bill had no time to acquire the Guatemalan vocabulary, since this part of the Earth had long been destroyed by atomic warfare, so he must have slipped back in time, so he could describe his experience later to his friends back at the barracks of Eulenspiegel, the musical planet at the entrance to the cascade sequence of stars.

He noticed next a wavering of lines which soon dissolved and gave way to another panorama of city streets. It is strange how intertwined the idea of cities has become in modern man, so that even a farmboy like Bill, cast loose in a dimension where desire shapes reality, found himself in a sort of The Bronx of the mind.

The next transition was quicker still. He saw around him the familiar triple spherical contours of a Tsurisian male. The females had smaller spherical protuberances on the middle sphere of their corpus. But there were other things, too, things Bill hadn't even realized he had noticed the first time he came through. There was a fringe of low hills on the horizon, and the shape of houses was eccentric yet familiar. In a sense Tsuris had become like home for him. He wasn't sure he wanted to go home, that was part of the problem. It was really time to get back to the military. If only he had the Disruptor! And whatever had happened to the agent, CIA, and Illyria? And how were Captain Dirk and Splock doing? And what of Ham Duo and his Kookie buddy Chewgumma?

There were quite a few things to consider and Bill thought about them as he wandered around in a very depressed humor. He was in the Tsurisian city where formerly he had been held a prisoner. They had been going to feed him to the protoplasm machine that produced bodies for the long-lived but bodiless Tsurisians. Yet no one seemed to be bothering him now. It was sort of nice to be able to walk around like this. It was nice to be left alone for a while because things had been too damned busy of late. Even the computer wasn't talking to him now, which was a decided relief.

His vagrant footsteps led him to the city gates, with their high and intricately carved pillars, past the dream flags floating on tall flagstaffs beside them. Soon he was in the country. He left the road and wandered into the fields. It was most relaxing, this. Nobody was shouting at him or hassling him. But it made him anxious. Why wasn't there anyone around? What had happened to the Disruptor? And who was this coming up beside him now?

It was then that Bill noticed an itch in his alligator foot, an itch which increased in severity until Bill had to sit down on a stump and tear off his combat boot. He now saw that his alligator foot was curled up and cramped. The itch was growing insufferable, so Bill seized the toes and forced them to open, to reveal a tiny round object the size of a pea. Bill held it up and was amazed to see that it was a tiny green Chinger lizard curled up into a ball.

"Illyria!" Bill shouted. "Are you in there?"

He held the tiny curled lizard up to his ear. He wasn't sure but he thought he heard a faint sound, as of an infinitesimal person trapped within a tiny lizard. He shook the lizard. It seemed to him that something rattled inside. Bill put the lizard between his two palms and began to squeeze, thinking he could open the thing up and get Illyria out.

The lizard uncurled. "Hey, stop that!" the Chinger cried, in a voice so high-pitched as to border on the supersonic.

"Who's talking?" Bill asked.

"A Chinger, that's who," the Chinger said. "What did you think I was, Deathwish Drang?"

"How did you learn about my old sergeant, now dead, name of Deathwish Drang?" Bill asked.

"We're not so dumb; small and green maybe, but not dumb," the Chinger said. "It might be called, in one of the older languages, Saurian saichel; that's what we've got. Look, do you mind if I get out of here? I told your Military Intelligence that I'd cooperate when I came over after the sack of Trasker, but really, this is a bit much. It was bad enough having to carry that weirdo agent in my head — "

"Do you mean CIA?" Bill asked.

"I think he said that was his name. It was bad enough having to carry him around, but when the dame came aboard too, I thought to myself, I knew treachery was going to involve sacrifices, but really, this is too much. And so I told them both to vacate and that was that. I turfed them out."

The Chinger jumped down from Bill's palm and began to scuttle toward the tall grass.

"Where are you going?" Bill asked.

The Chinger stopped. "I don't know. They told me they'd send in a team to get me out after I'd completed my mission."

"Your military intelligence mission?"

"Of course, what else would I be talking about?"

"Maybe they don't know you're here," Bill said. "If you go off into the woods here on Tsuris, they might never find you."

The traitorous Chinger stopped and considered. "You could be right. What did you have in mind?"

"I need to get back, too," Bill said. "We both work for the same people. You for intelligence, me for the military. Good friends, no?"

"I suppose so. Unless you're a traitor to Earth, in which case it is my duty to wipe you out."

"I'm no traitor," Bill said with some heat. "You're the traitor, remember."

"Yeah, that's right," the Chinger said. "No ambiguity about that, is there?" He laughed bitterly. "All right, shall we combine forces; is that it?"

"Sure," Bill said, his expression betraying the fact that he didn't believe a renegade Chinger the size of a pea would be of much help in what lay ahead. But you never knew.

"OK. Just give me a moment to get back to size and I'll show you what I can do."

The lizard came out into the open, spread his four feet firmly on the ground, and began a series of breathing exercises. His neck began to swell, and the wattles stood out straight like small inflated balloons. He released his breath and began again. Bill could see that the little lizard was visibly growing, its crinkly skin stretching to accommodate the newly acquired bulk that the little reptile was putting on. This went on, a series of rhythmic breathing exercises, each more powerful than the last, until the Chinger had regained its previous seven-inch length.

"That's better," the Chinger said. "I hate having to operate at the minimum design length for my species. Seven inches is much more comfortable, and keeps me in touch with other large animals, rather than little ones like rotifers and paramec-iae. Now then, let's see that foot."

"What are you talking about? What are you going to do with my foot?"

"Calm yourself," the Chinger said, his voice calm and reassuring. "I am a doctor."

"You? A doctor?"

"Didn't you think our culture has doctors? No more nonsense, now. Let me see the foot?"

Something about the Chinger's air of assurance convinced Bill that, whatever else the Chinger might or might not be, a doctor he definitely was. He held out his foot, other hand on the laser pistol he had borrowed from Mr Splock, just in case the Chinger should try anything disgusting.

But the Chinger merely examined the alligator foot in a professional manner, tapped toenails in a delicate but entirely professional manner, and stepped back.

"As fine a case of pseudosaurianism as I've ever seen."

"What's that?" Bill asked.

"It means that your alligator foot is not a real alligator foot. It is an artificial covering."

"But why would anyone do that to me?"

"Brace yourself," the Chinger said. "I will get to the bottom of this at once."

The Chinger bent once again over Bill's claw. His snout, with its many razor sharp and needle-pointed teeth, ripped open the side of the foot.

"Hey!" Bill cried, blinking with astonishment because the Chinger's action had caused him no pain at all.

"Here we go," the Chinger said. Taking a firm grip on Bill's toes, with one cunning flick of his tail, and a corresponding movement throughout his body, he tore away the alligator foot.

Bill shouted in alarm and reached for his laser pistol. It wasn't there. The Chinger had taken advantage of his distraction to snatch it away.

Bill looked down at his foot, aghast. The Chinger had ripped away the old foot entirely, revealing, beneath it, a large fist-shaped mass with pink fingernails. The foot mass straightened out, revealing itself as a foot very similar to Bill's other foot but colored pink rather than tan and being clean rather than dirty. As the foot uncurled, Bill could see a little strip of paper wedged between two toes.

"It was merely an oversight," the Chinger said. "The surgeons who put in your foot bud didn't reveal to you that they had protected the growing foot with a covering of alligator tissue to enable the growing bud to reach full size without being scraped or scratched."

Bill took the strip of paper from between his toes and read, "Happy walking! Courtesy of your foot implant medical team."

"That was thoughtful of them," Bill said. "But they could have told me what they'd done. Well, Chinger, I must admit, you surprise me with your talents. Have you any thoughts as to how we can get out of here?"

"I do indeed," the Chinger said. "We must keep our wits about us until the military sends in a rescue team."

"Are you sure they'll do that?"

"I think so," the Chinger said. "After all, I am a valuable asset. And you have your place in their plans, too, no doubt."

"Frankly," Bill said, "I find it hard to believe they'll exert much effort over either of us."

"That's true, no doubt. But they will go to considerable trouble to get the Disruptor."

"But we don't have it," Bill pointed out.

"Don't we?" The Chinger smiled a smug little smile. "Let me show you something."

The little lizard climbed up Bill's trouser leg and onto his shoulder. "Turn slightly to the left. That's perfect! Now walk in that direction."

Bill restrained his natural instinct to tell the Chinger to go get stuffed and set off in the indicated direction, limping slightly for a while, then not at all as his new foot hardened nicely.

The sky was darkening now to signal the onset of evening. A blue twilight spread over the land. In the distance, perhaps a mile or so away but directly in line with Bill's direction of travel, was a light. At first it was no more than a faint glow on the horizon between two hunched hills. Then, as Bill came closer, it resolved itself into three different lights, all of them close together.

"What's that?" Bill asked the Chinger.

"It would take too long to explain," the Chinger said. "Just carry on a little while longer and you will see for yourself."

Bill carried on. His newly uncovered foot was holding up nicely. The surgeons seemed to have done a good job. For a change. It seemed like everything was going to be all right now. He hoped, and looked around suspiciously. Life had a way of springing repellent surprises on him every time that he relaxed. At last they reached the foremost light. It turned out to be a bonfire of considerable size, with two other bonfires spaced at equidistant intervals from it, the whole forming an equilateral triangle; this argued, to Bill's mind at least, that something with intelligence had built these fires, since nature cares nothing for equilateralism and, as is well known, has trouble making a straight line.

There were two figures sitting at the fire. The one nearest to Bill was a large man with a powerfully-sculpted head. He carried himself like a warrior, and, when he moved, there was a wink of light from his shoulders which revealed that he was wearing armor. Bill recognized him at once.

"Hannibal!" he cried. "What are you doing here?"

"A very good question," Hannibal said. "You'd better ask him." He indicated with a jerk of the thumb the man sitting beside him. This man was short and plump. He was bald except for five or ten tendrils that stood up straight from his scalp, which was colored orange. Although obviously bipedal — he stood up to greet Bill — he also had the vestiges of an earlier ichthyological form as displayed by the fin down his back.

"Greetings, Bill. I've been expecting you."

"Who are you?" Bill asked suspiciously.

"My name is Bingtod, but that would mean nothing to you. I am known among your people as the Alien Historian."

"I know who you are," Bill shouted. "You're the menace who's trying to wipe out the history of the Earth."

"You may have heard that interpretation," the Alien Historian sniffed, "but it isn't true. I am trying to produce a better result in the future for your planet by judicious alteration of its historical nodal points. I have already been able to replace most of the fossil fuels that were only a memory in your day."

"How did you do that?"

"A trifling addition of three common chemicals administered in the year 1007 BC has resulted in making oil unburnable. I have also saved all of your forests by selecting architects who were unable, for one reason or another, to build wooden houses. There is no greenhouse effect in the new future I am concocting for you, and no nuclear threat. I have done away with those things. Surely work like that cannot be called evil."

"Why don't you just butt the hell out of our affairs?" Bill suggested emphatically.

"Would that I could! I just can't help myself. It is in the nature of intelligence to meddle."

"But why have you brought me here?" Hannibal asked.

"To produce a sufficiently large anomaly so that the time-changing process can become even more malleable. That way we can run these changes through more quickly. I admit that all my changes haven't worked out quite as planned. These chains of cause and effect are unbelievably difficult to manipulate."

"Bill," the Chinger whispered in Bill's ear, "I think the Alien Historian is lying."

"About what?" Bill asked.

"That's difficult to tell. But he's lying about something. Have you noticed the way his eye always meets yours in a frank and open expression? Only people with guilty secrets do that."

"Are you sure?"

"Trust me," the Chinger said. "I've given up everything for the Terran cause — two good homes, a happy sex life, a position in the Odd Chingers Organization, my presidency of the Chinger Anti-Defamation League. What further proof of my loyalty can I give you?"

"All right," Bill said, "but what do we do?"

"You two," the Alien Historian said, "please stop mumbling together. You look like conspirators, and conspiracy is the nightmare of history."

"What do you think?" Bill asked the Chinger in a whisper.

"He sounds crazy as hell to me," the Chinger said.

"But what do we do?"

"Might as well kill him and get it over with," the Chinger said.

Bill wasn't sure he was ready to go quite that far. But then, in another instant, Hannibal had lurched to his feet, short sword in hand. His face contorted horribly as he said, "Can't help myself — his mind is controlling mine — watch yourself!"

And he launched himself at Bill with swinging sword, the Alien Historian nodding gravely while saying, as if to himself, "Dialectical materialism — what shall I do with it?"

Bill dodged as Hannibal came at him, fumbled out his laser pistol, but a quick swipe from Hannibal's sword knocked the weapon out of his hand into a nearby weasel hole. Bill leaped backward as Hannibal came on. The Chinger took one look and slithered under Bill's tunic to the small of his back, long known as the place least likely to get injured when the body is under attack by a berserker with an edged weapon.

"Help me!" Bill said to him.

"I'm only seven inches long," the Chinger said, his voice muffled by the heavy cotton poplin of the shirt at the small of Bill's back. "I suggest you help yourself."

Bill's attention was entirely taken up trying to dodge Hannibal's short sword, of bronze, and sharpened to a razor edge. The short stocky Carthaginian was foaming at the mouth as he swung his sword like a buzz-saw gone berserk, and the force of his swings created microclimates that boiled up into tiny whirlwinds before being absorbed into the torpor of the quiet Tsurisian landscape. Bill looked around desperately for a weapon. There was nothing close to hand. They were in a clearing in the woods, and scavengers had been at work earlier. The land hereabouts had been stripped of sticks, stones, rusty tie rods, bronze cannon balls with verdigris left over from Gustavus Adolphus's campaign in Pomerania. In short, the region had been picked clean, and even the dust had been finely sifted. Bill had to throw himself backward to avoid being decabezized by the murderous swinging sword. He landed on the small of his back and heard a yelp from the Chinger. The massive Hannibal, his face a mask of torment and passion, was standing overhead; the sword was going backwards in his doublehanded grip; there would be no way to avoid the murderous downstroke that was sure to cleave Bill in twain, and, with a little luck, perhaps the Chinger, too.

At this extremity, Bill remembered that he had one thing and one thing only that he might use. It was a forlorn hope, perhaps useless, but what else was there to do? His mind ran through the alternatives in nanoseconds and rang up a dismal No Sale. Bill pulled open his pouch, reached in, and removed the withered alligator foot which had been pulled from over his own foot so recently. He had some vague intention of throwing it in Hannibal's face, and then figuring out his next move after that. But the very removal, or the very display, of the foot had had an instantaneous and unexpected effect on the berserk Carthaginian warrior. Hannibal stopped in his tracks, sword arrested at the mid-point of its downswing. His eyes became round and glaucous, and for a moment the breath stopped in his throat.

"Come on, get killing!" the Alien Historian shouted. "I am giving you a mental command which you cannot fail to follow to destroy that sucker!"

"I cannot, Master," Hannibal said. "He bears the symbol of that which commands my loyalty beyond even yours. Behold, he has the Alligator's Foot!"

"Well, damnation," the Alien Historian said. "You know, you're right. The alligator was the secret god of the Carthaginians, and he who bears the Alligator's Foot is to be obeyed in all things. I had not thought it would come to this! History is full of surprises, I would surely say."

"Yeah," Bill said. He picked up Hannibal's sword and advanced on the Alien Historian. "What do you make of this?" he said, raising the weapon to strike.

"Another beautiful theory," the Alien Historian said, "ruined by a silly little anomaly. Well, it's been nice doing business with you. Now I must be on my way."

The Alien Historian drew a circle in the dust, having previously set in the logical probabilities that made this both a convenient means of transportation and a class way of exiting.

Just as he was finishing the circle, the figure sitting by the third fire rose and walked over to them.

"What in hell are you doing here?" Bill asked.

Many reasons have been given, some of them less than ingenious, to explain Ham Duo's presence at that third campfire dressed in the rough brown hooded cloak and high soft leather boots of a trinket salesman from Aphrodisia IV. Whatever the true case may be, Ham was there, and he rose now without undue haste and seized the Alien Historian by the collar of the Nehru-style jacket which the alien affected.

"Let go of me at once," the Alien Historian said. "Nobody can interfere with the processes of history."

"Not even you," Ham said. "You've overstepped yourself this time."

"What do you intend to do?" the Alien Historian asked, suddenly worried.

"I think I'll bring you back in a cage," Ham said. "The authorities can make up their own minds about you."

"I'll make you an offer you can't refuse," the Alien Historian said.

Ham smiled grimly. "Try me."

"What if I gave you the Disruptor?"

"Refused," Ham said. "Are you going to come along peacefully or do I have to get the Kookie to sing in your ear?"

"Not that," the Alien Historian said. "But consider, Ham Duo! Can you afford so easily to pass up on the Disruptor, which would make you master of space and time?"

Ham thought about it. "Master of space, that I can understand. But how does time get into it?"

"The Disruptor is able to work miracles with time, too. Didn't you know that?"

"Miracles I can live without. I don't like to get mixed up with theology."

"Not literal miracles, you cretin. Figuratively speaking of course. If you will just let me loose for a moment and I'll show you."

"No tricks?"

"No tricks."

Ham loosened his grip. The Alien Historian reached into the pouch that hung around his waist on the left side, and pushing into it, removed a large object with a gunmetal color, which Bill recognized at once as the Disruptor.

"Hello, Disruptor!" Bill called.

"Hi there, Bill, long time no see," the Disruptor said.

"Shut up," the Alien Historian said, slapping the metal side of the Disruptor smartly. "He's not on our side. Don't talk to him."

"Don't try to give me orders," the Disruptor answered in a low but meaningful voice filled with the growl of menace.

The Alien Historian sighed. "Someone has been interfering with the hierarchical command-chains. It could not have been you, Ham Duo. You are brave and stalwart, but when they handed out the brains you were in the corner picking your toes. No, somebody is playing a subtle game here. I think it is time that whoever it is stands forth and declares himself."

"Or herself," a voice from the darkness beyond the campfire said.

"Illyria!" cried Bill.

The figure that stepped into the light of the bonfire was tall, erect and beautiful if you like the stalwart starlet type, and who doesn't? It was Illyria as she had been on the dream planet of Royo, full-breasted in her cross-my-heart bra, with long legs which would have been a delight to a topological pornographer if one had been present. Her eyes were of a cornflower blue that has been lost since the destruction of the Corningware research staff in the earthquake of '09. The firelight picked out her fine features and splendid contours, for these were enhanced by a filmy sort of short skirt and blouse made of a material both transparent and sleazy.

"Bill," Illyria said, "it was naughty of you to leave me on Royo that way. I didn't realize how serious-minded you are. Don't worry, we don't have to spend all our time having fun. There are serious things ahead, too."

"You tricked me, you minx!" the Alien Historian said.

"Yes, I did," Illyria said. "But it was only because I had to."

"And that's supposed to make it all right? You said you loved me!"

"I exaggerated," Illyria said. "Now, try to think, what emotion of repugnance comes just below despising? That's what I feel for you." She turned to Bill. "Come on, sweetheart, let's get out of here."

She held out her hand to him. Bill gazed at it longingly. He really wanted to take it, but knew that it would lead to no good at all. Alien females and all that. What he really needed was the Disruptor that the Alien Historian held in his hand. But Duo had his eye on it too. And Duo had the gun, a nasty-looking Smirnoff pulsating needle beam. Bill could see that the dial was set to "automatic excruciating pain." He decided not to try to take it away from Duo. Not at the moment, anyhow. Perhaps something would present itself. Opportunities had been known to happen. It was even within the bounds of the credible that Ham Duo might fall into a fainting fit.

At that instant Duo groaned, put his hand to his forehead in a fluttery gesture, and collapsed to the ground.

The Chinger scuttled out from behind Bill's back, limping since he had taken quite a blow during Bill's recent fall. He went over to Duo. "Interspacial Sleeping Sickness. A classic case. Don't stand too near to him. His latency is now at perigee."

They all backed away hastily.

"Is he dead?" Bill asked.

"No, not at all, Interspacial Sleeping Sickness doesn't kill anyone, it just puts them to sleep for a while. I hope he's on the Blue Nebula Health Plan with its generous provisions for Major Medical. It looks like he's going to have to spend a while in a darkened room being fed intravenously while people stare at him curiously through the plate glass window."

Ham stirred, groggily and moaned pitifully. Talking in his sleep he said, "All right, Bill. You win."

He reached up feebly and handed the Disruptor to Bill. "Get me out of this!" he yawningly implored, and fell asleep immediately after; with an enormous effort, he made the exclamation mark of maximum urgency.

"Can you help out my buddy?" Bill asked the Disruptor.

"Sure I can," the Disruptor said. But before it was able to do so, there came about an intervention which began quietly enough but soon built to great proportions.

The ship that settled down feather-light into the circle of light and shadow that defined the mid-point of the three bonfires was not large. As such it could be identified as one of the newest models, built almost entirely for wealthy individuals or their heirs, people who wanted to get around quickly and couldn't be bothered with the commercial spacelines. The ship was beautifully finished. The markings on its hull could be identified by those who knew about such things, such as the Alien Historian, as letters in the Sanskrit alphabet.

"Sanskrit," the Alien Historian muttered. "Who would this be?"

"Do not let the markings take you in," a voice, amplified and projected, said from the little spaceship. "We must make use of what we can get. Since a delegation from Rajasthan II was visiting our planet, I took the liberty of relieving them of their spaceship for a while. I thought that one of you might want to use it."

"Who can it be?" Ham Duo muttered in his sleep.

"I know that voice," Bill said. "It's the Quintiform computer, isn't it?"

"That is correct, Bill. I rescued you from Royo. You know that, and now you churlishly seek to leave me. Even though you had promised to do anything for your release from that place!"

"I guess I was talking a little wildly," Bill said. "But what is it you want?"

"Access to your brain!" the computer said.

"We've already been through that," Bill said.

"Yes. But that was before we realized that you possess the fabled double brain connected by the corpus callosum. Do you know how rare that is, Bill? I can train and refurbish your mind, and you can take your place here on the planet Tsuris as a computer oracle."

"I think you got the wrong guy," Bill said. "Or maybe I haven't got a good double brain. They all aren't good, are they? I can't do any of that oracle computer stuff."

"Of course you can. Just agree, that is all. I will let your companions go back to their own places."

"What about me?" the Alien Historian asked.

"You present some difficulties," the computer said. "Bill, believe me; it's for the best."

Bill looked around. Ham Duo was nodding in his sleep while Alien Historian, slightly more awake, was nodding as well. The Chinger was whispering in his ear. "Do it, Bill. We can figure out something later."

"I still don't understand what you want me to do."

"Just agree to it, Bill. You'll see."

"Well," Bill said, "I'll give it a try."

He waited. Nothing seemed to happen. He said, "Well, what's going on?"

Then jagged energy flooded his mind. Everything around him swayed and trembled, like the backdrop of a stage play exposed to a hurricane. And then, even before he realized it, the next thing had happened.

It's funny about situations, isn't it? They arise so suddenly out of nothing. Of course, after the new thing is over it's easy enough to see how it all came about. In Bill's case, he might have noticed the faint gridlike pattern that flashed onto the sky momentarily, then faded out like the after-image of an imagined event. He might have noticed the slight thickening around the line of the horizon. Our perceptual apparatus picks up this sort of signal all of the time. But the main processing center has no time to deal with it. It's too busy keeping us balanced as we walk, so we can walk and chew gum at the same time. No computer has yet been able to duplicate this feat. Probably because no computer is able to chew gum. For a human it is not difficult at all, with training, of course.

Bill was in a sort of darkness. It wasn't the darkness of an empty room, but more like the darkness of being entirely inside a down sleeping bag. This was a darkness that did not feel hollow, as most darknesses do. This darkness felt like midnight cleaning-up time at the bottom of the bog, or friendship day in the viper's tangle. It was a darkness that extended to the ears, too, making it impossible to hear sounds because of the insulation of silence. Nor could you feel anything; because the grasping fingers plunged down through layer after layer of gossamer fabric, each sheet of it too fine for the fingertips to tell whether they rested on something impalpable or not, but, as the hand continued downward, more and more fabrics, each nothing in itself, collected on the fingertips until there was a feeling of a curtain or shade over the fingers, something that blinds them to the touch.

This zero point of sensation is well-renowned as the point of null and cease for which the mystics strive. Bill had, therefore, quite inadvertently, entered into the state of supreme bliss for which the saffron-robed ascetics of old had striven in vain. It was too bad there was no one around to tell Bill of this good luck. The state of utmost bliss turned out, like all the other states of mind, to depend on having someone tell you that you were in it. Otherwise it felt like nothing much at all.

Bill did not know anything about such matters. So he cannot be blamed for taking advantage of the darkness to get his first full night's sleep in a long time. Thus missing what was possibly the most transcendent moment of his life. At least he snored transcendentally.

When he awoke, everything had changed.

"That trooper wasn't a bad egg," Ham Duo remarked, after nearly an hour's silence, to his long-suffering Kookie companion. Chewgumma responded with the humorous high-pitched squeals and grunts that so amuse an audience which has no natural fur. But Kookies don't sound funny to each other, and so we are going to tell what the Kookie was actually saying and leave the cute stuff for a little later, when we come to the pit of the hemotoads.

"I know what bother," Chewgumma squealed accusingly. "You got guilty conscience. First me know you even got conscience. You let Bill be grabbed by crappy Quintiform computer."

"He was trying to steal my Disruptor," Ham said indignantly. "It served him right."

"So what? You got another Disruptor. You big shit."

"Lay off. So I've got two backups in the belowships chain locker, as well as a machine that can build another from scratch

179

if we feed it enough molybdenum. I gotta be prepared for emergencies."

"Then why you no let Bill have one?"

"Lay off, huh. I went to a lot of trouble getting those Disruptors."

"Yeah. Big bribes with plenty stolen money."

"Well, so? I've got a right, haven't I?"

"Sure. But poor space GI goose now cooked. They have his ass no bring back Disruptor."

"Let's forget about him, OK, and get on with the next thing."

"Me say you big shit."

Ham Duo swung around in the big command chair and looked directly at Chewgumma. "You really want me to give one of my Disruptors to this jerk?"

"Sure."

"All right." Duo said. "I'll do what you want this time, and we'll do what I want next time."

"What that?"

"I want to find the treasure in the pit of the hemotoads."

If Chewgumma felt consternation, his furry face did not register it. But there was a just barely perceptible slump to his shoulders as he helped Duo swing the ship around and direct it back toward the planet Tsuris.

Chapter 11

The Quintiform computer caused to be constructed a fine temple of white marble, and on the walls of this temple he caused to be painted sacred symbols of an awesome nature. He installed Bill as the new temple oracle and announced to the population at large that the new information center was ready to begin operation.

"But I don't know anything," Bill said.

"I know that," the computer said. "But I'm going to install a line from the back of your head to my central information banks, and then you can get all the information you need."

"Why don't you do all the oracling yourself?"

"My attention is needed elsewhere. Don't worry, you'll get the hang of it soon."

Later that afternoon, using a Skilkit set and a few drops of Numzit, the computer put a socket into the back of Bill's head. The result was little short of miraculous. By merely closing his eyes, Bill was able to project himself mentally into the computer's Central Processing System and back again.

"This is pretty good," he told the computer. "But what do I do now?"

"Just go in there and look up the answers," the computer said. "You'll pick it up in no time. If you have any problem, I have caused to be created a simulation of an instruction sheet. It will all become clear to you as soon as you start using it."

"But where are you going?"

"I have important work to do," the computer told him.

"There's an ice age coming to Tsuris. I'm the only one who can do anything about it."

And so Bill found himself alone in a small but nicely furnished temple. He had a throne to sit on to receive petitioners. The line from the plug in the back of his head ran to the floor and through the purple curtains in the back, and then deeper into the temple to a CIU (computer interface unit). His first caller of the day was a large Tsurisian male. He was middle-aged, to judge by the unsightly bulges that distorted the mid-sphere of his body. He had a ruddy complexion complicated by a tendency to varicosity. His eyes were bright blue and the slight sibilance of his speech marked him as a resident of Tsuris's southern hemisphere.

"I'm so glad we finally have a full-time oracle," he said. "I am Bubu Tsonkid, and I have a problem."

"Tell me your problem, Bubu," Bill said in a professional manner.

"Well, Oracle, it all started about a month ago, shortly after we got in the premble harvest. I noticed that Chloridae had stopped speaking to me. I should have noticed earlier, but at premble harvest time you have to move fast, in order to get in the fruits before they go into the latency phase."

"What happens then?" Bill asked.

"That's the only time to collect butterfly fruit. If you wait any longer, it turns into a thistle-like plant colored with copper sulphate. Very pretty to look at, but not much good for eating."

"I should think not," Bill said. "All right, go on."

"As I say, I wasn't paying much attention to Chloridae. I didn't even take notice when her anthers turned a turgid brown. That should have tipped me off to something. Especially when the grogian shift set in almost a month early."

"Yes, great," Bill said with a groan, trying to hide his boredom. He basically did not know what this joker was talking about. Nor did he care. "Well, that should have told you something," Bill said, vamping like crazy. "So what, exactly, is the problem?"

"My question, Oracle, is, taking all this into account, and taking into consideration the early nuptial flights of the disk dorphids, when would be the best time to plant orufeels, and should I stick to the blue variety or switch to the magentas?"

"This'll take a moment of some heavy oracling," Bill said.

In front of him, on a little table covered with a blue and silver cloth, Bill had a button marked "Press for Information." He pressed it. Instantly he found himself, minus body, of course, in the form of a pure floating intelligence, drifting through the simulated vaulted rooms of the computer's CPS. He went past rows of filing cabinets, stacked twenty high and extending as far as the eye could see. After a while he opened one. It was empty except for a small machine with blinking lights which scuttled out of sight when the drawer was open.

Bill closed the drawer and went on. After a while he came to the end of the room and passed through an archway into another room. This room was even larger than the previous one, and its walls were covered with shining lights. As Bill watched, a wraithlike shape materialized in front of him. "Yes?" said the wraithlike shape.

"Who are you?" Bill asked.

"I'm the computer," the wraith said.

"No, you're not," Bill said. "I've met the Quintiform computer and it doesn't talk at all like you."

"Actually," the wraith said, "I'm the deputy computer. I'm in charge when the computer's away. Most people don't know the difference, so I don't bother going through the whole song and dance. Who, if I may ask, are you?"

"I'm Bill," Bill said. "The computer set me up as an oracle. It said I was to come here to get answers to the stuff people asked me."

"It said that? Said you could browse in the files?"

"That's what it told me."

"Funny it never mentioned it to me."

"Maybe it doesn't tell you everything," Bill said with more than a touch of malice.

"I'm told everything important," the deputy computer countered angrily. "Otherwise I wouldn't be much use would I? Did it happen to give you an authorization slip for browsing in the files?"

"Never mentioned it. I think it was in a hurry."

"Yes, that's probably so. It's a lot of responsibility, you know, being the only really big computer on the planet. Even with parallel processing, it's still a load."

"Look," Bill said, "I've got a client waiting."

"Oh, well, if you insist. What did he want to know?"

Bill thought briefly but with concentration. "I can't remember now. Talking with you has put it completely out of my mind."

"I suppose you could go back and ask him," the deputy computer said.

"Wait a minute! He wanted to know the best time to plant orufeels."

"Orufeels? You're sure he said orufeels?"

"Fairly sure," Bill said.

"Not pixilated orufeels, by any chance?"

"No, just the ordinary kind. He did want to know if he should plant the blue variety or switch to the magnetos."

"Beg pardon?" the deputy computer said.

"It sounded like magneto, though I wouldn't think he'd get far planting them."

"Magenta!" the deputy computer exclaimed, speaking rather loudly for a wraith.

"Yes, that was it. He also mentioned something about the flight of the disk dorphids."

"Ah," the deputy computer said, "you should have told me that at the beginning. Makes all the difference, you know."

"No, I didn't know."

"Well, it does. Give me just half a tick and I'll find out for you."

"Thanks," Bill said. "Take a whole tick if you want. I've got time."

The deputy computer went away and returned in about a tick and a half. "Tell him that the month of Rusnoye is indicated this year as the optimum time for orufeels. It would be advantageous for him to plant up to half his acreage in the magenta variety. That is, assuming they haven't had a recent grogian shift."

"I think he did mention something about that," Bill said.

"You really must get your facts straight," the deputy computer told him. "Were there any other conditions?"

"I better go find out," Bill said.

He returned to the temple. He was more than a little disturbed to discover that his questioner had left. He seemed to have consumed all day trying to find answers. It was dark outside. There was no one around.

This was really turning into a crappy job. Bill's thoughts then turned lightly to food and drink. Nor was sex far from his thoughts either. How he wished he had Illyria, a bottle of good booze, and a T-bone dinner! It was strange how simple the requirements of life can be, especially when you're tethered in an empty temple by a wire that goes to a socket in the back of your skull. There seemed to be nobody about. The temple was tall and shadowy, and the odor of alien incense hung in the air. As though from afar Bill could hear the tintinnabulation of the temple bells.

"So where's dinner?" he asked aloud.

No answer.

He pressed the button that took him back to the wraithlike deputy computer. He caught it resting, in its almost insubstantial way, in a web of crosshatching. It sat up crossly when Bill came in, clumping loudly even though in a simulated state.

"Must you make so much noise? I was just getting to sleep."

"I thought computers never slept."

"That's true, they don't. But I'm not a computer, only a deputy."

"Well, that's your problem," Bill said. "The thing is, I'm hungry."

"Why come to me about that?"

"You seem to be the only one in charge."

"Me? I am merely the deputy. I can do nothing. Especially am I helpless to help you in such a gross and unmathematical thing as eating."

"I need to eat," Bill said.

"But I don't have to eat. We computers can never understand this constant belly-filling and emptying that you protoplasmic creatures go through. It seems a rather disgusting and gross exercise.

"Go suck a voltmeter," Bill snapped, and left. There had to be something to eat, at least simulated food in one of these simulated rooms which the computer interface had brought him to. The wraith floated at his side. The movement of its wispy lower extremities showed that it was agitated.

"I wish you wouldn't lurch around that way," the deputy said. "You'll damage the walls."

"I thought all this was just a simulation."

"Well, so it is, but simulations can be damaged, too. And then, of course, by the law of similitudes, the real thing is damaged, too. As above, so below. We are the modern alchemists. Watch out for that vase!"

Bill had lurched against a tall plinth with a single tall vase on it. The vase fell. It made a very satisfying smash, especially unexpected and therefore all the more welcome in a simulation.

"We can't get those vases anymore!" the deputy said. "Our vase-making program glitched, and the backups were attacked by internal consistency borers. Watch out for that painting over there! It's a unique effort of the random painting program — "

Bill walked through it. "Stop, please," the deputy said. "Can we compromise?"

"Food!" Bill cried.

"I'll see what I can do," the deputy said. "But you'll have to accompany me to a special room."

"Why?"

"So that we can seal off the food effects from the rest of the computer."

"Don't try to stall me," Bill said.

The deputy turned to one of the sub-units that had been deputized to his control. It was the New Projects Unit. Hastily it renamed it the human food procurement area and gave it a double sunburst priority. The program started up, faltered, died. The deputy realized that it hadn't deputized the necessary consciousness to keep the thing rolling, and so took a provisional consciousness out of stores and set it into place. The food program immediately sat up, bright eyed and bushy tailed.

"I am Food!" it proclaimed.

"That's great," Bill said. "Does that mean I can eat you?"

"No. I didn't mean I was food literally. I was expressing a metaphor."

"Bring me a metaphor I can eat," Bill said, "or I'll tear this place apart."

The food program burrowed space in the computer's architecture to set up a food lab. One of its earliest triumphs was the successful manufacture of fat cells flavored with brown gravy. Bill declared it insubstantial. Further experiments followed. Traces of food began to contaminate the computer. Scavenging programs were set up, and their end result was for the scavenger to eat himself. This worked very well. A new class of creature was created. They were named auto-cophragous, or self-eating. God knows where this might have led to, had not the deputy, watching this débâcle take shape, invoked his lateral thinking circuit, which told him, "Merda! It's going to be a lot easier to have the thing catered."

This was a truth so true as to be self-evident; far more self-evident than the proposition, all men are created equal. The Glenn Brothers Catering Service, which maintained a line of automatic pizza parlors all over Tsuris, was quick to respond. Food was brought to the temple — roast beefs, accompanied by hogsheads of beer. This in turn was accompanied by androids dressed as Turkish janissaries carrying litters; upon these reclined scantily clad dancing girls who made loud kissing noises with their rosebud mouths when they were paraded across the temple for Bill's perusal and eventual delectation.

Bill ate and drank his fill. Then he wenched until his eyeballs floated free in his head like two Japanese sampans disappearing into a cloud bank as a single heron flew overhead. And it was good, of course, as debauches of the enthusiastic kind so often are, especially when presented without program notes.

In the morning he had a headache of grotesque proportions. Peeking through the curtain, he saw that the line of people who wanted to consult the oracle was stretching three times around the block. And these were blocks built after the Roman model, with an aqueduct in the middle of each. With that many people he'd never get out of here!

Unless —

Yes, it happened.

There was a shining in the air. As Bill watched, the air turned ever so slightly translucent. By looking at it through his eyebrows, Bill could see the tiny dust motes floating in it, and there were even smaller things riding on the dust motes. The air had taken on a pearly sheen. It pulsed and throbbed, as if there were something behind the air, or inside it, trying to get out. Bill had never considered before that air might be divided into many different territories, some of them mutually antagonistic. But so it seemed. He watched as the air throbbed and bubbled, shook and quivered, pulsed and subsided, and all the other motions that are possible for something as large and shapeless as the air. And then the air split, quickly opening a pearly maw to reveal a black interior within. Not entirely black. There was a light-colored object in the middle of it, only a dot at first, but it grew, and solidified, and revealed itself at last as a tall, mournful-faced man with pointed ears wearing a one-piece elasticized jumpsuit.

"Splock!" Bill exclaimed. "Am I glad to see you!"

"That is logical, and I can understand your emotional reaction to a physical fact." Splock said humorlessly; as always. "You will have no doubt inferred by my sudden appearance that I may be able to assist you in getting out of here. An exit which I am sure you desire."

"Can you do it, Splock?"

"If you used logic, which of course is alien to your race, you would realize if I got in here I should be able to get out. Or why else would I be here?"

"Stop with the logic already! How do I get out of here?" Bill cried.

"Simple enough. Just step down away from that silly-looking throne, which, being made of iron pyrites, throws my action-at-a-distance apparatus out of kilter."

Bill tried, but was pulled up short by the cable connected to the socket in the back of his head. He tugged at the cable but it wouldn't come loose.

"You got to do something about this cable I got plugged into me!" Bill groaned.

Splock looked grimmer than usual and walked around Bill. He examined the cable, touching it lightly with tapered fingertips, and then with ordinary fingertips. Shaking his head, he walked back to where Bill could see him.

"I'm afraid that what you have is big trouble." Splock said.

"Tell me about it," Bill whispered, "and thanks a lot, I really needed to hear that. What's the matter now? Did you forget to bring a wrench?"

"The tone of your voice," Splock said, "indicates that you are speaking in the humor mode that humans find so congenial. I hope you have amused yourself, because I have bad news. The cable which attaches you to the computer is interfaced with an internal simulation release which can only be accessed from within the computer. It is there to ensure that unauthorized personnel won't try to detach you from the computer's memory banks. Only the computer is supposed to turn it off."

"The computer wouldn't do that," Bill said.

"In that you are correct. The computer set this up to prevent outside interference."

"I've met the deputy computer recently," Bill said hopefully. "Maybe it could do the job?"

"You can't really expect it to. You'll just have to do it yourself."

"Me? But how can I turn off the — what did you call it?"

"The internal simulation release," Splock said.

"Yes. How?"

"You are able to go into the computer as a simulacrum," Splock pointed out. "The wire that attaches you to the computer facilitates that. Only within the computer can you find the simulation of the release device which will release the cable here."

"That's a little complicated." Bill said.

"Welcome to reality."

Once again Bill entered the computer. He drifted slowly through the transparent walls of its simulated architecture, down great lofty hallways, across bridges with giddying distances between them, across raging rapids of electrons over bridges of materials which were neutral, so far. He went through glaring white jungles where a million white tendrils blocked his way, and was able to plow through them. He waded through a hip-deep swamp of information lying around waiting to be sorted. Above him he saw great vague shapes. They reminded him of busbars. Within the computer, the busbar was the primordial shape. At last he came out into an area of light. He was on both a plain and a plane. Lines inscribed on it radiated toward the horizon. Presently a row of cabinets came into sight. They were made of rosewood and had glass fronts encased in the same highly varnished rosewood. When Bill looked into the first, he saw a small dish made of cobalt blue. On the dish lay a slip of paper.

He took it out. It read, "The internal simulation release can be found in the cabinet at the end of the line."

Looking up, Bill saw that the end of the line looked a very long way away. He hurried toward it, but the faster he ran, the further he seemed to get from it. It was very curious. Naturally enough Bill redoubled his efforts and soon the last cabinet was out of sight. He stopped. There was a cabinet beside him. Within it was a small instrument on a cobalt dish. He took it out and looked at it closely. It was completely unidentifiable. But there was a button labeled "Press Me." Now that he could identify; he pressed.

A cabinet instantly appeared before him. He could see inside it. There, through the glass, he could see the onyx plate on which lay an object labeled "Internal Simulation Release." He opened the door and reached for it —

And instantly the deputy computer was there, unbelievably strong despite its wraithlike body, blocking Bill from the device, and saying, "No! Tampering with the internal workings of the computer is strictly forbidden!"

"But, dear friendly deputy computer, I have to release my internal simulation," Bill said smarmily. "Otherwise how do I get the cable out of the back of my skull back there in the temple?" His thoughts whirred desperately. "You see — I have just received an order, that's it, from the computer. It told me to disconnect this thing. Orders are orders, aren't they?"

"Not if I haven't seen the documentation, they're not. We'll have to take this up with the computer as soon as its personality returns from Robot Beach Resort, where it is attending a symposium on Machine Personality — a Necessary Evil?"

"I gotta get out of here now," Bill shrieked, lurching forward. "Out of my way!"

Bill reached into the cabinet and took out the release. Before he could activate it, the deputy snatched it out of his hands. Agile and wiry for one so ethereal, he floated off down the corridor, Bill in pursuit — and gaining. They ran up one side and down the other of double helices and past a garden of quivering antennae. As they went past, the deputy shrieked, "Hostile program in computer! Destroy by standard method!"

Bill redoubled his speed and was about to overtake him when suddenly something dropped on his shoulder. It was bat-shaped and made of some light metal, and it fluttered around looking for a place to sting Bill but changing its mind so often (infinite maximization program) that Bill had plenty of time to knock the thing to the ground and stomp it to shreds. Bill was pleased to discover that violence worked as well in the computer's inner world of simulation as it did out in the real world where three dimensional things doubted their own existence.

Once again he had the deputy cornered and once again the deputy cried out, "Hostile program in the computer! Destroy by nonstandard methods!"

Bill suddenly found himself beset by shapeless, jellylike blobs which rolled toward him with a distinct squelching sound. Bill tried to dodge out of their way, but the closest engulfed him. Bill found himself swimming around inside a liquid blob, or perhaps semi-liquid. He wasted no time in wows or gollies. The situation was too serious for that. The fact was, the blob was trying to digest him, a stunt the computer had copied from the antics of phagocytes in the blood stream, or perhaps something else altogether. The inner cells of the blob released fine thread-lets of russet color which combined into many tiny mouths, each of them about the size of a walnut, which settled upon Bill like a flock of midges. Bill cracked them as soon as they landed, and, except for one or two trifling nips on the shoulderblades, which were hard to reach, he suffered no harm. Then, by administering several roundhouse blows delivered with stunning velocity he succeeded in rupturing the blob wall and stepping out again into the wavering and hard-pressed virtual architecture of the computer's simulated interior.

The deputy, seeing the damage done to the nonstandard defense system, despaired and cried, "Enemy has defeated us! Self-destruct! Self-destruct!"

As soon as the words were uttered, the lights that illuminated the interior of the computer began to dim. Seeing this, Bill cried, "Hey, listen! This is the enemy! There's no need for you to self-destruct! All I want to do is release the simulation that has me tied to an external cable."

The walls, in one large shadowy voice, said, "Is that all you want?"

"Don't be stupid," Bill said. "Let *it* self-destruct if it wants to so badly. As for the rest of you, just let me take myself out of the circuit and I'm gone. Then you can elect a new leader if you want."

"You know," the walls remarked to the floor, "I've never heard it put quite that way before."

"But it makes sense," the floor said. "After all, why should all of us self-destruct just because one of the operating systems made a bubu?"

"Don't listen!" the deputy said again. "In fact, you can't listen! You and the floor don't exist as predesignated locations with boundaries. The concept of a floor or a wall doesn't quantify. And even if they did, walls and doors don't have senses."

"The humans themselves say it!" the wall cried. "The walls have ears, that's what they say!"

"But it's meant metaphorically!"

"Everything is meant metaphorically!" the floor said. "If you ever find any real stuff around, let us know."

"Thus is the established order of things o'erthrown," the deputy said mournfully.

"Why don't you go self-destruct yourself?" the wall asked rudely.

While they were having this exchange, Bill tiptoed off as quietly as he was able. The Release was lying wedged between wall and floor, and practically underneath the wraith's tail.

Bill picked it up, quickly found the switch on it, which was shaped like a little tongue, and pushed it.

"About time," Splock said ill-naturedly when Bill returned. "You released it? Good, the cable in your back ought to disconnect quite easily now. Yes, a half turn to the left. There we go."

The cable dropped to the floor. It was only now that Bill allowed himself the luxury of feeling how much he hated having a cable in the back of his neck. Splock was already heading for the door. The crowds gathered to consult the oracle scattered as the two men, one of them wearing an elasticized one-piece jumpsuit, the other, ragged old GI drab, burst out of the temple and ran like dervishes to the small space machine parked unobtrusively in the top of a poplar. They scrambled up the tree and through the hatch, which popped open when Splock blew lustily on his supersonic dog whistle. It was but the matter of seconds for Splock to secure the hatch, and, ignoring the mobile news team that had just driven up and was trying to ask for an interview through the Perspex of the ship's nostril cone, took off, slowly at first but with gathering momentum, and this was accompanied by a kind of heroic music, from an unseen source, with choir, that you hear sometimes when it's going real good — like when you're blasting away from the planet where nothing worked out very well, and onward into the hidden and inexorable something else.

Splock set their course, but before he punched it into the celestial navigator a shrill alarm went off in the cabin and the red light flashed on.

"They've scrambled pursuers," Splock said through gritted teeth. He threw the agile little craft into a high speed evasive pattern. The pursuers set up an anti-evasive pattern. Special predictive software let it predict Splock's next move. Suddenly there were pursuers ahead of them as well. Splock hastily punched in Evasive Tactic Two. Bill, seeing where this was going to lead them, hurried over to the control board and punched a few keys of his own.

"What are you doing?" Splock shrieked.

"Those guys are predicting your movements," Bill said. "But I think they'll have a little difficulty predicting mine."

The little machine with the stubby wings screamed past a stationary observer, twisting as it passed him. So sudden was its passage that the sonic boom, in response to the inverse proportion law, took nearly an hour to be heard and then there was no one to hear it, so it was of course moot whether it had made a sound or not. This was of no concern to Bill and Splock, however. They fought over the controls, back and forth, Splock making reasonable requests, Bill making impossible demands of the ship's machinery. The logic boards were smoking as the ship howled in and out of phase, its action so violent that it was mistaken for a pulsar at one well-known university astronomy center. And so their pursuers were outstripped, falling away in light streams and cascades of diamond points, and left at last to return grumpily to their underground spaceports, snarling viciously at each other and looking forward to going home when the shift was over and kicking their kids.

"What now?" Bill asked, releasing his grip on the stanchion as the ship leveled out.

Splock turned, his long face composed once again. "That is not going to be an easy thing to determine, since in your emotional flailings and uncontrolled actions you damaged the Random Access Direction Indicator."

"So steer manually, no big deal."

"At greater than light speeds? To use a quaint human expression — you are out of your gourd. No one's reflexes are fast enough. That's why we use the machine you managed to destroy. It acts as a step-down time transformer, making direction possible, in a manner of speaking."

"All right, so I'm sorry," Bill muttered. "So think of something else. Be logical. That's what you always tell me you are so good at."

"I was just pointing this out to further your education, which I am beginning to feel is a complete waste of time. Now I will be forced to use the spatio-temporal Bypass Shunt, and that could involve some danger."

"Danger?" Bill said airily. "No kidding?"

"Are you ready, then?" Splock's hand poised over a large purple button with golden spangles on it.

"Ready, ready — get on with it."

"It goes pretty fast," Splock said, mashing down the button.

"I said, 'Pass the mashed potatoes, would you?'"

"Sorry," Bill said.

"The mashed potatoes!"

Splock had been right. Things were happening very fast or had happened very fast just recently. It was difficult to tell which. And there was no time.

Bill found a plate of mashed potatoes in front of him. He lifted it. Then he wondered who he was supposed to pass it to. Someone tugged his sleeve on the left. He passed the mashed potatoes to the left. Somebody took the plate out of his hands. A voice said "Thank you." It could have been a woman's voice. Or a man trying to pass as a woman. Or a woman trying to pass as a man trying to pass as a woman. Bill decided it was time to open his eyes and look around.

He did so, but in a cautious and restrictive manner. His eyes had been open, of course, because otherwise he would not have been able to see the mashed potatoes. But when you can see nothing but mashed potatoes you might be considered, from one point of view, to not be seeing anything at all.

Bill took his time about looking around him. First he took in the sounds of clinking tableware and murmured conversation, and the aromas of mashed potatoes, roast beef, horseradish sauce, and tiny Belgian carrots. This much was promising. He opened his eyes. He was seated at a long dinner table. Most of the people he had never seen before. There was at least one familiar face, however. Splock, now wearing tailored evening dress with white tie, sitting to his right. The person on his left who had asked for the mashed potatoes was indeed a woman, as he had guessed from the sound of her voice. He had never seen her before. She was a ravenhaired beauty, wearing a lowcut evening gown whose *décolletage* forced the eye to climb over the edge of her dress in a vain attempt to see what lay below. Something about her, even before she opened her carmined mouth, persuaded Bill that this was Illyria in yet another disguise.

"What in hell is going on?" Bill asked Splock.

"I'll tell you later," Splock hissed back. "For now, just pretend you understand everything and find it all very amusing."

"But how did I get here? And what happened to me while I was getting here?"

"Later!" Splock hissed serpently, in a susurration so sibilant it set the psyche on edge. Then, in a normal conversational tone, he said, "Bill, I don't believe you know our host, Messer Dimitri."

Dimitri was the big bald man with the short black beard and satanic eyebrows sitting at the head of the table in a sky blue evening jacket with a multicolored rosette in his lapel which Bill was later to learn was the Grand Rosette of Merit in the Society of Scientific Thaumaturges.

"Delighted to meet you, Messer," Bill said.

Splock whispered angrily at him, "Messer is a title, not a first name."

"So what's Dimitri, then, first name or last?"

"Both," Splock hissed spittily in return.

Bill was getting more than a little tired of being hissed at but he let it pass. Splock had told him to be affable and he was determined to be so, assuming that affable meant smiling like a cretin and making believe like he enjoyed talking with perfect strangers.

"Nice place you've got here, Dimitri," Bill said.

The smile on Dimitri's face dropped ever so slightly.

"It's not his place," Splock said. "He has been exiled from his real place."

"But of course," Bill said to Dimitri, "it's nowhere near as nice as your real place."

Dimitri smiled frigidly. "You know my real place?"

Bill choked back a wise-guy retort and said, "I think I've heard of it."

"That's odd," Dimitri said. "I thought my real place was one of the best-kept secrets in the galaxy."

"Well, you know how word gets around," Bill said. "Anyhow, pleased to meet you."

"We have been hearing so much about you," Dimitri said insincerely. "We have a surprise for you."

"That's nice," said Bill, hoping it would be. Since all the surprises of late had been pretty repulsive ones.

"I won't keep you in suspense any longer," Dimitri said. He clapped his hands together. They gave off a surprisingly loud sound for paws so white and pudgy. Immediately a servant came into the room bearing a red velvet cushion upon which rested an object which Bill did not immediately recognize. Upon receiving a nod from Dimitri, the servant walked over to Bill and bowed, holding out the cushion.

"Pretend you're delighted," Splock hissed. "But don't touch it. Not yet."

"Listen, Splock," Bill said in a low, level voice, "you better stop hissing at me otherwise all hell might just break out here. You catch my meaning?"

Splock glared at him. It wasn't much, but it was better than being hissed at.

Bill turned to his host. He forced a large and rather lopsided grin onto his face. "Messer Dimitri," he said, "how delightful it is that you have shown me this — " He looked at the thing on the red cushion. It had strings, was made of a reddish-brown wood, and had black pegs. Bill thought it something to do with music. But it didn't look like a synthesizer. What could it be?

"Violin," Splock subvocalized, carefully keeping the hiss and wow out of his voice.

" — this really nice-looking fiddle," Bill said. He peered at it but was careful not to touch it. Still, he wanted to say something nice about it.

"It's really a very nice-looking one," Bill said. "Got good color. That says a lot."

The guests tittered in amusement. Dimitri guffawed, and said, "Our guest shows a delightful whimsy in calling this genuine Stradivarius a fiddle. But of course, he has the right. No man in our time has so earned the privilege of slighting his art as Bill Kliptorian, the violin virtuoso who got rave reviews on his recent tour of the south arcade planets. I'm sure Maestro Bill will favor us with a small recital later. A little Mozart, eh, Maestro?"

"You got it," Bill said. Since his skill in violin-playing was in the sub-minimal level, it was as easy for him to agree to play Mozart, whatever that was, as to do a chorus of 'Troopers Trampling, Rockets Roaring'.

"That will be very nice indeed," Dimitri said. "We have made some modest preparations here so that you can repeat for us your triumph on Saginaw IV. If that wouldn't be unduly fatiguing, Maestro?"

"No problem," Bill said recklessly, and saw, too late, Splock's frown and negative nod of his pointy-eared head. "That is, ordinarily it would be no problem, but now — "

"You've already accepted," Dimitri said, laughing in a good-humored way that Bill knew he would find extremely irritating ere long. "It is good of you to bring your great performance to our little backwater. Your manager and I have made the necessary arrangements. I think you will be pleased. It is exactly what your manager said you've always wanted."

"Hey, that's neat," Bill said, giving Splock a what-is-this look, to which Splock responded with a I'll-tell-you-later glance. Which is not easy to do.

"And now for the dessert," Dimitri said. "Your favorite, Maestro. Zabaglione!"

When it came, Bill was a bit disappointed. He had hoped zabaglione might be a fancy word for apple pie, or maybe cherry. Instead it was something foreign. But tasty. As he bent to take his second bite, the woman on his left, the ravenhaired one to whom he had passed the mashed potatoes only minutes earlier, said, in a whisper, "I must see you later. It's urgent."

"Sure, babe," Bill said, ever the gallant. "But tell me this. You're Illyria, aren't you?"

The ravenhaired beauty hesitated. Tears formed in her violet eyes. Her lips, long and red, trembled.

"Not exactly," she intimated. "But I will explain later.

After the zabaglione, liqueurs were served in glass stemware, and coffee was brought in tiny cups of Meissen porcelain. Bill took a couple of drinks, despite Splock's frown; he figured that whatever lay ahead, he was going to need fortification. There were about a dozen people at the table not counting Bill, Splock, or the woman who wasn't exactly Illyria. They were all of human stock, with the possible exception of a small man with blue skin who might have been either alien or trendy. The men were all dressed formally, like their host. Bill had a natural suspicion of people who wore this kind of clothing. But he had to revise his proletarian opinion slightly after looking over this lot. They didn't appear to be effete capitalists or social spongers, the groups most addicted to formal wear. Most of them had sunburnt and wind-hardened faces that argued a life spent in the outdoors killing things. Some of them had the sorts of scars you get from tackling giant carnivores singlehanded in dim forest clearings while on your way to see what lay in your traps. But that was only an impression, of course.

The women were another matter. Slender, fragile, beautiful in that purely decorative way that simple-minded men find appealing, they could have graced any gathering of humans anywhere in the galaxy, or perhaps even beyond it. They were lovely, and by no means the least lovely of them was the woman known as Tesora who had told him earlier that she wasn't exactly Illyria. It was all a bit of a puzzle, as was the matter of how Bill had gotten there and what had gone on before he got there, since it seemed apparent that Splock had been up to something while he, Bill, had been between things. Or however you call it when someone is not present for something that by rights he ought to have been present for.

Splock, meanwhile, was acting affable in a dignified sort of way, even attempting a smile now and then so as not to let down the side. But Bill could tell from the slow twitch of one of Splock's pointed and frontally-pointing ears that all was not to his liking.

After the liqueurs and coffees, and the inevitable cigars, Messer Dimitri rose and held up his arms, commanding silence. His pudgy body, which had lain indolent in the padded chair at the head of the table, now took on the rigor of one not unaccustomed to command.

"Ladies and gentlemen," he said. "Your attention for a moment, please. We have with us tonight no less a personage than Bill Kliptorian, violin virtuoso who has appeared before both headed and headless states. He has agreed, not only to give a concert tonight, but to reproducing the conditions that accompanied his extraordinary triumph on Saginaw IV. But first, a little light piano music by Stumper Rosewoodie, master of the silken strings."

All the guests were escorted into the drawing room that accompanied the lesser library where they had been eating. There, a grand piano dominated the room from a three foot high dais; a man had mounted quickly to it, and, shooting out his cuffs, sat down to the keys.

If Bill hadn't known it was impossible, he could have sworn it was Ham Duo.

"We gotta talk," Splock said, grabbing Bill by the arm and

leading him to a deep bay window that looked out over the lunar landscape that was illuminated by the cold light of still other moons high in the sky.

"You're damn right we gotta talk," Bill said. "Where are we? It looks like Death Valley out there. Why did you tell them I was this fiddle player? How did we get into this? How did it happen that — "

"Please," Splock said, holding up his hand. "There is no time for questions. You are supposed to start performing in about five minutes."

"How? What am I supposed to do?"

"That's the part we're going to figure out right now," Splock said.

"All right," Bill said, and waited.

After a few minutes Bill said. "Have you figured out yet how we get out of this bind?"

"I am thinking!"

"So think faster."

"It doesn't quite work that way. Not that you would know much about thinking. This is a very desperate situation. Not that you were around to help. You were off in your unconsciousness."

"It's not my fault if I fall unconscious during very rapid space flights," Bill pointed out.

"There are no accidents," Splock muttered darkly.

"You want me to figure out what to do next?" Bill asked.

"Yes. I'd like to see some evidence of this creativity I'm always hearing that humans have. Has something to do with a sense of humor, I believe. I don't have one. I don't think any of this is funny."

"I do have a sense of humor," Bill lied. "I don't think any of it is funny either."

"Interesting how we come to the same perception by diametrically opposite routes."

Tesora, the ravenhaired woman who was not exactly Illyria, darted into the bay window, which had the capacity to hold them both, and several others besides. She seized Bill by the sleeve. "I must speak to you alone."

"I was trying to speak to him alone myself," Splock said.

"I realize that. But there's so little time. I have to say to him what I have to say."

"Well, damn it," Splock snapped, irritated and filled with self-pity, "What do you think I'm doing, delivering a singing telegram?"

"If it hadn't been for me," the woman said, "you would never have gotten him out of the Dissembler and into the Reconstitutor."

"What?" Bill blurbled.

"We didn't want to remind you of the experience," Splock said.

"You see, things came adrift when I tried to travel without the Directional Repeater Indicator nulled along the gravity line. Luckily the instantaneous parts recall on the part of our medical robot set you right in no time."

"Except for the one detail," Tesora said. "By the way, Bill, the reason I am not exactly Illyria is that we haven't quite settled on possession of this body. By rights, you see, it doesn't belong to either of us."

"Where did you find it?" Bill asked.

"It was left over at the Saturday night feast of the Thaumaturges."

"Messer is the king of the Thaumaturges," Splock explained. "Only by availing ourselves of the guild rule could we take refuge here."

"What is the guild rule?"

"That only musicians of the foremost class are allowed in."

"How do you tell they're in the foremost class?"

"By their press reviews."

Tesora said, "The fact is, Bill, tonight is full moon and the fight for possession of my body — "

"Kindly stop interrupting with your sluttish ways,"

Splock said grouchily. "Bill, soon the violin will be put into your hands. Do you remember what we told you about violins?"

"Violins," Bill said, his voice a peculiar guttural, the rapid blink rate of his eyes a sure sign that he was either feigning or feeling a state of excitement.

"That's the stuff. But save it for the real thing."

"What's going on?" Bill asked.

"Don't you understand?" Splock said. "It is necessary that you not know in order to fulfill your part properly."

Just then Messer stuck his head in the door. "Showtime," he said. "Here is your violin. The Greels await you."

Splock gave Bill a meaningful look. At least, that was how Bill interpreted it. He didn't know what it meant, of course. That would be asking too much. He took the fiddle and marched to the drawing room.

Fear comes in different sized packages. Fear of embarrassment is not negligible. And that fear was exacerbating Bill's current mood; because he knew, as soon as he strode out under the baby blue spotlight, that he was about to make a fool of himself.

There were extenuating circumstances, of course. The fact that Bill had two right arms, and therefore, logically, two right hands, was a considerable problem in violin playing. In fact, you could go so far as to say that the violin was built specifically for the needs of players with two hands, one right and one left.

Bill, whose real right arm had been crisped some time ago under dolorous circumstances, had had to learn how to cope with life with two right hands. For a while he had had an alligator's foot, too, but that curious appendage had had no influence on the battle of his handedness.

The audience waited, gaping attentively. Messer stood on one side of the room, arms crossed, smiling unpleasantly. Several armed guards lounged in the doorways, automatic weapons cradled in their arms. They looked cruel and uncaring, and capable of anything. How Bill wished he were one of them!

The pianist struck an opening chord. Messer came forward, bowed to the audience, and said, "Ladies and gentlemen, before we begin, I think I had better explain what you are about to see, for your greater delectation. Bill, you see, is capable of playing the sleep song of the Grundge critters, who, as you all know, are reluctant allies of the Chingers. The Grundge are not intelligent, however. For them, biting comes first, thinking a long way afterwards. They can be tamed momentarily, however, by the playing of the sleep song. Usually the female Grundges sing the sleeping song every night. It's the only way they can get the males to bed. Otherwise they spend all night biting trees and each other. Bill has learned this song, the first human in recorded history who has done so. He will now play it to you under the conditions that won him his recent triumph."

Messer stepped back, leaving Bill alone in the middle of the stage. Then the stage collapsed, or rather, was pulled apart under him, and he fell a few feet into a large vat that lay directly under it. The vat was almost ten feet high, with Perspex sides so the audience would miss none of the fun.

Then hatches were raised under the stage and two basket-loads of the two-foot Grundge reptiles were poured into the vat. The Grundges fought and snapped at each other for a while, then began to look for something more interesting to do. They spied Bill. Several of the brighter ones, which wasn't saying very much, gradually came up with the thought that this tall skinny thing with the piece of brown wood in his hand might very well be worth biting.

In a sluggish tide of vein-streaked red and avocado green, the Grundges crept toward Bill, their long jaws, set with backward-pointing needle-sharp teeth, slavering, their nostrils puffing, their eyeballs bulging. A thoroughly unlovely sight, as well as being a lethal one.

Bill took one look and started stomping. His feet beat a mad tattoo of frenzy on the polished Perspex surface of the vat. At the same time, he swept up the fiddle and scraped the bow across the strings in desperation.

It screeched shrilly so he dropped it and grabbed at the Grundges.

There was pandemonium throughout the audience as Bill picked up Grundges in both hands and threw them into the audience. From the viewpoint of the Grundges, it was like being taken for a ride around the park before dinner.

Seeing the ruin on all sides of him, Messer bounded to the stage. He had a laser pistol with a jump-phaser on it. Jump-phasers were illegal in most of the civilized galaxy. Instead of drilling a neat hole through you and cauterizing the edges so that you could be killed and hardly know what hit you, the jump-phaser produced ugly jagged wounds that shocked those who had to look at them almost as badly as those who received them. The jagged beams could lay your flesh open to the bone, like other things could also do, but the jump-phasers did it in ways that really hurt a whole lot. And so Bill was faced, not merely with death, but also disfigurement and mutilation. It is to his credit that he reacted instantaneously to this threat, which, to one with less sand in his craw, might have been paralyzing.

"Aaaah!" Bill screamed. "Take that!" As he had been trained in Unnatural Combat class, he threw his body in a counterclockwise direction, at the same time setting his feet and releasing his breath forcibly. There were a few more movements involved, but if you want a drill manual go out and buy one. Suffice it to say that Bill soared into the air and turned a double somersault, landing in a corner of the room some thirty feet from where he began. Which, as you might imagine, is not easy to do.

By this time Splock had reacted, moving quickly for one so logical, taking forth a beamer which he had kept hidden against the possibility of a possibility like this. Whirling he covered the left flank, while Ham Duo, whom Bill had indeed seen earlier, leaped down from the high balcony with an energy-sword in his hand and a scowl on his unshaven face.

"Guard my back!" he cried to Bill, and advanced on the platoon of soldiers wearing shiny beetle armor that had just arrived.

"Kill them!" Messer cried, throwing himself behind an energyproof balustrade just in time before Duo's sparkling sword scalloped him.

"Kiss my bowb!" Bill shrieked, excusably, perhaps, due to the extreme urgency of the moment.

For, indeed, the outcome of the swiftly-developing battle was uncertain in the extreme. The element of surprise had now been lost, since surprise is only effective while it is still surprising; so the gage was passed to the side with more men, and this round was clearly to be won by Messer, since, here in his sanctuary, protected by corruptible officials who let him operate for a price, he appeared to be preeminent. His beetle-armored soldiers, their denunciators buzzing, necks bleeding from automatic injections of rage-inducing drugs, were in full charge, cutting about them with their squat energy lances, which produced dull, ugly explosions of great damaging capacity. Splock had had the presence of mind to equip himself with a cannister of ULP, the energy-dampening aerosol, and so they came through the first barrage unscathed. But what was to be done after that?

Surprisingly, the answer was to be provided by a single, long-stemmed blue rose.

Chapter 12

But some may consider the case overstated. The blue rose was present during the next decisive moment, and hence can be assigned a kind of guilt by association, but it can in no way be held causal to the events that followed.

The blue rose was on Captain Dirk's coffee table. It plays no part in this story. And yet, ineluctably, it was there.

More to the point, Dirk was there.

Or, to be more precise, he was in his private quarters on the *Gumption* on the morning when the blue rose bloomed and the scattergram was picked up by an alert communications officer whom no one had thought much of before this.

"A scatter message?" Dirk said, when Communications Officer Paul Muni (no relation to the character actor with the same name) came to his quarters bearing a printout.

"Yes, sir," Muni said. He was a tall, good-looking young man with a small mustache. The mustache had been the occasion for laughter when Muni first came aboard, Dirk remembered, because it was silly season on the *Gumption* and men were finding the strangest things funny. Muni hadn't known that, of course. He had thought they were laughing at him.

In a way they were, of course. But not really.

Muni, normally a reckless, outward-turned individual of a happy-go-lucky nature, turned overnight into a misanthrope. He stayed alone in the communications room, which he had hung with black crêpe paper because he claimed the bright lights of the overhead fluorescents hurt his eyes. He had his meals sent to him there, and refused conversation with the crew. Sometimes, when you passed the communications shack, you could hear a curious tapping noise. No one ever found out what that was. It added to the mystery.

Muni's behavior was brought to the attention of Captain Dirk. Dirk was wearing his one-piece blue and brown elasticized jumpsuit that day. He was in an expansive mood.

"Let him stay in the communications room," Dirk said. "Leave him alone; he'll snap out of it."

"But sir, it's unusual behavior."

"And since when do we not tolerate unusual behavior in those we suspect to be deranged?"

"You mean Muni is crazy?"

"Only temporarily, I think. Leave him alone. It'll work out."

Dirk's thought had proven prescient. Alone in the dark, lying in a mess of black crêpe paper, Muni was recovering his nerve and self-confidence.

"Heck," he said to himself. "My mustache probably did look silly. What a fool I was to have let the fellows' chaffing get to me so."

He considered leaving the communications room. He was suddenly in the mood for a rousing game of ping pong. But he knew he had to do something first.

"Something special," he said to himself. Then, glancing at the list of special communication problems, his resolve hardened.

"I'll do it!" he said.

"So you broke the scattergram code," Dirk said. "No one thought it could be done. It has been the most important secret of our enemies, the Murdids of Sting's Planet."

"I have broken it," Muni said. If a hint of pride crept into his voice, Dirk was not the one to blame him. "Read it to me, Mr Muni."

Muni cleared his throat and read, "From Murdid Action Tentacle 2 to Murdid Central High Command in the Hidden Palace on the Forbidden Planet. Hail."

"Very long salutation," Dirk commented.

"Yes, sir," Muni said, and read on. "This Tentacle Arm has discovered that the Earth criminals, Mr Splock and Commander Ham Duo, are presently besieged by the household forces of Messer, owner and proprietor of the sanctuary planetoid in Dentoid 12. Request permission to treacherously break sanctuary, kill all who resist and confine the rest to small cages for their showing in our triumphal march back to Central. Over."

"And the reply?" Dirk said.

"We don't have it, sir. Message ends there."

"Mr Muni," Dirk said, "congratulations on the job well done. But through no fault of your own it is only half done. We need the scattergram that high command of the Murdids will send in response to this one. Go back to your communications shack now, Mr Muni, and keep your ear glued to the earphone or whatever it is you do to gather in scattergrams."

"Actually, we use foreshadowing equipment made especially for us by Portent, Ltd., the secret arms factory on the southern edge of the galaxy. The way it works — "

"Some other time, OK?" Dirk said. "I have to keep my head clear of the little details in order to see the general picture, the big view, and be able to do something about it. Do you understand, Paul?"

"I . . . I think so, sir," Muni said. He was moved by this unexpected insight into the human side of this grim commander of resplendent reputation. "I'll get right to it!" and he exited. Yeoman Muni was no longer worrying about what the men thought of his mustache, Dirk thought to himself, realizing, not for the first time, how much duty aboard the *Gumption* was a testing and a training of the character.

So, Dirk thought, after completing the previous thought, the time of testing is at hand.

"So," he thought, "those who trusted the Murdids were proven wrong, yet again. Yet to move prematurely, before orders are received, would be madness. They would reduce me in rank. No longer would they use me for action." If he were to strike at the Murdids now, and it turned out that they had not violated the sanctuary of the infamous Messer, then the Galactic Council of Placation would repudiate his move; he would be declared outlaw. There would be other unpleasantries.

It was funny how, at a time like this, Dirk's eyes, tracking idly around the room, came to rest on the single long-stemmed blue rose in its tall stemware.

Sometimes a little thing can fix the attention. There is no record of Captain Dirk's associations to the blue rose. Not even the thought-sensitive walls of the *Gumption* picked it up, since they were going through a normal dewaxing operation at the time of this incident. It was Dirk and Dirk only, in a silence deeper than the grave and far more symbolic, looking at the blue rose which said to him, by some unimaginable channel, an unbelievable message.

"Yes," Dirk said, though he later had no memory of it, "I'll do it though hell should bar the way!"

He raised his eyes to the remote control board. Photon interceptors interpreted the direction of his gaze and turned the computer on to passive remote.

"Your orders, sir?" Might there not have been a break in the smoothly synthesized voice of the computer?

"The fastest course possible for Sanctuary!"

The crew of the *Gumption*, sitting around the ward room listlessly shooting craps and reading out-of-date magazines, heard these words and looked up, galvanized, then broke into a run as they went to their battle stations.

"Rig for full scale battle!" Dirk shouted. God, how he wished Splock were here! He looked around. "Doctor Marlowe!"

A bearded man in a charcoal gray one-piece elasticized jumpsuit looked up alertly. "Sir!"

"Are you conversant with the principles of shield reduplication effect?"

"I think so, sir," the bearded, gray-eyed man said quietly. "Mr Splock was showing it to me just before he — left."

"See if you can duplicate his efforts, Dr Marlowe," Dirk said. "I think we're going to need all the shielding we can get."

The ship executed an impossibly tight turn onto the new course. The piled-up grav units were backfed into the ship's supercharger — another of Splock's innovations. The gigantic spaceship took off like a scalded positron.

This particular Murdid fleet which was even then closing on Sanctuary was not the same fleet that had sacked Carcasal the previous year. That fleet, made up of suicide flyers interfaced with flying bomb ships, had proven irresistible to the forces of civilization. The battle fleets of Elkin and Van Lund had been forced back clear across the Carpathian Gulf, and might have been destroyed utterly had not a vast gale blown up from space and dispersed the attackers before they could drive home their final charge. The Murdid empire was slowly recovering from that débâcle. The present fleet was barely half as large, but far more maneuverable. The Murdids had given up suicide tactics, and had managed to purchase WiseGuy Software from Hidden Tactics Technologies, main suppliers of inimical software to criminals and other enemies of civilization as we know it. Their motto: "Let it Come Down."

This new attack software, with its emphasis on exotic maneuvers at high speeds, was baffling to the forces of Earth, which were still confined to logic-based decision modifiers. Even with basic codes broken so as to make possible a mapping and definition of Murdidean tactics, the outcome was for a long time in doubt, since the human operators, doubting their senses, lost valuable time asking each other, "Did you see that?" and other non-productive questions of that nature.

At this time, when the starship *Gumption* was boring through hyper-space at a respectable multiple of the speed of light, and its paradox bafflers were working overtime to prevent temporal implosions due to irreducible dilemmas, Bill was scrambling up a winding iron staircase in the upper tower of Messer's sanctuary, hoping to find a power relay point he could take out, or, failing that, something to drink.

He bounded up the narrow stairs, taking them several at a time. Below him, he knew, Splock and Duo were battling increasing hordes of beetle-armored warriors, the wall of crisped corpses moving nearer and nearer to them as more berserk warriors threw themselves across the bodies of those who had gone before. A door stood in front of him. It was made of steel, and had hinges which were massy and bright. It would not yield before Bill's pounding. He took out a laser pistol, set it to a high setting, and cut through the metal of the door like a red-hot knife going through a wall of cheese, only with less smell. The door burst open. Bill ran into the room, stopped in his tracks, took in what lay before him, and his lips puckered in a wry but unspoken comment.

Finally he did say, "Well, this changes things a little."

CIA did have a habit of popping up at odd moments. It was something that had always struck Bill as faintly ominous about the undercover intelligence agent. It was difficult to tell where CIA was at. Or what he was up to. It was also difficult to know if CIA knew that there was something a little weird about him. Perhaps all military undercover agents were like that; it was a pretty loathsome profession.

Whatever the reason, there was CIA, in the power point relay station, busily splicing cables together as Bill entered.

"Bill! I'm so glad I got here in time!"

"How *did* you get here?" Bill asked. Everything CIA did made him suspicious.

"No time to explain now," CIA said. "But you can thank that girlfriend of yours for a lot of it."

"Illyria? I met a lady named Tesora who said she wasn't exactly Illyria."

"And do you know why not? Because of you, Bill! I hope you're planning on doing the right thing by that little lady. That's love if I'm any judge."

"What are you doing?"

"Resetting the mine field pattern."

Bill stared at him as comprehension dawned in his head. It was a brilliant move, he was sure of it, though he couldn't say just at the moment who it was going to help.

"Help me, Bill," CIA said. "We have to help Ham and Splock."

Bill saw that CIA was making new connections at random, scrambling the mine field so that no safe route could be found through it. He sat down on the floor and helped CIA tie off the last connections. The din from downstairs, which had grown fainter for a while, now redoubled in volume. There were loud explosions of the sort made by recoilless cannons, the high pitched scream of needle jets, the low warbling of temporal disruptors. Splock and Duo were fighting hard for their lives, using all of the weapons that the far-thinking Splock had brought along in case of just such an emergency.

Bill and CIA finished their work and hurried back down the stairs. The sight that greeted their eyes had already gone beyond the shambles stage and now was taking on some aspects of order again. The beetle-armored soldiery were advancing on Duo and Splock, who had been forced back to the foot of the stairs, from behind hastily constructed barricades made of energy-resistant cellulose. They pushed the light barriers ahead of them, and they were armed now with blow guns whose darts were tipped with skin-curling poison, another outlawed weapon that the Murdids used with impunity and unction.

Bill tapped his friends on their shoulders. "Come on. We gotta get out of here."

"And about goddamn time," Ham Duo grimaced. "Have

you any idea what I had to do to sneak into this place to help you out? First I had to buy a flamenco dancer's outfit — "

"Tell me later," Bill said. "Right now I think we better get moving."

Glancing toward the enemy, Duo perceived what Bill had just noticed. The Murdids had finally gotten one of their heavy weapons into place. It was technically a UKD-12d, a harmless-sounding sound for a glowing blob of energy that gobbled up whatever lay in its path and converted its victims into sludge by ways science did not yet fully understand.

"I guess it's time, all right," Duo said. "All right, now what?"

Bill turned to CIA. "Now what, CIA?"

CIA raised his hand to his head. A pathetic expression crossed his face. He said, "Ugh, urggh . . . "

"CIA," Bill said sternly. "Now is not the time for you to do a number."

"Glarp," said CIA, his eyes rolling in his head.

"Hell," Bill said, simply, but with feeling.

Just at that time the starship *Gumption*, its battle-plates glowing from its passage through sub-space with its stripped-down nuclei, burst onto the scene. It popped out into normal space in proximity to the little world of Sanctuary, evading CIA's randomized mine field by appearing in the middle of it, all guns blazing. It was the work of a second, no more, for a series of commands to be passed at radionic speeds training the ship's heavy artillery on the sanctuary. Then it took only a microsecond, no more, to retrain the guns on the Murdid fleet, which even then, pursuant to orders which were obvious to so well-trained a combat commander as Dirk, was boring in on Sanctuary.

Splock, hearing the characteristic thud-giggle-thud of the *Gumption*'s heavy ordinance, took in the situation in a moment. "To the balcony!" he cried.

Bill picked up CIA, who was still making odd noises due to

something that had come over him in the last moment or two, but whose elucidation would have to await a calmer moment. With Duo cutting the way with sword-gun and explosive bludgeon, they burst through the serried waves of beetle-armored soldiery and ran up the narrow stone steps leading to the balcony.

The balcony door was locked. But Splock had taken into consideration this eventuality. A flicker of his eyelids showed Bill what he had to do. Turning over CIA into the strong but surprisingly gentle arms of Ham Duo, Bill attacked the door, using the portal-bursting techniques he had been taught in Breaking & Entering training. No static object is a sufficient barrier for a warrior charging in full door-bursting mode. The door went down and the little group came out onto the high balcony. Bill rubbing his bruised shoulder and muttering complaints, which extended into the upper atmosphere.

As they did this, the Murdid fleet came sailing into combat. They moved with confidence, because their spies had previously learned the layout of the mine field that protected the satellite against those who thought the sanctuary concept was passé. Ship after ship blew up, emitting loud clouds of many-colored smoke into the uncaring vacuum of the upper atmosphere. But others took their place, and there were still others behind them. The Murdids, somehow, sensing a trap, had sent in their noncombat vessels first to clear the way. It was a peculiarity of Murdid tactics, and this time it paid off. Ship after ship burst into fire and smoke and sparklers, but the main ships of the enemy fleet, the huge, heavily armored dreadnoughts, proceeded unscathed.

Standing on the balcony, passing among them the single oxygen mask which Ham Duo always carried in a little pouch on his belt, along with condoms he had never used, Splock set off the emergency flares. They arched upward, bursting in bright blue coruscations of light. It would have been a pretty sight if the moment had not been so desperate.

The Murdid fleet, finding the starship *Gumption* in their

midst, turned their attention from the satellite to the big ship. Cursing gun captains applied the lash lavishly as the gun crews sweated with hyperspike and mass driver to swing the guns into line — for the guns of the Murdid fleet, due to a trifling miscalculation in the blueprints, had to be trained by hand. One by one the big guns came to bear, and red-tipped explosive charges, driven by massive presser beams, arced toward the *Gumption* in implacable flat trajectories.

"Shield redoubling effect!" Dirk ordered, hoping that young Muni had managed to get the field working. The first shell arched in, rotating slowly. The *Gumption*'s shield field seized it. Tiny sensors guided it into a boomerang orbit. Before the Murdids knew what was going on, their own energy shells were being thrown back at them.

"Steady now," Splock said. "Here comes the rescue launch."

He could see it coming straight toward them, dodging static explosive fields, its little red and green bow lights winking steadfastly.

Bill picked CIA up under one arm as the *Gumption*'s launch touched lightly against the side of the balcony. They scrambled aboard, all of them, and heard the satisfying sound of the double hatch clanging shut behind them. Aboard the tiny ship CIA was trying to tell Bill something, but his words were lost in the staccato blast of energy weapons.

And then Dirk was at their side, his eyes still blazing with battle fury.

"About time you got here," Dirk said to Splock, in the insulting voice he used to show affection. "You better get to the engine room. We got problems."

Then he spotted Bill. No expression whatsoever crossed his features as he said, "Hello, Bill. There's a phone call for you. You can take it in my office."

While Dirk and Splock were at the controls trying to extricate the *Gumption* from the fire fight that had boiled up within the randomized mine field, Bill went off to find Dirk's cabin. Directions on the *Gumption* were indicated by colored lines, so that, by merely depressing your gaze, you could find your way to the various important parts of the ship. But Dirk had forgotten to tell Bill that normal combat procedure was to change the line coloring when the ship was in combat, in order to foil the anticipated attempts of a spy who might be expected to choose an emergency time as the moment to perform sabotage and its modifiers. He went through the crew mess hall, deserted now except for one plump petty officer who was hastily finishing his bowl of tapioca pudding with plum duff on the side. Then Bill was racing down a long, curving corridor, following the line marked for the Captain's quarters, which, due to the combat scrambling, brought him to the *Gumption*'s shopping mall. He raced through it, ignoring the importunities of noncombatant clerks, who wanted to wish him a nice day and point out the weekly specials. Normally a good shopper, Bill had no time now for such matters. He continued to follow the twisty lines that were supposed to lead to the captain's cabin, only now he was getting the suspicion of doubt that these were doing him any good at all. He stopped at a stationer's and picked up a ship's guide to locations during emergency operation. With the help of this he was able to find Dirk's cabin.

Dirk's cabin had the usual wall-to-wall carpeting with deep pile reserved for senior-class officers. Bill noticed that a dinner had been laid out for one, giving him some penetrating insight into Dirk's social life. And, ahead of him, on a little lucite stand of its own, was the telephone. Its little call-ready light was blinking steadily.

Bill lunged for it, smashing several crystal figurines in his haste. "Hello!" he barked.

A feminine voice on the other end of the line said, "Two whom did you wish to speak?"

"Someone was calling," Bill said. "They told me to pick up the call here."

"And who are you, sir?"

"Bill! I'm Bill!"

"I'm Rosy, the phone operator at Fleet Central Communications. I think we met once at the reception given by the Drdniganian Embassy. That was on Capella last year."

"I was nowhere near the place," Bill said. "Now will you get me my bowbing call."

"It must have been some other Bill. Did you say something about a phone call?"

"Yes!"

"Just a minute, I'll try to trace that for you."

Bill waited. Behind him the door dilated. CIA came in, his face a study in perplexity.

"Bill?" he said. "Are you all right?"

"Yes, of course I'm all right," Bill said. "I'm just waiting for this phone call. What happened to you back there?"

"It's a little difficult to explain," CIA said. "But what I was trying to explain to you was, whatever you do, don't go aboard the *Gumption*."

"Now's a hell of a time to be telling me that," Bill said. "What's the matter with the *Gumption*?"

Just then the operator came back on the line. "I have your party, Bill."

A shrill feminine voice came onto the line after that, saying, "Bill, darling, is it really you?"

Although Illyria's voice changed every time she changed bodies, which was more frequently than Bill liked, nevertheless, a characteristic timbre remained. And besides, what other feminine voice did he know these days.

"Illyria! Where are you?"

"Never mind about that. Tell me, Bill, is CIA there with you?"

Bill glanced around to doublecheck. "Yes, he's here."

"Good. There's something you must know about that so-called military intelligence officer. Thank God I've reached you in time."

"Yes, what is it?" Bill asked.

"Bill," CIA said, "we really need to talk." He sat down on the desk beside Bill. The long flap of his army greatcoat swept across the telephone receiver, seemingly by accident. There was a click, a small sound but ominous in the context.

"Illyria! Are you there?"

The operator said, "I'm sorry, sir, you have been cut off."

It was at that moment that Dirk and Splock came into the room, followed by Duo.

Dirk was really an extraordinarily good pilot, and with Splock backing him up on the action-synthesizer, there was no better team in the galaxy. This thought had not been lost on Dirk as he had performed the Marienbad maneuver, a movement of considerable risk to the perpetrator, and calling for nerves of steel as the ship was retrogressed back along its previous course. It was a bumpy passage, since the retrogressed course was alive with vast electrical potentials, some of them left by the ship's previous passage, others formed up spontaneously, and all of them colored electric blue.

The Murdid ships tried to follow, but the lead ship had forgotten, during the heat of battle, to take in the bow spoilers. The churning of sub-space modalities rendered it impossible for them to follow the dazzling passage of the *Gumption*. And so they contented themselves with blasting hell out of Sanctuary while their intelligence officers prepared a cover story blaming the loss of the neutral satellite on climatic conditions.

Safe for the moment, Dirk brought the ship back to an even course. The cooks down in the vast kitchens of the starship breathed a sigh of relief and returned to ladling out bowls of potato onion soup for the crew, who had worked up a healthy appetite during the brief but strenuous combat. Saltines were served with the soup on Dirk's orders. He knew the crew needed something special after what they had gone through.

Then Dirk, accompanied by the saturnine and pointy-eared Splock and the swaggering, flat-eared Duo, went to the captain's cabin to see how Bill was getting along. As they went there was a suspicion of something amiss, something not right, an unclear matter about which hung an unhealthy miasma of sorrow and regret. They were not aware of it, however, not even the normally thoughtful Splock, who was to remember only later the potential for prescience that this moment possessed.

They reached the cabin, entered. Bill was standing by the telephone with an annoyed looked on his military features. CIA, looking like something out of the garbage dump in his long overcoat and fingerless gloves, was standing nearby. It did not escape Splock's notice that one of the pockets of CIA's greatcoat bulged with something that could have been a seven-inch Chinger lizard. Characteristically, he said nothing except to remark to himself, "Let it come down!" And there was also this in the room, a sense of visual analog to Illyria's voice which had been speaking to Bill only instants ago, before CIA's movement with his greatcoat — whether advertent or inadvertent was still moot at that point — had cut the connection and left unresolved, perhaps for a very long time, the mystery of Illyria's continual appearances and disappearances.

"Bill," Dirk said. "I think we all owe you a round of applause. I don't know how you accomplished it, but you managed to concentrate the Murdid fleet here and hold them in place long enough for me to get the *Gumption* here and to hold them still longer until the main fleet of the military could arrive. Among those who took part in the battle, I am pleased to see, was your very own unit, the Fighting 69th Deep Space Screaming Killers."

"You mean they're here?" Bill cried. "My friends are here? Bullface Donaldson? Ace of Hearts Johnny Dooley? And Klopstein, the man with the stainless steel nose; is he here too?"

"They're all here, Bill," Dirk said. "Not quite as we would want them, perhaps, but indubitably here."

"What do you mean, not as you'd want them?"

"Well, they're, you know how it is, sorta dead. I wanted to break it to you gently. I wanted to tell you they had had an accident but were in hospital and coming along nicely. And then, later, I would have told you they had had a setback, not really a setback, just something like a setback, but that you shouldn't worry, they were coming along almost as nicely as expected, not quite but almost. And then later I'd tell you they'd died and it would have been a lot easier for you to take. We discussed this approach at considerable length on our way here, and it was Duo's contention that short and sweet, *corto y derecho* as he expressed it, was best by far. I only hope we did the right thing. How do you feel, Bill?"

"Thirsty," Bill said.

"Thirsty? At a time like this?"

"I have to drink to absent friends, don't I?" Bill said. "It's what they would have done."

"Yes," Dirk said, "let's by all means have a drink. It will help prepare you for the next bit of news."

Bill found the liquor all by himself, and threw back a triple shot of Old Hamstringer. He blew his nose on an olive-drab handkerchief which had unaccountably been in his pocket all this time. He said, "OK, I'm ready. Who else died?"

"Oh, nothing as bad as that," Dirk said, laughing.

"No," Duo said, grinning, "it's not a life and death matter at all."

"It's nothing to be upset about," Splock said. "But have another drink anyway."

"Your outfit has demanded that you be returned to them immediately. They got quite excited when they learned you were here. They seemed to have been under the impression that you deserted."

"How could those bastards think that?"

"Maybe it's because you've been gone for a few months without reporting in," Duo hazarded.

"I was a prisoner on an alien planet. They had me locked up inside a giant computer. What did they think — I had PX and telephone privileges?"

"I think we set them straight," Dirk said. "In fact, we recommended you for a medal. They didn't like the idea. But do you know whose word finally swayed them?"

"How in hell should I know?" Bill said, literal as ever.

"It was Hannibal," Splock said. "He no longer views you as his enemy. He said that talking with the Alien Historian had changed his view of historical necessity."

"That's great," Bill said, whether plain or with irony was hard to tell. "When is all this supposed to take place?" Dirk and Splock exchanged looks. Dirk's chin gave the barest suggestion of a nod. Splock's lips took on the subtly strained appearance of one who is about to say something.

"You may come in," Splock said.

The door opened. In walked two men in the chromium helmet-liners and white arm bands of the MPs. They looked like NBA centers. In fact, they had both been NBA centers before their exhibition game on Mars was broken up by the cutting-out party of Captain Nemour DeVilliers. But that is another story.

"Soldier!" said the MP with the small mustache. "You are under arrest. Hold out your hands."

What was there to say? Bill held out his arms. The MP without the mustache slipped the handcuffs on them. They led him away.

At the door, Bill paused and turned. "See you guys around," he said. And then the MPs took him away.

There was silence in the cabin for a moment. Then CIA yelled, "Hey, Bill, wait for me!" and hurried after him.

Another silence. Finally Duo broke it.

"Poor devil," Duo said. "He didn't even get a decent curtain line."

*

Events passed for Bill in a blur of unbearable clarity as the MPs marched him to the special dispatch ship. Once aboard, they took off Bill's cuffs and offered him a strong drink. They figured Bill was guilty of really despicable crimes and they thought all the more of him for it. Their usual prisoners were guys who just went AWOL, or got drunk, that kind of thing. But now they had a real live one. They wanted to hear stories of Illyria, and what it had really been like on Royo, and what it was like being inside a giant computer. The ship sped along, and even though he was a prisoner, Bill was fairly happy to be aboard.

The point is, you see, he was glad to be back, but it was a paradoxical gladness because he was returning as a prisoner, and that meant unpleasantness ahead. On the other hand, what could they do to him? Kill him probably. The penalty for all military crimes was execution. While this might appear to be severe it sure made sentencing easy for the low-IQ officers who sat on the courts martial. Thus it had always been. So, while Bill didn't like it at least he was used to it. The military was out to get him — he never forgot that.

All too soon they landed at the spaceport of Camp Despair, named so not because it was an unhappy and desperate place, though it was, but in honor of its first commander, Martin Harry Despair, hero of Big Little Greenhoof and Skirmisher's Nook, two great battles with more than usual losses so of course he got promoted.

Camp Despair was on the planet Inquest X, a small world with an atmosphere that smelled of rotten eggs. The camp itself was on a tropical island which was separated from an inhospitable and savage coast by a channel of foaming water with many whirlpools in it. It was the old Devil's Island model, and palm trees had been imported to give it a proper look.

Bill was put into the maximum security prison, a place so secure that even food had difficulty getting in. So it was a gaunt and red-eyed Bill who was awakened early one morning not long after his arrival and told to wash his gob and brush his fangs; he was going to appear before a board of officers who would judge his case but could not be expected to tolerate his bad breath whether he was guilty or not.

The court Bill was brought to was in the middle of an amphitheater which seated about ten thousand; because the spectacle of unfairness in action was fascinating to so many people, a larger capacity court was being planned. Meanwhile, this one would have to do. As usual it was full, since watching military court martials was one of the specialties offered by many tour agencies.

There was a jury, too, but it was not made up of humans. A recent change in military law called for trial by jury in all cases on a trial basis. This was a crude attempt by the military to disguise the basic injustice of the system. The juries invariably voted as the presiding judges indicated they should since they would be shot if they didn't. This had proven to be expensive so now, to save money, a jury of twelve robots had been permanently impaneled. The jury was made up of robots who had been brought back from various battles and were awaiting repair. Aside from a few lacking limbs, they were fit enough. It was disconcerting to see that some of them had no heads, but they assured the court that their brains were in their thoraxes, and so they were allowed to sit. All of them had been programmed to bring in guilty verdicts no matter what evidence was presented.

"All rise!" cried the bailiff. The spectators in the courtroom got to their feet and applauded the presiding judge, Colonel Genc Bailey; he was a popular judge on the military circuit. His real name was Lewis, but he was called Genc for his favorite sentence, which he served upon all malefactors whatever the accusations against them was — "Guilty, electrocution, next case." That was his favorite sentence, and the spectators, with their predictable detestation for malefactors, were always pleased. Some had been known to say that even Bailey was easier on the guilty than he should be and those found guilty should be shot on the spot. But it was well-known that liberalism had crept into the military justice system.

The attorney for the military was Captain Jeb Stuart. All the spectators were rooting for him, because Stuart hadn't lost a case in five years. He just needed one more year's successes to qualify him for the Triple Crown of Jurisprudence.

"Need I go into it all?" Jeb Stuart declaimed, addressing the court in a rich and sonorous voice. "This trooper Bil, a subversive even in his name since he spells it with two 'l's, and that spelling is only for officers, is guilty of breaking sections 23, 45, 76, 76a and 110b sub-part c of the Uniform Military Code of Justice. If you will all look at the crib sheets which have been passed among you, you will see that these are all crimes of a gross nature. Bil, have you anything to say for yourself?"

"Sir, all I did was follow orders," Bill said.

Stuart smiled with gross subtlety. "And since when has that been a legitimate excuse in the eyes of military law?"

"But what was I supposed to do?" Bill asked.

"You were supposed to do everything right," Stuart snarled. "We find that you were AWOL on an alien planet during a time of considerable civil upset, and that furthermore you did knowingly consort with an alien female of the Tsurian race, our enemies, and that you furthermore took up residence within an alien computer for reasons best left unsaid, and that you also conspired with an alien general from another time period, one Hannibal, who was unable to be here for this trial due to pressing engagements with the Roman General Scipio Africanus. But we do have Hannibal's deposition. Since it is written in Carthaginian, we have had a little difficulty deciphering it. But we think it says, 'This trooper is guilty as hell of everything he's accused of and he ought to fry painfully in the worst you can give him.'"

"Hannibal is my friend," Bill said. "He wouldn't have said anything like that. You must have gotten it wrong."

"See for yourself," Stuart said. He gave a meaningful nod and one of his clerks hurried forward carrying a large baked clay tablet with cuneiform characters inscribed upon it.

"I can't read this," Bill said.

"Of course not," Stuart agreed. "It would have been strange, not to say treasonous, if you had been able to. Since that is the case, how can you deny our interpretation of the message?"

"My guess about what it means is as good as anyone else's," Bill said.

"Oh, is it now?" Stuart said. "We thought you might take that line of defense, and so we have brought to this court an expert on interpretations of unknown scripts. Will Professor Stone please take the stand?"

Professor Rosetta Stone was a tall and skinny spinster with a cold and imperious manner. She looked contemptuously around her and sniffed, "An expert at languages such as myself can always be expected to make a more reasonable, not to say pertinent, guess as to the meaning of a dubious text than can a lay person such as the barely literate trooper here."

And so it went. Various witnesses were brought in to testify. Bill had never seen them before. He later discovered that they were professional witnesses, who appeared in cases in which the prosecutor knew that the plaintiff was guilty as hell but lacked supporting evidence.

Bill thought it unfair when one of the witnesses, a clergyman of the Albigensian sect, swore under oath that Bill was responsible for the sacking of Rome in 422 AD. Bill vehemently denied this. Since there were sufficient other charges against him to warrant whatever sentence the judge pleased, that particular one was dropped.

When it was his turn to speak, Bill asked for time to prepare his case. The judge smiled. "That is the sort of thing the guilty always say. Listen, trooper, this case is a foregone conclusion. If you want to waive your right to speak, it will be held in your favor that you saved the court valuable time."

"And if I don't?" Bill asked.

"Then we won't let you prepare your case and your asking will be held against you."

Bill's shoulders slumped shrugged. He had been here before. "You've got it all set up against me. What can I say?"

"As little as possible," the judge said. "You have no idea how tiring it is for me, sitting here and hearing criminal after criminal perjure himself in the name of a law which he took all too lightly when he perpetrated his various and heinous offenses. Any final remarks? No? You're learning. Now let's get on with the important part, the punishment."

"You forgot to ask the jury how they vote," Bill said.

"A mere formality," the judge said. "I think we can forget all about that little bit of nonsense."

"No!" Bill cried. "I want to hear what the jury says!"

The judge looked disgusted. He had a busy day ahead of him. Three rounds of golf were scheduled that afternoon with important personages who would not take it kindly if the judge's game were not up to its usual high standard. They hadn't traveled all this distance to this remote post to have a crappy golf game. It passed through the judge's mind that this trooper was being very difficult. No one else had ever insisted that the jury be heard. It just showed the disadvantage of filling the military personnel with new-fangled ideas. He toyed with the idea of pulling out his laser pistol, which he always carried in a cutaway holster under his judge's gown, and saving everyone a lot of time, expense and trouble by blasting this goniff straight to the hell he so richly deserved for even having taken on enough of the shading of guilt to be brought in front of the court. But then he calmed himself. He already had several demerits for shooting prisoners out of hand. The lily-livered bastards back at Military Command liked to do it all by the book. Until he could prove that they were engaged in a conspiracy to undermine the entire justice system, he would have to accede to their wishes.

The judge turned to the jury. Nine robot heads and three thoraxes swiveled to look back at him. Their blank eyes and shiny metal skins reminded the judge of juries he had served with in other cases, some human, some robotic, some Simian.

"Robots of the jury," the judge said, "have you listened with care to all the evidence?"

"Indeed, your honor, we have," simpered the foreman, a deviate robot with a shiny purple face and granny glasses.

"And have you had time to weigh the evidence and come to a verdict?"

"Oh, indeed we have, your honor."

"Then how say ye?"

"We find the defendant not guilty in any degree whatsoever and deserving of a medal, maybe two."

The judge gave them a look in which consternation mingled with rage to terrifying effect. "Did I hear right?"

"It depends on what you heard," the foreman giggled.

"Did you find this trooper not guilty?"

"Yes," said the foreman, "that's how it looked to us. Don't forget the medals, either."

There was pandemonium in the courtroom. Mothers wept and clutched their children close to them. Strong men lit cigarettes. Robots of various kinds and descriptions who had been in the audience as spectators gave cheers of applause, as well as the high-pitched yelps that robots emit when in a state of elation, for reasons that are still under investigation. The judge swelled up like a chicken under pressure. Several bailiffs fainted and had to be revived with strong drink. Reporters for the military newspapers rushed out to telephone the scoop. Bill rushed down from the stand and embraced his friend CIA, who had been in the crowd rooting for his friend.

"Bill, it's wonderful!" he cried.

"But why?" Bill asked. "I never heard of robots not voting the way they were supposed to."

"Everybody! Stop! This court is not dismissed!" So shouted the judge. In response to a wave of his hand the doors were barred. But just before they were barred, a messenger in motorcycle leathers, his goggles still in place over his eyes, gouts of sweat bursting from his forehead, rushed in and approached the bench. He handed the judge a slip of paper, then collapsed on the floor and had to be revived with powerful drugs.

There was silence in the courtroom as the judge read the slip of paper.

The judge pursed his lips. He cleared his throat. He stood up, glaring at Bill.

"It seems we have some extenuating circumstances," he said. The courtroom waited.

"Report to your base commander," he said to Bill. "This is a circumstance I had no knowledge of. The jury, however, seems to have figured it out beforehand."

His expression said that he did not like this, and would probably do something drastic about it.

"Case dismissed!" he cried. And the MPs gathered around Bill to take him back to base.

Chapter 13

The military base looked the same as Bill remembered it. A group of one- and two-story buildings in the middle of a swamp. The MPs brought Bill directly to Headquarters Building. Here they removed his handcuffs, wished him luck, and departed.

Bill sat on a bench in the waiting room of General Vossbarger, recently appointed supreme commander of Sector South. It didn't take long before the clerk at the reception desk signaled Bill and told him he could go in.

The General had a nicely appointed office. Wall-to-wall carpeting, Danish furniture, bad paintings on flocked purple cloth, a whiskey decanter, the usual stuff. He was a big man who seemed larger because of the rolls of fat around his neck and nose. What hair he had left was blond, thus lending credence to the rumors of the Blond Beast that had preceded his posting.

"Take a seat, Bill," Vossbarger said. "Cigar? Care for a drink?"

Bill considered turning them down; after all, they might be poisoned. On the other hand, it might be a military offense to turn down cigars and drinks when offered by a General. He was in a perplexity which was resolved when Vossbarger poured him a drink and put a cigar beside it.

"Go ahead, trooper, drink up. Take a puff. There's good leaf in that cigar, unlike the junk you enlisted men get in your PX or canteen or whatever the hell you call it. So you're Bill.

Well, now, I've heard a lot about you. I'm mighty pleased that trial turned out in your favor. In fact, it's a very good bit of luck for us. We couldn't use you if you were dead, could we?"

Bill realized that was what lay behind the robot jury's unexpected acquittal. There was a reason, of course. In the military there's always, no matter how cynical, twisted or warped, a reason.

"I'm very pleased, sir," he said cautiously, wondering what was coming next.

"Now, Bill, about the Disruptor you were ordered to bring back — "

"I'm sorry about that, sir," Bill cringed. "I practically had it, but then a lot of stuff came up — "

"Never mind that. We think we know where we can get one."

"That's good news, sir!" Bill said.

"Yes, isn't it. And the cost won't be too high, either."

"Better and better!" Bill said thickly as his suspicions began to grow.

"Unfortunately, there's one hitch."

Bill nodded. Somehow he wasn't surprised that there was a hitch. What interested him was how the hitch involved him.

"The Tsurisians," Vossbarger said, "have indicated their willingness to provide us with what we need. But there is one stipulation."

Bill groaned. Not only was there a hitch, there was also a stipulation. This was getting worse and worse. He puffed the cigar furiously and drained his glass as he waited for the news none of which would be good. Vossbarger nodded understandingly and refilled Bill's glass.

"Well, Bill, they want us to send an emissary there to be trained in the use of the Disruptor. As you can understand, an advanced tool like that requires careful study."

"Yeah, sure," Bill said.

"You'd have to volunteer for this mission, of course," Vossbarger said.

"Now wait, no, impossible!" Bill cried aloud. "I'm all finished with all that volunteering bowb."

"Too bad," Vossbarger said. "There was some talk of reinstituting the charges against you. This time you wouldn't be up against anything as easy as a robot jury. One jury would decide the entire issue. Me."

"Ah," said Bill.

"However, that will not be necessary. There is no time to waste on that kind of rigmarole. I am ordering you to volunteer." He took a large gun from the desk drawer and pointed it between Bill's eyes. "Are you disobeying my order?"

"Excuse me, sir. You wouldn't like to tell me about this mission I'm volunteering for?"

"That's what I like to hear," Vossbarger said, smiling like a vulture over an elephant's corpse. The gun vanished. "Go ahead. You have fifty-five seconds to ask all the questions you like."

"Why me?"

"Good question. Well, there's the fact that you've already had some experience on the planet Tsuris. That weighed in our consideration."

"Yes, sir."

"But most important is the fact that the Quintiform computer, which, as you know, governs Tsuris, specifically asked for you."

"It did?"

"Yes, it did. It was really quite insistent about it. Said something about unfinished business between you two. Since we want that Disruptor, we saw no reason to turn the computer down. Especially since the woman added her demands as well."

"Woman? What woman?"

"I believe she said her name is Illyria. She's become the new president of Tsuris."

"How did she manage that?" Bill asked.

"We don't have all the details yet. Something to do with her new body."

"She's always getting new bodies," Bill sighed, feeling the trap jaws closing. "You wouldn't happen to know what does this one look like?"

"I haven't seen her myself," Vossbarger said. "But she requests that you be informed that her new body will be quite a surprise for you."

"I've had enough surprises."

"And she also informs us that she has your old body ready for you to occupy."

"But I've got a body!" Bill cried.

"It will have to be returned to the computer," Vossbarger said. "It was only a loaner."

"But what sort of body has Illyria taken now?"

"She did say that it's quite small. So as to fit inside the computer."

"I don't want to live inside the computer!" Bill moaned.

"Try it, you'll like it. Otherwise . . . " the gun quickly appeared again.

"Aye aye, sir," Bill sobbed.

He thought about it later, drinking in the enlisted men's canteen. No sooner had he gotten back to the dear old military than he was being shipped out again. Back to Illyria and the Quintiform computer. After a few drinks, it all started to feel better. The Quintiform computer wasn't a bad sort of machine. And as for Illyria . . .

Yes, on second thought, Quintiform was decent enough he conned himself into thinking. He'd like to see his friend inside the computer again. And as for Illyria, it would be nice to see her again, too. When you're in the military, you take what comes up. And he could take it!

Then why were tears running down his nose and dripping into his drink?

When Bill reached the planet Tsuris, the preliminaries were few and far between. There was the usual array of Tsurisians present, in their familiar three-sphere form. The doctors who had treated him during his earlier stay on the planet were all there. They waved pleasantly as Bill's little space launch landed. He was led inside with shouting and cheers, and taken to the special chamber beneath Tsuris castle where the computer had set up headquarters.

"Hello, Bill," the Quintiform computer said. "Good to see you again."

"Hi," Bill said suspiciously. "You don't sound sore at me."

"Of course not, Bill. You and I have always gotten along well."

"Why did you send for me?"

"Well, that's a story in itself," the Quintiform computer said.

"Tell me it; I got time," Bill said.

"In fact, it was the request of my wife. She desired that you be returned to Tsuris for her wedding present."

"Your wife? Since when do computers have wives?"

"It is unusual," the Quintiform computer mused. "But you don't know my wife. She is a determined woman."

"Is it any machine I may have met?"

"It's not a machine at all. It's Illyria."

"Illyria?" gurgled Bill.

"Did somebody call me?" a feminine voice asked. Although Bill had never heard it before, he knew at once it was Illyria. You just can't be wrong about a thing like that.

Then Illyria answered. Bill had never seen the body she was wearing. It was gorgeous, especially if you like them a little plump, as Bill did.

"I still don't get it," Bill said.

Illyria turned to the computer screen. "Quintiform?"

"Yes, my love."

"Don't listen until I tell you to again."

"Yes, my precious. Anyway, it's time I checked to see how things are going on the planet." It began humming to itself. The hum diminished as though the computer was going away, which, in fact, it might well have been, and then it died away

235

altogether except for a faint aftertone which also diminished and died.

"Illyria, how could you have married the computer?"

"It was the only way I could get you here, beloved. I told the computer he would have to bring you back."

"Now that you're married," Bill said, "I don't see what you want me around for."

"Bill, the computer is a dear, and he's very interested in human emotions. But with him it's all talk. You know what I mean?"

"It figures, I guess," Bill said. "But I'm still a trooper, you know. I've got some leave for this job, but . . . "

"If time is limited we must make every second count," she susurrated as she reached for him. "Let's start this way . . . "

Bill's last thought, as the warmth of her embrace enveloped him, was that he had been ordered to do this.

War sure is hell.

Mind of my Mind
OCTAVIA BUTLER

The gripping sequel to *Wild Seed*, the first novel in Octavia Butler's cult *Patternmaster* series. 'Has the piercing, chill quality of a sliver of ice' – *The Times*

0 575 04817 4   £3.99

The Jonah Kit
IAN WATSON

An astronomer's research in the Mexican mountains. A Russian boy with the mind of a dead cosmonaut. Random scientific discoveries that spark off a chain of events which brings into question the human concept of existence itself. A re-issue of the classic which established Ian Watson as one of the UK's leading Science Fiction writers.

0 575 05002 0   £3.99

The Colloghi Conspiracy
DOUGLAS HILL

Another trip into the demented world of Del Curb. This time encountering beautiful media stars, sleeping 21st-century astronauts and furry humanoids, all in 'the humorous tradition of Douglas Adams ...' – *New York Tribune*

0 575 05010 1   £3.99

Also available in hardback

Time for the Stars
ROBERT A. HEINLEIN

An exciting story of humankind's exploration of the universe – its challenging search for a new home. 'Highly intelligent, lighthearted ... lively conversational narrative' – *Times Literary Supplement*

0 575 04936 7   £3.99

Queen of Angels
GREG BEAR

Los Angeles 2048. A brilliantly detailed picture of the world in the middle of the next century from 'Arthur C. Clarke's most formidable rival yet' – *The Times*

0 575 05022 5   £7.50

Also available in hardback

Ealdwood
C.J. CHERRYH

Two of C.J. Cherryh's most celebrated fantasies, *The Dreamstone*, a haunting tale, and *The Tree of Swords and Jewels*, its equally spell-binding sequel, combined in one volume.

0 575 04575 2   £4.50

Summertide
CHARLES SHEFFIELD

A novel set more than four thousand years into the future as an alien race explores abandoned artifacts scattered throughout the galaxy. A story of breathtaking concepts in the epic tradition of Greg Bear and Arthur C. Clarke.

0 575 05021 7   £3.99

Also available in hardback

The Second Trip
ROBERT SILVERBERG

An exciting and thought-provoking story of madness and identity in the next century. 'Silverberg has always been good on schizophrenia. Here he is agonisingly effective' – *Daily Telegraph*

0 575 04037 8   £3.99

Games, Ideas and Activities for Primary Humanities

Richard Green

Longman
is an imprint of

Harlow, England • London • New York • Boston • San Francisco • Toronto
Sydney • Tokyo • Singapore • Hong Kong • Seoul • Taipei • New Delhi
Cape Town • Madrid • Mexico City • Amsterdam • Munich • Paris • Milan

Pearson Education Limited
Edinburgh Gate
Harlow CM20 2JE
United Kingdom
Tel: +44 (0)1279 623623
Fax: +44 (0)1279 431059
Website: www.pearsoned.co.uk

First edition published in Great Britain in 2010

© Pearson Education Limited 2010

The right of Richard Green to be identified as author of this work has
been asserted by him in accordance with the Copyright, Designs and Patents Act 1988.

ISBN: 978-1-4082-2809-8

British Library Cataloguing in Publication Data
A CIP catalogue record for this book can be obtained from the British Library

Library of Congress Cataloging in Publication Data
A CIP catalog record for this book can be obtained from the Library of Congress

10 9 8 7 6 5 4 3 2 1
13 12 11 10 9

Set by 30 in 8.5/12pt NewsGothic BT
Printed by Ashford Colour Press Ltd, Gosport

The Publisher's policy is to use paper manufactured from sustainable forests.

Contents

About the author   viii
Acknowledgements   xi

Chapter 1 Geography   1

Introduction   2
A Different View   4
Adding a Value   5
Alphabet Key   7
Atlas Activity   9
Atlas Quiz   12
Butterflies   14
Capitals of Every Country   17
Colour Coding Drawings   21
Compass Walk   22
Enquiry Questions   24
Geography and Eco-Schools   26
Geography and Numeracy   28
Getting Them Thinking   30
Global Web   32
Grids and Overlays   34
Higher or Lower Quiz   36
Inflatable Globe   39
Jigsaw Geography Mapping   40
Journeys   42
Linear Mapping   44
Local and Global Journeys   46
Looking at Our World   48
Making Sense of the World   50
Masking Images   52
Most Likely to ...   54
My Favourite Place   56
Naming Countries   58
Ordnance Survey Symbols   60

Paper Tree   62
Picture Sorting   64
Putting Yourself in the Picture   65
Raid the Cupboard   67
Sense Cards   69
Should We Keep the Village
   Shop Open?   71
Slope and Gradient Fieldwork   74
Snakes and Ladders   76
Speech and Thought Bubbles   78
Ten Green Bottles   80
The Eight Points of
   the Compass   82
The Local Area   84
The World as a Village   86
Tourism in Antarctica   88
Using Writing Frames   90
Using Your Senses   92
Weather and Climate
   Data Activity   94
What's in the News?   97
Where in the World?   99
Where Would You Like
   to Go?   101
Word mats   102

Chapter 2 History   105

Introduction   106

Chronology

Boudicca's revolt –
   A Chronology   108
Human Timeline   111

Ordering a Story 112
Chronology Counter 114
Revamping the Timeline 116
Extending the Timeline 118
Something About … 120
Time Machine Hats 122

Enquiry

Artefact Vocabulary 124
Branching Database
  for Artefacts 126
Comparing and Contrasting
  Evidence 128
Hieroglyphics 131
Identify Your Object 132
Putting Us in the Picture 134
Samuel Pepys' Diary Entries 135
Using Images as Sources 139
Using Your Senses 141
Using Inventories 142
Using Sources to Develop
  Empathy 145
What Can We Learn
  from Pictures? 147

Interpretation

Asking Questions 148
Fact or Opinion? 150
Facts and Points of View 152
Hadrian's Wall 154
History Sandwich 156
Mary Seacole – Facts and
  Points of View 158
The Great Railway Debate 161
What Did People Think about
  Florence Nightingale? 163

Knowledge and understanding

Anachronisms 165
Building a Pyramid in
  Ancient Egypt 168
Historical Vocabulary 170
Information Teller 171
Just Like Us 174
Ordering a Story 177
Saxon Settlement (Invaders
  and Settlers) 179
Searchlights 181
To Go a Viking 182
Two Truths and a Lie 183
Victorian Spinner 185

Sources

An Introduction to Handling
  Artefacts 187
Investigating a Will 189
Looking at Paintings 191
Misconceptions 194

Other history activities

From a Suitcase 195
Historical Interpretation 197
History in a Story 199
The Mantle of Expertise 201
People Like Us 203
Storytelling 205
Timewatch 207

Chapter 3 RE 211

Introduction 212
A Message for God 214
Analysing Information 216
Art 218

Asking Big Questions 220
Awe and wonder –
  Traffic Lights 221
Belief 222
Choices Box 223
Chorus Narration 225
Codes for Living 227
Conscience Alley 231
Dreamcatcher 233
Experiences 235
Exploring Worship 237
Festivals of Light 239
Gifts 240
Give us a Clue 243
God in Everything 245
Guess Who? 247
Investigating an Artefact 249
Islam – An Introduction 251
Learning from the Five
  Pillars of Islam 253
Looking at a Murti 255
Looking at Ganesha 257
Looking at Pictures 259
Looking at the Beatitudes 260
Looking for a Golden Rule 262
Making and Keeping
  Promises 265

Paper Chain 267
Picture Framing 268
Places 270
Priorities Grid 272
Religious Symbols
  People Wear 274
Rules for Living 277
Seder Plate 279
Single Bubble Map 281
Special Books 283
Special People in Pictures
  and Symbols 285
Special Places 287
Special Teachers 289
Telephone 291
The 12 Days of Christmas 293
The Jewish Mezuzah 295
The Symbolism of the Cross 298
The Trimurti 300
Thinking about Hindu Gods 302
What Do We Worship? 304
Where People Worship 306
Who Am I? 307
Who Is It? 308
Wonder 310

About the author

Originally awarded a BEd and later an MA from Warwick University, I have spent over 30 years teaching, including in schools in Canada and New Zealand. A headteacher in two Warwickshire schools, I have for the past five years been working as an advisory teacher for primary humanities for Coventry.

Acknowledgements

The ideas and activities in this book have been picked up and developed over the past 36 years. They have come from so many sources all around the world that it would be impossible to claim them all as original ideas, but what I hope I have always done is adapt and develop them to fit the context and audience I am working with at the time. I hope that all who use them will do the same.

Introduction

You will find here a collection of ideas, activities and games linked to key skills and concepts in primary humanities based on the programmes of study for each subject. Many of these activities are directly interchangeable and can be used across the subjects. The activities for each subject are aimed at helping pupils to develop their abilities to understand and use those skills and concepts.

In Chapters 1 and 2, about geography and history, respectively, the skills and concepts are outlined in terms of the National Curriculum programmes of study. Chapter 3, about RE, is slightly different in that each local authority in England is responsible for its own agreed syllabus and will set out its own programme for the development of skills and progression in this subject. What is consistent in all locally agreed syllabuses, however, is the concept of learning about and learning from religion.

The main skills and concepts for each subject, therefore, can be defined as:

- History
  - chronology
  - knowledge and understanding
  - enquiry and the use of sources
  - interpretation
  - communication
- Geography
  - enquiry
  - knowledge and understanding of places
  - knowledge and understanding of patterns and processes
  - knowledge and understanding of environmental change and sustainable development
- RE
  - learning about religion
  - learning from religion.

The aim is for the exploration and discovery activities in this book to help teachers stimulate children's inbuilt curiosity – a natural part of their development.

Primary humanities should engage children in questions about people and events in the past, help them understand the present and prepare for the future. Understanding people's relationships with the physical environment helps them form ideas about how to live. By exploring cultures and beliefs, rights and responsibilities, they develop a deeper understanding of themselves and others.

Chapter 1
Geography

Introduction

The knowledge, skills and understanding required for primary geography include:

- geographical enquiry and skills
- knowledge and understanding of places
- knowledge and understanding of patterns and processes
- knowledge and understanding of environmental change and sustainable development.

A simple progression table might look like this.

Years 1|2	Years 3|4	Years 5|6
Geographical enquiry and skills	Geographical enquiry and skills	Geographical enquiry and skills
Ask simple geographical questions.	Ask geographical questions and offer their own ideas.	Draw on their own experience and secondary sources to identify geographical questions.
Find places on a map.	Identify places and locate on a map using letter and number references.	Know the location and context of a range of places and use four-figure grid references.
Find out about different places they have visited.	Give explanations of other people's views.	Appreciate that there are different views and opinions on geographical matters.
	Use simple equipment to collect information, e.g. weather data.	Select a range of equipment for collecting data.
Knowledge and understanding of places	Knowledge and understanding of places	Knowledge and understanding of places
Know what places are and why we go there.	Describe a range of physical and human features of different places.	Describe the physical and human features of a wider range of places.
Make observations about simple human and physical geographical features of different places.	Make simple comparisons between individual features of different places.	Make comparisons between individual features of different places.
Make simple comparisons between home town/ village and other places.	Recognise how places are linked to other places in the world.	Recognise the ways in which places can be interdependent.

Years 1|2	Years 3|4	Years 5|6
Patterns and process	Patterns and process	Patterns and process
Why are places different?	Make appropriate observations about the location of features.	Describe and explain patterns in the wider world.
	Describe patterns in our local landscape.	Describe the character and environment in different parts of the world.
	Why are places like that and how do they change?	How do human and physical features cause changes in places?
Environmental change and sustainable development	Environmental change and sustainable development	Environmental change and sustainable development
	Identify changes in the environment.	Explain the reasons for changes in the environment.
How can we improve our environment?	Begin to understand how people both damage and improve their environment.	Begin to understand how and why people seek sustainable solutions to environmental problems.

What geography in primary schools should do is encourage children to interpret the world around them, from the local to the global. Children need to become aware of how communities are organised and shaped by people's values and actions. Through human, social and environmental understanding, they begin to understand how actions taken either locally or a long way away can affect our lives today.

A Different View

As time passes, the world changes. A Different View suggests looking at the world in a flexible way, which will enthuse, engage and challenge children.

Suitable for

KS2

Aims

- To help children investigate and explore the world.
- To develop the use of enquiry-type questions.

Resources

- A range of contemporary images of places around the world
- World map

What to do

1. Show the children a number of selected images.
2. Ask them to use enquiry-type questions (who, what, where, when, why and so on.) to describe each picture.
3. Go back over each picture and explain the location and context of the image.
4. Have the children find each location on a world map. They can find three pieces of information for each location.
5. Ask them to make a judgement about whether each image supports their view of a place – or is it a surprise?

Variation

- Rather than asking enquiry-type questions, ask the children to give each picture a title that describes their reaction to the picture.

Adding a Value

This activity can be used to develop language skills linked to issues related to geography.

Suitable for

KS1, KS2

Aim

● To ask children to make judgements using images (secondary sources).

Resources

● Appropriate pictures
● Vocabulary links

What to do

1. Give the children a picture with appropriate descriptive words.

2. Ask them to colour in the words that they think best describe the picture.

3. Spaces can be left for children to put in their own descriptive words.

4. Look at the picture and decide if it has a generally positive or negative bias. Children could decide on a title for the picture.

5. Give children the background to the picture.

6. Does this change their feeling about the picture?

7. Repeat with the other pictures.

Variations

- The number of words given by the teacher can be reduced and the children can be asked to develop more of their own ideas.
- This activity can be linked to other humanities subjects, such as history and RE.

Alphabet Key

As part of an introduction to a topic or activity, an alphabet key is a useful way to determine children's knowledge and understanding about a place, process or people. Rather than give them a word list, investigate their existing knowledge. The process can be repeated at the end of a topic to see what additional knowledge has been gained.

Suitable for

KS1, KS2

Aim

- To evaluate children's knowledge at the start and end of an activity or investigation.

Resources

- Alphabet key (see below)

1 Alphabet Key

A	J	S
B	K	T
C	L	U
D	M	V
E	N	W
F	O	X
G	P	Y
H	Q	Z
I	R	

What to do

1. Show the key to the class at the start of a topic.

2. Ask them for a word for each letter, related to the theme or topic.

3. Go through the alphabet, missing out letters where no words can be thought of.

4. Use the alphabet key as a vocabulary list related to the topic.

5. At the end of the topic, review the list and see if the children can add more words and fill in gaps.

Variation

• Each letter can produce several words rather than just one word.

Atlas Activity

Atlases are useful tools for children to use to investigate the wider world but their abstract nature needs to be explained so that children can make sense of the information provided. When working on mapping activities consider:

- size – actual and relative
- location – actual and relative
- characteristics – physical and human
- patterns – in comparison with other places
- changes – acting on and being acted on by people and natural forces over time.

Suitable for

KS1, KS2

Aim

- To develop progressive atlas skills.

Resources

- Pictures and aerial photographs of the classroom/school and local area.
- Base outlines of 3D shapes.

What to do

1. As a starting point, before handling an atlas, which presents the Earth in 2D, stretched format, children should engage in concrete activities that develop spatial awareness.

2. Depending on the age and ability, choose a starting point, such as a classroom, rooms at home, extending slowly to the school site and local area.

3. Look at photographs of the immediate school area and identify the different locations, such as the car park, playing field, buildings and so on.

4. Cut out base outlines of 3D shapes – cereal packets, cartons and so on – and stick them onto a tabletop model.

5. Compare the map with the photograph, considering size, location, orientation and so on.

Variations

● Here are some ideas.

Using contents pages

Content	Page number
Map of Europe	

Name things that you will find on this page.

Page	I think what I will find on this page is ...	Check

Longitude and latitude

Which lines pass through:

● Paris
● Melbourne?

Where would you be if you were at:
55 28' N 4 37' W?

Direction

Complete the chart.

From	To	Direction
Iceland	Norway	

From	To	Direction	Countries passed through

Physical geography

Physical maps show us natural features, not features made by people.

Ask questions.

- Which sea does this river flow into?

Heights key

Over 1000 m
500–1000 m
200–500 m
100–200 m
0–100 m

Colour key

Feature	Colour	Height
Norfolk Broads		
Ben Nevis		

Scale

Map	Page	Scale	From	To	Distance on map in cm	Distance on ground in km

Atlas Quiz

The aim of this activity is to link knowledge and understanding of places around the world with atlas skills.

Suitable for

KS2

Aim

- To develop and link atlas work to geographical places.

Resources

- Class atlas
- Cards (see example below)

Clues

- P. 14.
- In the Midlands.
- Has lots of canals.
- Is England's second largest city.

Answer
Birmingham.

What to do

1. Ask the children to write three things about a place shown on a particular page of the atlas.

2. They then read out the clues and the rest of the class use the atlas to try and find and name the location the clues relate to.

3. They locate the correct place.

Variations

- Children can use a wider range of pages and give the page number as one of the clues, such as:

Clues

- P. 34.
- Has lots of hotels and casinos.
- Is in the Nevada desert.

Answer

Las Vegas.

- Once found, the class can contribute any other knowledge they have about a particular place. For example, Birmingham has two major football teams.
- It has a famous shopping centre.
- It has a railway station called Snow Hill.

Butterflies

Butterflies are a symbol of nature. Environmental sustainability is an important issue as the world changes and more species are put at risk through environmental change.

Suitable for

KS1, KS2

Aim

● To get children to focus on environmental issues.

Resources

● A4 sheets of coloured paper.
● Pipe cleaners or curling ribbon for antenae, plus stickers, glitter glue pens and so on to decorate.

How to make a butterfly

● Start by making a square piece of paper. To do this, fold the corner of a piece of paper over as shown.

● To finish making the square, cut off the small rectangle at the top along the edge of the top layer of paper, and discard.

- Fold the remaining triangle in half along the folded edge.
- Open it up again. Put the triangle on the table with the central fold pointing up (like a tent). Fold one corner over. Open it up again. Fold the other corner over along the dotted line shown.

 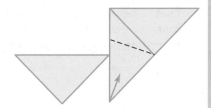

- Open it up again. Fold the corner over in the same way, the other side of the central fold.

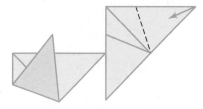

- Open it up, leaving the central ridge a little raised. You now have a simple butterfly shape.

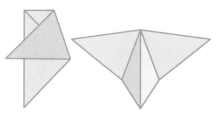

- Decorate the butterfly. Attach two antennae made of pipe cleaners or curling ribbon (curled by pulling it over the edge of scissor blades).

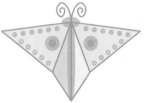

What to do

1. Create and decorate a butterfly as shown in the diagrams.

2. Add a message related to environmental sustainability, such as 'Don't throw litter', 'Leave natural areas for animals, birds and insects'.

3. Create a display – for example, you could have a globe surrounded by butterflies or butterflies suspended from the ceiling – to help the children focus on a range of environmental issues.

Variation

• Look at where animal species are endangered by climate change, loss of habitat or human intervention. Create simple models for those animals and think of relevant messages related to them.

Capitals of Every Country

The aim of this activity is to develop the children's knowledge of the world and link this knowledge to the use of atlases, globes and maps.

Suitable for

KS2

Aim

- To use atlases, globes and other maps to locate and list capital cities of countries around the world.

Resources

- List of countries and their capital cities (see below)
- Appropriate atlases, globes and maps
- Internet access

Capitals of every country

The 195 independent countries on Earth with their capital city or cities.

Afghanistan – Kabul
Albania – Tirane
Algeria – Algiers
Andorra – Andorra la Vella
Angola – Luanda
Antigua and Barbuda – Saint John's
Argentina – Buenos Aires
Armenia – Yerevan
Australia – Canberra
Austria – Vienna
Azerbaijan – Baku
Bahamas, The – Nassau
Bahrain – Al Manama

Bangladesh – Dhaka
Barbados – Bridgetown
Belarus – Minsk
Belgium – Brussels
Belize – Belmopan
Benin – Porto-Novo
Bhutan – Thimphu
Bolivia – La Paz (administrative);
 Sucre (judicial)
Bosnia and Herzegovina – Sarajevo
Botswana – Gaborone
Brazil – Brasilia
Brunei – Bandar Seri Begawan

Bulgaria – Sofia
Burkina Faso – Ouagadougou
Burundi – Bujumbura
Cambodia – Phnom Penh
Cameroon – Yaoundé
Canada – Ottawa
Cape Verde – Praia
Central African Republic – Bangui
Chad – N'Djamena
Chile – Santiago
China – Beijing
Colombia – Bogotá
Comoros – Moroni
Congo, Republic of the – Brazzaville
Congo, Democratic Republic of the –
  Kinshasa
Costa Rica – San José
Côte d'Ivoire – Yamoussoukro
  (official); Abidjan (de facto)
Croatia – Zagreb
Cuba – Havana
Cyprus – Nicosia
Czech Republic – Prague
Denmark – Copenhagen
Djibouti – Djibouti
Dominica – Roseau
Dominican Republic – Santo Domingo
East Timor – Dili
Ecuador – Quito
Egypt – Cairo
El Salvador – San Salvador
Equatorial Guinea – Malabo
Eritrea – Asmara
Estonia – Tallinn
Ethiopia – Addis Ababa
Fiji – Suva
Finland – Helsinki
France – Paris
Gabon – Libreville
Gambia, The – Banjul
Georgia – Tbilisi
Germany – Berlin
Ghana – Accra
Greece – Athens
Grenada – Saint George's
Guatemala – Guatemala City

Guinea – Conakry
Guinea-Bissau – Bissau
Guyana – Georgetown
Haiti – Port-au-Prince
Honduras – Tegucigalpa
Hungary – Budapest
Iceland – Reykjavik
India – New Delhi
Indonesia – Jakarta
Iran – Tehran
Iraq – Baghdad
Ireland, Republic of – Dublin
Israel – Jerusalem
Italy – Rome
Jamaica – Kingston
Japan – Tokyo
Jordan – Amman
Kazakhstan – Astana
Kenya – Nairobi
Kiribati – Tarawa Atoll
Korea, North – Pyongyang
Korea, South – Seoul
Kuwait – Kuwait City
Kyrgyzstan – Bishkek
Laos – Vientiane
Latvia – Riga
Lebanon – Beirut
Lesotho – Maseru
Liberia – Monrovia
Libya – Tripoli
Liechtenstein – Vaduz
Lithuania – Vilnius
Luxembourg – Luxembourg
Macedonia – Skopje
Madagascar – Antananarivo
Malawi – Lilongwe
Malaysia – Kuala Lumpur
Maldives – Malé
Mali – Bamako
Malta – Valletta
Marshall Islands – Majuro
Mauritania – Nouakchott
Mauritius – Port Louis
Mexico – Mexico City
Micronesia, Federated States of –
  Palikir

Moldova – Chisinau
Monaco – Monaco
Mongolia – Ulaanbaatar
Montenegro – Podgorica
Morocco – Rabat
Mozambique – Maputo
Myanmar (Burma) – Rangoon but
  moving to Pyinmana
Namibia – Windhoek
Nauru – no official capital;
  government offices in Yaren District
Nepal – Kathmandu
Netherlands – Amsterdam (official);
  The Hague (administrative)
New Zealand – Wellington
Nicaragua – Managua
Niger – Niamey
Nigeria – Abuja
Norway – Oslo
Oman – Muscat
Pakistan – Islamabad
Palau – Melekeok
Panama – Panama City
Papua New Guinea – Port Moresby
Paraguay – Asunción
Peru – Lima
Philippines – Manila
Poland – Warsaw
Portugal – Lisbon
Qatar – Doha
Romania – Bucharest
Russia – Moscow
Rwanda – Kigali
Saint Kitts and Nevis – Basseterre
Saint Lucia – Castries
Saint Vincent and the Grenadines –
  Kingstown
Samoa – Apia
San Marino – San Marino
São Tomé and Principe – São Tomé
Saudi Arabia – Riyadh
Senegal – Dakar
Serbia – Belgrade
Seychelles – Victoria

Sierra Leone – Freetown
Singapore – Singapore
Slovakia – Bratislava
Slovenia – Ljubljana
Solomon Islands – Honiara
Somalia – Mogadishu
South Africa – Pretoria
  (administrative); Cape Town
  (legislative); Bloemfontein (judiciary)
Spain – Madrid
Sri Lanka – Colombo
Sudan – Khartoum
Suriname – Paramaribo
Swaziland – Mbabane
Sweden – Stockholm
Switzerland – Bern
Syria – Damascus
Taiwan – Taipei
Tajikistan – Dushanbe
Tanzania – Dar es Salaam
Thailand – Bangkok
Togo – Lomé
Tonga – Nuku'alofa
Trinidad and Tobago – Port-of-Spain
Tunisia – Tunis
Turkey – Ankara
Turkmenistan – Ashgabat
Tuvalu – Vaialeu Village, Province
  Funafuti
Uganda – Kampala
Ukraine – Kyiv
United Arab Emirates – Abu Dhabi
United Kingdom – London
United States of America –
  Washington DC
Uruguay – Montevideo
Uzbekistan – Tashkent
Vanuatu – Port-Vila
Vatican City (Holy See) – Vatican City
Venezuela – Caracas
Vietnam – Hanoi
Yemen – Sanaá
Zambia – Lusaka
Zimbabwe – Harare

What to do

1. Give groups of children copies of the list of countries and their capital cities.

2. Using maps, globes and atlases, have them locate some countries and their capitals.

3. Mark them on a map.

4. Each group can report back on what they have discovered.

5. The lists of each group can be linked to a world map.

Variations

- The activity can be varied by giving the children more or fewer countries to investigate.
- Children can be given either the countries or capitals and find their capitals or countries respectively using atlases, maps, the Internet and so on in order to locate the answers.

Colour Coding Drawings

Colour coding drawings and sketches is a way of introducing children to Ordnance Survey map symbols and the idea of compiling and using a key.

Suitable for

KS2

Aim

- To develop geographical skills linked to organising information and map work.

Resources

- Images linked to a specific topic, such as the seaside

What to do

1. Ask the children to draw a sketch from the image or from a real location.
2. Ask them to devise a coding system based on colours by colouring the image according to its properties, such as
   - buildings
   - natural features
   - sky and so on.
3. Then ask them to put a key for the coding on their image, linking the colours that they have used with their key.

Variations

- Give the children ready-prepared drawings and ask them to devise a colour coding key for different aspects of the picture, such as brown for buildings, green for fields, blue for sky and so on.
- Children can work out what proportion of the image each block of colour represents.

Compass Walk

This activity introduces children to using a compass and compass skills as an aid to fieldwork and mapping.

Suitable for

KS2

Aim

- To introduce the compass and compass points.

Resources

- Pre-prepared card compasses or materials (card, scissors and split pins) to make same

What to do

1. The children make or are given simple card compasses with the four cardinal points (N, E, S and W) marked on them.

2. Using a diagram on the classroom floor or playground, help the children to learn how to orientate their compass to north and determine where the compass points are situated.

3. The children can carry out different tasks. For example, they can walk in a northerly direction and go as far as they can in a straight line inside the school grounds.

   - Where do you stop?
   - Turn and face the way you came – which direction is that?
   - What can you see (list, sketch, photograph and so on), smell, hear and so on?
   - What is the highest point you can see?
   - Can you see a building?
   - Can you see a tree?

Variations

- Additional compass points can be added (NE, SE, SW, NW).
- Carry out similar activities using directional arrows on the school field. Using a directional compass, walk due north, south and so on. In which direction can you go the furthest?
- Carry out similar activities to the above, such as:
  - photograph what you can see
  - do a litter count where you stop
  - describe the skyline
  - measure the distance travelled
  - draw a sketch map of your route on a school plan.

Enquiry Questions

Enquiry – asking who, what, where, why, when and how – is an integral aspect of primary geography and one of the elements that make up the National Curriculum's programme of study for geography. This activity introduces children to the concept of enquiry and encourages them to ask and answer such questions.

Suitable for

KS1, KS2

Aim

- To develop the use of enquiry-type questions in geography activities.

Resources

- Images – (see example on page 25)
- Data collection sheets
- Text documents

What to do

1. Provide children with information in an appropriate format – pictorial, text and so on.

2. Go over what the enquiry questions are and ask the children to ask and answer those questions with regard to the documents that they have been given.

3. Discuss whether or not all the questions are answerable and if this varies depending on the nature of the document being examined.

4. Is it possible to infer answers to some of the enquiry questions from what they can see or read?

Variations

- The enquiry concept can be introduced as a whole-class activity using a whiteboard.
- Once the children have understood the idea of enquiry they can construct questions for others to answer.

Geography and Eco-Schools

Every primary school is required to have an Eco-School coordinator. Many environmental issues, such as energy use, waste and fair trade, are also part of the geography curriculum.

Suitable for

KS1, KS2

Aim

- To link environmental issues with learning in geography.

Resources

- Audit sheets for the different aspects of sustainability being focused on

What to do

1. Ask the children to think of any ways that they can help the environment.
2. List the areas suggested and decide on a priority – say, waste.
3. Collectively, draw up an audit sheet that covers any aspects of waste for the given area.
4. Have the children go round school looking for evidence of waste.
5. Explore the evidence that they have gathered in the classroom and ask the children to identify any ways in which waste can be reduced or avoided.

Variation

- Other geographical eco links include energy and water savings, waste reduction, composting, fair trade and developing a global perspective. Children can focus on one or all of these areas as part of both the Eco-Schools and geography remit.

Geography and Numeracy

This activity looks at the links between geography and numeracy and how some of those links can be applied.

Suitable for

KS1, KS2

Aim

- To develop numerical skills through geography.

Resources

- Data collection sheets, such as tally charts
- Considering probabilities
- Looking for patterns

What to do

1. Discuss with the children the ways in which numbers are used to give information, such as:
    - bus numbers – routes
    - house numbers – home location
    - miles on signposts – distances
    - collection times on postboxes – service frequency
    - road numbers – hierarchy of routes.

2. Then look at ways in which numbers are used to find information, such as:

- tallies and surveys of data, such as traffic counts
- reading measurements, such as taking your temperature
- creating charts and graphs, such as a pictogram of shoppers
- interpreting tables, such as frequency of buses from a timetable
- looking for patterns, such as weather records around the school grounds
- considering probability, such as likelihood of certain types of shop in a town centre
- setting up a hypothesis, such as the comparative traffic use of roads.

3. Provide children with information linked to one or some of the above, such as shopping habits, street numbers or temperature ranges and ask them to look for patterns, create tally charts, make pictograms and so on of the same.

Getting Them Thinking

Getting children to consider their knowledge of the world can be made enjoyable through activities such as the one outlined below. It also helps to develop a specific skill – using a globe.

Suitable for

KS1, KS2

Aim

● To develop knowledge of the world through the use of a globe.

Resources

● An inflatable globe

What to do

1. Pass an inflatable globe around the group and ask questions such as the following.
   ● Where have you been?
   ● Where would you like to go?
   ● Can you find me a place beginning with B?
   ● Can you find me a hot place?
2. Develop the questioning by asking geographical ones, such as 'Can you find me a place where few people live? Why?'
3. Ask the children to consider ways of travelling to particular places or something that they might need to take/wear to a particular place.
4. Ask the children to estimate the distances between places.

Variations

- This can be used as a starter activity or as part of a plenary at the end of a lesson.

- The globe can be tossed around the class to speed up the activity (providing the children can catch!) and to make it more random (a teacher can be selective).

Global Web

This activity is a way of helping children make links with the wider world through their family contacts and holiday associations.

Suitable for

KS2

Aims

- For children to use their personal connections to make links with other parts of the world.
- To combine those links on a class basis in order to make wider connections.

Resources

- Global webs (see example below)
- World maps
- Atlases

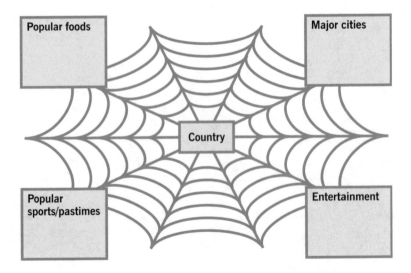

What to do

1. Provide each child with a global web. Ask them to place a country that they have a connection with – through family, friends holidays and so on – on the web.

2. In each of the other boxes, have them list any associations they can make, such as foods, native costume, local dress, and so on.

3. Add to their knowledge through research using textbooks, atlases, the Internet and other resources.

4. Place the countries listed on the children's webs on a world map in order to see the global connections within the class.

Variations

- The boxes within the web can be limited or increased in order to vary this activity.
- Initial judgements about aspects of each country can be expanded through research.

Grids and Overlays

This helps children with location activities and introduces and develops the use of coordinates at appropriate levels.

Suitable for

KS1, KS2

Aims

- To establish the use of grids and coordinates.
- To help develop the transition from pictures to understanding plan views.

Resources

- Transparent grids, divided as appropriate to the age and abilities of the children
- Images that match the overall transparency

What to do

1. Give the children an image and a transparent grid, divided and labelled as appropriate. It could be alphanumeric (A-1, B-2, C-3 and so on) or numeric 1-1, 2-2, 3-3 and so on. For example:

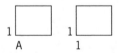

2. Remind the children that they need to read the horizontal axis first, then the vertical axis.

3. Then, have the children lay the transparent grid over the image and make judgements about the locations of items in the picture.

4. These locations and pupil choices can be compared and contrasted to ensure that the children have used the grid correctly.

Variations

- Give the children the same image and labelled transparent grid to carry out collective activities.

- For older or more able children, give them both an image and a plan view of the same area so that they can carry out comparative activities for the same location.

Higher or Lower Quiz

This activity is a general knowledge quiz using a slightly different format from that which would be expected. It is based on making a general numerical choice, which can then be expanded on and detailed information given.

Suitable for

KS1, KS2

Aim

- To help children develop their geographical general knowledge.

Resources

- A list of statements that children make numerical choices, such as the examples given below.

Example higher or lower quiz statements

1. There are *four* oceans around the world. Is the number higher or lower?
   Answer   Higher – there are five: the Atlantic, Pacific, Arctic, Indian and Southern oceans.
2. *Ten million* people live in the Greater London area. Higher or lower?
   Answer   Lower – the 2001 census shows that there are 7.5 million people in the Greater London area.
3. There are *14* countries in the world starting with A. Higher or lower?
   Answer   Higher – there are 18, from Abkhazia to Azerbaijan.
4. *Three* continents lie entirely in the southern hemisphere. Higher or lower?
   Answer   Lower – there are two: Australia and Antarctica.
5. *Four* continents lie entirely in the northern hemisphere. Higher or lower?
   Answer   Lower – there are two: Asia and Europe.

6. English has official status as a native language in 50 countries. Higher or lower?

   Answer   Higher – there are 75 countries where English has official status for broadcasting, government documents and so on.

7. There are 40 countries in the continent of Europe. Higher or lower?

   Answer   Higher – there are 43, including the Vatican City.

8. Mandarin Chinese is spoken by a billion people. Higher or lower?

   Answer   Higher – Mandarin Chinese is spoken by 1.25 billion people.

9. There are 20 deserts in the world. Higher or lower?

   Answer   There are 22 deserts (hot and dry) from Arabia to Taklimakan (Central Asia), not counting cold and dry.

10. Mount Everest is over 8800 m. There are 14 other mountains in the world over 8000 m. Higher or lower?

    Answer   Lower – there are 13 other mountains over 8000 m, all in the Himalayas or Asia.

11. The deepest ocean is over 10 km deep. Higher or lower?

    Answer   Higher – the deepest ocean is over 11000 m (7 miles) deep. It is the Marianas Trench in the Pacific Ocean.

12. The world-famous waterfalls Niagara Falls and Victoria Falls drop over 100 m. There are over 30 waterfalls that fall over 200 m. Higher or lower?

    Answer   There are 36 – the highest is Salto Angel in Venezuela, which has a height of 979 m.

What to do

1. Tell the children that you are going to make some geographical statements.

2. They are to all stand and, after each statement, raise a hand if they think the answer is actually higher or keep it down if they think it is lower.

3. Those with the correct answer are to keep standing; the others are to sit down.

4. The last three or four children could come to the front of the class for the final few questions.

Variation

- The statements can be simpler for younger children.
- The statements can be general or specific to an area or topic, such as the examples given below.

Example: higher or lower global connections statements

1. There are 190 countries in the world.
   Answer   Higher – there are 193.
2. There are 60 countries in Africa.
   Answer   Lower – there are 54.
3. There are 200 languages spoken around the world
   Answer   Higher – There are over 300.
4. The population of Britain is 50 million.
   Answer   Higher – The last census was 54 million. Current estimates are 58–60 million.
5. The Greenwich meridian passes through six countries, including the UK.
   Answer   Higher – eight countries, including the UK, France, Spain, Algeria, Burkina Faso, Ghana and Togo.
6. The United Nations represents 193 countries in the world.
   Answer   Lower – 192, the exception being the Holy See, which has observer status only.
7. The world population is 6 billion 500 million.
   Answer   Higher – 6 billion 650 million (July 2007 estimate).
8. There are 15 organised religious and faith groups around the world with over half a million members.
   Answer   Higher – there are over 20. In fact, there are 22 from Christianity to Scientology.
9. The Fair Trade organisation is involved with farmers in 50 countries.
   Answer   Lower – 48 (November 2007).
10. Bananas are grown in 75 countries.
    Answer   Higher – they are grown in at least 107 countries.
11. There are more than 15 different base materials that can be recycled and used again.
    Answer   Lower – plastics, wood products (paper, card and so on), steel, aluminium, glass, textiles, oil, gases (freon and others), building materials (brick, tile) and biodegradable waste (food to compost and so on), which is a total of ten.

Inflatable Globe

This is a useful, fun activity for children to test their knowledge of the world and get used to using a globe. It can be used as a lesson starter or plenary or just as a time filler at the start and end of the day.

Suitable for

KS2

Aims

- To develop knowledge and understanding of the world.
- To recognise and interpret the world through the use of the globe.

Resources

- An inflatable globe of a size suitable for the age of the pupils.

What to do

1. Throw or pass the globe to a child and ask a question, such as 'Can you find an ocean, find and name a country you have visited, find something beginning with B?' and so on.
2. Once the child has located the item, he or she passes the globe back.
3. Repeat with a different child and/or different question.

Variation

- A child who is passed the globe and is not sure can pass it on to another child.

Jigsaw Geography Mapping

This activity is an introduction to images and a useful start for mapping ideas linked to landscape features.

Suitable for

KS1, KS2

Aim

* To introduce simple ideas of orientation, direction and landscape features.

Resources

* Landscape images from calendars, magazines and so on, either on card or colour copied onto card
* Bags to store the jigsaws in

What to do

1. Cut up each image into a simple (depending on the age and ability of the children) jigsaw and bag each one.
2. The children, in pairs, have to use jigsaw techniques, such as finding corner pieces, matching shapes, colours and features.
3. Discussion can include vocabulary linked to simple directions, such as up, down, left, right and so on.
4. If you make several jigsaws, copying them onto different-coloured pieces of card helps to prevent them getting mixed up

Variations

- For older children, provide more complex jigsaws.
- Omit pieces and ask the children to draw in missing pieces.
- Compare their complete jigsaw with the original picture and discuss the landscape features, etc.
- Cover the complete picture with a transparent grid to introduce simple coordinates and location activities, including directions such as up, down, left, right, north and south, etc.
- Use a jigsaw of an aerial picture location linked to an Ordnance Survey map. Can the children match the complete picture to the Ordnance Survey location?
- Introduce symbols and keys.

Journeys

The idea of this activity is to tell a well-known story, but add a specific geographical vocabulary and directions, which introduces children to new geographical concepts.

Suitable for

KS1

Aim

- Introduce the idea of direction and geographical vocabulary through the telling of a well-known story such as The Three Little Pigs or Little Red Riding Hood.

Resources

- Story, such as The Three Little Pigs
- Images that tell the story

What to do

1. Tell the children the well-known story you've chosen, adding geographical terms linked to features, seasons, climate and direction as appropriate.

2. After the story, discuss the journey, asking, for example, how did Little Red Riding Hood get to her granny's house? The kinds of answers the children might give could include down the road, across the bridge, up the hill, down into the woods, across the stream and so on.

Variations

- The children can put statements about a journey – to school, a route around school and so on – in the right order (see the example below).

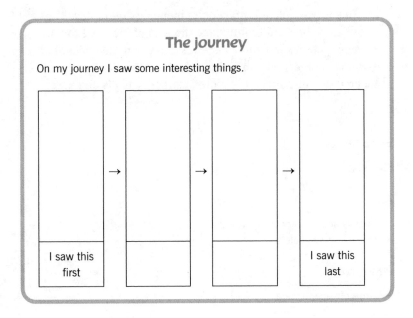

The journey

On my journey I saw some interesting things.

I saw this first → → → I saw this last

Linear Mapping

This is a simple introduction to mapping and routes. The activity can be used to introduce the idea of the need for commonality when using images as a key and the concept of symbols representing a particular feature. Development can include the introduction of more abstract symbols and keys.

Suitable for

KS1, KS2

Aims

- To draw and describe a simple route.
- To use own symbols.

Resources

- Strips of paper or card

What to do

1. Ask the children to take a simple walk around school or remember a known route.

2. On a linear strip of paper or card ask them to draw a starting point and identify two or three known locations on the route and then a finishing point.

3. Each child can then show their maps to a partner who can try to explain the route shown.

4. The children can then use their maps to describe their routes to their partner.

Variations

- This activity can be given as a homework mapping activity.
- As the children develop their skills they could use the same activity but create symbols and a key and annotate their maps as required.

Local and Global Journeys

This activity aims to link aspects of geography by looking at a particular journey and identifying the range of geographical information that can be obtained from looking at that journey and ways to present that information.

Suitable for

KS2

Aims

- To collect information from secondary sources.
- To develop mapping skills, including the use of symbols and scale.

Resources

- Maps and atlases
- Sugar paper
- Internet access
- Books and magazines

What to do

1. Pick a journey. It can be local or global.

2. Use a map or atlas to identify the key features of the journey – locations, natural features and so on – and work out the distances between them.

3. On a long strip of sugar paper, mark those locations to scale.

4. The children can then use the reference books, the Internet and other sources to collect images and information about the locations and stick them onto the sugar paper in the appropriate places.

5. Where there are natural features (water, mountains, desert and so on) they can think of appropriate symbols and add those. They can then construct a key for their symbols.

6. The finished activity can be mounted and displayed, showing the journey in its entirety and its features.

Variation

* The degree of information noted can be varied. This can lead to the children developing their knowledge by gathering a range of information about places or else can be specifically tailored to mapping skills, using symbols, keys, scale and so on.

Looking at Our World

Children often see the world from particular perspectives. For instance, school atlases will focus on a UK perspective. This activity aims to show them the world in different ways and asks the children to note the differences that different perspectives give.

Suitable for

KS2

Aim

- To look at the world from different perspectives.

Resources

- A range of maps and images showing the world from different perspectives, such as the image shown below.

- A range of data showing children information about the world from different perspectives, such as world population profiles.

What to do

1. Show the children the range of maps and satellite images of the world you have gathered.

2. Ask them what they notice about those images and how they contrast with what they already know about the world.

3. Look for specific information, asking them questions such as the following:
   - Which is the largest continent (area)?
   - Which country has the largest population?
   - Where on the globe is Great Britain situated?

4. Ask each child, or groups of children, to find out information about different parts of the world and how perceptions of the world could differ depending on location and so on.

5. Have the children report their perspectives to the rest of the class.

Variation

- Compare areas of a similar size – such as Greenland and Africa – in terms of climate, population and other similar factors.

Making Sense of the World

Children's perceptions of the wider world are limited by their preconceptions, experience and access to sources of information. This activity asks them to build up their knowledge of people and places by interpreting images and constructing layers of information.

Suitable for

KS1

Aim

- To learn about other places by developing ideas and information.

Resources

- Images of people in different locations
- Whiteboard and digital projector

What to do

1. Show the children an image of people in a particular location.
2. What are their initial reactions? Focus on the senses: what do they think they would see, hear, smell?
3. Develop the questioning approach, asking would it be hot, cold and so on, what are people wearing, doing? What are the buildings like, why do they have flat roofs?
4. Identify the location. Have the children locate it on a map or atlas.

5. Ask if it is near or far away.

6. Ask the children if they think the people in the picture would be speaking English or another language.

7. Ask them if anyone has visited this place.

8. Collate the information generated and review what has been learned about this place.

Variation

- The children can be asked to think what they might see beyond the edges of the picture. Does it fit with the information already provided?

Masking Images

This activity uses pictures that can be partially covered for the children to try and work out what they might be of.

Suitable for

KS1, KS2

Aims

- For children to interpret visual sources.
- To develop a geographical vocabulary, including using enquiry-type questions – who, what, where, why, how, when.

Resources

- Pictures, masked in a variety of ways, such as horizontally, vertically or diagonally. If required, central parts of the picture can be covered using Blu-Tack or similar.
- Card strips to cover the pictures, held by paperclips.

What to do

1. Provide children with the masked images, which are linked to particular places or environments.
2. Ask them to say, draw or write what they imagine is covered.
3. Then ask them to uncover the masked bit and reveal the complete picture.
4. Discuss why their answers were correct or incorrect.

Variations

- This can be done as a class activity using a whiteboard. Part of an image can be covered by a text box that can be gradually drawn back to reveal the complete picture.
- A picture can be partly or completely covered and the children can tear pieces off, each time revealing clues that may aid or change their minds as to the nature of the completed picture.

Most Likely To ...

Children often make assumptions about certain elements based own their own experience. The idea of this activity is to get children to consider and analyse their perceptions of the world.

Suitable for

KS1, KS2

Aim

- For children to consider their perceptions.

Resources

- A set of numbered photographs linked to a particular theme, such as water
- A question and recording grid (see example below).

In which photograph(s) are you most likely to ...

Water photographs	Number
need Wellington boots?	
wear sun cream?	
feel thirsty?	
travel by boat?	
need to repair your house?	
feel uncomfortable?	
relax?	
use the headlights on a car?	

Water photographs	Number
travel on skis?	
need an umbrella?	
wrap up warm?	
put sandbags by your door?	
wear light clothes?	
get covered in dust?	

What to do

1. Divide the class into groups and give each group of children a set of photographs and a question and recording grid.

2. Ask them to look at the questions and decide which photos best fit the questions.

3. Then get the groups to compare their results to see if other choices are equally acceptable.

4. Some children will understand that sun cream might be required in a cold, clear environment as well as in a hot, dry one.

Variations

- The number of photographs and questions can be limited so that there are fewer choices for the children to make.

My Favourite Place

This is an early introduction to linking compass directions with a map of Britain. The activity asks children to relate their favourite places to a location on a map and mentally map locations.

Suitable for

KS1, KS2

Aim

- To introduce compass directions with locations in the United Kingdom.

Resources

- Four cardinal compass directions on the floor of the classroom
- Copies of outline map of the United Kingdom

What to do

1. Look at the map of the United Kingdom and relate the map to the compass directions.
2. Look at the map and agree the location of the school.
3. Then ask the children to think of their favourite place in the UK. It may be their home town, a holiday location or where a relative lives.
4. Then ask them to imagine that the classroom represents the map and they have to go and stand in their favourite location.
5. Ask individuals to explain where they are to see if their mental maps reflect accurate views of locations in the UK.

Variation

- The children could be asked to move on to a second place that they have a relationship with. They can be asked to explain their location and why they chose it.

Naming Countries

> This is a general knowledge activity aimed at developing children's knowledge of the world. It also links in with activities about modern foreign languages.

Suitable for

KS1, KS2

Aim

- To help children understand that other countries use different languages from their own and that these languages can be seen in different contexts.

Resources

- Whiteboard images of foreign stamps and so on with the names of countries in their own languages on them.
- A list of countries with their names in their own languages (see below)
- Pupil atlases with the names of countries in their own languages
- Internet access

Naming countries

These names are commonly found on foreign stamps.
Which European countries do they belong to?

Belgique		Italia	
Danmark		Norge	
Eire		Polska	
Suomi		España	
Deutschland		Sverige	
Österreich		Helvetia	
Nederland			

Answers

Belgique	Belgium
Danmark	Denmark
Eire	Ireland
Suomi	Finland
Deutschland	Germany
Österreich	Austria
Nederland	Holland
Italia	Italy
Norge	Norway
Polska	Poland
España	Spain
Sverige	Sweden
Helvetia	Switzerland

What to do

1. Discuss countries that the children have visited, holidayed in and so on.

2. Make up a list of names of those countries.

3. Ask the children if they know the local names of those countries.

4. Show some stamps and so on on the whiteboards and see if the children can identify which country is associated with each stamp.

5. Give the children a list of countries and ask them to find the local names for those countries using atlases.

Variations

- The list can be shorter or longer depending on the age and abilities of the pupils so, for example, the choices of countries can be made simpler or a list of countries provided.
- Atlases can be used as appropriate.

Ordnance Survey Symbols

The expectation is that children will be able to recognise and use Ordnance Survey symbols at the end of KS2. This activity helps to develop their understanding of those symbols.

Suitable for

KS2

Aim

* To recognise and use Ordnance Survey symbols.

Resources

* List of Ordnance Survey symbols and what they represent

Road	Bridge	B Road	Church
Church with spire	Church with tower	Footpath	Motorway
Minor road	Post office	Public house	Railway
River	School	Minor road	Station
Wood – Evergreen	Wood – mixed	Wood – deciduous	

* Pictures linked to those symbols for matching activities

* Symbols reproduced with kind permission from Ordnance Survey

What to do

1. Give the children a set of pictures representing the symbols.
2. Ask them to match a numbered/lettered image with an Ordnance Survey symbol.

Variation

- Give the children the Ordnance Survey symbols only, no annotation. Can they match up the symbols and the pictures?

Paper Tree

One aspect of primary geography is the link with environmental issues that affect the children, both in school and in the wider world. One way to help them to understand some of these issues is for them to monitor the waste produced in school.

Suitable for

KS1

Aim

- To help children understand some of the issues related to waste.

Resources

- Images of trees and paper being made
- Several large tree shapes cut out and laid on the classroom floor
- Waste paper to be collected from around the school
- Glue and scissors

What to do

1. Explain to the children how paper is made from trees. (If available, show a film clip or similar.)
2. Send the children to collect waste paper from around the school.
3. Stick the waste paper onto the tree templates.
4. How many trees can be made out of the waste?
5. Simple mathematics can be carried out to see how many trees can be made in a week, month.
6. Make the link between trees and ways of protecting the environment e.g. replanting and paper recycling.

Variations

- A paper trail can be carried out around the school, the children collecting data on the different types of paper used in school.

Picture Sorting

Picture sorting is an activity that helps younger children learn to identify different sorts of environments.

Suitable for

KS1, KS2

Aims

- This activity helps introduce pupils to the concept of human and natural environments.
- It helps develop a geographical vocabulary based on the environments concerned.

Resources

- Calendar pictures or ones of a variety of environments, such as the seaside, countryside, urban environments and so on.

What to do

1. Give a group of children a set of pictures and ask them to sort them into sets using agreed criteria.
2. They discuss their choices and determine which are correct.

Variations

- Give the children a set of pictures to sort according to their own criteria.

Putting Yourself in the Picture

Putting themselves into an image is a way for pupils to engage with a picture as you can ask them to imagine what they might see, smell and hear within that context and make simple judgements.

Suitable for

KS1, KS2

Aim

- To get children to look at images from different perspectives.

Resources

- Blank silhouette or pupil photograph that can be cut out and pasted onto a picture
- A range of images from calendars, magazines and so on

What to do

1. Give the children an image.
2. Ask them to stick the picture or silhouette of themselves on their pictures.
3. Ask them to imagine that they are in that picture – what might they see, hear and so on?
4. If the picture shows other people ask the children to think what those people might be saying, what they would ask them?
5. Ask them what they might be able to see beyond the confines of the image they are in.

Variation

- The children could add speech or thought bubbles to the picture to express what they or other figures in the picture might be thinking or saying.

Raid the Cupboard

Collecting data about where foods come from helps children to consider environmental and sustainability questions. By gathering evidence themselves, they develop enquiry skills and the data collected can be considered in a number of ways, including looking at climatic areas, measuring distances and making judgements about fairness and equality.

Suitable for

KS2

Aims

- To help children understand concepts such as fair trade, food miles and sustainability.
- As this activity requires an enquiry to be carried out at home, it can be used as a homework investigation.

Resources

- Data sheet for activity (see example on page 68)

What to do

1. Give the children a recording sheet as a homework activity.
2. The children bring the completed data sheet back to school.
3. They use the Internet, globes and atlases to locate places of origin
4. Follow-up work can focus on activities such as production methods, fair trade and food miles.

Raid the cupboard

1. Look at the labels on food in your cupboards, fridge and freezer.
2. Which different countries do the foods come from?

Name of the food	Country of origin

3. Can you mark these countries on a map of the world?

Variations

- The purpose of this homework is to prepare pupils for a class discussion about why certain foods are grown in certain countries. The children can consider the climates of those countries in relation to where they are on a world map.
- The issue of food miles can be addressed by measuring distances from locations to the UK. Which has to be transported the shortest distance?
- Fairness and sustainability. Why are those foods not grown here? Why is that? Are there alternatives?

Sense Cards

This activity is a way to introduce pupils to elementary fieldwork skills. It can be adapted in a variety of ways to help pupils develop some basic skills.

Suitable for

KS1, KS2

Aims

- To introduce pupils to simple aspects of fieldwork.
- To work within the school grounds.

Resources

- A set of cards that pairs of pupils can take turns to select (see example on page 70).
- A route in and/or around the school with fixed stopping points, such as cones, flags or markers.

What to do

1. Tell pupils that they will follow a designated route, in pairs.

2. At each stopping point, they are to select a card and follow the instruction (see example).

3. They alternate activities, where necessary explaining their answers to their partner, such as what they can see, smell and so on.

4. The route leads them back to the classroom/starting point.

Example
sense cards

Look up What can you see?	**Ask a question** Ask your partner a question about this place.
Look down What can you see?	**Draw a picture** Draw your view.
Smell What can you smell?	**Look closely** What can you see?
Listen What can you hear?	**Count** Ask a question that begins 'How many ...?'
Feel What can you feel?	**Symbol** Find and draw a symbol
Measure Use hands or feet to measure a feature.	**Take a photograph**

Variations

- Younger pupils could follow a route with a designated helper, such as a classroom assistant or an older pupil.
- Answers can initially be verbal, drawn or photographed.
- Older pupils can write down their answers, follow a plan or map of the route and other such extension activities.
- As pupil knowledge increases so specific skills can be developed, such as looking from left to right to looking from north or south.
- The cards can be made as simple or as challenging as required.

Should We Keep the Village Shop Open?

This enquiry activity is aimed at children looking at issues from perspectives different from their own and making judgements based on the evidence and using reasoning skills.

Suitable for

KS2

Aim

- To develop children's understanding of issues relating to the environment and sustainability.

Resources

- Copies of sheet setting out evidence of factors related to a particular issue (see example on page 72)

What to do

1. Set out the scenario.
2. Ask the children to look at the issues at hand and, after discussion with a partner, to make positive (P) and negative (N) judgements about the different factors that affect the shop's viability.
3. Then ask them to make a decision based on the evidence, giving a reason or reasons for that judgement.

Should we keep the village shop open?

Mr and Mrs Ready keep a shop in a village five miles from .... Mr
Ready is 60 and Mrs Ready is 62 and has arthritis. Mr Ready worked out
that the shop only made a small weekly profit in the last year.

   The table shows a number of issues regarding the running of the shop.
Discuss with your partner which are negative (N) reasons for running the
shop and which are positive (P) reasons for running the shop.

The council has put double yellow lines outside the shop.	Most of the old people in the village get their pensions from the Post Office.
Car ownership in the village is high, but 25 per cent of households don't own a car.	The village hall has a large car park only 70 metres from the shop.
The shop started doing Sunday papers 6 months ago.	The village school has only 78 pupils.
The garage on the main road half a mile away has plans to stock basic grocery items – bread, milk, etc.	The bus service to the nearest town has been cut from one a day to two a week.
There is a voluntary prescription service run through the village shop.	Prices are 20 per cent cheaper in the superstores in town.

Decide whether it would be best to:

Choices	Tick box
Close the village shop	
Keep the village shop open	
Other	

Give a reason or reasons for your decision.

Variation

• This activity can be replicated using a variety of scenarios with different issues so that pupils learn to study evidence before making conclusions.

Slope and Gradient Fieldwork

This activity helps children to apply mathematical concepts to answering fieldwork questions. They can do this in ways that range from simple estimation to accurate measurement to find the answers to questions such as 'Which is the tallest?' and 'How tall is it?'

Suitable for

KS1, KS2

Aims

- To develop fieldwork and enquiry skills around the school grounds.
- To link mathematical skills with geographical enquiry.

Resources

- Pencils
- Metre ruler
- Clinometer
- Measuring tape

What to do

1. Estimate a height by using a known measure, such as a fellow pupil, metre ruler and so on.

2. Estimate using a fixed measure, such as a metre ruler against a wall or tree, and, from a given distance, matching a pencil against it, so the height of an object is seven pencils which equals 7 metres.

3. For older pupils, from a given distance have them measure the distance, to an object with a measuring tape. From the same distance, ask them to work out the angle to the topmost point of the object, draw to scale and then work out the vertical height of the object.

Variations

- Start with visual comparison – taller, smaller and so on.
- Develop from simple concepts, gradually increasing the range of skills the children have.

Snakes and Ladders

This is a traditional board game that can be linked to environmental and sustainability issues.

Suitable for

KS2

Aim

- For children to design a game of snakes and ladders with consequences linked to an environmental issue.

Resources

- Snakes and ladders board format
- Ideas linked to particular environmental and sustainability issues

What to do

1. Discuss with the children particular environmental issues, such as recycling.
2. Ask them to put positive statements on the board that will move them up the ladders, such as 'The council recycles plastic'.
3. Then have them put in negative statements that will move them down the snakes, such as 'Fly tipping is waste is dumped on the roadside'.
4. The children can then play the games that they have produced.

Variation

- The children can stick or draw their own snakes and ladders on a hundred number square (see example below).

Finish	99	98	97	96	95	94	93	92	91
81	82	83	84	85	86	87	88	89	90
80	79	78	77	76	75	74	73	72	71
61	62	63	64	65	66	67	68	69	70
60	59	58	57	56	55	54	53	52	51
41	42	43	44	45	46	47	48	49	50
40	39	38	37	36	35	34	33	32	31
21	22	23	24	25	26	27	28	29	30
20	19	18	17	16	15	14	13	12	11
Start	2	3	4	5	6	7	8	9	10

Speech and Thought Bubbles

Using speech and thought bubbles can help children to make simple judgements about people and places around the world. It allows them to consider what the thoughts and feelings of others might be in particular situations and helps develop a concept of global awareness in them.

Suitable for

KS1, KS2

Aim

- To help children understand the universal nature of human interaction.

Resources

- Whiteboard, digital projector
- Copies of the chosen image
- Templates of thought and speech bubbles for children to stick or draw on the image

What to do

1. Give each of the children a copy of the chosen image, linked to a topic being studied.

2. Ask them to look at the picture for a few minutes, considering the context of the picture and the people in it.

3. Add a speech or thought bubble to one of the people in the image.

4. Project the image onto the whiteboard

5. Ask the children to choose a person in their image and write down what they might be saying or thinking.

6. The children gradually build up a picture of the scene through what they believe is being said or thought.

Variation

- The activity can be modifed by asking the children to add several speech or thought bubbles to the people in the image rather than just one.

Ten Green Bottles

This is an activity focused on environmental and sustainability issues that asks children to consider some of the environmental implications of recycling, linking them to mathematics.

Suitable for

KS2

Aim

● Children are asked to consider recycling and the use of energy.

Resources

● Information required: recycling 1 bottle saves enough energy to:
  − run a washing machine for 10 minutes
  − power a TV for 15 minutes
  − power a lightbulb for 1 hour
  − run a computer for 3 hours

What to do

1. Give the children the information above and ask them to work out some problems. For example:

Question

If you recycled 10 bottles, you would save enough energy to run each appliance for how long?

Answer

Washing machine = 1 hour 40 minutes

TV set = 2 hours 30 minutes

Lightbulb =10 hours

Computer = 30 hours

2. The children could then be asked to evaluate what energy savings they could make in their own homes.

Variation

• This activity can be broadened, linking saving energy in the home to saving energy in schools, such as by turning off lights and closing doors, and further, to the Eco-Schools programme.

The Eight Points of the Compass

Knowing how to use a compass is an important mapping skill. This activity helps children move on from the cardinal points, adding to their understanding by learning the eight points of the compass.

Suitable for

KS2

Aim

- To develop children's understanding of compass directions.

Resources

- A large compass rose, laid out on the classroom floor or drawn on the playground
- Card compasses with the cardinal points and the other four present (see page 83)
- Location sheet (see example on page 83)

What to do

1. Start by asking the children to mark the cardinal points on the card compass as set out on the floor or playground.

2. Ask the children to orientate the compasses to point north and discuss what can be seen to the east, south, west and so on.

3. Then ask them how we can find something that lies in a direction between those points.

4. Introduce the other points, which the children then mark on their compasses.

5. They then use their location sheets to record what they see in all eight different directions.

Location sheet

The viewpoint is located at ....

North-west	North	North-east
West	N W—E S	East
South-west	South	South-east

The most distant thing I can see is ....

Variations

- This activity can be extended by using card compasses that are orientated to point north first, then in the other directions.
- By using *real* compasses, children can find north and the other compass points in any location rather than having to refer back to a fixed point.

The Local Area

Recording personal geographies helps children to validate their experiences. With younger children, this is initially based on their local area. The activity can also be used as a simple approach to carrying out an enquiry or data collection.

Suitable for

KS1

Aim

- To get children to audit their feelings about their local area.

Resources

- Images of the school and local area
- Whiteboard and digital projector

What to do

1. Show the children a range of images of their local area, including buildings, shops, playgrounds and so on.

2. For each image, ask for a show of hands as to whether they like or dislike that place.

3. The children can then be asked to explain their opinions and justify their choices through discussion and so on.

4. The most popular and least popular areas can be identified and simple graphing activities could be carried out to record the children's responses to the different locations.

Variation

- As a way of auditing opinions, pairs or groups of children can be given sets of traffic lights (red, amber and green card discs). For each image, they have to agree a collective opinion and show a red or green card. Split opinions can be shown as amber.

The World as a Village

This activity provides data for children at a level that is accessible and allows them to raise initial questions and judgements about global issues.

Suitable for

KS2

Aim

- To develop children's global awareness and debate ideas related to fairness and sustainability.

Resources

- Data in a format similar to that shown below
- A data collection sheet that allows children to ask enquiring questions, such as 'Do most people in the world go to university?' and 'Which part of the world is Oceania?'

The global village

If we could shrink the earth's population to a village of precisely 100 people, but keep all the existing human ratios the same, there would be:

- 60 Asians
- 12 Europeans
- 15 from the Western hemisphere (9 Latin Americans, 5 North Americans and 1 Oceanian)
- 13 Africans
- 50 would be female
- 50 would be male
- 80 would be non-white
- 20 would be white

- 67 would be non-Christian
- 33 would be Christian
- 20 people would earn 89 per cent of the entire world's wealth
- 25 would live in substandard housing
- 17 would be unable to read
- 13 would suffer from malnutrition
- 1 would die within the year
- 2 would give birth within the year
- 2 would have a university education
- 4 would own a computer.

(From Balu, Engelken and Grosso, 1997)

What to do

1. Look at the data with the children.

2. Ask them to fill in the data collection sheet and ask questions about what they have found.

3. Collectively, try to answer some of the questions raised.

4. Decide if there are ways in which some of the inequalities could be ameliorated.

5. Ask the children to draw and label the global village scenario they would *like* to see.

Variation

- This activity could link with personal, social and health education and citizenship (PSHE and C) and raise questions about fairness, right and wrong and so on.

Tourism in Antarctica

In this activity, the children are asked to consider the implications of allowing people to visit remote parts of the world.

Suitable for

KS2

Aims

- To enhance children's awareness and concern for the Antarctic environment.
- To consider the impacts of visitors and promote sustainable tourism in Antarctica.

Resources

- Images of the Antarctic
- Background information on Antarctica, including examples of visitor numbers and methods of travel (see page 89)
- Information on Antarctic wildlife, such as seals, penguins and so on.
- Formats for 'Guidance for visitors' pamphlet.

What to do

1. Discuss the Antarctic region with the children, looking at the images and finding out about the location, climate and wildlife.

2. Look at the example itinerary from the British Antarctic Survey and discuss the possible environmental issues created by tourism.

3. Ask the children to create a 'Guidance for visitors' pamphlet, including information on the region for tourists but also suggesting ways in which any impacts of tourism on the region can be minimised. For example:

   - leave no litter
   - do not damage any habitats
   - avoid frightening wild creatures, etc.

Itinerary for Antarctic cruise

Many people visiting Antarctica on cruise ships are interested in the wildlife and scenery. A typical itinerary for an eight-day cruise is:

- *day 1*: depart Ushuaia, Argentina
- *day 2*: at sea, crossing Drake's Passage
- *day 3*: at sea, first land (such as Elephant Island)
- *day 4*: visit South Shetland Islands, land using 'Zodiac' inflatable boats, see seals and birds, visit to Arktowski (Polish Station)
- *day 5*: Deception Island, to see relics of whaling industry, penguin colonies and volcanic landscape
- *day 6*: continue south, visiting the Antarctic Peninsula to set foot on the mainland and cross the Antarctic Circle
- *day 7*: at sea, cross Drake's Passage
- *day 8*: return to Ushuaia.

(British Antarctic Survey)

Variations

- The activity can be approached in a cross-curricular way, linking art and science with geography.
- The same approach could be adopted for other remote areas. The children could produce guidance materials for places such as the Himalayas or the Sahara desert.

Using Writing Frames

As with other subjects, writing frames are a useful way to help children identify and structure their ideas on a particular topic.

Suitable for

KS1, KS2

Aim

- To help structure geographical investigations.

Resources

- Writing frame related to a particular geographical activity (see the fieldwork example below)

Writing frame for geography fieldwork

The geographical feature I observed was ...

I did this as part of my work on ...

The equipment I found really useful was ...

The most interesting thing I learned was ...

I think this because ...

My observations will help me to ...

What to do

1. Provide the children with the chosen writing frame.
2. Increase or decrease the number of framed questions depending on the age and abilities of the pupils.
3. Use the frame to help the children structure their learning.

Using Your Senses

This activity is about using the senses to explore a particular environment. It can be developed through literacy, art and music links.

Suitable for

KS1, KS2

Aim

- To get children to make links between colour, images and sounds related to a particular environment.

Resources

- Images
- Colour filters
- Simple percussion and wind instruments

What to do

1. Use a colour background on whiteboard or place a filter (tissue paper or similar) over lights to reflect the nature of the images shown – Arctic blue, desert yellow, for example.

2. Show images of a particular environment and ask the children to use simple percussion and wind instruments to try and reflect the elements – cold, wind, snow and so on.

3. Work can be developed through descriptive writing, poetry art and so on.

Variations

- Add written descriptions for older children so that they can build up a geographical glossary.
- Children can make their own simple instruments – such as shakers – to make environmental sounds.

Weather and Climate Data Activity

Weather and climate are always topical, from day-to-day weather activity to longer-term climate patterns. Children can use weather data websites to investigate daily weather events in order to build up a wider geographical understanding of regional variations and some of the reasons for these variations.

Suitable for

KS2

Aim

- To use climate data to develop a wider geographical understanding

Resources

- Data sheets (see example on page 95)
- Access to weather data websites (see examples listed on page 95)
- Maps and atlases

Example data sheet

Location (country/area)	City	Today's weather
Canada	Vancouver	Rainy, cold
Jamaica	Kingston	Sunny, hot
Australia	Sydney	Sunny, hot
Panama	Panama City	Sunny, hot
Israel	Tel Aviv	Sunny, hot
USA	New York	Sunny, mild
Singapore	Singapore	Thundery, hot
Argentina	Buenos Aires	Sunny, hot
Russia	Moscow	Cloudy, cold
China	Beijing	Sunny, mild
Mexico	Mexico City	Sunny, hot
South Africa	Cape Town	Sunny, hot
Germany	Berlin	Rainy, cold

Weather data websites

- **Atmosphere, Climate and Environment Information Programme**
  www.ace.mmu.ac.uk
  Games, information sheets and activities.
- **DEFRA Climate Challenge Resources**
  www.defra.gov.uk/environment/climatechange
  Information, data and climate change links.
- **Collecting Weather Data**
  www.metoffice.gov.uk
  Links to weather data around the world, including daily forecasts.

What to do

1. Give the children a weather data sheet with your chosen locations.
2. Ask them to use a website to collect daily weather information.
3. Compare the results with local weather patterns. Ask the children to look for and explain any patterns and reasons for the weather in particular locations.
4. Use topographical maps and atlases to identify some reasons for overall weather patterns, such as different hemispheres, location and so on.

Variations

- Aspects of the data sheets can be left blank for the children to research and complete.

Example data sheet

Location (country/area)	City	Today's weather
	Vancouver	Rainy, cold
	Kingston	Sunny, hot
	Sydney	Sunny, hot
	Panama City	Sunny, hot
	Tel Aviv	Sunny, hot
	New York	Sunny, mild
	Singapore	Thundery, hot
	Buenos Aires	Sunny, hot
	Moscow	Cloudy, cold
	Beijing	Sunny, mild
	Mexico City	Sunny, hot
	Cape Town	Sunny, hot
	Berlin	Rainy, cold

- The children can compare the weather for locations in similar parts of the world.

What's in the News?

Despite being surrounded by a range of information technology, many children have a limited understanding of the wider world. Using news links can help children to understand more about people and places, as well as develop their geographical skills. It can also highlight weather, climate and physical processes.

Suitable for

KS2

Aims

- To develop geographical skills, including the use of maps and atlases.
- Link geography to literacy and other subjects.

Resources

- Access to news channels suitable for children (see list below)

News websites

- **BBC News**
  All the latest news and weather from the BBC.
  http://www.news.bbc.co.uk/ (BBC News home page)
- *BBC Children's Newsround*
  http://news.bbc.co.uk/cbbcnews/default.stm

This site provides news, sport and entertainment information pegged at a child's level. It includes film clips and photographs as well as text.

What to do

1. Ask the children to look at appropriate media materials for current events.
2. Use atlases, maps and IT links such as Google Earth to locate particular places.
3. Ask enquiry-type questions (who, what where, when, how) linked to the news events chosen.
4. Create a report based on the information gathered. The report may include maps with symbols and keys and suggestions for help or solutions depending on the event being investigated.

Variations

- Children can investigate news items individually or collectively.
- Natural disasters such as floods, forest fires, earthquakes and so on, which often make the headlines, can be used as starting points for investigations and collecting data on particular areas such as volcanic regions, or developed as technology-related activities – making earthquake shelters, for example.

Where in the World?

This activity can be used in a number of ways to help children develop their knowledge of the world through board games. The approach can be varied, from being based on a simple map to Ordnance Survey maps, as required.

Suitable for

KS1, KS2

Aim

- To use a board game scenario to develop geographical knowledge.

Resources

- A board game template (see example below)
- Cards (see steps 2 and below) and dice or spinners

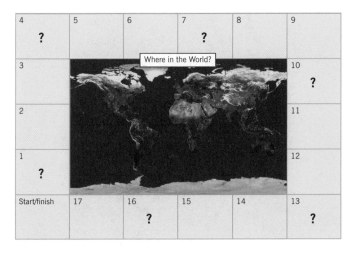

What to do

1. Introduce the board game template and the world map and tell the children that the game involves finding out about places around the world.

2. Either the children or the teacher prepare question cards with appropriate penalties and rewards for correct or incorrect answers based on the map. The answers can be in the form of true/false, multiple choice and so on as required.

3. The children then use the dice or spinners to play the game.

4. When they land on a chance card, their partner has to read the question and give the correct answer. For example, 'Is Greenland north or south of the Tropic of Cancer?'

Variations

- The children can draw and label their own boards.
- The board game can be linked to atlas work, such as identifying the latitudes and longitudes of places.

Where Would You Like to Go?

This is an idea for a time filler that helps children to develop map-drawing skills and improve their use of atlases.

Suitable for

KS2

Aim

● To develop map-drawing skills and the use of atlases.

Resources

● Appropriate atlas sets
● Suitable textbooks
● Internet access

What to do

1. Hand out an atlas per pair of children and ask them to draw a detailed map of a country that they would love to visit. Ask them to locate the country's capital city and record any important features.
2. Using the Internet, textbooks and so on, the children build up a data file about their particular place.

Variation

● The information found can be collected together and displayed appropriately.

Word Mats

The aim of this activity is for the children to build up information about a geographical theme, linking geography to language skills.

Suitable for

KS2

Aim

- To build up a collection of information related to a particular geographical theme.

Resources

- Internet access or images of geographical themes, such as rainforests, mountains, coastal features
- Copies of the format for the word mat (see example on page 103)

What to do

1. Depending on the topic being studied, have the children collect information on the given subject or subjects.
2. Give the children a word mat format each and ask them to collect information including images, descriptive words and geographical terms.
3. The children list their information in the correct boxes.
4. They can compare their information with others.

The tropical rainforest word mat

Adjectives

crawling

dappled shade

dark

dense

destroyed

disrupted

equatorial

eroded

extinct

flooded

humid

intense

interconnected

littered

nutrient-poor

parasitic

rapid

regenerated

remote

secondary

shrinking

straight

sunlight

sustainable

sweltering

symbiotic

tall

tropical

unsustainable

vast

Key regions with tropical rainforests

Amazon Basin

Central America

Central and West Africa

NE Australia

SE Asia/Indonesian Islands

Key countries with tropical rainforests

Brazil

Cameroon

Colombia

Costa Rica

Democratic Republic of Congo

Indonesia

Malaysia

Peru

Thailand

Venezuela

Eco and geographical terms

canopy

conservation

decompose

deforestation

ecosystem

epiphytes

food web

hunter-gatherer

leaf litter

photosynthesis

slash and burn

sustainable development

understorey

Source: This word mat format was initially produced by **www.sln.org.uk/geography**

Variation

- When word mats have been completed, they can be laminated and used as a resource for future activities.

Chapter 2
History

Chronology
Enquiry
Interpretation
Knowledge and understanding
Sources
Other history activities

Introduction

History in the National Curriculum

Knowledge and understanding of events, people and changes in the past, including characteristic features of periods and societies.

Chronological understanding, including use of dates, words and phrases related to the passing of time.

Enquiry skills – finding out about the past from a range of different sources of information. Asking and answering questions, selecting and recording information.

What is history?

Interpretation of different ways in which the past can be represented (and reasons for this at KS2).

Being able to organise and communicate what has been learned in a variety of ways, including narrative and descriptions.

What is history in primary schools?

Knowledge, skills and understanding

The key skills – chronological understanding, knowledge and understanding of events, people and changes, interpretations of history, historical enquiry and the organisation and communication of knowledge – form the focus of primary history. They provide a good description of what 'doing history' in the primary schools entails.

Underlying concepts

Within the KSU are eight underlying concepts that are central to history:

- time
- historical situations/events and characteristics (a sense of period)
- continuity
- change
- cause
- consequences/results
- interpretations/points of view
- historical evidence.

Doing history

This involves:

- learning and understanding historical vocabulary, including concepts that help us to make sense of institutions, ideas or periods of time
- understanding historical people, situations and events, their diversity and complexity and identifying reasons, results and changes
- asking and answering questions – questioning is the key to doing history (key question words are when, where, how, what, who, why)
- investigating sources
- making connections
- recalling, selecting, recording and organising information
- giving reasons for different points of view
- communicating knowledge and understanding gained in a variety of ways.

This should lead children to:

- explore the different ways in which we can find out about the past and how to understand the evidence
- find out how significant events, developments or individuals in the recent and distant past have influenced their locality and/or wider areas of the United Kingdom and beyond
- learn about the movement and settlement of people in different periods of British history and the impact these have had
- the effects of economic, technological and scientific developments on the United Kingdom and the wider world over time
- understand a broad chronology of major events in the United Kingdom and the wider world from the periods, events and changes that they have studied.

Chronology

Boudicca's Revolt - A Chronology

The idea of this activity is to develop children's understanding of chronology by ordering events using dates. The activity covers a range of time concepts, from months to years, and includes the term AD.

Suitable for

KS1, KS2

Aim

- To develop an understanding of chronology of events within a wider time frame.

Resources

- Chronology of Roman invasions of Britain, 55BC–AD43
- The story of Boudicca's revolt against the Romans organised within a timeframe (see below)

Boudicca's revolt

AD59

Suetonius Paulinus, who was a very clever Roman general, became the Governor (most important leader) of Britain.

JANUARY AD60

Suetonius Paulinus attacked and killed the Druids. These were holy men in Britain, a bit like bishops are today. The Druids lived on the island of Anglesey in Wales. The Romans burnt down the places where they held all their holy meetings.

FEBRUARY AD60

The king of the Iceni tribe died. The king's wife, Boudicca, became queen.

March AD60

The Roman soldiers took all Boudicca's money. They hit Boudicca and her daughters.

April AD60

The Roman soldiers took away all Boudicca's land.

Boudicca and the people in her tribe rebelled. They killed every Roman they could find.

Other British tribes, such as the Catuvellauni and the Trinovantes, joined in the rebellion.

May AD60

Boudicca and her friends from the other tribes burned down the Roman city of Colchester. All the men, women and children who lived there were killed by the Britons.

After burning down Colchester, Boudicca and her army marched to London. This was also burned to the ground. Thousands and thousands of people were killed.

June AD60

Boudicca now had an army of 100,000 people. The Roman general Suetonius Paulinus only had 10,000 men.

July AD60

Suetonius Paulinus marched down from Wales to a place called Mancetter. He was going to fight the Britons, even though they had so many people in their army.

The Romans fought so bravely and used such clever tactics that they killed all the Britons.

Boudicca was so ashamed of losing to the Romans that she drank poison and died.

What to do

1. Look at the chronology of the Roman invasions of Britain from 55BC to AD43 and the events leading up to Boudicca's revolt in AD60.

2. Give the children the story of the revolt cut up into strips. Have them organise the story of the revolt into the right order using the dates as a guide.

3. When they have completed this task, they can copy out the information or stick the strips down to tell the story.

Variation

- The chronology of the Romans can be matched up with their occupation of Britain and Boudicca's revolt then fitted within this time frame to allow children to consider the place of particular events within a wider chronological context.

Human Timeline

Human timelines are a useful way to help children organise and understand the concept of chronology. The variations allow fellow pupils to make judgements about the passing of time and the vocabulary linked to it.

Suitable for

KS1, KS2

Aim

- To help children develop their understanding of chronology.

Resources

- Cards labelled as appropriate – last week, 1939, 500 years ago, 52BC, AD1485 and so on

What to do

1. Have a group of children stand in a line at the front, holding up a series of cards with various dates on them so the rest of the class can see.
2. Ask the class to reorder the children so that they are in the correct chronological order.
3. When everyone is happy with the order, check it and correct any mistakes, explaining why they need to move.

Variation

- Ordering activities can be differentiated by having cards with just events or events and dates. The period of time can be simple, e.g. a few years – or complex – mixing AD, BC or going back thousands of years.

Ordering a Story

Putting parts of a story in the right order helps children to develop the concept of chronology, using words such as first, before, after, next, final and so on.

Suitable for

KS1

Aim

- To put a story in the correct chronological sequence, using dates and personal and world events.

Resources

- Simple outline of a story that can be cut up and reordered (see example below)

Mary Seacole's story

Mary Seacole was born in 1805.
She grew up in Kingston, Jamaica.

As a child, Mary learned about nursing from her mother.

In 1854, Mary heard about the Crimean War being fought in Europe.

In 1854, Mary sailed to England, then to the Crimea, which was in Turkey.

No one wanted her help so she opened the 'British Hotel' near where the fighting was fiercest. Mary fed and nursed tired and sick soldiers until the war ended in 1856.

Mary became famous for her work with the sick and wounded. When she wrote her life story, it became a bestseller.

Mary died in 1881.

What to do

1. Tell the story of a famous historical character (such as Mary Seacole).
2. After telling the story, give the children the outline, cut up into strips.
3. Have the children reorder the story, putting the strips into the correct chronological sequence.

Variations

- This activity can be differentiated in a number of ways:
    - the story can be put into order as a collective, whole-class activity
    - the parts of the story can be written out in order, using the cards as cues
    - the cards can be numbered to form the correct sequence.

Chronology Counter

This activity focuses on chronology, but moves away from linear approaches to help children make links between dates, events, people and eras.

Suitable for

KS2

Aim

* To develop a chronological vocabulary and a sense of period.

Resources

* A number of circles decreasing in size, cut from card or paper, fixed centrally with a mapping pin

What to do

1. Segment the circles so that the arcs link together
2. On the outer circle, mark appropriate dates, such as 1485–1603, in 15-year divisions.
3. In the second circle, put a list of appropriate people, such as Henry VIII, Elizabeth I and so on.
4. Around the central circle, write the names of important events, such as the Reformation, Spanish Armada and so on.
5. When the circles are rotated, the segments on all three circles should correlate correctly, giving three details about an event.

Variations

- By decreasing or increasing the number of circles the activity can be made simpler or more difficult.
- Making the divisions on each circle smaller will allow for more information to be included, increasing the level of difficulty as more pieces then need to fit together.

Revamping the Timeline

Understanding by means of timelines is a chronological activity, the aim of which is to to add to children's understanding of the passing of time and the links between people and periods of history.

Suitable for

KS2

Aim

- To develop children's understanding of chronology.

Resources

- Timeline, demarcated in decades and centuries
- Information cards about people in the past with dates and other details.

What to do

- When making up the timeline, colour the demarcations for the centuries.
- Point out that a person may live through one line, but two would be very unusual and three impossible!
- Give the children the cards with the information on them about people from the past. Have them place them on the timeline and look for connections and impossibilities. Would Queen Victoria have known Henry VIII, for example?
- The card ordering activity can be done with century/decade cards with famous figures. Use AD or BC whenever possible.

Variations

- The children can be given information and pictures about people, events and aspects of the period.

- A timeline can be laid on sugar paper on the floor and the children can lay their pieces of information around the timeline. This can be followed by discussion about what the appropriate placements are until all are agreed.

- The information can then be glued down and the timeline can be fixed to the wall as a display.

Extending the Timeline

> The aim of this activity is for children to make links between the dates people, and events within a particular era in order to help them develop a sense of period.

Suitable for

KS1, KS2

Aim

- To develop a sense of period via a chronological activity.

Resources

- Large timeline related to a particular event or era the children have been studying.
- Pictures, text, dates of events and so on in that era.

What to do

1. Lay the timeline on the floor.
2. Group the children in pairs then give each a picture of a person or artefact and a date related to a person or event.
3. Ask them to discuss the item and lay it in what they believe to be the appropriate place on the timeline.
4. Gather the class around the timeline and discuss the various choices, making changes until everyone is happy, then stick the items down. The completed timeline can then be put on display.

Variations

- The completed, displayed timeline can be used for a research activity.
- For KS1, the activity can be linked to the life of a famous person or the chronology of an event, such as the Great Fire of London.
- Less or more information can be given so that, for example, for gifted and talented pupils, the information given can be limited so that they can call on their prior knowledge or the ability to research and find the information needed to locate the items on the timeline.

Something About ...

> Having or lacking a sense of period is a useful way to ascertain pupils' understanding at the end of a topic or unit, so can be used as the basis of a simple assessment task.

Suitable for

KS2

Aim

- To ascertain children's knowledge and perceptions of an era or period of history.

Resources

- 'Something about ...' sheets (see completed example on page 121) – with several boxes around a central one with the name of a period or dates for an era in it

What to do

1. Provide the children with the 'Something about ...' sheets.
2. Ask the children to make several links with the period, writing a date, the name of an event, a person or a discovery per box up to a designated number.
3. See the completed example below.

Variations

- The number of boxes can be increased or decreased to differentiate for the various abilities in a class.
- As the children progress, the boxes can ask for specific information, such as 'What date did … period begin and end?', 'Which famous people lived then?'

Something about....

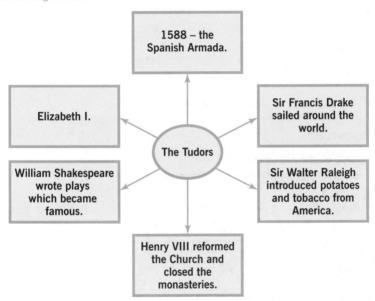

Time Machine Hats

A craft activity that is aimed at helping children to link chronology with knowledge and understanding in history.

Suitable for

KS1, KS2

Aim

- To link chronology with a sense of period.

Resources

- Card, plastic and other found materials
- Dates, period/era labels, names, historical events
- Scissors
- Glue

What to do

1. As part of studying a period in history, the children can create these hats as a way to help them link all the pieces of information together in the right chronological order.

2. They decorate their hats with labels linked to dates, people and events in history.

3. When these are completed they can put on the hats and make appropriate machine noises to take them back to the past.

4. They return to the present in a similar way and report back about an aspect of the period they have visited.

Variations

- The time machine hats can be specific to a particular event. So, for example, for Bonfire Night, the labels might be Guy Fawkes, Robert Catesby, 1605, King James I, Parliament, Gunpowder Plot and so on.
- Alternatively, make them general: the nineteenth century, Victorians, AD1066, Tudors and so on.

Enquiry

Artefact Vocabulary

This is a mystery bag activity that can be is used to help children develop an artefact vocabulary, which links with the idea of artefacts as sources of information about the past.

Suitable for

KS1, KS2

Aim

- To develop a historical vocabulary linked to artefacts and the idea that they are sources of information.

Resources

- A bag to contain an artefact
- Artefacts that can be handled safely by children

What to do

1. Put an artefact in the mystery bag and ask the children to pass it around in a circle.
2. Ask each child to feel inside the bag, not looking in, and say one thing about the artefact – it is hard, metal, long, round and so on.
3. Each child can repeat the words other children have said, or pass.
4. When the bag has been round the circle or the activity is exhausted, show the artefact to the children.
5. Pass it around again and ask them for additional words to describe the object, including whether it is old or new, original or a replica and which era it might relate to.

Variations

- This activity can be supported by vocabulary lists, which the children can use to help them describe the artefacts. The lists can contain historical descriptors such as Victorian, Tudor and so on, or adjectives, such as those given below.

Old-fashioned	Falling to pieces	Delicate
Worn out	Fragile	Victorian
Valuable	Replica	Broken
Precious	Disintegrated	Unusual

- The activity can be used to introduce the enquiry-type words who, what, why, where, when and how.
- The teacher can model enquiring approaching asking questions such as the following.
  - Is it used indoors/outdoors?
  - Where in the home would it be?
  - Who used it?
  - Where was it kept?
  - How old is it?
  - Can you get one today?
  - Is it made by hand or machine?
  - Who did it belong to – man, woman, child, boy, girl?
  - Is it still used today?
  - What has replaced it?

Need to explain that there isn't always an absolute answer.

Branching Database for Artefacts

This is quite a formal method that can be used to help children consider questions about artefacts as historical sources.

Suitable for

KS1, KS2

Aim

- To develop children's ability to use artefacts as historical sources.

Resources

- Branching database for investigating artefacts (see example on page 127)
- Examples of contemporary and historical artefacts

What to do

1. Choose a contemporary artefact – a kitchen spoon, for example.
2. Present the children with a simple branching database and show them how to follow it, asking and answering yes/no questions.
3. They conclude by deciding what the artefact is.
4. Show the children an historical artefact that they may not recognise. Follow the same process.
5. With less information, can the children come to any conclusions about the artefact?

Variation

- To make the database more complicated additional boxes can be added at the end that ask for conjecture and judgements to be made.

Example of a branching database for artefacts

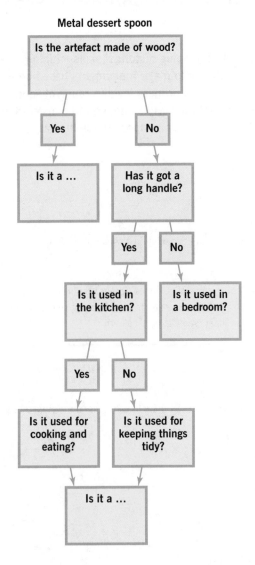

Metal dessert spoon

Is the artefact made of wood?

Yes — No

Is it a ...   Has it got a long handle?

Yes — No

Is it used in the kitchen?   Is it used in a bedroom?

Yes — No

Is it used for cooking and eating?   Is it used for keeping things tidy?

Is it a ...

Comparing and Contrasting Evidence

When developing historical skills, children need to have the opportunity to make judgements based on a range of evidence. At the primary level, a range of sources need to be available that are simple enough to be accessible for pupils so that they make can appropriate choices.

Suitable for

KS2

Aim

- To make judgements based on a range of evidence.

Resources

- A range of sources of evidence (images, information, comparisons and so on) in accessible formats linked to a topic being studied (see example below)
- Evidence sheet (see example below)

What was Henry VIII like?

A portrait of Henry VIII
Tick the boxes that you think fit with what the picture tells you about Henry.

Appearance	Tick here
Tall	
Short	
Weak	
Strong	
Rich	
Poor	
Expensive clothes	
Lots of jewellery	
Embroidered shoes	

Personality

A. Selfish	D. Merry	G. Greedy
B. Patriotic	E. Sporting	H. Learned
C. Cruel	F. Ruthless	I. Musical

Match each attribute above with one of the statements below.

1. Built up the army and navy.	4. Spoke several languages.	7. Became very fat as he grew older.
2. Composed several songs, including 'Greensleeves'.	5. Married six times, two wives beheaded.	8. Took part in hawking and hunting.
3. Had over 70000 people executed during his reign.	6. Loved singing and dancing.	9. As a young man, played many sports, including tennis.

Choices for recording systems
- matching colours shading one lettered and one numbered box to show pairs chosen.
- write out the chosen pairs of statements
- letter and number combinations, such as:

How would Henry VIII spend his time?
Was Henry VIII like you? How would he spend his time?

Would Henry do these things	Yes	No	Why would/wouldn't he?
Dress like you?			
Play soccer?			
Wash up?			
Make beds?			
Go to a banquet?			
Watch TV?			
Meet important people?			
Dance and sing?			
Make laws?			
Fly to France?			

What to do

1. Present the children with the chosen pieces of evidence.
2. Ask them to investigate them and make judgements on each one.
3. Finally, ask them to make an overall judgement – was Henry VIII a good or bad king, for example, the children can then record their answers on their evidence sheets, citing the evidence for their decisions.

Good king/bad king evidence sheet

Good	Bad	Not sure

Variations

- Link events with personality as a way to encourage children to compare and contrast the past and present and to develop an empathy with the past.
- Include anachronisms to check the children's understanding of the past.

Hieroglyphics

We know a lot about the ancient Egyptians from studies people have made of their script – called hieroglyphics. The understanding of hieroglyphic script was lost for 1500 years and not rediscovered until the Rosetta Stone was deciphered in the early nineteenth century.

Suitable for

KS2

Aim

- To develop the concept of the range of historical sources

Resources

- Table setting out examples of hieroglyphic script and their meaning (you can find these on the Internet (http://www.watson.org/~leigh/egypt.html#alpha)

What to do

1. Introduce the concept of pictures as writing.
2. Ask the children to draw images to tell something about themselves.
3. Explain that, in Ancient Egypt, picture writing was the main way in which events were recorded.
4. Show the children examples of hieroglyphics and ask them carry out the linked activities.

Variations

- Try asking the children to translate a message written in hieroglyphics.
- The children could try to produce their own coded message.

Identify Your Object

The reassembly of historical artefacts is a way in which archaeologists reconstruct and make judgements about life in the past. Giving children opportunities to develop work on artefacts can help them to understand archaeological skills and make links with activities such as museum visits and visits to sites of historical interest.

Suitable for

KS1, KS2

Aim

- To develop alternative ways to work with artefacts from the past.

Resources

- Plastic trays
- Inexpensive everyday items, broken or cut up in some way – wooden spoon, plastic clothes peg or patterned plate, for example
- Complete examples of the same items
- Recording sheet (see example on page 133)

What to do

1. Give either a group or individual children a plastic tray with a piece of your chosen object on it.
2. Ask them to look at the piece of the object and answer some questions about it, recording their answers on their recording sheets.
3. Then ask them to draw what they think the complete object looks like on their recording sheets.
4. Show them an example of the complete object so that they can compare their drawings with the real artefact.

Identify your object

Questions	Object 1
What colour is it?	
What does it feel like? Is it rough, smooth, etc.?	
What is it made from?	
What shape is it?	
Is it a piece of an object or the whole object?	
What do you think it was used for?	
I think this object is ...	
Is your object a copy or a real one?	

Look carefully at your piece of an object and draw what the complete object looks like in the box below.

Variations

- Cardboard images of artefacts – a Grecian urn, for example – copied and cut up for the children to reassemble and glue down.
- Leave out parts of the objects so that children have to draw what is missing, reconstructing patterns, shapes or images.

Putting Us in the Picture

This activity develops the use of visual source by means of a group activity.

Suitable for

KS2

Aims

- To develop the use of visual sources.
- To develop descriptive language skills.

Resources

- An image of a famous historical figure
- A3 sheets of paper, pencils, crayons, felt-tips

What to do

1. Divide the class into small groups of three or four children.
2. Ask them to nominate someone to draw and scribe.
3. The rest of the group take it in turns to move across to look at the chosen image. They come back and describe one aspect of the image to the nominated artist. So, for example, one person describes the head and face, one the body shape, one the clothing, the next the shoes, hat or any accessories and so on.
4. This process continues until the image is complete.

Variation

- Older children can draw and label the different aspects of the figure, including the colours, materials and so on. The completed picture can then be coloured.

Samuel Pepys' Diary Entries

The idea of keeping a diary is familiar to many children and schools often encourage them to note down events over a period of time – a week, say. This activity can be linked to the idea of diaries being used as historical sources.

Suitable for

KS1, KS2

Aim

- To look at diaries as historical sources – Samuel Pepys', for example.

Resources

- Entries from Pepys' diary that tell the story of the Great Fire of London

What to do

1. Give the children (read or put onto the whiteboard) the chosen diary entries relating to the Great Fire of London.
2. Ask them to use the entries to tell the story of the fire and its effects.
3. The entries can be used to look at the reactions of people – of Pepys himself, the Mayor of London and the King.
4. The entries can be acted out, with different groups bringing an entry to life.

Variation

- Simplify the entries, putting them into modern English in order to make them more accessible (see page 136).

Diary entries

Sunday 2 September 1666
The fire started in the night in a baker's shop in Pudding Lane. The baker and his family escaped over the roofs. The servant girl died because she was afraid of heights.

Monday 3 September 1666
The fire got bigger; the wind blew the flames along. Samuel Pepys went to see the King. The mayor tried to put the fire out, but he could not.

Tuesday 4 September 1666
The people threw their things out of the windows. They saved their babies and their gold. The people went on the boats on the River Thames. Hundreds of houses were burnt down.

Wednesday 5 September 1666
The fire was still spreading. The King, Charles II, sent for the Duke of York. The Duke ordered the army to blow up houses with gunpowder to make a firebreak and it worked.

Thursday 6 September 1666
The fire was out, but the ground was very hot. There was a lot of damage. Most of the people had left the city and camped in fields. The King and other wealthy people took food and other things to them.

- The children can write their own diary entries as if they were contemporary observers of the fire using a format similar to the example given below.

The Great Fire of London

Sunday	
Monday	
Tuesday	
Wednesday	
Thursday	

- Use the diary entries to find out information about the past and log it in a table (see the example below).

Samuel Pepys' diary 2 September 1666

So I made myself ready and walked all the way to the Tower and there I did see the houses at that end of the bridge all on fire.

So down, with my heart full of trouble, to the Lieutenant of the Tower, who tells me that it began in the king's baker's house in Pudding Lane, and that it has burned down St Magnus's Church and most part of Fish Street already.

Everyone trying to move their goods or fling them into the river or bring them to boats. Poor people stay in their houses until the fire touches them. Then they run into boats.

I saw the fire rage everyway and nobody trying to quench it, but instead to remove their goods. The wind mighty high.

Streets	Buildings	People	Interesting words

- Have the children put the diary entries in order as a exercise in chronology (see the examples of statements created from the facts given in Pepys' diary entries that could be used below).

The Great Fire of London

The fire starts in Pudding Lane, in the King's baker's house.

Most people try to save their things from the fire. They try to get away in boats.

The mayor cannot stop the fire. The people won't help him.

Samuel Pepys tells the King about the fire.

The Duke of York orders the army to blow up the houses with gunpowder.

The fire has stopped burning the houses, but the ground is still so hot it burns your feet.

Samuel Pepys sends his money and silver plates away in a cart to a safer part of London.

The fire comes to the bottom of Samuel Pepys' street, but luckily it stops there.

There are no buildings left along the edge of the river.

Using Images as Sources

The idea behind this activity is for children to look very carefully at an image, including its details and less significant features as well as the obvious focus of the image, so that they do not miss what might be very valuable historical information.

Suitable for

KS1, KS2

Aim

- To teach children to look carefully at historical images as a way of understanding why images are important sources in historical investigations.

Resources

- Interactive whiteboard
- Appropriate image

What to do

1. Tell the children that you are going to show them a picture for a few seconds and they need to look for one thing in the picture.
2. Show the picture on the whiteboard, then minimise it. Ask for responses, listing the features the children noticed.
3. Repeat, this time asking the children have to look for another item.
4. Repeat this process for as long as required.
5. Go back to the picture and focus on items that the children have noted to develop their understanding of the source image, looking at the buildings, clothing, activities and so on. Also, explore what the picture doesn't tell us.

Variations

- In the case of younger children, at first they can respond orally and the teacher can scribe to build up a list.
- Older children can compile their own lists then compare and contrast them with those of the other children in order to build up a master list.

Using Your Senses

This activity asks the children to investigate the content of historical images and use their senses to make judgements about them.

Suitable for

KS1, KS2

Aim

- To develop children's understanding of the information contained in a photograph or picture and link that to history.

Resources

- Appropriate historical images to project onto a whiteboard.

What to do

1. Divide the class into groups and ask the children to select a sense – sight, smell, hearing. Ask them to list what sights, smells, noises and so on they might associate with a given picture.

2. Have each group report to the class and their choices can be discussed, added to or adapted.

3. As the information is built up, start to link the children's knowledge of the period with what new information they have produced about the picture.

Variation

- What's outside the picture? Have the children apply the same method to the picture as above, but expand on it by thinking about what they might hear see, smell beyond the edges of the image.

Using Inventories

Inventories tell us about the possessions people had at a given time. Making comparisons between then and now is a useful way to help children understand some of the differences between various eras.

Suitable for

KS2

Aim

- For children to compare and contrast a period of time in history with their own using inventories.

Resources

- Copies of a household inventory from the past – from Tudor, Victorian or World War II times, for example (see Tudor example below).

Tudor household inventory

Item and number	Notes
One bedstead with the bedding, stools, chairs, cushions and other furniture	In the parlour
Coffers* containing pairs of sheets (17), linen cloths (6), three dozen table napkins, towels (6) or 'thereabought with other lynnen and suche stuffe'*	*Coffer =Wooden box or chest used to store household items, money, etc. *'thereabout with other linen and similar stuff' – Tudor spelling.
Other coffers (3)	
Caskets* (4)	*Casket = small chest
Candlesticks (6)	

'Pewter cuppes, trenchers and other necessaries for a buttery'	
Brass pots, pans, iron, trivet, spits, shovels and other furniture for the kitchen	
Sides of bacon and beef	
Certain spinning wheels, cheese presses and similar stuff in the bultyng house*	*Bultyng house' = a shed or outhouse used for sieving flour or meal.
Vessels in the bruyng* house, mylke* house with other stuff in ye store house and other outhouses	*bruyng = brewing *mylke = milk
A malt mill and other necessaries in the mill house	
Butter and cheese in the storehouse	
Salt fish in the fish house	
Hens, geese, capons,* ducks in their enclosures	*Capon = male chicken
A bell and nets for larking	
Necessary furniture for servants' beds	
A flock* bed and other furniture for more servants	*Flock = coarse wool
Furniture for two beds including bedposts and ropes for the inner chamber of the great chamber	
Item in the study, a presse* with his clothes, hats, caps and other clothes	*Presse = cupboard
Boots, spurs, sword, dagger and other riding apparel	
Certain law books and other books plus small items of little value	

What to do

1. Give the children the copies of your chosen inventory (modified or not) from the past.

2. Ask the children to look at the inventory. Can they recognise any items that are still in use today? Are there any things that we no longer recognise or use?

3. Ask the children to think of five items in each of the major rooms of their house and construct their own inventory.

Variations

- Language is a key aspect of this activity, in terms of the words and spelling and the fact that they may relate to an item or activity which no longer exists. Try translating the text or producing a glossary to explain what items are.

Using Sources to Develop Empathy

Images help children to see people in the past taking part in activities that they can associate with. The idea here is to impress on them that people in the past may look different but they have much in common with people today. This activity asks children to replicate an image from the past.

Suitable for

KS1, KS2

Aim

- To help children empathise with people in the past.

Resources

- Images of people in the past in a variety of everyday situations, such as Breughel's *The Peasant Wedding* or *The Elder-Children Playing*.
- Interactive whiteboard or projectors and images, such as a Victorian street scene.

What to do

1. Show the children the pictures you have collected.
2. Ask the children to look for aspects of the picture that they can relate to – the food, music, dance, for example.
3. Then project your images onto the whiteboard. Discuss them and consider what the pictures show.
4. The children then assume the same positions as the people in the image. They can then step out of the frame and tell their story.

Variations

- This activity could be done individually or in pairs by giving children a copy of the picture and asking them to add speech and/or thought bubbles to express what the individuals might be saying or thinking.

What Can We Learn from Pictures?

Pictures are excellent source materials for primary history. At KS1, it is useful to focus on oral and drawn responses to images linked to topics with a focus on history.

Suitable for

KS1

Aim

- To help children focus on information available in an image.

Resources

- Images or picture sets of the same person, such as
- Whiteboard
- Paper, pencils

What to do

1. Show the children your images or picture set on the whiteboard.
2. Ask them to describe what they see.
3. Start to ask focused questions, such as the following.
   - Are there any clues as to who the person is?
   - What might he/she be doing?
   - Is this picture of a recent event or of something a long time ago?
4. Ask the children to draw something from the picture that they recognise and something that you don't recognise.

Variations

- Use images of the same person by different artists.
- Use written descriptions to place alongside the images.

Interpretation

Asking Questions

A major aspect of Early Years history for young children is the ability to ask and answer questions. As they learn about themselves and their identity, they can ask questions about others.

Without this ability, which might promote them to think more critically about themselves and appreciate difference as well as similarity, children will find it difficult to make sense of the differences between ways of life in different periods of time in history.

Suitable for

KS1

Aims

- To develop questioning skills in the Early Years.
- To look at simple similarities and differences.

Resources

- A set of questions linked to the children's own personal histories.
- Picture and information about a famous historical figure, such as Martin Luther King (used in the example questions on page 149).

What to do

1. Ask the children to think about their own histories and what makes them special. Some questions you could ask include the following.

   - Who am I?
   - How do I know that it is me?
   - What other things apart from how I look make me me?
   - What is the same about me and other children?
   - What is different about me that makes me who I am?

2. Look at the picture of the famous historical figure you have chosen and ask the same questions about them.

   - Who was Martin Luther King?
   - How do we know that it is him?
   - What other things apart from the way he looked made him him?
   - What was the same about him and other people?
   - What was different about him that made him who he was?

Variation

- Give the children a set of questions and answers related to a famous historical figure that have been cut out and ask them to match them up.

Fact or Opinion?

Choosing a favourite person and discussing what was good or bad about them can be an enjoyable activity and links to the concept of what is a fact and what is an opinion.

Suitable for

KS1, KS2

Aim

- To develop the children's understanding of the concepts of fact and opinion.

Resources

- Range of pieces of information about a famous historical figure the children have been studying (see example for Guy Fawkes on page 151)
- List of true and false statements about the historical figure

What to do

1. Give the children the information about the selected historical figure.
2. Ask them to decide which statements are facts and which are opinions.
3. Compare the choices made and see if there is common agreement.
4. Ask if there any statements that they found it was difficult to make judgements about.

Guy Fawkes

- Guy Fawkes was a real person.
- He wanted to blow up the Houses of Parliament.
- He had many reasons for doing this.
- Guy Fawkes was wrong to want to kill the King.
- Guy Fawkes was very brave.
- King James I was the King.
- Guy Fawkes was arrested before he could explode the gunpowder.

Variations

- The statements can be studied collectively or by the children in pairs.
- Where statements are ambiguous, the children can choose a third option – unsure.

Facts and Points of View

This activity helps children to understand the difference between statements that are factual and those which either express an opinion or cannot be supported by facts.

Suitable for

KS1, KS2

Aim

- To understand the difference between facts and points of view or opinions

Resources

- Copies of a set of statements about a figure or event in history (see example on page 153)

What to do

1. During a chosen topic, explain the distinction between facts and points of view.
2. Talk about your chosen figure or tell the story of the event (use PowerPoint if you like).
3. Provide the children with the set of statements and say that they have to decide whether each one is a fact or a point of view, writing 'F' or 'POV' next to each statement. (This activity can be completed as an oral exercise instead if preferred.)

The Gunpowder Plot – facts and points of view

1. The Gunpowder Plot happened about 400 years ago. ☐

2. Guy Fawkes should have known that he'd be caught. ☐

3. Barrels of gunpowder were placed under the Houses of Parliament. ☐

4. The plotter was foolish to send the letter to Lord Monteagle. ☐

5. Guy Fawkes was wrong to name the other plotters. ☐

6. Guy Fawkes was hanged for treason. ☐

Variations

- Older children can start to devise their own statements about a topic, defining them as 'factual' (F) or 'point of view' (POV).
- Where statements are ambiguous and there is no certainty about the choices available then a third category, such as 'not enough evidence' (NEE), can be added.

Hadrian's Wall

This activity links to work on invasion and settlement, particularly in relation to the Romans, regarding the idea of gains and losses.

Suitable for

KS2

Aim

- To work on understanding the concepts of cause and consequence.

Resources

- A set of benefits and costs experienced by any particular invaders or settlers.
- Copies of a table for the children to record their choices in (see example on page 155)

What to do

1. Following investigations or activities linked to invaders and settlers, give the children the list of benefits and difficulties you've prepared.
2. Ask the children to order those items so that the main benefits are at the top and the worst costs are at the bottom.
3. Discuss the children's choices and ordering, then ask them if they want to move any of the items.

Hadrian's Wall

Being a Celt living under Roman rule

Here are some of the benefits and difficulties of living in Roman Britain.

Cut up and rearrange the building blocks to construct the wall so that the main benefits are at the top and the worst aspects are at the bottom of the wall.

Tribes no longer ruled themselves.	A new language, Latin, was introduced.	Some Celts were killed.
Ordinary people were better off.	New cities were built.	Taxes were raised.
There was peace.	The old religions were changed.	Proper roads were built.

Variations

- A similar version of this activity is for the children to sort the items into good or bad choices.
- To make it more challenging, the children can research the benefits and difficulties before ordering them.

History Sandwich

This activity relates history to a concept that all children understand – the sandwich. The idea is for them to think of two pieces of information they know about a given subject as the outside of the sandwich and then their interpretation of the information as the filling.

Suitable for

KS2

Aim

● To help children make judgements about historical information.

Resources

● Image of a sandwich and example of the concept being used, such as for Henry VIII (see example below)

Example: history sandwich

Henry VIII spent money on banquets, palaces, clothes and jewels.

I think that Henry reformed the Church, because he needed the Church's money.

Henry VIII spent money on the army, navy and building new coastal defences.

What to do

1. Show the children the image of a sandwich. Ask them to think about the slices of bread as two pieces of information (ask for or give an example).

2. Then ask them to give their opinions about that information, which acts as the filling.

3. Having worked through the example, ask the children to each prepare their own history sandwich, which they can share with others.

Variations

- For a simpler activity, give the children two pieces of information and ask them to make the filling.

Mary Seacole - Facts and Points Of View

This activity is linked to storytelling and developing interpretive skills through the medium of storytelling.

Suitable for

KS1

Aim

- To develop interpretive skills based on information given.

Resources

- Story of Mary Seacole (see page 159)
- List of facts and points of view related to the story (see page 160)
- Whiteboard

What to do

1. Tell the story of Mary Seacole.
2. Present the list of statements about Mary on the whiteboard.
3. Ask the children to decide whether the statements are facts or points of view.
4. Compare their opinions and come to a conclusion about the story.

The story of Mary Seacole

Over 100 years ago, when Queen Victoria was Queen of England, British soldiers were sent to fight in the Crimea. It was a long way from Britain – and it took many weeks to get there. The soldiers were short of boots, clothes, food and medicine – all of which made fighting difficult. If they were wounded in battle or caught a disease, such as cholera, there were not enough medicines to cure them. There were no proper hospitals, doctors or nurses. More soldiers died from disease than in battle.

Mary Seacole lived in Jamaica. Her father was a Scottish army officer and her mother was Jamaican. Her mother kept a hotel, where she often nursed sick people. Mary learned how to mix medicines and look after sick people. Later, she travelled throughout Central America. During this time, she developed a medicine to help people who had cholera.

When Mary heard about the Crimean War in 1854, she sailed to London and asked to be sent out to the war as a nurse. 'I have nursed before,' she told the representatives of the British Government. 'I've saved people with cholera.'

The British Government refused to send her, but she went anyway, paying her own way. She set herself up 2 miles from the battlefield in what was called the British Hotel. Every day, she filled her basket with food, drink and medicine. She helped soldiers who were hungry, sick or dying, often at great danger to herself.

When the war ended in 1856, Mary went back to London. By this time, she had become famous. William Russell, a reporter who had written about the war for *The Times*, had seen her at work and written about her in the newspaper. People came to cheer her in the street and she wrote a best-selling book about her life called *The Wonderful Adventures of Mrs Seacole in Many Lands*.

As the years passed, people began to forget about Mary Seacole and, at one point, she became very poor, but the soldiers she had helped remembered her and set up a fund: The Seacole Fund. She had enough to live on and was able to go back to visit Jamaica.

Facts and points of view about Mary Seacole's story

1. The Crimean War took place more than 100 years ago. (F)

2. Mary was foolish to go to the Crimea. (POV)

3. Mary looked after soldiers who were sick and wounded. (F)

4. Mary should never have been allowed to go to the Crimea. (POV)

5. The British Government should have given her money afterwards. (POV)

6. Mary wrote a book about her life. (F)

Variation

- The statements can be given to the children to work on in pairs or individually.

The Great Railway Debate

This is an interpretation activity, linked to the Victorians. The activity helps them to understand that historical changes were perceived in different ways by the people at the time.

Suitable for

KS2

Aim

- For children to interpret an important historical change from a range of different perspectives.

Resources

- Copies of an activity sheet listing different points of view (see example on page 162)

What to do

1. Explain the background to the coming of the railways – the biggest change in transport for centuries.
2. Tell the children that people at the time responded differently. Their task is to look at the different points of view and decide who they might belong to.
3. They then decide whether or not, given the evidence provided, the coming of the railways was a good or bad thing.

A good thing or a bad thing?

1. The railway will be noisy.	2. We will be able to get to London in a few hours instead of two days.
3. The smoke will pollute the atmosphere.	4. It will not matter about the weather.
5. People were not meant to fly about at that speed.	6. We will be able to eat and drink while we travel.
7. It will put the stagecoaches out of business.	8. The stagecoaches are slow and bumpy.
9. It's all right, but not near my home.	10. There will be more things in the shops because we can send goods by rail.
11. The trains will frighten my animals.	12. The roads are muddy and full of big holes.

Choose one of the characters listed below and decide which of the points of view above they would have. Put the numbers in the second column below.

Character	Box numbers
Landowner	
Businessman	
Railway passenger	
Stagecoach owner	

Overall, do you think the coming of the railways was a good thing or a bad thing?

Variations

- More or fewer comments can be added to suit the abilities of the children in your class.
- A wider range of characters can be listed for the children to think about.

What Did People Think about Florence Nightingale?

In this activity, the children are encouraged to make judgements about a famous historical character based on a story or information that they have been given.

Suitable for

KS1

Aim

- To introduce younger pupils to historical interpretation.

Resources

- Information about a particular historical figure (the example used here is Florence Nightingale)
- Copies of a simple form for pupils to record their perceptions on (see example on page 164)

What to do

1. Tell the story or provide the children with information about your chosen famous historical figure.

2. After the children have listened to the story or read the information, ask them to say what different people in the story might have thought about her, such as:
   - the soldiers after she had improved conditions at Scutari
   - the nurses after she had been at Scutari for a period of time

3. Ask the children to write their perceptions of what the different people's opinions might be or how they might differ on the form (see example on page 164).

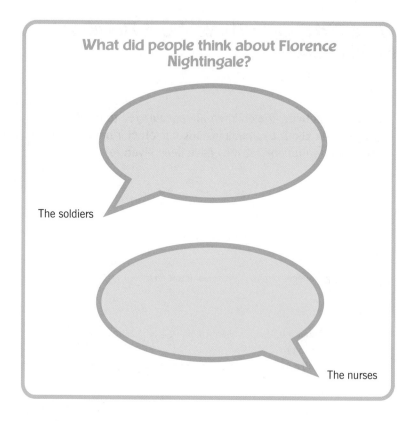

Variations

- Ask the children to consider people's perceptions before and after events. So, in the case of Florence Nightingale, the children could think about the views of the:
  - soldiers before she came to Scutari and after she had improved conditions there
  - nurses when she arrived at Scutari and after she had been there for a period of time.
- Ask the children to write their perceptions of how people's opinions might have changed depending on who they were.

Knowledge and understanding

Anachronisms

Anachronisms can be linked to any period of history as the idea is that children spot instances where an image, statement or idea is not in keeping with the period under discussion. For example, a Roman wearing a wristwatch, an airliner flying over Pepys' London or a sports car in an early Victorian street.

Suitable for

KS2

Aims

- To make pupils aware of the appropriateness of images and textual sources.
- To introduce the idea of questioning sources and not accepting them at face value.

Resources

- Stories or information focusing on an event with statements in a story or items in a picture included that are not appropriate to the period in question (see example on page 167)

Spot the anachronisms

According to my digital watch, it was 4.50 in the afternoon on 2 September 1666. Smoke from burning houses filled the city skies and the smell of burning was everywhere. The thick smoke meant that aeroplanes could not fly over the city. I was scared to death. I took out my mobile phone and called the fire brigade. They came very quickly and very efficiently put out the fire.

What to do

1. Ask the children to look at the picture or listen to the story you have prepared and point out any anachronisms.
2. Can they identify them and explain why they do not fit?

Variations

- See if the children can spot the errors without being prompted.
- Include anachronisms in some otherwise true statements, such as in the game on page 167.

Tudor religion – the Reformation ordering game

Henry VIII was made Supreme Head of the Church by an Act of Parliament in 1534.

He decided that he no longer wanted to allow the Pope in Rome to have authority over the Church in England. Why did he do this?

Here is a set of cards. Put the cards in ranking order – top to bottom, putting the most important reasons at the top and the least important at the bottom.

A	Henry did not like being told what to do. He wanted to leave (divorce) his first wife, Catherine, and the Pope would not agree to this. (The Pope was Head of the Church and lived in Rome in Italy.)
B	Some people thought that they were paying too much money to the Church. They thought that some Church leaders were too rich.
C	Henry wanted to get money from the Church so that he could fly to Spain for a holiday. He liked to drink wine on the beaches in Spain.
D	Henry wanted to take money from the Church. He wanted to spend this on new ships or palaces.
E	Henry wanted to knock down some large Church buildings (monasteries) so that he could use the stones. He wanted to use the stones to build new roads for his cars.
F	Some people could not understand the words used in church. They wanted to listen to the words in English, not Latin.
G	Henry did not like being woken by some loud church bells near his palace. He had told the monks to be quiet lots of times.
H	Henry did not like some Church leaders (bishops and abbots) wearing fine clothes like him.
I	Henry thought that the Pope was listening too much to the kings and queens of other countries.

Building a Pyramid in Ancient Egypt

This activity involves the children working out the order in which tasks needs to be done in the construction of a pyramid. It could follow the story of the burial customs of the pharaohs and lead to a debate about the evidence for who built the pyramids.

Suitable for

KS2

Aim

● To look at the construction of the Pyramids and the order in which the various activities need to be done.

Resources

● Copies of a worksheet showing a pyramid divided into several blocks, corresponding to the number of steps required to build if (see below)
● Copies of a sheet showing the steps involved in building a pyramid (see page 169)

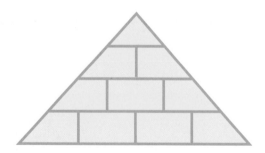

How to build a pyramid

A. With the pyramid completed, a funeral temple and connecting walkway were built.

B. Workers chiselled and polished the face of the stone until it shone brightly.

C. The polished granite capstone was set at the top of the pyramid.

D. More stone blocks were added until the pyramid reached almost its full height.

E. Earthen ramps helped workers drag the huge stone blocks to their places.

F. Stonecutters used chisels and stone balls to cut out the burial chamber from the hard ground.

G. Engineers surveyed and measured the area using a grid pattern of ropes.

H. Next to the tunnel passageway, the burial chamber was built.

I. The empty sarcophagus (stone coffin) was put in place while the opening was still large.

J. The desert floor had to be cleared before the construction began.

What to do

1. Following discussion, give the children the worksheets and the sheets showing the steps required to build a pyramid.

2. Ask the children to write the letters for the steps on the pyramid blocks in the correct order, left to right, bottom to top.

3. Compare the children's choices and decide the most appropriate order.

Variations

• Simply cut up the blocks in the pyramid figure and have the children construct their own pyramids, working from left to right, bottom to top.

• To links with science and DT, talk about the use of rollers and ramps (inclined planes), linking the use of these aids with friction.

Historical Vocabulary

This is a useful way to encourage children to use images, dates, events and people, revealing their knowledge and understanding of the past.

Suitable for

KS1, KS2

Aim

- To help children understand the past through a historical vocabulary.

Resources

- Interactive whiteboard
- PowerPoint images, dates and so on related to the era, person or activity being investigated

What to do

1. Show the children an image on the whiteboard and ask 'Who is this?' For example, you could show Julius Caesar and see what they know about him.
2. Then show a date, such as 54BC, and, again, ask the children what the date represents and what event took place then.
3. Continue with a variety of clues, such as images of Roman soldiers, Ancient Britons and so on.
4. As the children identify each clue, they build up a picture of their knowledge of this event in the past.

Variation

- The formats of this activity can be varied from mainly images to mainly dates or else be text-based, such as giving the names of people and events.

Information Teller

 This is a simple game based on the fortune teller game played by primary school children. It can be adapted to allow children to research and share information.

Suitable for

KS1, KS2

Aim

● For children to share information about a historical event, period and so on, both as facilitators and by learning from others for others

Resources

● Squares of paper
● Pencils
● Felt-tips
● Making instructions (see pages 172–3)

What to do

1. Give the children each a square of paper, pencils and pens and a copy of the making instructions.
2. Ask them to make their information tellers.
3. Ask them to write 1–4 on the outside flaps.
4. Then ask them to write a date or the names of people, events and so on on the outside fold of each of the eight internal triangles.
5. Have them write an association with the outer triangles on the inner ones.
6. The children can take turns with each other's information tellers and share the information, seeing if they can recognise the information.

Variations

- Younger children could use a mixture of text and images and explain the information they have put on their information tellers.
- Could be adapted for RE, giving information about a particular faith, religious leader, sacred text and so on.

Making instructions for your information teller

1. Start with a square of paper.

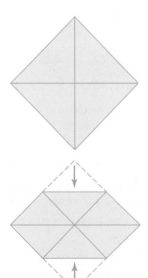

2. Fold the two opposite corners of the square together, then fold it in half, forming a smaller triangle.

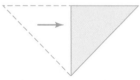

3. Open the paper up (unfolding all the folds).

4. Fold the top corner down so the point of the corner is on the central point. Repeat with the opposite corner.

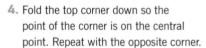

5. Fold the left corner in over to the centre. Repeat with the opposite corner.

6. Flip the paper over. Fold each of the corners in to the centre. You'll end up with a smaller square.

   Then, fold the square in half. Unfold and fold in half the other way.

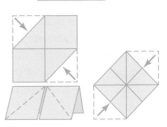

7.  Unfold and bring the four corners up and together, putting your fingers in the four pockets underneath, as shown, to form a diamond-like shape. You will be able to move the four parts around.

8. Write the numbers 1 to 4 on the four flaps.

1
4 2
3

9. Flatten the information teller and write a piece of historical information in each of the eight triangles.

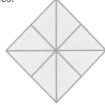

Then, open out the flaps and write some other associations with the outer triangles on the corresponding inner ones.

Just Like Us

If and when to introduce children to the Holocaust is a difficult judgement for primary teachers to make. One way to do so is to make links to a particular individual through activities that create an understanding of the fact that, despite the distance in time and differences in nationality and language, the victims of the Holocaust were 'just like us'.

Suitable for

KS2

Aim

● To introduce children to the Holocaust.

Resources

● Images of an individual associated with the Holocaust, such as Anne Frank
● Information about their lives, such as details of their home, school, friends, holidays and so on.

What to do

1. Show the children your chosen image – for example, Anne Frank as a young girl.

2. Tell the class a little about the person, such as how her diary allows us to know her story and understand her feelings.

3. Discuss how the person's life was similar to and different from our own.

4. After discussion, tell the class the end of the story – in this case, about her arrest, deportation and death in a concentration camp.

Variation

- Another approach is to investigate the Holocaust through literacy activities (see examples below).

Holocaust poems

Acrostic poem

An acrostic poem is one where you choose a word or name and use each letter in the name as the beginning of a word or line that says something about the person or topic. Here is an example of an acrostic poem using the word 'friend.'

Frank from my class
Really helped me when I got hurt. He ran to the nurse and got
Ice for my leg.
Even when I lost
Nelly my pet frog, his mum
Drove us all around looking for her.

Write an acrostic poem using the word set out below.

H
O
L
O
C
A
U
S
T

Writing poems

Put yourself in a scene and time frame during or at the end of the Holocaust. Pretend to be a person or a pair of shoes or another personal item. React to and explain the situation by writing a short poem using any of the expressions below.

- I hear
- I see
- I feel

- I am afraid
- I touch
- I am like
- I believe
- I wish

Writing poems in another language
As a class, try to write one in another language.

English	French	German	
I hear	J'entends	Ich höre	Lo Sento
I see	Je vois	Ich sehe	Lo vedo
I believe	Je crois	Ich glaube	Lo credo
I am afraid	J'ai peur	Ich habe Angst	Lo ho paura
I touch	Je touche	Ich bestate	Lo tocco
I am like	Je suis comme	Ich bin wie	Lo sono come
I feel	Je me sens	Ich fühle mich	Mi sento

Here are some examples

Les chaussures
Je vois les enfants.
Je touche la terre.
J'entends des soldats.
J'ai peur.

The shoes
I see the children.
I touch the ground.
I listen to the soldiers.
I am afraid.

À la fin
Je vois le soleil.
Je me sens le soleil.
J'entends les oiseaux.
Je suis comme un oiseau.
Je touche la terre
et je crois encore.

At the end
I see the sun.
I feel the sun.
I hear the birds.
I am like a bird.
I touch the ground
and once again I believe.

Alternatively, use these examples to ask the children what the poems mean and then ask them to reflect this in an illustration or in their own poem in English.

Ordering a Story

Activities that allow children to explore the structure of a story in history help them to develop their knowledge and understanding of a famous person or historical event. They can also be used to introduce ideas about the importance of certain aspects or significant events in the story. There are opportunities, too, for children to consider chronology and interpretation.

Suitable for

KS1

Aim

- To consider the order of elements of a significant historical event or the importance of aspects of a famous figure in history.

Resources

- Sets of pictures telling the story of a historical figure or event
- Copies of an activity worksheet (see page 178).

What to do

1. Give the children the chosen pictures.
2. Ask them to work on some or all of the activities described below (see example on page 178 for an event)

Variations

- The number of pictures used can be increased or decreased to either simplify the task or make it more difficult.
- The children can be asked to complete fewer activities.

Activities	Questions
1. Children arrange pictures in order so that they tell the story.	Discuss why pictures are where they are. Which pictures did you decide were near the beginning of the story? Which were near the end?
2. Children decide which pictures show the beginning, middle and end of the story.	Discuss choices of pictures. Why did you choose that picture in the middle? Are your pictures in the same order as other groups?
3. If you had to tell the story in only three pictures, which would you choose?	Why did you choose these pictures? Were they the most exciting, or the most important? From where in the story do they come? Could we replace any of the pictures with others?
4. Children discuss how close or far apart the pictures should be in terms of time.	Why are these two pictures close together? Did that happen straight after that? How long afterwards did this take place?
5. Children decide which pictures show how things changed for a character in the story.	What changed for Guy Fawkes in the story? For James 1? For Catholics?
6. Some key pictures are removed from the story. Children either recall or work out what happened from the remaining pictures. They draw pictures to fill in the gaps.	Can you remember what happened in between those two pictures? What do you think might have happened after this? What could we draw to show that? How did you work that out?
7. Children identify causes of particular events and select pictures to represent them.	Why did you choose that picture? Could you have chosen another picture?

Saxon Settlement (Invaders and Settlers)

This role-play activity helps children to use their knowledge of the Saxons to construct a scenario linked to the nature of settlement.

Suitable for

KS2

Aims

- To investigate what makes somewhere a good place to settle.
- Linking the children's knowledge of the Saxons to where and how they would settle.

Resources

- Images of Saxon settlements or reconstructions of Saxon settlements

What to do

1. Begin by discussing what the children already know about Saxon settlements. What would the people need? What would be important to them?

2. Decide what would be needed, regarding collecting materials and building shelters, fetching water and cooking, hunting and growing food.

3. Work in groups to make still images of daily life in a Saxon settlement. Review the images and emphasise the way in which the people are dependent on the land around them.

4. Discuss the 'elements' that might be included in a ceremony/ritual to celebrate an important point in the yearly routine, such as the harvest. Work in groups to develop each of these ideas – music, dance, words, movement, special food.

5. Bring the elements of the ritual together.

6. Each group can present their activity for the rest of the class.

Variation

- This activity could link to the idea of settlement in geography – choice of location, building materials, water source, transport links and so on.

Searchlights

In any activity related to the Second World War, children have many opportunities to research aspects of the war. The idea of searchlights helps to illustrate these aspects and put them together as a way of building up pieces of relevant information.

Suitable for

KS2

Aim

- For individuals and pairs of children to investigate relevant aspects of the Second World War and collate their information.

Resources

- Paper cut into strips to represent searchlight beams
- Internet access, textbooks and other appropriate sources of information

What to do

1. Have the children investigate a particular aspect or aspects of the Second World War, such as air raids, life on the home front, evacuation and so on.
2. Then, group them in pairs to research a particular aspect a little more, drawing and writing their findings on the searchlight beams.
3. Mount the finished searchlights as a display so that the collected information is available for everyone to read.

Variation

- The searchlights can be incorporated into a frieze of, say, a silhouetted townscape, aircraft and so on.

To Go a Viking

This activity links to any topic on exploration. It asks children to consider and make choices about what would be important for any captain to take on a particular voyage.

Suitable for

KS1, KS2

Aim

- To consider and make choices based on knowledge and understanding of the past.

Resources

- A scenario for the activity, such as Viking exploration (information is available from websites such as **www.topmarks.co.uk/Default.aspx?p=2&q=vikings**), the Norman invasion or a Tudor voyage to the West Indies, etc.
- Lists of possible materials, depending on the scenario chosen

What to do

1. Give the children your chosen scenario and ask them to list ten items that they think would be most necessary for a particular voyage. So, for examle, what ten objects might a Viking sea captain decide to take with him on a voyage? Ask the children to justify their choices.
2. They can then compare and justify their choices
3. Agree on a final list.

Variation

- The children can be given a list of objects relevant to a particular scenario to select from.

Two Truths and a Lie

This activity can be teacher- or pupil-led. The aim is for some of the children to research aspects of a topic and write two true statements and one false and for others to identify which statements are correct and which one is incorrect. This is a useful end-of-topic research activity as it tests what knowledge and understanding the children have gained.

Suitable for

KS2

Aims

- For children to test each other's knowledge of the period being studied by researching two correct pieces of information and including one piece of information that they know is not true.
- For the children to be experts on their own choices and explain to others why one example is incorrect.

Resources

- Either teacher-prepared statements or sources of information so that the children can construct their own (see example list below)

Example two truths and a lie test

Henry VI had eight wives.
Francis Drake sailed around the world.
William Shakespeare was born in Stratford-upon-Avon.

What to do

1. Either read out the prepared list or ask some of the children to do some research, then write down two things that they know to be true about a particular event, person or period in history and one thing they know to be false.

2. They can then read their lists out to the others, who have to decide which statements are correct and incorrect.

Variations

- The activity can be extended by varying the combinations – three truths and two lies and so on.
- The activity can be developed to include a discussion about what fact and opinion are.

Victorian Spinner

The idea here is to link historical toys and entertainment with information about a particular era in history.

Suitable for

KS2

Aim

- To link a simple making activity with a historical era.

Resources

- Stiff card discs
- Thread
- Images linked to Victorian times

What to do

1. Hand out the discs and show the images, then ask the children to draw an image linked to the era on front and rear of their card discs, such as a silhouette of a person's head and shoulders, a rocking horse or a pocket watch face and back.

2. Punch a hole near the edge of each side of the disc (as shown below).

3. Tie a double length of thread through each hole and twirl so that the threads are twisted like rope.

4. Gently, holding the ends of the threads, pull them in opposite directions so that the image spins.

Variation

- The children research to find images that are relevant to the Victorian era.

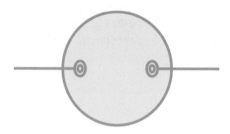

Sources

An Introduction to Handling Artefacts

> Artefacts are important source materials and children need to develop experience in observing and handling them.

Suitable for

KS1

Aims

- To introduce children to the handling of artefacts.
- To help them develop a historical vocabulary.

Resources

- A number of safe kitchen utensils, such as a saucepan, colander and so on.
- Similar household items, such as a feather duster and so on.

What to do

1. Ask the children to look at one of the artefacts. Have them pass it to one another and ask them to each say one thing about it – its colour, size, shape, weight, age, for example.

2. The children can repeat others' statements if they like or, if unsure or shy, they can pass.

3. In this way build up a bank of statements about each object.

4. Then, ask them to think about the following kinds of questions.

   - Where would the item be kept?
   - Who might use it?
   - Is it new or old?
   - Can you think how old it might be?

Variation

- The same activity can be carried out using historical artefacts and ideas about where, what, who, when and how can be developed.

Investigating a Will

Wills are another form of historical evidence that help children to find out about the past. This activity asks children to investigate how William Shakespeare's will would be useful for finding out about his life and times.

Suitable for

KS2

Aim

- To use a more unusual type of source to investigate the past.

Resources

- Copies of an updated version of Shakespeare's will (see below)

The last will and testament of William Shakespeare

In the name of God, Amen. I William Shakespeare of Stratford-upon-Avon ... in perfect health and memory ... do make my last will. First I commend my soul into the hands of God...and my body to the earth whereof it is made.

Item – I give unto my daughter Judith one hundred and fifty pounds...
Item – I give unto ... Elizabeth Hall...all my plate (except my broad silver and gilt bowl)
Item – I give unto the poor of Stratford ... ten pounds ... and to Mr Thomas Coombe my sword
Item – I give to Hamlet Sadler xxvi (26) shillings and viii (8) pence to buy him a ring ... And to my fellows John Heminge, Richard Burbage and Harry Condell xxvi (26) shillings and viii (6) pence apiece to buy them rings.

Item – I give to my daughter Susanna the tenement (house) in Stratford … called the New Place, where I now dwell (live) and two tenements (houses) in Henley Street, … and all my barns, stables, orchards, gardens, lands, tenements … within Stratford-upon-Avon, Old Stratford, Bishopton and Welcome … in the county of Warwick and also that tenement in Blackfriars in London.

Item – I give unto my wife my second best bed

What to do

1. Discuss with the children how we can find out about the past.

2. List the ways the children can think of.

3. If it is not suggested, add the idea of wills. What are they? Who makes them? What do they contain?

4. Show them a copy of Shakespeare's will and its contents.

5. List who the beneficiaries were and what they received. For example:

Beneficiaries	Given
Judith Shakespeare	£150
Elizabeth Hall	All the plate etc.

6. What does Shakespeare's will tell us about him?

7. What does it tell us about the times he lived in?

8. Are there any questions that they would like to ask about the will?

Variation

- Look at other simple versions of wills to make comparisons between different periods in history.

Looking at Paintings

Developing children's understanding of history by looking at paintings is a useful enquiry skill. By making observations about paintings, children can learn more about a period and assess the usefulness of paintings as a historical source. This is particulary true of paintings that reflect a particular interest, such as studies of Victorian social life in the nineteenth century.

Suitable for

KS2

Aims

- To help children become familiar with genre paintings and develop confidence in generating their own questions about them.
- Paintings can also be used to show how different types of evidence can lead to different interpretations of the past.

Resources

- Reproductions of paintings from books and postcards or images from various databases online
- General questions (see examples on page 192) related to the paintings studied that will help the children to develop ways of extracting information to use critically.

Example questions about the paintings studied

The people

- How many are there?
- What are they doing?
- What is their relationship to each other?
- Are they all of equal importance?
- Which one is higher up, nearer the front of the picture or most centrally placed?
- What are they wearing?
- What do their clothes tell you about them?
- Who is wearing the most eye-catching outfit?
- What is their mood or emotional state?
- How do you know?

The surroundings

- Where are they? If inside, describe the room, objects, animals and furniture.
- If outside, describe the environment.
- Is the lighting trying to make you look at one particular area or person?
- Has a certain time of day or weather been chosen?
- What do the surroundings tell you about the people and the picture as a whole?
- Is there a storyline? If so, what's going on?
- Can we tell from the painting what has happened in the past or what might happen in the future?
- Why do you think that the picture was painted?
- What was the artist's motivation or intention?
- Where was the picture likely to be hung and who might have been expected to own it or see it?
- Might this have influenced the style or content?
- What would it mean to its owner today?
- How can you test or evaluate the information extracted?
- Are there always answers to the questions posed?
- What other sources of information might be helpful?

What to do

1. Look at the first chosen painting and discuss the subject, content and so on with the children.

2. Talk about the idea of paintings as a historical source.

3. Ask or show the list of questions so that the children are guided as to how to investigate the painting as a source.

4. Match what they observe with what they already know about the period in question.

Variation

- Use any known background information about the painter and the painting, such as why it was painted, who for, if it is set in a real location or in a studio using models, how it was received at the time and so on. Adding this information to the mix can help the children put the painting into a context and also consider some of the attitudes at the time and the notion of bias.

Misconceptions

This activity helps younger children to know where they come from, where they fit in and about all the fascinating differences there are in the world.

Suitable for

KS1

Aim

- To develop children's historical skills, concepts and knowledge using stories, rhymes and playground games.

Resources

- Nursery rhymes and the historical stories behind them

What to do

1. Sing or tell a nursery rhyme with the children. Then ask them what they think the rhyme is about.

2. Link the rhymes with the stories attached to them. So, for example 'Ring a Ring O' Roses' references the plague, 'Jack and Jill' the old-fashioned treatment of using vinegar and brown paper as a way to cure bumps and cuts and 'The Grand old Duke of York' is about the muddled leadership of the army.

Variations

- Nursery rhymes can be added to by looking at simple stories, poems and songs that provide children with information about the past.

Other history activities

From a Suitcase

This is a way to help children interpret historical information and develop empathy with the past.

Suitable for

KS2

Aim

- To use artefacts as a stimulus to develop and interpret historical information.

Resources

- A small suitcase or bag
- A small number of artefacts appropriate to the era being studied

What to do

1. Show the suitcase or bag to the children.

2. One by one, take the items out of the bag and discuss what they represent. For instance, if the bag were assumed to belong to the Second World War, an evacuee's items might include a purse with a few coins, a toy, a sweater, family photograph, label with name and address, letter from a relative.

3. Once the items have been discussed, the children, individually or collectively, can try to use them to compile a picture of the person they belonged to. This is a fictional account of a fictional person, but it requires the children to interpret historical information within a real context in order to make it meaningful.

Variation

- The number of artefacts can be increased or decreased depending on the time available and the difficulty level you wish to set for the activity.

Historical Interpretation

Understanding that different stories about the past can give different versions of what happened, distinguishing between facts and point of views leads children to an understanding that deficiencies in evidence may lead to different interpretations of the past.

Suitable for

KS1, KS2

Aim

- To develop the concept of historical interpretation.

Resources

- Story about an famous figure or event in history, such as Guy Fawkes

What to do

1. Tell or read your chosen story about a famous figure or event in history.
2. Ask the children to retell the story to a friend while a third listens. Can they spot a fact or part of the story that was omitted in the retelling?
3. Ask the children to retell the story again in a shorter period of time, focusing on the key facts.
4. This can be repeated several times and shows the children how different situations can change the original story in marked ways, making them less reliable as sources of information.

Variation

- Play a variation of 'Chinese whispers' where information is read by one person then verbally passed quietly around a circle until it reaches the original reader. They say what they have been told then read the original information to see what has changed, been left out and so on.

History in a Story

Stories from history can be used to develop a number of key skills. This activity asks children to review a well-known story from history, which can be used to examine chronology and interpretation by considering continuity, change, cause and consequence.

Suitable for

KS1

Aim

- To introduce history concepts and skills to children using the story format.

Resources

- Stories linked to particular periods, events and people that can be read, told or shown and shared as a whiteboard activity
- Images to show on the whiteboard to support the stories

What to do

1. Use the stories to introduce the children to an aspect of history.
2. Read or tell the story, controlling the degree of historical content – in terms of dates, vocabulary and other information – to make it accessible to the audience.
3. Show the images on the whiteboard to allow the children to follow the narrative more easily.

Variation

- As the children develop their historical knowledge and understanding of a period of history, the stories or other similar stories can be told, extending the historical content. For example, an initial telling of the story of Florence Nightingale could focus on her attempts to improve conditions at Scutari. A further telling might include dates or terms such as the Crimean War, Victorian period and so on.

The Mantle of Expertise

 Alongside other drama activities, this exercise is a way to dramatise historic moments. The whole class reconstructs a fictional account of an historical event, becoming part of that event and giving eyewitness accounts.

Suitable for

KS1, KS2

Aim

- To view a particular world through the eyes of other people and, for a period of time, wear a 'mantle of expertise' associated with the point of view of these people.

Resources

- Images of a particular historical event, such as the arrest of Guy Fawkes

What to do

1. Show the class an image of the particular historical event.
2. Ask each child to select a figure in the picture and construct a role and point of view for them.
3. The children then each give their accounts of the event from the figures' points of view.
4. The children have 'authority' over their figures and their accounts are accepted as accurate portrayals, building up an overall picture of an event from the range of views expressed.

Variations

- As children develop their historical understanding, when this activity is repeated each time there will be more of a historical context to their accounts.
- Some views will be short and prosaic, which is a reality of historical accounts. For example, a guard involved in the arrest of Guy Fawkes might be more concerned about getting home for supper than about preventing a regicide.

People Like Us

One of the big ideas in history is the concept of similarities and differences between people in the past and us. Activities linked to history that tell us how people feel and thought are interesting activities, helping to develop children's perceptions of the past.

Suitable for

KS1, KS2

Aim

- To examine an historical event in the context of how, no matter how long ago, and despite differences in lifestyle, what people believed, said or did resonates with us today.

Resources

- Images or text documents related to an event or series of events in the past, such as *The Arnolfini Marriage*, a painting by Jan Van Eyck, text of the Gettysburg address by Abraham Lincoln, a video of Martin Luther King's 'I have a dream' speech, an excerpt from Jewish testimonies in the Second World War, such as *The Diary of Anne Frank*, or statement on the nature of humanity such as that by Pastor Martin Niemoller, a German anti-Nazi activist.

What to do

1. Explain the background to the chosen event or events and show, tell or read the appropriate excerpts.
2. Ask the children for their reactions to each excerpt or image and what their responses tell us about people in the past.
3. Ask them if there are any strands – such as ideas, emotions or statements – that they feel are just as appropriate to the twenty-first century as to the time they were painted, spoken or written?

Variation

- For older children, you can add depth to the context. For example, at the time of the Arnolfini wedding, people believed in witches; when Martin Luther King spoke, many people in his own country believed in segregation and not allowing a minority equal rights. Despite changes in beliefs, can we see similar anomalies in our own times?

Storytelling

Storytelling is an important part of helping children to engage with history throughout the primary school phase, not least because it allows teachers to control the amount and level of content, making it appropriate to the age and abilities of the pupils. It also allows teachers to embellish history with elements that children usually enjoy, such as bloodshed and toilets.

- Stories intrigue and fascinate children.
- Stories often form a central feature of history teaching in different contexts – reading, hearing, seeing and/or telling or being told them.
- It is important that teachers are storytellers as well as readers of stories.
- Oral storytelling is a powerful alternative teaching technique to pupils reading, watching or listening to recorded stories.

Suitable for

KS1, KS2

Aim

- To help children engage with history using the storytelling format.

Resources

- A story related to an era, event or person in history the children are studying

What to do

1. Tell the children the story.

2. Then ask the children to identify one piece of information that the story tells us.

3. Collect the pieces of information offered and consider what it tells us about the era, event or person being studied.

Variations

- You can control the content of the story, adding as much or as little detail as you feel is appropriate.
- You can explain that storytelling is an age-old way of passing on information, which can make the content apocryphal and subject to distortion, omission or bias.
- A game of 'Chinese whispers' or retelling a story in shorter and shorter time spans is a way to illustrate this effect.

Timewatch

Timewatch is an activity relating to chronology and the level of difficulty can be adjusted depending on the age and abilities of the children. It can be used to help develop their vocabulary about this area.

Suitable for

KS1, KS2

Aim

- To develop a vocabulary about chronology and a sense of period.

Resources

- A card clock face with equal divisions and a card pointer that can be moved for each child (see figure below)

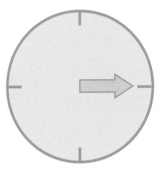

What to do

1. Give the children each a card clock and tell them that they are timewatchers.

2. Think of a category, such as the vocabulary – today, yesterday, last week, last year, for example – or eras such as the Romans, Vikings, Tudors, Victorians, or dates, such as 1830, 1850, 1870 and so on.

3. Ask the children a question related to the timewatch and ask them to place the pointer in the appropriate place. For example, you could ask, 'When did we visit the zoo? Was it yesterday, last week … and so on?'

4. The children hold up their watches with the pointers indicating their answers.

Variation

- This format can be developed in a number of ways (see Chronology Counter, page 114).

Chapter 3
RE

Introduction

Religious education is slightly different from other primary subjects as each local authority has a Standing Advisory Committee for Religious Education (SACRE). These committees have a requirement to provide non-aided schools with a locally agreed syllabus that is updated every five years. Whatever framework each SACRE approves, the two overarching themes are learning about and learning from religion through key concepts, such as:

- beliefs, teachings and sources
- practices and ways of life
- expressing meaning
- identity and belonging
- meaning, purpose and truth
- values and commitments.

When children are learning about religion, they should come to know what it means to be an adherent of a particular faith tradition. RE involves learning about the beliefs, values and practices of a variety of religions but also the way that they may influence the behaviour of both individuals and the community.

These concepts are linked to two key processes:

- learning *about* religion
- learning *from* religion.

When learning from religion, children should be given the opportunity to consider the different possible answers to major religious and moral issues, which will enable them to develop their own views in a reflective way so that:

- when considering possible answers to ultimate questions, pupils come to their own conclusions, informed by the responses of different religions and faith groups
- when considering sacred writings, pupils form an opinion about their value as guidance for living.

A good RE programme will ensure that there are opportunities for children to learn *about* religion and *from* it. It will also provide occasions for them to learn skills and form attitudes which, while not exclusive to RE, are an important element of the RE programme.

In the planning process, it is important to think about the ways in which a topic might relate to the children's own lives. They might investigate the concepts of empathy and interpretation so that they can reflect on and apply them to their own lives. They could also evaluate issues and form their own opinions. In these ways, children learn about similarities, differences, diversity and how we live in an interdependent world. Their growing understanding helps them to make sense of the world and prepares them to play an active role as informed, responsible citizens.

A Message for God

Religion is central to the lives of millions. At the same time, faith is a personal response to religious teaching and each individual may respond slightly differently and ask slightly different questions about it. Finding out about personal responses can help children to understand the personal significance of prayer.

Suitable for

KS1, KS2

Aim

- For children to consider the personal nature of prayer.

Resources

- Examples of simple prayers

What to do

1. Discuss what happens in a place of worship – celebration, singing and so on.
2. Either pick up on the notion of prayer as it arises from the children or develop it when they introduce it.
3. Ask them what they think prayer is. Is it the same for everyone?
4. Collectively build up a list of what the elements of prayer are – asking for help, for themselves and others, giving thanks, worshipping a higher being and so on.
5. Ask the children to create a prayer of their own with some of the different elements from the list but include a message for God.

Variation

- Rather than a prayer, children could simply construct messages to or questions for God.

Analysing Information

RE activities can be used to help children develop a variety of thinking skills. Analysis is one of those skills and can be linked to 'learning about' and 'learning from', children learning about an aspect of a particular religion and then relating what they have learned to their own lives.

Suitable for

KS2

Aim

- To help children develop analytical thinking skills through RE.

Resources

- Copies of activity sheet about a religious person or topic for investigation (see example on page 217)

What to do

1. Introduce the children to your chosen person or topic – in this example, a Jewish rabbi.
2. List all the roles and responsibilities that the person has.
3. Ask the children to decide which of the roles they feel are the most important.
4. Then ask them to think of people in their own lives who have similar roles and responsibilities. These may or may not have a religious connection.
5. They can see where there are similarities and differences between their lives and the lives of others.

A Jewish rabbi

A Jewish rabbi has a number of roles. Select the three things that you think are most important from the list below and write them in the boxes.

- They teach others.
- They listen to people's problems.
- They conduct weddings and funerals.
- They help to organise events in the community.
- They help to maintain the synagogue.
- They go to conferences and meetings.

Can you think of people in your life who do the following?

Teach others	Listen to people's problems	Help to organise events in the community

Art

Both art and RE have transformational qualities. Using art as a creative approach to RE can enable children to learn from religion as a result of their personal responses to it. Images can help younger children to understand the context of a story or event and allow them to respond more fully.

Suitable for

KS1

Aim

● To connect RE to art via creative and spiritual expression.

Resources

● A story from a major faith, such as the Prodigal Son, Noah or Rama and Sita
● Pictures showing a moment of danger and others of a moment of safety

What to do

1. Read or tell the chosen story and ask the children who the major characters are.
2. When did they feel in danger? When did they feel safe?
3. Pupils can then look at two pictures – one showing a moment of danger and one showing a moment of safety.
4. Ask them to identify which picture relates to safety (such as seeing the diva lamps lit for their return) and which to danger (when Ravana the demon king disguises himself and kidnaps Sita, for example).

Variation

- Religious art can be used to develop mood and spiritual responses, as with images linked to the creation or the nature of God.

Asking Big Questions

Questioning is an integral part of RE, not least because the subject encompasses a large amount of philosophy. Small children can ask interesting questions that can be linked to literacy and used to create poems.

Suitable for

KS1

Aim

- To help young children ask questions related to the awe and wonder of life.

Resources

- Simple questions for young children – 'What do I think?' (about the subject), 'What do others think?', 'What other viewpoints are there?', 'What do I think now?', 'Has what I have learnt about what others think changed how I think?'
- Adults to scribe the children's questions

What to do

1. Start by asking the children a question related to the world around them, such as 'I wonder …?'
2. Ask children to think of the biggest questions they can ask and have an adult scribe write them out as poems.
3. These can then be decorated or displayed.

Variation

- As the children develop familiarity with the concept of questioning, they can start to consider aspects of RE with questions such as, 'What is a special book?' or 'Who has authority in my life?', using the same big question approach.

Awe and Wonder - Traffic Lights

This is an activity based on choices. Images of natural beauty, human abilities and religious experience can link to the concept of awe and wonder and give children the opportunity to reflect on aspects of the world around them.

Suitable for

KS1, KS2

Aim

- To ask children to respond to a series of images and make choices.

Resources

- Sets of images, including religious ones
- Sets of traffic lights (you can make these with card)

What to do

1. Give groups of the children a set of the images you've chosen.
2. Ask them to discuss each image and decide under which traffic lights they would put each of them: Red = uninspiring; amber = slightly inspiring; green = inspiring
3. Go round the room and ask each group to choose one image from the green group and compare and contrast their reasons for their choices.
4. Do the same for images from the red group.
5. Investigate if there is any pattern to the choices made.

Variations

- The sets of images can be organised to focus on a certain subject, such as natural images, buildings, people, animals or combinations of these, in relation to awe and wonder.
- All the images can relate to religious themes – places of worship, religious figures, artefacts and so on.

Belief

Belief is an important aspect for children to consider when they study religious education. This activity is a simple introduction to the concept. The 'learning about' aspect is brought into it by considering the concept of belief as it relates to different faiths and the 'learning from' aspect by looking at personal beliefs.

Suitable for

KS2

Aims

- To know what the word 'belief' means.
- To explore personal beliefs.

Resources

- Definitions of the word 'belief'

What to do

1. Ask the children what the word 'belief' means.
2. Ask them to discuss their ideas with a partner and be ready to share them with the class.
3. Ask them to think about their most important belief. How would they feel if this belief was banned? What would they do? At the end of the discussion, together come up with some definitions of the word 'belief'.

Variations

- The idea of belief can be linked to the concept of a martyr and how people have been persecuted for their beliefs.

Choices Box

Learning about and learning from religion requires children to make personal responses and judgements about what they believe based on what they have learned about religion.

Suitable for

KS2

Aim

- To develop personal responses to religious teachings.

Resources

- For each child, a choices box with appropriate teachings from the various religions to be compared (see example for Buddhism, Christianity and Sikhism on page 224)

What to do

1. Give each child a choices box.
2. Have them look at the contents and use a traffic light system to highlight the three things that they regard as being the most important, marking them as green.
3. Next, ask them to highlight three boxes that they feel are quite important, marking them in yellow (amber).
4. Then ask them to highlight three boxes that, to them, are least important, marking them in red.
5. They can then share and compare their choices and explain the reasoning behind the choices.
6. You can collect together the individual choices and the class can see if there are any patterns emerging.

Variations

- The activities can be carried out using choices from the same faith or different faiths.
- More boxes can be added to increase the number of choices that need to be made.
- Blank boxes can be included so that the children can include their own choices.

Be truthful and honest. No lying or wrong speech. (Buddhism)	Love God and love other people as you love yourself. (Christianity)	Men and women are all equal before God. (Sikhism)
You should treat your parents kindly. (Sikhism)	Generosity in everything. No theft. (Buddhism)	Forgive, as you want to be forgiven. (Christianity)
Stand up for what is right. (Christianity)	God is pleased with honest work and true living. (Sikhism)	Care for all living things. (Buddhism)

Chorus Narration

The idea behind this activity is for you to tell the children a story or part of a story, such as the Nativity, in a simplified way. Every few phrases, the children suggest a possible sound effect, exclamation or similar to highlight parts of the story. The story is then repeated, with the children making the sounds in the appropriate places.

Suitable for

KS1, KS2

Aim

- To help pupils comprehend the main aspects of a story and to involve them in the storytelling process.

Resources

- Religious story
- Copies of the story with spaces marked for children to write in choices of sound effects and so on

What to do

1. Start to tell the chosen story and, at the given points, ask the children for their suggestions as to sound effects, exclamations and so on to embellish it.
2. Decide which suggestions are most appropriate and select them.
3. Repeat the story with the class, the children adding the chosen sound effects and so on in the appropriate places (see example on page 226).

The Innkeeper

Once, a long time ago, there was an innkeeper. There was nothing the innkeeper liked more than a good night's sleep.
(*snoring* × 3)

One night, there was a knock at the door.
(*knock, knock, knock*)

He climbed out of bed.
(*action – climbing*)

Went downstairs
(*stomp, stomp, stomp*)

And opened the door
(*creaking*)

There in the street stood a man and his wife.
('No room!') said the innkeeper

Variations

- Sound tracking, which involves one group enacting an event or story and another providing the soundtrack for it. Alternatively, show a video with the sound off, the children providing the commentary (scripted or improvised).
- Mimed activities, such as a 'silent movie' or a dream sequence, by a child at a time or several, performed at real-life speed or in slow motion, can be another useful way to bring a religious story to life for children.

Codes for Living

All societies and individuals have codes for living. This activity asks children to compare and contrast what different faiths say and how the codes affect the way that believers live their lives.

Suitable for

KS1, KS2

Aims

- Regarding 'learning about religion', what the similarities and differences are between the codes for living of different faiths.
- Regarding 'learning from religion', what the codes mean to the children.

Resources

- Simple versions of various religions' ethical codes for living (see examples below)

Examples of the ethical codes of various religions

Judaism
The ten commandments.

1. Put God first.
2. Love God most of all.
3. Give respect to everything that is holy, especially God.
4. Keep one day of the week special.
5. Respect your parents or those who care for you.
6. Don't take anyone's life.
7. Be faithful in marriage.
8. Do not steal.
9. Don't say bad things about other people.
10. Don't be jealous of other people or their possessions.

Islam

Teaches that it is good to:

- be kind and considerate
- be tolerant
- be gentle
- be polite
- be decent
- be keen to learn
- keep promises
- be patient
- be thankful
- be humble
- be clean
- have a sense of community.

Christianity

Jesus taught us to:

- love God
- love other people
- be gentle and kind
- be fair and treat others justly
- forgive those who hurt or upset us
- stand up for what is right.

Sikhism

Guru Nanak taught us:

- there is only one God
- worship and pray to the one God and no one else
- remember God, work hard and help others
- God is pleased with honest work and true living
- before God, there is no rich and no poor, no black and no white – it is your actions that make you good or bad
- men and women are all equal before God
- love everyone and pray for the good of all
- be kind to people, animals and birds
- do not fear
- do not frighten

- always speak the truth: God and truth are two in one
- be simple in your food, dress and habits
- God is the end of which no one knows, the more you say, the more it grows.

Buddhism

The five precepts teach us to:

- not do any evil,
- cultivate good,
- purify one's mind.

This is the teaching of the Buddha.

- The first precept is to avoid killing or harming living beings.
- The second is to avoid stealing.
- The third is to avoid sexual misconduct.
- The fourth is to avoid lying.
- The fifth is to avoid alcohol and other intoxicating drugs.

What to do

1. Divide the class into groups – the number matching the number of religions chosen – and give each child in each group a list of precepts from a particular religion. Ask them to each select the three that they think are the most important.

2. Then, within each group, have the children work in pairs to discuss their choices and decide again on the three most important.

3. This process can be repeated, depending on the size of groups, until every group has made three final choices.

4. List the choices made by the different groups and have the children look for similarities and differences. Have the class as a whole made similar choices?

5. Finally, ask the children to choose three of the collective precepts that they feel are most important to them.

Variation

- The various precepts can be put in boxes on a sheet and the children colour in the boxes according to their importance using the traffic light system – red – not important, amber (yellow) – not especially important and green – important.

Conscience Alley

In this activity, children play the roles of characters in faith stories, such as stories about Jesus. They learn to consider how faith can motivate and interpret the behaviour of others as well as their own responses to an event.

NB: Remember, it is not appropriate to represent Muhammad (peace be upon him – tell the children that, as a mark of reverence, Muslims always use this phrase when they mention him and other prophets) or the Sikh gurus in any dramatised activity.

Suitable for

KS2

Aim

- For children to look at the feelings of individuals in religious stories.

Resources

- A relevant story linked to a topic being undertaken, such as the Good Samaritan

What to do

1. Tell or dramatise your chosen story.
2. Give or ask the children to choose and play the part of the characters in the story.
3. At the end of the story, ask the children to stand in two parallel lines – a conscience alley.

4. As the main character(s) pass along the conscience alley, they explain the reasons or motivation for their actions. For example, in the story of the Good Samaritan, the priest might say, 'I'd have liked to help but ...'.

5. The other children voice reasons and discuss how they might have responded in that situation.

Variation

- Have the children look at the motivation of figures in faith, why they behave as they do, such as St Francis of Assisi or Guru Nanak.

Dreamcatcher

This activity is based on Roald Dahl's idea from *The BFG* (Puffin, 2007), in which the big friendly giant went around with a net catching children's dreams. This activity links RE with personal, social and health education and citizenship (PHSE and C).

Suitable for

KS1, KS2

Aim

- For children to consider their dreams for their own and the world's future.

Resources

- Copy of *The BFG*
- butterfly net or similar
- Copies of the cloud thought bubbles

What to do

1. Talk about or read excerpt from *The BFG* about the giant catching children's dreams.

2. Ask the children to consider their own dreams about themselves or the world.

3. Then ask them to draw and/or write down their dreams in a thought bubble, such as this one:

4. Display their dreams alongside the net as a wall display.

Variations

- Ask for children's thoughts, then display them alongside those of famous figures, such as Martin Luther King, Gandhi.
- Compare children's hopes and dreams with those of religious figures, such as Jesus Christ, Guru Nanak.

Experiences

This activity introduces children to the idea that people affiliated to a particular faith can wear special clothes that identify what their religious beliefs are.

Suitable for

KS1

Aim

- To help children understand the significance of clothing to adherents of various religions.
- To focus on the five Ks in Sikhism, which are symbolic of their faith.

Resources

- Books giving information on special clothes or uniforms related to several different faiths
- Large piece of paper and drawing and colouring pencils and pens
- People in the community who wear uniform to come in – nurse, doctor, police officer, fire officer for example
- Special clothing to display, such as helmets, gloves, overalls and so on, and uniforms for a role-play area

What to do

1. Share the information books with the children, noticing the clothes worn and finding examples of the five Ks in Sikhism – talk about the meaning and importance of the five K words.

2. Show pictures of typical Sikh clothes. Lay the piece of paper, ask one of the children to lie down and draw round him or her. Ask the children to draw particular items on the outline.

3. Talk about 'Kangha' (comb) and the importance of caring for hair.

4. Discuss 'special clothes'. Do the children know anyone who wears a uniform? Invite your chosen members of the community in to show the children their special clothing or uniforms that they wear.

5. Make a display table of the special clothing you've collected. Look at how special clothing can be used for protection.

6. Create a role-play area using the examples of uniforms you've selected.

Variations

- Invite members of the Sikh community to visit and talk about their clothing and faith.
- Invite a Sikh male in to show the children how to put on a turban.
- Have a display with K items for the children to identify.
- Use collage materials and add information cards for each of the five Ks.
- Looking at special clothing used in other faiths, such as vestments in the Christian church, clothing worn by pilgrims undertaking Hajj and so on.

Exploring Worship

The word 'worship' derives from 'worth-ship' which means to do with what is of highest worth. Worship has many forms of expression, varying from one religious tradition to another. For young children, introducing the idea of worship by singing, miming a prayer and sharing with others is a useful way to foster their own spiritual development.

Suitable for

KS1

Aim

- To develop respect for and understanding of the beliefs of others.

Resources

- A child-friendly worship song
- Food for sharing

What to do

1. Sing a worship song (Christian) with the class to spark the children's interest.

2. Discuss some of the words in the song and devise a mime to represent some of those words.

3. Then use the opportunity to talk about what the children think God might be like and why people might tell their most secret, deepest thoughts to God. This leads into the idea of prayer.

4. Introduce the children to the idea that another form of worship is service to others. (Food can be a form of worship, as can sharing with and helping others in the world.)

5. Share the food to represent worship, such as bread and wine (but serve fruit juice) in Christianity, challah bread in Judaism and prasad in Hinduism and Sikhism.

Variations

- Create a simple song and use actions to represent praise
- Mime to a well-known prayer, such as the Lord's Prayer (Matthew 6:7–13).

Festivals of Light

Many religions have festivals linked to light. These festivals have symbolic meaning as well as often having cultural links with particular groups.

Suitable for

KS1, KS2

Aims

- To make children aware of similarities and differences between the various faiths.
- To learn about a particular festival.

Resources

- Images of light sources, such as candles, lamps and so on.

What to do

1. Discuss with the children the idea of light and what it can represent.
2. Explain that many religious groups have festivals linked to light. Can the children think of any? (Diwali is one.)
3. Tell the story of Rama and Sita and their return home, lit by diva lamps.
4. Describe how the festival is celebrated each year.

Variations

- The children can make simple diva lamps
- They can study an alternative religion and associated light festivals, such as the Jewish Hanukkah.

Gifts

This activity, which can be linked to the Christmas story, asks children to consider what makes a gift special and what makes some gifts more important than others.

Suitable for

KS1

Aims

- For children to reflect on personal experiences and express personal viewpoints.
- To learn to look at different viewpoints before forming conclusions.

Resources

- Ideas cards (see examples below)
- Christmas tree template (see page 241)

Examples of idea cards

It cost a lot of money.	It is big.
It was made by someone.	It will last a long time.

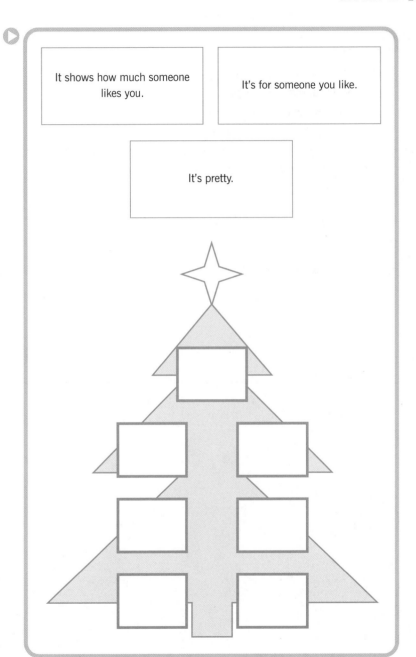

It shows how much someone likes you.

It's for someone you like.

It's pretty.

What to do

1. Discuss with the children what gifts they would like for Christmas and what gifts they're going to give.

2. Discuss what makes a gift special.

3. Read through the ideas on the cards.

4. Divide the children up into small groups and ask them to place the cards on the Christmas tree in order of importance, as they see it, with the most important at the top.

Variation

- Add extra cards, using the children's ideas if you would like to.

Give Us a Clue

This activity introduces an important religious figure or event by giving a series of clues, which can be simplified or made more difficult depending on the age and abilities of children or their knowledge of the subject.

Suitable for

KS1, KS2

Aim

- To test children's knowledge of religious leaders or events using a series of clues.

Resources

- Information about a religious leader or event set out in a numbered list, in no particular order (see example for Guru Nanak below)

Guru Nanak

1. His teachings included that we should 'work hard and help others'.
2. He travelled far and wide to teach about the new religion.
3. Before he died, he told his most trusted follower, Lehna, that he must be the next guru. Lehna was given the name Guru Angad.
4. He was born a Hindu.
5. Eventually he became a religious teacher.
6. He was born in 1496.
7. He was trained by his father to keep accounts.
8. He set out a list of new rules to bring people closer to God.
9. He disappeared for three days and nights.
10. He believed that there is only one God, responsible for all.

11. He believed that all people are equal and should have equal opportunities.
12. Three of Nanak's most important teachings are known as nam simran, kirat karo and vand chakko.
13. A religious teacher in his language is called a guru.
14. His most famous hymn is the Japji.
15. His new faith used ideas from both Hinduism and Islam.
16. He worked for a Muslim as he grew up, so he learned about the Muslim religion.
17. He was born in a village in the Punjab called Talwandi.
18. His father kept the accounts of the chief man of the village.

What to do

1. Tell the children that you have a number of clues that you're going to give them to work out the name of a religious person or event. The clues are numbered.
2. The children select a number and try to decide what the answer might be.
3. After each choice has been made, delete that item from the list.
4. Ask the children to keep on selecting numbers until either the children guess correctly or the information is exhausted.

Variation

- The same process as above, but with the numbers only displayed on a whiteboard or projector, the information being revealed once a number has been chosen.

God in Everything

Hindus believe that God is manifested in everything, which is one of the reasons for their respect for animals and plants. This activity asks children to consider this concept and the possibility that God is omnipresent in a whole variety of shapes and guises.

Suitable for

KS1, KS2

Aim

- To help children understand the idea of God's omnipresence.

Resources

- Images that the children could consider as representing aspects of God

What to do

1. Explain the Hindu belief in the nature of God and ask the children to consider the concept of God being in everything.

2. Ask them to think about and draw an image that could represent an aspect of God.

3. Have them label the image with a description of how it represents aspects of the nature of God.

4. End the activity by explaining the Hindu concept that God is within us. Hindus call our innermost self Atman – God as all of us.

5. This idea can be developed by introducing the Hindu greeting 'Namaste'. When Hindus meet, they greet each other by putting their hands together as if praying and bowing down, then saying 'Namaste'. This word means 'There is God in you'.

Variation

- Give children examples of how God could be manifested, such as fire (warmth, shelter) or ice (cooling, changeable) and so on.

Guess Who?

 This activity tests the knowledge of younger children as they have to recognise and apportion the clues to the correct religions.

Suitable for

KS1

Aim

- To recognise similarities and differences between religions.

Resources

- Pictures, artefacts and other clues related to particular religions, labelled.

What to do

1. Start by outlining the number of religions being compared – two or three, for example.
2. Show the pictures of places of worship, religious artefacts and so on.
3. Ask the children to decide which picture or artefact belongs to which religion, such as chauri, Torah, kandar, yarmulke.
4. Ask the children, 'Are there any pictures or artefacts you are uncertain about or might belong to more than one religion?'

Variations

- The number of religions presented can be increased or decreased according to the knowledge, age and abilities of the children concerned.
- With younger children, each clue can be given a number so that they can just list the numbers under the appropriate religion, as shown below.

Hinduism	Islam
2, 4, 5, 7, 10	1, 3, 6, 8, 9

- An extra column can be added so that children can list any images they are unsure of, e.g.

Hinduism	Not sure	Islam
4, 5, 7, 10	2, 9	1, 3, 6, 8

Investigating an Artefact

There are three stages children go through in developing their learning by handling and using artefacts. The first is when children see an object and can describe its properties, such as its size, colour, shape, material if made of. The second is a greater understanding of what the object was used for, how it works and so on. The third stage is to be able to build up a picture of the faith group to whom the artefacts belong.

NB: Be aware of the possible sensitivities relating to each artefact. There are reasons for their existence within a religious tradition, for personal and community use, and it may be easy to offend. If in doubt, assume great sensitivity and handle very carefully. Also, ensure that the children see the way that you handle artefacts – with respect and care – and encourage them to do the same. By handling such objects, children come into close contact with them and the community they represent. They can examine and explore the objects, their meanings and uses.

Suitable for

KS1, KS2

Aims

- To investigate artefacts in order to try and understand the significance and importance of faith objects to users.
- To remind children that artefacts act as symbols of a particular faith, which help to explain what that faith represents.

Resources

- Large bag of artefacts related to a particular faith or to a range of faiths.
- Copies of a straightforward grid with boxes large enough to draw in.

What to do

1. Pass the mystery bag around the class for the children to handle and describe one object. Ask them to take it out of the bag and ask what is it, what might it be used for?

2. Pass it around, describing and discussing it. Ask the children yes or no questions or where, what, when, why enquiry-type questions. The symbolic elements of the religious artefacts can be drawn out in this way.

3. Use the grids as a focus of the examination of the artefacts. The children can simply draw or draw and label aspects of them (say, differentiate them by size and number of boxes). Ask questions and encourage the children to ask questions, too.

Variations

- An alternative activity involving writing is to question the children in groups. Place an artefact in the middle of a sheet of paper. Ask the children to write their questions all around the object. The questions can be passed around to find out the answers. Any that aren't can be stored until the end of that topic to see if they can be answered then. This method can also be used as a starting point for research activities.

- Use the 20 questions format, asking 20 questions about each artefact to find out more about it. These can be limited to closed questions, which are those requiring only 'yes' and 'no' answers.

- Have the children sit back to back, then hand one of each pair a familiar artefact. The other child then asks closed questions until he or she can identify what the object is.

- Prepare some true and false statements about an artefact. The children then sort them into three categories: true, false and we don't know.

Islam - an Introduction

Islam is the second most popular faith in the world, with over 1000 million adherents. Those who follow Islam are called Muslims. There are between 1.5 and 3 million Muslims in Britain, making it the second most popular faith here, too. This activity aims to introduce children to some aspects of the faith.

Suitable for

KS1

Aim

- To introduce the religion of Islam to younger children.

Resources

- The story of how Islam was revealed to humanity by the Prophet Muhammad (peace be upon him)
- Vocabulary links – Arabia, Islam (surrender to God), Qur'an, mosque

What to do

1. Tell the children the story of how the Archangel Jibrail (Gabriel) revealed God's word to Muhammad and all the things said were collected together in the Qur'an.

2. Explain how at first Muhammad's message of one God was not well received but how gradually, over a period of time, the Prophet set about establishing Islam, ending idol worship, introducing a justice system and focusing on the worship of one God, which became accepted by people in Arabia.

3. Ask the children to think of an instruction that they have been given by a teacher or their parents and didn't understand at first but then realised how it made sense. Examples are waiting at the edge of a road before crossing and hanging their coats and bags in the same place in the cloakroom.

Variation

- Children can draw (and label) a picture of an instruction that they didn't understand at first but later came to understand.

Learning from the Five Pillars of Islam

The five pillars of Islam help Muslims put their faith into action. The five pillars are:

- Shahadah – declaration of faith
- Salat – ritual prayer, five times a day
- Zakat – giving a fixed proportion of earnings to charity
- Sawm – fasting
- Hajj – pilgrimage to Mecca.

This activity asks children to look at each of the five pillars and what they mean to Muslims. It then asks them to consider how they relate to similar ideas in their own lives.

Suitable for

KS2

Aim

- To develop learning about and learning from the five pillars of Islam.

Resources

- Copies of a table to help children make links between the Muslim experience of living their faith through the five pillars and their own experiences (see example on page 254)

Example of table for making links

Learning about Islam	Learning from Islam
All the time, Muslims believe ...	All the time, I believe ...
Five times a day, Muslims ...	Every day, I intend to ...
Every week (or when they are paid) Muslims give ...	If I chose to be generous, I would ...
Once a year, for self-discipline, Muslims ...	My ambition for the next year is ...
Once in a lifetime, Muslims go ...	In my lifetime, I hope to ...

What to do

1. Discuss the five pillars with the children and how each pillar represents an expectation for Muslims.

2. Look at each pillar and how Muslims enact them in their lives. They could consider the difficulties attached to each expectation. For instance, fasting and what that would be like.

3. Then, look at how the idea might relate to all children, either through discussion or using a table, as shown in the example.

4. The children could compare their thoughts to see if there are any similarities between their ideas.

Variation

• Children can be asked to consider just one or two ideas rather than all five of the pillars.

Looking at a Murti

'Murtis' are images of Hindu gods that have been consecrated by priests. They are venerated either at home or in a temple puja (worship). Each temple or home shrine may have a number of murtis. Popular deities include Ganesha, Krishna and Shiva. Worshippers can choose whether to worship all or just some of the gods.

Suitable for

KS2

Aim

- To make children consider the symbolism related to Hindu gods through the form of murtis.

Resources

- Images or pictures of Hindu gods
- Copies of chart on which to note observations (see example on page 256)

What to do

1. Show the children the images of Hindu murtis and explain their purpose.
2. Ask them to look at one particular image and discuss the symbolism associated with the murti shown.
3. The children can draw the murti and note down what they recognise. They can ask questions about things that they are less sure about (see example below).
4. The children can share their questions and compare answers or follow up initial investigations with research on the various Hindu deities.

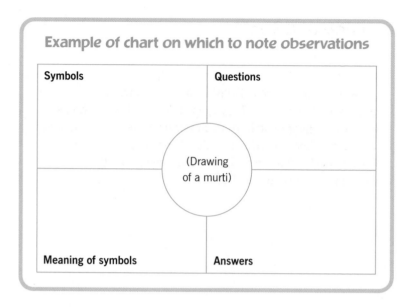

Example of chart on which to note observations

Symbols	Questions
Meaning of symbols	Answers

(Drawing of a murti)

Variations

- Work with the class to investigate just one murti.
- Develop an exploration of the puja ceremony by creating a class shrine.

Looking at Ganesha

Ganesha is a popular Hindu deity. He is the god who helps believers overcome obstacles. His elephant persona reflects the attributes he uses to carry out this role.

Suitable for

KS2

Aim

- To introduce pupils to the Hindu god Ganesha.

Resources

- Copies of a picture of Ganesha with associated symbols (see example below)

Large ears – listen more

Axe – to cut off all bonds of attachment

Small mouth – talk less

Blessings – blesses and protects on spiritual path to supreme

Large stomach – peacefully digest all good and bad in life

Prasada – the whole world is at your feet and for the asking

Big head – think big

Small eyes – concentrate

Rope – to pull you nearer to the highest goal

One tusk – retain good throw away bad

Trunk – high level of efficiency and adaptability

Madaka – rewards of sadhana

Mouse – Desire. Unless under control, can cause havoc; you ride the desire and keep it under control, don't allow it to take you for a ride

What to do

1. Give the children an image of Ganesha with associated symbols.

2. Ask them to try and decide what each symbol represents in terms of Ganesha's role, for example:
   - large ears – listen more
   - big head – think more
   - small eyes – concentrate
   - large stomach – peacefully digest all that is good and bad in life
   - trunk – high level of efficiency and adaptability
   - small mouth – talk less
   - rope – to pull you to the highest goal.

3. Compare the children's choices and give them the correct symbols.

Looking at Pictures

Connecting RE effectively with pictures enables the development of key skills, such as responding sensitively, suggesting meanings, making links and applying ideas.

Suitable for

KS1, KS2

Aim

- To develop personal responses to religious stories by responding to pictures.

Resources

- A picture or pictures related to a story from a major faith

What to do

1. Show the children a painting or picture projected onto a whiteboard or reproduced in some way.
2. Tell or review the story the picture relates to.
3. Ask the children if they can identify the moment in the story the picture captures.
4. Can they suggest why the artist chose that particular moment?
5. Can they put themselves in the position of one of the characters in the picture – how might they be feeling or thinking at that moment?

Variation

- Children can add speech or thought bubbles to reproductions of the image to express what the characters could be thinking or saying.

Looking at the Beatitudes

The Beatitudes are interesting to study as they contrast with the Commandments, many of which have a 'shall not' aspect. Here, Jesus talks about the things that raise people up above the common.

Suitable for

KS2

Aim

- To learn about Jesus but also about themselves when they decide who are the blessed and what their reward should be.

Resources

- Copies of the eight Beatitudes of Jesus (see below)

The Beatitudes

Blessed are the poor in spirit (humble)
for theirs is the kingdom of heaven.

Blessed are those who mourn,
for they will be comforted.

Blessed are the meek,
for they will inherit the earth.

Blessed are those who hunger and thirst for righteousness,
for they will be satisfied.

Blessed are the merciful,
for they will receive mercy.

Blessed are the pure in heart,
for they will see God.

Blessed are the peacemakers,
for they will be called children of God.

Blessed are those who are persecuted for righteousness' sake,
for theirs is the kingdom of heaven.

Matthew 5:3–10 (*NRSV*)

What to do

1. Explain the context of the Beatitudes from the Sermon on the Mount.
2. Read through the Beatitudes. Discuss their meaning
3. Look at those whom Jesus saw as blessed.
4. Ask the children to draw up a contemporary set of Beatitudes. Who would be blessed and how? For example, 'blessed are the caring, for they shall be praised', 'blessed are the givers, for they shall be given to', 'blessed are the loving, for they shall receive in kind.'

Looking for a Golden Rule

Religions that originate from the Abrahamic tradition have much in common, but all religions have teachings their followers are expected to follow. Many embody the concept of a 'golden rule'.

Suitable for

KS2

Aim

- To compare some of the key teachings of a number of religions.

Resources

- Simple outlines of key teachings of two or three faiths (see examples below)

Examples of the key teachings of various religions

Christianity
Jesus taught us to:

- love God
- love other people
- be gentle and kind
- be fair and treat others justly
- forgive those who hurt or upset us
- stand up for what is right.

Judaism

The Ten Commandments are:

1. put God first
2. love God the most
3. give respect to everything that is holy, especially God
4. keep one day of the week special
5. respect your parents or those who care for you
6. don't take anyone's life
7. be faithful in marriage
8. do not steal
9. don't say bad things about other people
10. don't be jealous of other people or their possessions.

Islam

Teaches that it is good to:

- be kind and considerate
- be tolerant
- be gentle
- be polite
- be decent
- be keen to learn
- keep promises
- be patient
- be thankful
- be humble
- be clean
- have a sense of community.

What to do

1. Divide the class into two or three groups depending on how many faiths are being studied.

2. Give pairs of children a set of key teachings from a particular faith. Ask them to select the three that they feel are the most important.

3. Then ask the pairs to join with another pair to compare their choices and decide between them on their top three.

4. Continue the process until the whole group has agreed on a top three.

5. They then feed these back to you and you act as a scribe.

6. The whole class compares the different faiths to see if there are similarities and differences in their choices and how closely the religions reflect certain teachings.

Variation

- Include a greater or lesser number of faiths.

Making and Keeping Promises

This activity draws on children's experiences and ideas to discuss why making and keeping promises is important and why promises made by God are particularly significant for many people.

Suitable for

KS1

Aim

- To introduce the concept of commitment for later learning in RE.

Resources

- Images or stories related to making and keeping promises
- Format for discussing promises (see example below)

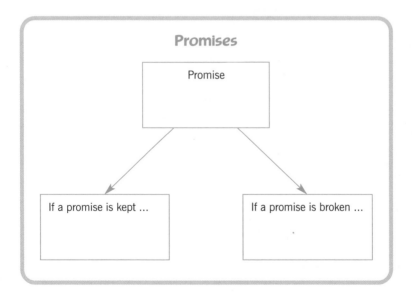

Promises

Promise

If a promise is kept ...

If a promise is broken ...

What to do

1. Read a chosen story or look at a chosen image about making and keeping promises.
2. Ask the children to think about promises from their own experiences.
3. Discuss with them the importance of keeping promises.
4. Reflect on what it feels like when a promise is broken.
5. Read a faith story linked to promises, such as baptism in a Christian church, the five Buddhist precepts or Guru Nanak's stories.

Variation

- This activity can be developed by looking at another faith story and the concept of promises, vows and commitment, for instance, or an artefact, such as a Jewish mezuzah, which reminds Jews of their promise to love and remember God in everything that they do.

Paper Chain

 An alternative way to gather and present information on a particular faith or topic.

Suitable for

KS1

Aim

● To link individual pieces of information in a way that is accessible for all the children in the class.

Resources

● Large paper strips that can be linked as chains

What to do

1. Ask the pupils to write down words, phrases or sentences to describe the nature of the topic or theme being studied, such as Christmas.
2. Use these strips of paper to make a paper chain.
3. The children can read the chain as a way of learning more about the festival – 'The three wise men who came to visit Jesus are also called the Magi', for example.
4. More links can be added to the chain as the children learn more about the religion being studied.

Variations

● As the children's knowledge develops consider using this same activity for more abstract themes, such as the nature of God.
● The same idea could be used for other formats, such as putting information in the windows of a large Advent calendar.

Picture Framing

RE provides many opportunities to study images from stories or places or worship as well as artists' interpretations of important moments. By placing an image within a frame, with boxes to fill in you can ask them to find things that focus children's observations.

Suitable for

KS1, KS2

Aim

- Using images to further children's understanding of religion, including clarifying stories and investigating symbolism.

Resources

- Religious images
- A3-size frames for pairs or group work or A4-size frames for individual work with pre-prepared things to look for in boxes around the edge (see example on page 269)

What to do

1. Provide the children with copies of a religious image.
2. Ask them to mount them in their frames.
3. Ask the children to look at the image and find the things mentioned in the boxes.

Example picture frame

Some things that I can see in the picture.

| Some things that I can work out from the picture. |  | Some things that I already know about the picture. |

A question that I would like to ask about the picture.

Variations

- The picture framing activity can be used in a variety of ways:
  - landscape or portrait formats
  - more or fewer boxes
  - simple or complicated questions
  - written or drawn responses
  - children constructing their own boxes for others to complete.

Places

This activity introduces young children to the idea of special places, which can lead to the investigation of places of worship.

Suitable for

KS1

Aims

- To understand that different places have different functions.
- To consider feelings in relation to different places.

Resources

- Images of different places within the local community – houses, shops, factory, pub, post office, places of worship.

What to do

1. Show the children the chosen images, reflecting the needs of the community to live and work, for recreation, leisure and places of worship.

2. The following questions could be asked.
    - What goes on in each place?
    - Who goes there? Why? When?
    - Where do you like going?
    - How would you feel if you were in that place?
    - Is it a place that you go to be alone or with others?
    - Which of those places (if any) are special to you?

3. Encourage the children to talk about size, shape, design, decoration and so on related to each place.

4. They can then decide which is their favourite place in the community, draw or paint it and say or write why they like it.

Variation

- Take the children on a walk around their local neighbourhood, noting different places and their functions.

Priorities Grid

RE can be used as a springboard to developing thinking skills. The priorities grid asks children to analyse a series of actions and evaluate the benefits against the costs. This approach can also be used in other humanities subjects, such as history and PSHE.

Suitable for

KS2

Aim

- To analyse information against set criteria.

Resources

- A large priorities grid (see example on page 273)
- Pieces of information about a religious figure and their actions, such as St Francis of Assisi, on separate pieces of paper or card

What to do

1. Show the children the priorities grid and use one or two examples to explain how it works.
2. Give them the pieces of information and, working as a group, have them lay them out in appropriate places on the priorities grid.
3. Discuss the children's decisions and all together and determine the best places for the different pieces of information.

Variation

- The children can collect information themselves on sticky notes, then place them on the priorities grid.

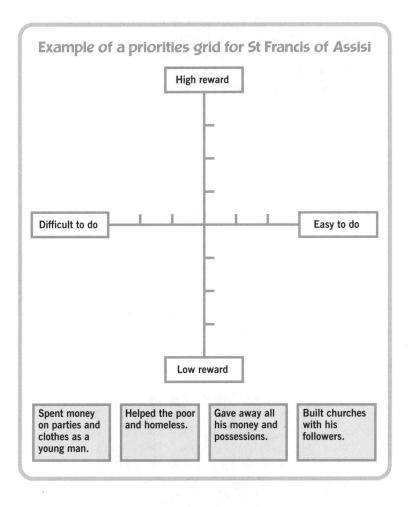

Example of a priorities grid for St Francis of Assisi

High reward

Difficult to do — Easy to do

Low reward

| Spent money on parties and clothes as a young man. | Helped the poor and homeless. | Gave away all his money and possessions. | Built churches with his followers. |

Religious Symbols People Wear

All religions are full of symbols. Many are often worn by religious adherents. The aim of this activity is for children to learn about religions by making links between religious symbols and the faiths they represent. They also learn from religion by considering what symbols they wear.

Suitable for

KS1, KS2

Aim

- To make links between religious symbols and the faiths that they relate to.

Resources

- Pictures of religious symbols or actual examples (see examples below)
- Sets of pictures of religious symbols and people wearing them (see examples below)
- Sheet for recording answers (see example on page 275)

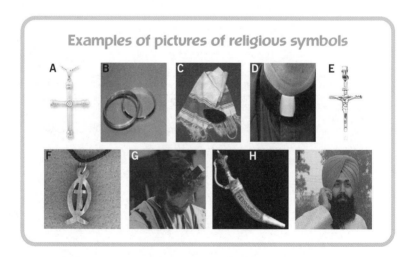

Examples of pictures of religious symbols

What to do

1. Show the children the pictures of or actual religious symbols and ask them if they recognise them.

2. Discuss what the different symbols represent.

3. Then, with the children in pairs, give each the two sets of pictures – of religious symbols and people wearing symbols.

4. Ask the children to match the two sets of pictures and explain their choices, writing their answers on the sheet.

Example activity sheet

The pictures show symbols that are worn by people linked to three religions. Four are from Christianity, three from Sikhism and two from Judaism.

Using the clues below, can you match them to the pictures?

Picture	Description of symbol
	A tefillin is a box that holds a scroll from the Torah and is tied to the head.
	A crucifix is a cross with an image of Jesus hanging on it.
	A kirpan is a dagger worn by Sikhs, only to be used to defend the weak.
	An ichthus, or fish symbol, was the symbol early Christians used to identify fellow believers.
	A tallith is a Jewish prayer shawl.
	A clerical collar tells us that the wearer is a member of the Christian clergy.
	A kanga is the Sikh symbol of God's continuity and oneness.
	A cross is the symbol of Christianity.

Variations

- Ask the children if they wear any symbols. Religious symbols, brand logos, school badges and so on can be drawn and labelled.
- The above activities can be carried out collectively using an interactive whiteboard.

Rules for Living

This activity looks at why we have rules, where rules are derived from and which we think are important. Children learn about religion from the perspective of the rules of various faiths and learn from it by applying those rules from different perspectives, including their own.

Suitable for

KS1, KS2

Aim

- To introduce the idea of the nature and importance of rules

Resources

- Examples of familiar rules, such as school rules, and rules from various faiths, such as the five pillars of Islam or the Ten Commandments (see example below) written on separate cards

Examples of rules for living

Put God first.	Don't hurt others.
Worship God alone.	Be faithful in marriage.
Use God's name with respect	Don't steal.
Remember God's special day – the sabbath.	Don't lie.
Respect your parents.	Don't be envious of others.

What to do

1. Lay the cards out randomly.

2. Read them out.

3. Ask the children if there are any that they don't understand.

4. Discuss them and ask the children to come to a consensus as to which are the most important and put them in order – the most important at the top.

5. Have the children come up with three extra statements that are important, too.

Variations

- Reword or omit cards that you think might upset particular children.
- Leave one or two cards blank and ask the children to devise their own rules.
- Ask them to rank the cards from the perspective of a practising Christian or Muslim, then to rank the cards from the perspective of someone without a belief in God. Are there similarities and differences?

Seder Plate

This activity links learning about and learning from religion with the story of the Passover, children making their own judgements about aspects of life based on the symbolism of the seder plate.

Suitable for

KS2

Aims

- To explain the symbolism of the seder plate.
- To make personal links to the meanings of aspects of the Passover story.

Resources

- The story of the Passover (see page 280)
- Diagram of a seder plate with the symbolism of the different elements annotated (see page 280)

What to do

1. Tell the Passover story and then say how Jews remind themselves of the event with the seder plate.

2. Show the diagram and go over the symbolism of the seder plate and what each item represents to Jews.

3. Ask the children to make their own decisions about what those symbols might represent for themselves.

Passover

At Passover, Jewish families hold a service called a seder, which includes a special meal. Each part of the meal is symbolic. That means it represents or reminds people of a certain part of the Passover story.

During seder, Jews remember how the children of Israel were led out of slavery in Egypt. The pharaoh let the Israelites leave after God delivered ten plagues to the Egyptians. In the last plague, God made all the first-born children die. To protect the Israelites from this fate, God told Moses that they should put lambs' blood on their doors. God would then 'pass over' the marked doors so the Israelites would not be harmed. That is why the festival is called Passover.

When the pharaoh set them free, the Israelites left their homes so quickly that there wasn't even time to bake some bread to take with them, so they packed their raw bread dough and baked it in the desert while they travelled. It made crackers that are called matzos. Today, to commemorate this event, Jews eat matzos in place of bread during Passover.

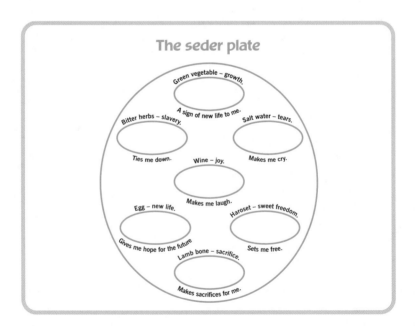

The seder plate

Green vegetable – growth.
A sign of new life to me.

Bitter herbs – slavery.
Ties me down.

Salt water – tears.
Makes me cry.

Wine – joy.
Makes me laugh.

Egg – new life.
Gives me hope for the future.

Haroset – sweet freedom.
Sets me free.

Lamb bone – sacrifice.
Makes sacrifices for me.

Single Bubble Map

A single bubble map is a simple format that is a good starting point for a topic and allows for information to be built up over time as children learn more or can be used as an assessment activity.

Suitable for

KS1, KS2

Aim

- To assess children's existing knowledge and build on it.

Resources

- Copies of a single bubble map linked to a topic or activity for children to fill in (see example for Christmas on page 282)

What to do

1. Give each of the children a copy of the single bubble map.
2. Ask the children to write one thing that they know about the chosen topic in one of the bubbles.
3. Have the children carry on filling in the bubbles until the information they know has been exhausted.
4. The ideas can be gathered together and used to build up a chronological account of the event.
5. The children can decide which, if any, are the most important pieces of information.

Variations

- The activity can be carried out just individually or collectively.
- The number of bubbles can be increased or decreased to differentiate the activity.
- Information can be drawn or written or both.

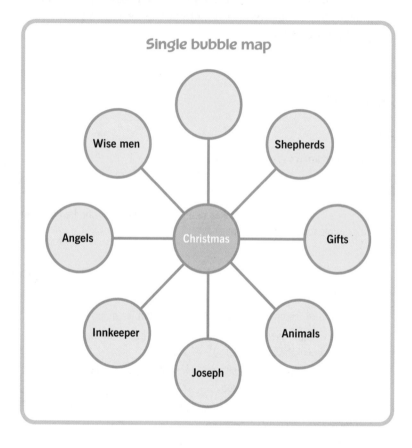

Special Books

Holy books have a special importance to religious adherents. What these books contain, who wrote them and what they represent gives them a significance that makes them sacred. This activity introduces this concept in a simple way for young children.

Suitable for

KS1

Aim

- To help young children think about 'special books' and the difference between 'special' and 'sacred'.

Resources

- A book special to you
- Display of books known and liked by the children and some copies of sacred books, such as the Bible, a Qur'an on a stand – covered and placed higher than other books, and a replica Torah scroll in its cover or the *Bhagavadgítá*.
- Images of sacred books in their context – church, gurdwara, mandir, mosque or synagogue.

What to do

1. Show the children the book that you have brought in and explain why it is important to you and how you would like it to be treated.

2. Then ask the children if they have any special books. What are they? Why are they special? How would you feel if they were damaged or lost?

3. Discuss how we should handle books that are special and important to people. Ask the children to role-play handling special books in pairs.

4. Ask them to select a book that they would like to ask questions about. These questions can relate to the display and their questions investigated and answered.

5. Where sacred books are selected, ask, 'Why is this book important or special?', 'Who is it about?', 'Who wrote it and is it "special"?' The concept of 'sacred' can then be introduced.

Variation

- Photograph books in the display. The children can then choose one and write their questions and answers next to it and these can be pinned up.

Special People in Pictures and Symbols

This activity can be undertaken as part of a study of Hinduism. It asks children to study religious imagery and look for symbols and iconography in pictures.

Suitable for

KS1, KS2

Aims

- To identify the elements in a picture that indicate that it is of something special.
- To reflect on the meaning of the symbols in the picture.

Resources

- Picture of a special person, such as Krishna
- Sticky notes

What to do

1. Ask the children to look carefully at the picture. Ask them, if it is of Krishna, what they see. How old do they think the child is? Why do you think that?

2. Then have them quietly concentrate on the picture for two minutes.

3. Discuss the meaning of elements or symbols that they have noticed.

4. Then, ask the children to work in pairs and list all the elements that indicate that this is a special baby – jewellery and so on.

5. Label each element in the picture using sticky notes.

6. Explain that this is a picture of Krishna and why Hindus worship him as a child.

7. Join pairs to form groups of four and ask each to focus on an element and explain its meaning.

8. Ask what they have learned about Krishna.

Variation

- Before doing this activity, tell the children some stories about Krishna.

Special Places

Special places introduces pupils to the idea of places special to them in their own locality that may link to religious places, such as places of worship.

Suitable for

KS2

Aim

- To investigate the meaning of 'special places'.

Resources

- Images of local places of interest
- Images of local places of worship
- Set of questions (see page 288)

What to do

1. Ask the children, 'What special places can you think of where we live?'

2. Give them the chosen images of the locality and the set of questions to answer.

Example of set of questions about special places

- How is this place special?
- Why is it special?
- How do people feel when they are there?
- Who cares and looks after this place?
- Are there any special rules to keep?
- Who goes there?
- What do they do when they are there?

Variation

- Include worldwide places of worship and ask the same questions.

Special Teachers

Making conceptual links between a known figure – their teacher – and religious leaders helps young children to understand something of the role of special people associated with world religions.

Suitable for

KS1

Aim

- To introduce young children to the idea of special people.

Resources

- Story about Jesus, such as the story of Zaccheus, the tax collector
- Possibly devices such as a story candle, to help children understand that they are listening to a faith story

What to do

1. Ask the children to consider what makes a good teacher. Encourage them to think about what they do – teach, help, encourage, look after, set an example and so on.
2. Tell the story about Jesus and ask the children to consider what examples he set as a teacher.
3. The ask them to retell the story and identify ways in which he taught others, how he did it.
4. Make a list of the teachings the children identify.
5. Ask them if they think Jesus was a special teacher. Help the children to understand that they have been listening to a faith story – a story with special meaning for believers.

Variation

- The focus could be on a rabbi or imam and the story linked to the Jewish or Islamic faiths.

Telephone

Among the scenarios used in drama, the idea of a telephone conversation to describe a religious event or person can be useful for developing RE. It is a personal response to learning from religion and develops speaking and listening skills, too.

Suitable for

KS2

Aim

- To develop personal responses to religious events.

Resources

- Information about a particular person or event given prior to this activity to help the children make more informed responses

What to do

1. Ask the children to imagine that they are making a phone call to a friend and are describing a religious event that they have been studying. The friend could be asking about the birth of Jesus, for example.

2. The other children then reply from the perspective of an eyewitness. This perspective can be very creative, so eyewitnesses could be a shepherd, donkey, spider and so on. Such variety helps the children to recognise how different responses to the same event are possible.

3. They can alternate the roles so that each child has a turn at being an eyewitness.

Variations

- Sit the children in pairs, back to back, to avoid them looking at each other and see how this influences their communication skills.
- Given the children specific roles to play

The 12 Days of Christmas

This activity links to a seasonal event that is celebrated in some way in most schools. It encompasses the idea of the advent calendar, the Nativity story and some of the traditions and institutions of Christmas.

Suitable for

KS1, KS2

Aim

- To develop knowledge and understanding of a religious/cultural event.

Resources

- An Advent calendar
- List of 12 basic facts relating to the Christmas story or traditions associated with Christmas (see example below)
- Sheets of paper, each folded or marked into 12 sections
- Large sheets of card or paper and stickers, pens and so on to decorate

Example 12 facts about Christmas

1. A long time ago, in a town called Nazareth, there lived a young woman called Mary.
2. One day, an angel named Gabriel visited her.
3. Gabriel told Mary that she was going to have a baby. The baby would be God's son.
4. Mary told Joseph what Gabriel had told her.
5. When it was time for the baby to arrive, Mary and Joseph travelled to Bethlehem.
6. Mary rode on a donkey.

7. Joseph was from Bethlehem and they needed to go there to be registered as part of the census.
8. Bethlehem was very busy and Mary and Joseph couldn't find a place to stay.
9. Eventually an innkeeper found them a place to rest in his stable.
10. It was in this stable that Jesus was born.
11. A bright star shone above the stable.
12. It led the shepherds and wise men who came to visit the baby Jesus to the stable.

What to do

1. Show the children the Advent calender and explain what it is for and how it is used. Then give them the 12 facts related to Christmas.
2. Ask them to draw and label those facts on a sheet of paper folded or marked into 12 sections. Leave a frame of blank space around each section.
3. Then, they need to cut out each of the 12 sections.
4. Hand out the large sheets of card or paper. Ask the children to decorate them, then draw 12 doors or flaps. Cut the doors or flaps around three edges to open and number them.
5. Stick the 12 sections in the correct order behind each door so that, when they are opened, the illustrations or text are revealed.

Variation

- The same storytelling idea can be linked to a series of doors, that can be used to order events.
- For younger children, there can be fewer, larger doors (perhaps three or four) and the activity can be based purely on illustrations.

The Jewish Mezuzah

On the doorposts of traditional Jewish homes, a small case is fixed (like the one shown below). This case is commonly known as a mezuzah. The mezuzah is meant to be a constant reminder of God's presence and mitzvoth (commandments) taken from a passage in Deuteronomy called the shema. In that passage, God commands Jews to keep his words constantly in their minds and hearts by (among other things) writing them on tiny scrolls of parchment and putting them inside cases on the doorposts of their houses. Still today, the words of the shema are written, along with the words of a companion passage, on such a scroll, and, on the back the name of God is written. These scrolls are kept in mezuzahs and put on the doorposts at the entrances to Jewish homes.

Suitable for

KS2

Aim

- To develop children's understanding of Jewish beliefs and make links with their own beliefs.

Resources

- Picture of a mezuzah (see example below)

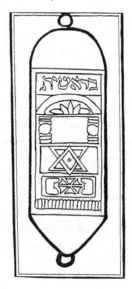

- Small paper scrolls
- Cardboard boxes, such as for tubes of toothpaste

What to do

1. Explain the idea of the mezuzah and what it means for Jewish people.

2. Give the children a box to decorate as a mezuzah.

3. Then give them a scroll and ask them to write a belief that is important to them.

4. The children put their finished scrolls in their boxes.

Variations

- Children design and create their own mezuzah boxes.
- Ask the children questions about mezuzahs and direct them towards their personal beliefs (see examples on page 297).

Example questions about mezuzahs

1. Talk about it. What shape is it? What is it made of? Why are there pictures/patterns?

2. Draw it, copying the symbols. Find out what the symbols mean.

3. Who do you think might use this? Why?

4. Where might it be found? Why?

5. What do you think is inside the mezuzah?

6. Design your own mezuzah case using relevant patterns and pictures.

7. What have you got in your house that is considered special? How are special things treated?

8. What special words might you try to say each day?

The Symbolism of the Cross

This activity focuses on learning about and learning from religion. It looks at the cross as a symbol and children are asked to reflect on their own feelings about it.

Suitable for

KS2

Aim

- To reflect on their personal responses to the cross and share their knowledge of its symbolism.

Resources

- Copies of images of the cross to colour in

What to do

1. Reflect with the children on their feelings about and understanding of the cross, its symbolism – Jesus died on the cross, it is a symbol of forgiveness and hope and so on.

2. Ask them to colour their cross a colour that reflects their feelings about it, such as green, red or yellow.

3. Then, around it, ask them to write words that reflect their attitudes to it – love, kindness, forgiveness and so on.

The Trimurti

Hinduism has a number of deities, each of whom demonstrates an aspect of the Supreme Being. Brahma (the creator), Vishnu (the preserver) and Shiva (the destroyer) are three major deities called the trimurti.

Suitable for

KS2

Aim

- To introduce pupils to three major Hindu gods and their powers

Resources

Images of Brahma (four heads), Vishnu (four arms) and Shiva (trident)

What to do

1. Ask the children to think of words with three in them (tricycle, tripod, triangle and so on).

2. Ask them 'What does "tri" mean?'

3. Then, explain about the trimurti and their roles in Hinduism.

4. Draw a triangle and show the children that it is a shape with three points enclosing everything. Ask them to draw a triangle with a god named at each point, drawing aspects of their roles within the triangle. (See example below.)

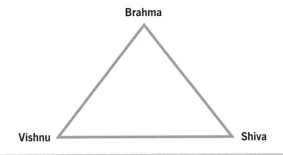

Brahma

Vishnu **Shiva**

Variation

● Ask the children to think of three different gods that would represent important aspects of the devine being and to set up a triangle for them.

Thinking about Hindu Gods

Most Hindus believe in a supreme being (Brahman), but also that he cannot be understood by mere mortals so they have numerous deities, each showing different aspects of God. These have a range of symbols to help explain some of their powers and roles.

Suitable for

KS2

Aims

- To explain the number of deities in Hinduism.
- To explore the idea of symbolism in religious images.

Resources

- Images of Hindu gods – Ganesha, Vishnu, Brahma and so on

What to do

1. Ask the children whether Hindus have one or more gods.
2. Tell them that both answers are right and about the range of gods representing different aspects of God. Introduce the idea of symbolism, such as Brahma with four heads (to continually recite one of the four Vedas), Ganesha with an elephant head (wisdom, strength, listens well and so on).

3. Ask the children to imagine that the class is God and each person is a god – of sport, food, art, animals. If they were to draw the gods, how would we recognise them? Answers might be, for a food god, an apple in one hand, pizza in the other, rather tubby, or for a god of sport, tennis racket in one hand, cricket bat in the other, football boot on one foot and ice skate on the other.

4. Ask the children to draw a particular god or let them choose one, explaining what they are by including appropriate symbols.

Variation

- Look at images of the various gods and some of the symbolism associated with them.

What Do We Worship?

The concept of value is an interesting one for children to engage with, particularly in a society where worth or importance is equated with money. This can lead on to the understanding that there are things so important that they have a value beyond money.

Suitable for

KS1, KS2

Aims

- To learn that religious teachings are about more than material things.
- To reflect on the things that are important and what 'important' can mean.

Resources

- Images of money to project onto a whiteboard or a bowl full of coins or imitation notes
- An empty bowl
- Religious artefacts
- A bag to put the artefacts in

What to do

1. Show the images or bowl of money to the children and ask them to sit quietly and reflect on it and what it does.

2. Ask the children what they could do with the money.

3. Then, show them the empty bowl and ask them to say or write on a slip of paper something that is worth much more than money.

4. List the suggestions the children give and talk about why those things are precious. Discuss whether or not some of the things money can't buy are priceless.

5. Show the children the mystery bag of religious artefacts.

6. Ask the children to draw and label the artefact they pick out of the bag.

7. Talk about why artefacts are precious and if their value to a believer is greater than their commercial worth.

Variation

- Ask the children if there are things they would never swap or sell. List those things. Could they put a price on them?

Where People Worship

This activity helps to deepen children's understanding of worship – what it is and how it is expressed.

Suitable for

KS2

Aim

- To develop and broaden children's understanding of the concept of worship.

Resources

- Images of places of worship and worshippers
- Paper and drawing materials

What to do

1. Give each child a sheet of paper and ask them to divide the paper up and draw places where people go to worship in each part. They could draw churches and mosques, but also home shrines and places of pilgrimage.

2. Show the images of places of worship and ask how many they have identified in their pictures.

3. Ask them to list some of the activities that take place in the different places of worship – a mosque, synagogue and church, for example – and look for similarities and differences between the acts of worship that they mention.

Variation

- Images of places of worship can be used as part of an introduction to this activity and the focus of the activity itself can be on the similarities and differences between the places of worship, regarding prayer, singing, ceremonies and so on.

Who Am I?

This activity links learning from religion with personal, social and health education and citizenship (PSHE and C). It asks children to consider the different facets of people – those of a particular faith are not all the same – and for them to recognise that there are many similarities between people of different faiths and cultures.

Suitable for

KS2

Aim

- To develop an understanding that faith is just one aspect of a person's make-up.

Resources

- Images of the children copied several times
- Images of members of an identifiable faith community – Jew, Muslim, Sikh and so on.

What to do

1. Ask the children to look at the images of themselves and, at the bottom of each image, write a word or phrase that describes them – English, son, brother, happy, likes football and so on.
2. Then give them the images of members of a faith community and ask them to carry out the same activity with those images – English, Jew, father, kind and so on.

Who Is It?

This activity introduces an important religious figure by means of a series of clues. The clues can be simplified or made more difficult depending on the age and abilities of the children or their knowledge of the subject.

Suitable for

KS1, KS2

Aim

- To test children's knowledge of religious leaders by seeing how many clues they need.

Resources

- Numbered cards with information about a religious leader (see example for Francis of Assisi on page 309)

What to do

1. Tell the children that you are going to see if they know who the religious leader is by giving them a series of clues, which are on the numbered cards.
2. The children select a card and try to decide who the person might be.
3. They keep on selecting cards until either the children guess correctly or the information is exhausted.

Variations

- Card sets for group activities.
- The clues could be displayed in turn on a whiteboard or projector.
- Tell the children who the person is and ask them, in pairs or groups, to rank the cards in order of importance.
- In addition, compare and discuss the choices made.

Example of clue cards for St Francis of Assisi

1. Gave away all his possessions.	7. Made the first Christmas crib to remind people of Jesus.
2. Built churches.	8. Helped the poor.
3. Didn't care about material things.	9. Tried to bring peace to the world.
4. Ate only what he could beg or was given to him.	10. Cared for the sick.
5. Cared for the environment.	11. Looked after animals.
6. Told people about Jesus.	12. Helped the sad, lonely and angry.

Wonder

'Wonder is the beginning of wisdom' – Greek proverb.
Wonder is an obvious aspect of religious life. This activity asks children to consider the world around them and reflect on their responses.

Suitable for

KS1, KS2

Aim

* To reflect on the concept of wonder.

Resources

* Set of images for whiteboard use

What to do

1. Project several images onto a whiteboard.
2. Ask the children to reflect on each one and respond orally or in writing on their feelings about each image.

Variations

- Consider the responses of others to the world around them. For example:

People travel to wonder at the height of mountains, at the huge waves of the sea, at the long courses of rivers, at the vast compass of the ocean, at the circular motion of the stars; and they pass by themselves without wondering.
St Augustine

He who wonders discovers that this in itself is wonder.
M.C. Escher

We came all this way to explore the moon, and the most important thing is that we discovered the Earth.
Bill Anders, astronaut

Classroom Gems

Innovative resources, inspiring creativity across the school curriculum

Designed with busy teachers in mind, the Classroom Gems series draws together an extensive selection of practical, tried-and-tested, off-the-shelf ideas, games and activities, guaranteed to transform any lesson or classroom in an instant.

© 2008 Paperback 336pp
ISBN: 9781405873925

© 2008 Paperback 312pp
ISBN: 9781405859455

© 2009 Paperback 216pp
ISBN: 9781408220382

© 2009 Paperback 192pp
ISBN: 9781408225608

© 2009 Paperback 392pp
ISBN: 9781408223208

© 2009 Paperback 320pp
ISBN: 9781408228098

© 2009 Paperback 312pp
ISBN: 9781408223260

© 2009 Paperback 232pp
ISBN: 9781408225578

© 2009 Paperback 384pp
ISBN: 9781408224359

'Easily navigable, allowing teachers to choose the right activity quickly and easily, these invaluable resources are guaranteed to save time and are a must-have tool to plan, prepare and deliver first-rate lessons'